The Tom Swift Omnibus #6

©2007 Wilder Publications

Wilder Publications, LLC.
PO Box 3005
Radford VA 24143-3005

ISBN 10: 1-60459-108-0
ISBN 13: 978-1-60459-108-8

First Edition

The Tom Swift Omnibus #6
By Victor Appleton

Tom Swift and His Giant Cannon
(Or the Longest Shots on Record)

Tom Swift and His Photo Telephone
(Or the Picture That Saved a Fortune)

Tom Swift and His Aerial Warship
(Or the Naval Terror of the Seas)

Tom Swift and His Giant Cannon
(Or the Longest Shots on Record)

TABLE OF CONTENTS:

ON A LIVE WIRE

"Now, see here, Mr. Swift, you may think it all a sort of dream, and imagine that I don't know what I'm talking about; but I do! If you'll consent to finance this expedition to the extent of, say, ten thousand dollars, I'll practically guarantee to give you back five times that sum

"I don't know, Alec, I don't know," slowly responded the aged inventor. "I've heard those stories before, and in my experience nothing ever came of them. Buried treasure, and lost vessels filled with gold, are all well and good, but hunting for an opal mine on some little-heard-of island goes them one better."

"Then you don't feel like backing me up in this matter, Mr. Swift?"

"No, Alec, I can't say I do. Why, just stop and think for a minute. You're asking me to put ten thousand dollars into a company, to fit out an expedition to go to this island—somewhere down near Panama, you say it is—and try to locate the lost mine from which, some centuries ago, opals and other precious stones came. It doesn't seem reasonable."

"But I'm sure I can find the mine, Mr. Swift!" persisted Alec Peterson, who was almost as elderly a man as the one he addressed. "I have the old documents that tell how rich the mine once was, how the old Mexican rulers used to get their opals from it, and how all trace of it was lost in the last century. I have all the landmarks down pat, and I'm sure I can find it. Come on now, take a chance. Put in this ten thousand dollars. I can manage the rest. You'll get back more than five times your investment."

"If you find the mine—yes."

"I tell you I will find it! Come now, Mr. Swift," and the visitor's voice was very pleading, "you and your son Tom have made a fortune for yourselves out of your different inventions. Be generous, and lend me this ten thousand dollars."

Mr. Swift shook his head.

"I've heard you talk the same way before, Alec," he replied. "None of your schemes ever amounted to anything. You've been a fortune-hunter all your life, nearly; and what have you gotten out of it? Just a bare living."

"That's right, Mr. Swift, but I've had bad luck. I did find the lost gold mine I went after some years ago, you remember."

"Yes, only to lose it because the missing heirs turned up, and took it away from you. You could have made more at straight mining in the time you spent on that scheme."

"Yes, I suppose I could; but this is going to be a success—I feel it in my bones."

"That's what you say, every time, Alec. No, I don't believe I want to go into this thing."

"Oh, come—do! For the sake of old times. Don't you recall how you and I used to prospect together out in the gold country; how we shared our failures and successes?"

"Yes, I remember that, Alec. Mighty few successes we had, though, in those days."

"But now you've struck it rich, pardner," went on the pleader. "Help me out in this scheme—do!"

"No, Alec. I'd rather give you three or four thousand dollars for yourself, if you'd settle down to some steady work, instead of chasing all over the country after visionary fortunes. You're getting too old to do that."

"Well, it's a fact I'm no longer young. But I'm afraid I'm too old to settle down. You can't teach an old dog new tricks, pardner. This is my life, and I'll have to live it until I pass out. Well, if you won't, you won't, I suppose. By the way, where is Tom? I'd like to see him before I go back. He's a mighty fine boy."

"That's what he is!" broke in a new voice. "Bless my overshoes, but he is a smart lad! A wonderful lad, that's what! Why, bless my necktie, there isn't anything he can't invent; from a button-hook to a battleship! Wonderful boy—that's what!"

"I guess Tom's ears would burn if he could hear your praises, Mr. Damon," laughed Mr. Swift. "Don't spoil him."

"Spoil Tom Swift? You couldn't do it in a hundred years!" cried Mr. Damon, enthusiastically. "Bless my topknot! Not in a thousand years—no, sir!"

"But where is he?" asked Mr. Peterson, who was evidently unused to the extravagant manner of Mr. Damon.

"There he goes now!" exclaimed the gentleman who frequently blessed himself, some article of his apparel, or some other object. "There he goes now, flying over the house in that Humming Bird airship of his. He said he was going to try out a new magneto he'd invented, and it seems to be working all right. He said he wasn't going to take much of a flight, and I guess he'll soon be back. Look at him! Isn't he a great one, though!"

"He certainly is," agreed Mr. Peterson, as he and Mr. Swift went to the window, from which Mr. Damon had caught a glimpse of the youthful Inventor in his airship. "A great lad. I wish he could come on this mine-hunt with me, though I'd never consent to go in an airship. They're too risky for an old man like me."

"They're as safe as a church when Tom Swift runs them!" declared Mr. Damon. "I'm no boy, but I'd go anywhere with Tom."

"I'm afraid you wouldn't get Tom to go with you, Alec," went on Mr. Swift, as he resumed his chair, the young inventor in his airship having passed out of sight. "He's busy on some new invention now, I believe. I think I heard him say something about a new rifle."

"Cannon it was, Mr. Swift," said Mr. Damon. "Tom has an idea that he can make the biggest cannon in the world; but it's only an idea yet."

"Well, then I guess there's no hope of my interesting him in my opal mine," said the fortune-hunter, with rather a disappointed smile. "Nor you either, Mr. Swift."

"No, Alec, I'm afraid not. As I said, I'd rather give you outright three or four thousand dollars, if you wanted it, provided that you used it for your own personal needs, and promised not to sink it in some visionary search."

Mr. Peterson shook his head.

"I'm not actually in want," he said, "and I couldn't accept a gift of money, Mr. Swift. This is a straight business proposition."

"Not much straight business in hunting for a mine that's been lost for over a century," replied the aged inventor, with a glance at Mr. Damon, who was still at the window, watching for a glimpse of Tom on his return trip in the air craft.

"If Tom would go, I'd trail along," said the odd man. "We haven't done anything worth speaking of since he used his great searchlight to detect the smugglers. But I don't believe he'll go. That mining proposition sounds good."

"It is good!" cried Mr. Peterson, with fervor, hoping he had found a new "prospect" in Mr. Damon.

"But not business-good," declared Mr. Swift, and for some time the three argued the matter, Mr. Swift continuing to shake his head.

Suddenly into the room there ran an aged colored man, much excited.

"Fo' de land sakes!" he cried. "Somebody oughter go out an' help Massa Tom!"

"Why, what's the matter, Eradicate?" asked Mr. Swift, leaping to his feet, an example followed by the other two men. "What has happened to my son?"

"I dunno, Massa Swift, but I looked up jest now, an' dere he be, in dat air-contraption ob his'n he calls de Hummin' Burd. He's ketched up fast on de balloon shed roof, an' dere he's hangin' wif sparks an' flames a-shootin' outer de airship suffin' scandalous! It's jest spittin' fire, dat's what it's a-doin', an' ef somebody don't do suffin' fo' Massa Tom mighty quick, dere ain't gwin t' be any Massa Tom; now dat's what I'se aÄtellin' you!"

"Bless my shoe buttons!" gasped Mr. Damon. "Come on out, everybody! We've got to help Tom!"

"Yes!" assented Mr. Swift. "Call someone on the telephone! Get a doctor! Maybe he's shocked! Where's Koku, the giant? Maybe he can help!"

"Now doan't yo' go t' gittin' all excited-laik," objected Eradicate Sampson, the aged colored man. "Remember yo' all has got a weak heart, Massa Swift!"

"I know it; but I must save my son. Hurry!"

Mr. Swift ran from the room, followed by Mr. Damon and Mr. Peterson, while Eradicate trailed after them as fast as his tottering limbs would carry him, murmuring to himself.

"There he is!" cried Mr. Damon, as he caught sight of the young inventor in his airship, in a position of peril. Truly it was as Eradicate had said. Caught on the slope of the roof of his big balloon shed, Tom Swift was in great danger.

From his airship there shot dazzling sparks, and streamers of green and violet fire. There was a snapping, cracking sound that could be heard above the whir of the craft's propellers, for the motor was still running.

"Oh, Tom! Tom! What is it? What has happened?" cried his father.

"Keep back! Don't come too close!" yelled the young inventor, as he clung to the seat of the aeroplane, that was tilted at a dangerous angle. "Keep away!"

"What's the matter?" demanded Mr. Damon. "Bless my pocket comb —what is it?"

"A live wire!" answered Tom. "I'm caught in a live wire! The trailer attached to the wireless outfit on my airship is crossed with the wire from the power plant. There's a short circuit somewhere. Don't come too close, for it may burn through any second and drop down. Then it will twist about like a snake!"

"Land ob massy!" cried Eradicate.

"What can we do to help you?" called Mr. Swift. "Shall I run and shut off the power?" for in the shop where Tom did most of his inventive work there was a powerful dynamo, and it was on one of the wires extending from it, that brought current into the house, that the craft had caught.

"Yes, shut it off if you can!" Tom shouted back. "But be careful. Don't get shocked! Wow! I got a touch of it myself that time!" and he could be seen to writhe in his seat.

"Oh, hurry! hurry! Find Koku!" cried Mr. Swift to Mr. Damon, who had started for the power house on the run.

The sparks and lances of fire seemed to increase around the young inventor. The airship could be seen to slip slowly down the sloping roof.

"Land ob massy! He am suah gwine t' fall!" yelled Eradicate.

"Oh, he'll never get that current shut off in time!" murmured Mr. Swift, as he started after Mr. Damon.

"Wait! I think I have a plan!" called Mr. Peterson. "I think I can save Tom!"

He did not waste further time in talk, but, running to a nearby shed, he got a long ladder that he saw standing under it. With this over his shoulder he retraced his steps to the balloon hangar and placed the ladder against the side. Then he started to climb up.

"What are you going to do?" yelled Tom, leaning over from his seat to watch the elderly fortune-hunter.

"I'm going to cut that wire!" was the answer.

"Don't! If you touch it you'll be shocked to death! I may be able to get out of here. So far I've only had light shocks, but the insulation is burning out of my magneto, and that will soon stop. When it does I can't run the motor, and—"

"I'm going to cut that wire!" again shouted Mr. Peterson.

"But you can't, without pliers and rubber gloves!" yelled Tom. "Keep away, I tell you!"

The man on the ladder hesitated. Evidently he had not thought of the necessity of protecting his hands by rubber covering, in order that the electricity might be made harmless. He backed down to the ground.

"I saw a pair of old gloves in the shed!" he cried. "I'll get them—they look like rubber."

"They are!" cried Tom, remembering now that he had been putting up a new wire that day, and had left his rubber gloves there. "But you haven't any pliers!" the lad went. "How can you cut wire without them? There's a pair in the shop, but—"

"Heah dey be! Heah dey be!" cried Eradicate, as he produced a heavy pair from his pocket. "I—I couldn't find de can-opener fo' Mrs. Baggert, an' I jest got yo' pliers, Massa Tom. Oh, how glad I is dat I did. Here's de pincers, Massa Peterson."

He handed them to the fortune-hunter, who came running back with the rubber gloves. Mr. Damon was no more than half way to the power house, which was quite a distance from the Swift homestead. Meanwhile Tom's airship was slipping more and more, and a thick, pungent smoke now surrounded it, coming from the burning insulation. The sparks and electrical flames were worse than ever.

"Just a moment now, and I'll have you safe!" cried the fortune-hunter, as he again mounted the ladder. Luckily the charged wire was near enough to be reached by going nearly to the top of the ladder.

Holding the pincers in his rubber-gloved hands, the old man quickly snipped the wire. There was a flash of sparks as the copper conductor was severed, and then the shower of sparks about Tom's airship ceased.

In another second he had turned on full power, the propellers whizzed with the quickness of light, and he rose in the air, off the shed roof, the live wire no longer entangling him. Then he made a short circuit of the work-shop yard, and came to the ground safely a little distance from the balloon hangar.

"Saved! Tom is saved!" cried Mr. Swift, who had seen the act of Mr. Peterson from a distance. "He saved my boy's life!"

"Thanks, Mr. Peterson!" exclaimed the young inventor, as he left his seat and walked up to the fortune-hunter. "You certainly did me a good turn then. It was touch and go! I couldn't have stayed there many seconds longer. Next time I'll know better than to fly with a wireless trailer over a live conductor," and he held out his hand to Mr. Peterson.

"I'm glad I could help you, Tom," spoke the other, warmly. "I was afraid that if you had to wait until they shut off the power it would be too late."

"It would—it would—er—I feel—I—"

Tom's voice trailed off into a whisper and he swayed on his feet.

"Cotch him!" cried Eradicate. "Cotch him! Massa Tom's hurt!" and only just in time did Mr. Peterson clutch the young inventor in his arms. For Tom, white of face, had fallen back in a dead faint.

"We'll Take a Chance!"

"Carry him into the house!" cried Mr. Swift, as he came running to where Mr. Peterson was loosening Tom's collar.

"Git a doctor!" murmured Eradicate. "Call someone on de tellifoam! Git fo' doctors!"

"We must get him into the house first," declared Mr. Damon, who, seeing that Tom was off the shed roof, had stopped mid-way to the powerhouse, and retraced his steps. "Let's carry him into the house. Bless my pocketbook! but he must have been shocked worse than he thought."

They lifted the inert form of our hero and walked toward the mansion with him, Mrs. Baggert, the housekeeper, standing in the doorway in dismay, uncertain what to do.

And while Tom is being cared for I will take just a moment to tell my new readers something more about him and his inventions, as they have been related in the previous books of this series.

The first volume was called "Tom Swift and His Motor-Cycle," and this machine was the means of his becoming acquainted with Mr. Wakefield Damon, the odd gentleman who so often blessed things. On his motor-cycle Tom had many adventures.

The lad was of an inventive mind, as was his father, and in the succeeding books of the series, which you will find named in detail elsewhere, I related how Tom got a motorboat, made an airship, and later a submarine, in all of which craft he had strenuous times and adventures.

His electric runabout was quite the fastest car on the road, and when he sent his wonderful wireless message he saved himself and others from Earthquake Island. He solved the secret of the diamond makers, and, though he lost a fine balloon in the caves of ice, he soon had another air craft—a regular sky-racer. His electric rifle saved a party from the red pygmies in Elephant Land, and in his air glider he found the platinum treasure. With his wizard camera, Tom took wonderful moving pictures, and in the volume immediately preceding this present one, called "Tom Swift and His Great Searchlight," I had the pleasure of telling you how the lad captured the smugglers who were working against Uncle Sam over the border.

Tom, as you will see, had, with the help of his father, perfected many wonderful inventions. The lad lived with his aged parent, his mother being dead, in the village of Shopton, in New York State.

While the house, which was presided over by the motherly Mrs. Baggert, was large, it was almost lost now amid the many buildings surrounding it, from balloon and airship hangars, to shops where varied work was carried on. For Tom did most of his labor himself, of course with men to help him at the heavier tasks. Occasionally he had to call on outside shops.

In the household, beside his father, himself and Mrs. Baggert, was Eradicate Sampson, an aged colored man-of-all-work, who said he was called "Eradicate" because he eradicated dirt. There was also Koku, a veritable giant, one of two brothers whom Tom had brought with him from Giant Land, when he escaped from captivity there, as related in the book of that name.

Mr. Damon was, with Ned Newton, Tom's chum, the warmest friend of the family, and was often at Tom's home, coming from the neighboring town of Waterford, where he lived.

Tom had been back some time now from working for the government in detecting the smugglers, but, as you may well suppose, he had not been idle. Inventing a number of small things, including useful articles for the house, was a sort of recreation for him, but his mind was busy on one great scheme, which I will tell you about in due time.

Among other things he had just perfected a new style of magneto for one of his airships. The magneto, as you know, is a sort of small dynamo, that supplies the necessary spark to the cylinder, to explode the mixture of air and gasoline vapor. He was trying out this magneto in the Humming Bird when the accident I have related in the first chapter occurred.

"There! He's coming to!" exclaimed Mrs. Baggert, as she leaned over Tom, who was stretched out on the sofa in the library. "Give him another smell of this ammonia," she went on, handing the bottle to Mr. Swift.

"No—no," faintly murmured Tom, opening his eyes. "I—I've had enough of that, if you please! I'm all right."

"Are you sure, Tom?" asked his father. "Aren't you hurt anywhere?"

"Not a bit, Dad! It was foolish of me to go off that way; but I couldn't seem to help it. It all got black in front of me, and— well, I just keeled over."

"I should say you did," spoke Mr. Peterson.

"An' ef he hadn't a-been there to cotch yo' all," put in Eradicate, "yo' all suah would hab hit de ground mighty hard."

"That's two services he did for me today," said Tom, as he managed to sit up. "Cutting that wire—well, it saved my life, that's certain."

"I believe you, Tom," said Mr. Swift, solemnly, and he held out his hand to his old mining partner.

"Do you need the doctor?" asked Mr. Damon, who was at the telephone. "He says he'll come right over—I can get him in Tom's electric runabout, if you say so. He's on the wire now."

"No, I don't need him," replied the young inventor. "Thank him just the same. It was only an ordinary faint, caused by the slight electrical shocks, and by getting a bit nervous, I guess. I'm all right—see," and he proved it by standing up.

"He's all right—don't come, doctor," said Mr. Damon into the telephone. "Bless my keyring!" he exclaimed, "but that was a strenuous time!"

"I've been in some tight places before," went on Tom, as he sat down in an easy chair, "and I've had any number of shocks when I've been experimenting, but this was a sort of double combination, and it sure had me guessing. But I'm feeling better every minute."

"A cup of hot tea will do you good," said motherly Mrs. Baggert, as she bustled out of the room. "I'll make it for you."

"You cut that wire as neatly as any lineman could," went on Tom, glancing from Mr. Peterson out of the window to where one of his workmen was repairing the break. "When I flew over it in my airship I never gave a thought to the trailer from my wireless outfit. The first I knew I was caught back, and then pulled down to the balloon shed roof, for I tilted the deflecting rudder by mistake.

"But, Mr. Peterson," Tom went on, "I haven't seen you in some time. Anything new on, that brings you here?" for the fortune-hunter had called at the Swift house after Tom had gone out to the shop to get his airship ready for the flight to try the magneto.

"Well, Tom, I have something rather new on," replied Mr. Peterson. "I hoped to interest your father in it, but he doesn't seem to care to take a chance. It's a lost opal mine on a little-known island in the Caribbean Sea not far from the city of Colon. I say not far—by that I mean about twenty miles. But your father doesn't want to invest, say, ten thousand dollars in it, though I can almost guarantee that he'll get five times that sum back. So, as long as he doesn't feel that he can help me out, I guess I'd better be traveling on."

"Hold on! Wait a minute. Don't be in a hurry," said Mr. Swift.

Mr. Peterson was an old friend, and when he and Mr. Swift were young men they had prospected and grub-staked together. But Mr. Swift soon gave that up to devote his time to his inventions, while Mr. Peterson became a sort of rolling stone.

He was a good man, but somewhat visionary, and a bit inclined to "take chances"—such as looking for lost treasure—rather than to devote himself to some steady employment. The result was that he led rather a precarious life, though never being actually in want.

"No, pardner," he said to Mr. Swift. "It's kind of you to ask me to stay; but this mine business has got a grip on me. I want to try it out. If you won't finance the project someone else may. I'll say good-bye, and—"

"Now just a minute," said Mr. Swift. "It's true, Alec, I had about made up my mind not to go into this thing, when this accident happened to Tom. Now you practically saved his life. You—"

"Oh, pshaw! I only acted on the spur of the moment. Anyone could have done what I did," protested the fortune-hunter.

"Oh, but you did it!" insisted Mr. Swift, "and you did it in the nick of time. Now I wouldn't for a moment think of offering you a reward for saving my son's life. But I do feel mighty friendly toward you—not that I didn't before—but I do want to help you. Alec, I will go into this business with you. We'll take a chance! I'll invest ten thousand dollars, and I'm not so awful worried about getting it back, either—though I don't believe in throwing money away."

"You won't throw it away in this case!" declared Mr. Peterson, eagerly. "I'm sure to find that mine; but it will take a little capital to work it. That's what I need—capital!"

"Well, I'll supply it to the extent of ten thousand dollars," said Mr. Swift. "Tom, what do you think of it? Am I foolish or not?"

"Not a bit of it, Dad!" cried the young man, who was now himself again. "I'm glad you took that chance, for, if you hadn't—well, I would have supplied the money myself—that's all," and he smiled at the fortune-hunter.

PLANNING A BIG GUN

"*But*, Tom, I don't see how in the world you can ever hope to make a bigger gun than that."

"I think it can be done, Ned," was the quiet answer of the young inventor. He looked up from some drawings on the table in the office of one of his shops. "Now I'll just show you—"

"Hold on, Tom. You know I have a very poor head for figures, even if I do help you out once in a while on some of your work. Skip the technical details, and give me the main facts."

The two young men—Ned Newton being Tom's special chum—were talking together over Tom's latest scheme.

It was several days after Tom's accident in the airship, when he had been saved by the prompt action of Mr. Peterson. That fortune-hunter, once he had the promise of Mr. Swift to invest in his somewhat visionary plan of locating a lost opal mine near the Panama Canal, had left the Swift homestead to arrange for fitting out the expedition of discovery. He had tried to prevail on Tom to accompany him, and, failing in that, tried to work on Mr. Damon.

"Bless my watch chain!" exclaimed that odd gentleman. "I would like to go with you first rate. But I'm so busy—so very busy— that I can't think of it. I have simply neglected all my affairs, chasing around the country with Tom Swift. But if Tom goes I— ahem! I think perhaps I could manage it—ahem!"

"I thought you were busy," laughed Tom.

"Oh, well, perhaps I could get a few weeks off. But I'm not going—no, bless my check book, I must get back to business!"

But as Mr. Damon was a retired gentleman of wealth, his "business" was more or less of a joke among his friends.

So then, a few days after the departure of Mr. Peterson, Tom and Ned sat in the former's office, discussing the young inventor's latest scheme.

"How big is the biggest gun ever made, Tom?" asked his chum. "I mean in feet, in inches, or in muzzle diameter, however they are measured."

"Well," began Tom, "of course some nation may, in secret, be making a bigger gun than any I have ever heard of. As far as I know, however, the largest one ever made for the United States was a sixteen-inch rifled cannon—that is, it was sixteen inches across at the muzzle, and I forget just how long. It weighed many tons, however, and it now lies, or did a few years ago, in a ditch at the Sandy Hook proving grounds. It was a failure."

"And yet you are figuring on making a cannon with a muzzle thirty inches across—almost a yard—and fifty feet long and to weigh—"

"No one can tell exactly how much it will weigh," interrupted Tom. "And I'm not altogether certain about the muzzle measurement, nor of the length. It's sort of in the air at present. Only I don't see why a larger gun than any that has yet been made, can't be constructed."

"If anybody can invent one, you can, Tom Swift!" exclaimed Ned, admiringly.

"You flatter me!" exclaimed his chum, with a mock bow.

"But what good will it be?" went on Ned. "Making big guns doesn't help any in war, that I can see."

"Ned!" exclaimed Tom, "you don't look far enough ahead. Now here's my scheme in a nutshell. You know what Uncle Sam is doing down in his big ditch; don't you?"

"You mean digging the Panama Canal?"

Yes, the greatest engineering feat of centuries. It is going to make a big change in the whole world, and the United States is going to become—if she is not already—a world-power. Now that canal has to be protected—I mean against the possibility of war. For, though it may never come, and the chances are it never will, still it may.

"Uncle Sam has to be ready for it. There never was a more true saying than 'in time of peace prepare for war.' Preparing for war is, in my opinion, the best way not to have one.

"Once the Panama Canal is in operation, and the world-changes incidental to it have been made, if it should pass into the hands of some foreign country—as it very possibly might do—the United States would not only be the laughing-stock of the world, but she would lose the high place she holds.

"Now, then, to protect the canal, several things are necessary. Among them are big guns—cannon that can shoot a long distance— for if a foreign nation should send some of their new dreadnaughts over here—vessels with guns that can shoot many miles—where would the canal be once a bombardment was opened? It would be ruined in a day—the immense lock-gates would be destroyed. And, not only from the guns aboard ships would there be danger, but from siege cannon planted in Costa Rica, or some South American country below the canal zone.

"Now, to protect the canal against such an attack we need guns that can shoot farther, straighter and more powerfully than any at present in use, and we've got to have the most powerful explosive. In other words, we've got to beat the biggest guns that are now in existence. And I'm going to do it, Ned!"

"You are?"

"Yes, I'm going to invent a cannon that will make the longest shots on record. I'm going to make a world-beater gun; or, rather, I'm going to invent it, and have it made, for I guess it would tax this place to the limit.

"I've been thinking of this for some time, Ned. I've been puttering around inventing new magnetos, potato-parers and the like, but this is my latest hobby. The Panama Canal is a big thing—one of the biggest things in the world. We need the biggest guns in the world to protect it.

"And, listen: Uncle Sam thinks the same way. I understand that the best men in the service—at West Point, Annapolis and Sandy Hook, as well as elsewhere—are working in the interest of the United States to perfect a bigger cannon than any ever before made. In fact, one has just been constructed, and is going to be tried at the Sandy Hook proving grounds soon. I'm going to see the test if I can.

"And here's another thing. Foreign nations are trying to steal Uncle Sam's secrets. If this country gets a big cannon, some other nation will want a bigger one. It's a constant warfare. I'm going to devote my talents—such as they are—to Uncle Sam. I'm going to make the biggest cannon in the world—the one that will shoot the farthest and knock into smithereens all the other big guns. That's the only way to protect the canal. Do you understand, Ned?"

"Somewhat, Tom. Since I gave up my place in the bank, and became a sort of handy-lad for you, I know more about your work. But isn't it going to be dangerous to make a cannon like that?"

"Well, in a way, yes, Ned. But we've got to take chances, just as father did when he invested ten thousand dollars in that opal mine. He'll never see his money again."

"Don't you think so?"

"No, Ned."

"And when do you expect to start on your gun, Tom?"

"Right away. I'm making some plans now. I'm going down to Sandy Hook and witness the test of this new big cannon. You can come along, if you like."

"Well, I sure will like. When is it?"

"Oh, in about a week. I'll have to look—"

"'Scuse me, Massa Tom," broke in Eradicate, as he put his head through the half-opened office door. "'Scuse me, but dere's a express gen'men outside, wif his auto truck, an' he's got some packages fo' yo' all, marked 'danger-ous—explosive—an' keep away fom de fire.' He want t' know what he all gwine t' do wif 'em, Massa Tom?"

"Do with 'em? Oh, I guess it's that new giant powder I sent for. Why, Eradicate, have him bring 'em right in here."

"Yais, sah, Massa Tom. Dat's all right; but he jest can't bring 'em in," and Eradicate looked behind him somewhat apprehensively."

"Can't bring 'em in? Why not, I'd like to know?" exclaimed Tom. "He's paid for it."

"'Scuse me, Massa Tom," said the colored man, "but dat express gen'men can't bring dem explosive powder boxes in heah, 'case as how his autermobile hab done ketched fire an' he cain't get near it nohow. Dat's why, Massa Tom!"

"Caesar's ghost!" yelled the young inventor. "The auto on fire, and that powder in it! Come on Ned!" and he made a rush for the door.

Koku's Brave Act

"Tom! Tom!" cried Ned, as he watched the disappearing figure of his chum. "Come back here! If there's going to be an explosion we ought to run out of the back door!"

"I'm not running away!" flashed back Tom. "I'm going to get that powder out of the auto before it goes up! If it does we'll be blown to kingdom come, back door or front door! Come on!"

"Bacon and eggs!" yelled Ned. "He's running an awful risk! But I can't let him go alone! I guess we're in for it!"

Then he, too, rushed from the office toward the front of the shop, before which, in a sort of private road, stood the blazing auto. And Ned, who had now lost sight of Tom, because of our hero having turned a corner in the corridor, heard excited shouts coming from the seat of trouble.

"If that's some new kind of powder Tom's sent for, to test for his new big gun, and it goes up," Ned said to himself, as he rushed on, "this place will be blown to smithereens. All Tom's valuable machinery and patents will be ruined!"

Ned had now reached the front door of the shop. He had a glimpse of the burning auto—a small express truck, well loaded with various packages. And, through the smoke, which from the odor must have been caused by burning gasoline, Ned could see several boxes marked in red letters:

Dangerous Explosive

Keep Away from Fire

"Keep away from fire!" murmured the panting lad. "If they can get any nearer fire I don't see how."

"Oh, mah golly!" gasped Eradicate, who had lumbered on behind Ned. "Oh, mah golly! Oh, good land ob massy! Look at Massa Tom!"

"I've got to help him!" cried Ned, for he saw that his chum had rushed to the rear of the auto, and was endeavoring to drag one of the powder boxes across the lowered tail-board. Tom was straining and tugging at it, but did not seem able to move the case. It was heavy, as Ned learned later, and was also held down by the weight of other express packages on top of it.

"Oh, mah golly!" cried Eradicate. "Git some watah, somebody, an' put out dat fire!"

"No—no water!" yelled Tom, who heard him. "Water will only make it worse—it'll scatter the blazing gasoline. The feed pipe from the tank must have burst. Throw on sand—sand is the only thing to use!"

"I'll git a shubble!" cried Eradicate. "I'll git a sand-shubble!" and he tottered off.

"Wait, Tom, I'll give you a hand!" cried Ned, as he saw his chum step away from the end of the auto for a moment, as a burst of flame, and choking smoke, driven by the wind, was blown almost in his face. "I'll help you!"

"We've got to be lively, then, Ned!" gasped Tom. "This is getting hotter every minute! Where's that Koku? He could yank these boxes out in a jiffy!"

And indeed a giant's strength was needed at that moment.

Ned glanced around to see if he could catch a glimpse of the big man whom Tom had brought from Giant Land, but Koku was not in sight.

"Let's have another try now, Ned!" suggested Tom, when a shift in the wind left the rear of the auto comparatively free from smoke and flame.

"You fellows had better skip!" cried the expressman, who had been throwing light packages off his vehicle from in front, where, as yet, there was no fire. "That powder'll go up in another minute. Some of the boxes are beginning to catch now!" he yelled. "Look out!"

"That's right!" shouted Tom, as he saw that the edge of one of the wooden cases containing the powder was blazing slightly. "Lively, Ned!"

Ned held back only for a second. Then, realizing that the time to act was now or never, and that even if he ran he could hardly save himself, he advanced to Tom's side. The smoke was choking and stifling them, and the flames, coming from beneath the auto truck, made them gasp for breath.

Together Tom and Ned tugged at the nearest case of powder—the one that was ablaze.

"We—we can't budge it!" panted Tom.

"It—it's caught somewhere," added Ned. "Oh, if Koku were only here!"

There was a sound behind the lads. A voice exclaimed:

"Master want shovel, so Eradicate say—here it is!"

They turned and saw a big, powerful man, with a simple, child-like face, standing calmly looking at the burning auto.

"Koku!" cried Tom. "Quick! Never mind the shovel! Get those powder boxes out of that cart before they go up! Yank 'em out! They're too much for Ned and me! Quick!"

"Oh, of a courseness I will so do!" said Koku, to whom, even yet, the English language was somewhat of a mystery. He dropped the shovel, and, heedless of the thick smoke from the burning gasoline, reached over and took hold of the nearest box. It seemed as though he pulled it from the auto truck as easily as Tom might have lifted a cork.

Then, carrying the box, which was now burning quite fiercely on one corner, over toward Tom and Ned, who had moved back, the giant asked:

"What you want of him, Master?"

"Put it down, Koku, and get out all the others! Lively, now, Koku!"

"I do," was the simple answer. The giant put the box on the grass and ran back toward the auto.

"Quick, Ned!" shouted Tom. "Throw some sand on this burning box! That will put out the fire!"

A few handfuls of earth served to extinguish the little blaze, and by this time Koku had come back with another box of powder.

"Get 'em all, Koku, get 'em all! Then we can put out the fire on the auto."

For the giant it was but child's play to carry the heavy boxes of powder, and soon he had them all removed from the truck. Then, with the danger thus narrowly averted, they all, including the expressman, turned in and began throwing sand on the fire, which now had a good hold on the body of the auto. The shovel, which Eradicate had sent by Koku, who could use more speed than could the aged colored man, came in handy.

Soon the fire was out, though not before the truck had been badly damaged, and some of its load destroyed. But, beyond a charring of some of the powder boxes, the explosive was intact.

"Whew! That was a lucky escape," murmured Tom, as he sat down on one of the boxes, and wiped the smoke and sweat from his face. "A little later and there'd only been a hole in the ground to tell what happened. hot work; eh, Ned?"

"I guess yes, Tom."

"I thought of the powder as soon as I saw that the truck was on fire," explained the expressman; "but I didn't know what to do. I was kinder flustered, I guess. This is the second time this old truck has caught fire from a leaky gasoline pipe. I guess that will be the last—it will for me, anyhow. I'll resign if they don't give me another machine. Will you sign for your stuff?" he asked Tom, holding out the receipt book, which had escaped the flames.

"Yes, and I'm mighty glad I'm here to sign for it," replied the young inventor. "Now, Koku, I guess you can take that stuff up to the shop; but be careful where you put it."

"I do, Master," replied the giant.

"What sort of powder is that, Tom?" asked Ned a little later, when they were again back in the office, the excitement having calmed down. The expressman had gone back to town afoot, to arrange about getting another vehicle for what remained of his load. "Is it the kind they use in big guns?"

"One of the kinds," replied Tom. "I sent for several samples, and this is one. I'm going to conduct some tests to see what kind I'll need for my own big gun. But I expect I'll have to invent an explosive as well as a cannon, for I want the most powerful I can get. Want to look at some of this powder?"

"Yes, if you think it's safe."

"Oh, it's safe enough if you treat it right. I'll show you," and working carefully Tom soon had one of the boxes open. Reaching into the depths he held up a handful of something that looked like sticks of macaroni. "There it is," he said.

"That powder?" cried Ned. "That's a queer kind. I've seen the kind they use in some guns on the battleships. That powder was in hexagonal form, about two inches across, and had a hole in the centre. It was colored brown."

"Well, powder is made in many forms," explained Tom. "A person who has only seen black gunpowder, with its little grains, would not believe that this was one grain of the new powder."

"That macaroni stick a grain of powder?" cried Ned.

"Yes, we'll call it a grain," went on the young inventor, "just as the brown, hexagonal cube you saw was a grain. You see, Ned, the idea is to explode all the powder at once—to get instantaneous action. It must all burn up at once as soon as it is detonated, or set off.

"To do that you have to have every grain acted on at the same moment, and that could not be done if the powder was in one solid chunk, or closely packed. For that reason they make it in different shapes, so it will lie loose in the firing chamber, just as a lot of jack-straws are piled up. In fact, some of the new powder looks like jack-straws. Some, as this, for instance, looks like macaroni. Other is in cubes, and some in long strings."

As he spoke Tom struck a match and held the flames near the end of one of the "macaroni" sticks.

"Caesar's grandmother!" yelled Ned. "Are you crazy, Tom?" as he started to leap for a window.

"Don't get excited," spoke Tom, quietly. "There's no danger," and he actually set fire to the stick of queer powder, which burned like some wax taper.

"But—but—" stammered Ned.

"It is only when powder is confined that it explodes," Tom explained. "If it can burn in the open it's as harmless as water, provided you don't burn too much at once. But put it in something where the resulting gases accumulate and can't escape, and then— why, you have an explosion—that's all."

"Yes—that's all," remarked Ned, grimly, as he nervously watched the burning stick of powder. Tom let it flame for a few seconds, and then calmly blew it out.

"You know what a little puff black gunpowder gives, if you burn some openly on the ground," went on Tom; "don't you, Ned?"

"Sure, I've often done that."

"But put that same powder in a tight box, and set fire to it, and you have a bang instead of a puff. It's the same way with this powder, only it doesn't even puff, for it burns more slowly.

"An explosion, you see, is the sudden liberation at one time of the gases which result when the powder is burned. If the gases are given off gradually, and in the open, no harm is done. But put a stick like this in, say, a steel box, all closed up, save a hole for the fuse, and what do you have? An explosion. That's the principle of all guns and cannon.

"But say, Ned, I'm getting to be a regular lecturer. I didn't know I was running on so. Why didn't you stop me?"

"Because I was interested. Go on, tell me some more."

"Not now. I want to get this powder in a safe place. I'm a little nervous about it after that fire. You see if it had caught, when tightly packed in the boxes, there would have been a terrific explosion, though it does burn so harmlessly in the open air. Now let me see—"

Tom was interrupted by the postman's whistle, and a little later Eradicate came in with the mail that had been left in the box at the shop door. Tom rapidly looked over the letters.

"Here's the note I want, I think," he said, Selecting one. "Yes, this is it. 'Permission is hereby granted,' he read, 'to Thomas Swift to visit,' and so on, and so on. This is the stuff, Ned!" he cried.

"What is it?"

"A permit to visit the government proving grounds at Sandy Hook, Ned, and see 'em test that new big gun I was telling you about. Hurray! We'll go down there, and I'll see how my ideas fit in with those of the government's experts."

"Did you say 'we' would go down, Tom?"

"I sure did. You'll go with me; won't you?"

"Well, I hadn't thought very much about it, but I guess I will. When is it?"

"A week from today, and I'm going to need all that time to get ready. Now let's get busy, and we'll arrange to go to Sandy Hook. I've had trouble enough to get this permit—I guess I'll put it where it won't get lost," and he locked it in a secret drawer of his desk.

Then the lads stored the powder in a safe place, and soon were busy about several matters in the shop.

OFF TO SANDY HOOK

"What's the idea of this government test of the big gun, Tom?" asked Ned. "I got so excited about that near-explosion the other day, that I didn't think to ask you all the particulars."

"Why, the idea is to see if the gun will work, and do all that the inventor claims for it," was the answer. "They always put a new gun through more severe tests than anything it will be called on to stand in actual warfare. They want to see just how much margin of safety there is."

"Oh I see. And is this one of the guns that are to be used in fortifying the Panama Canal?"

"Well, Ned, I don't know, exactly. You see, the government isn't telling all its secrets. I assume that it is, and that's why I'm anxious to see what sort of a gun it is.

"As a matter of fact, I'm going into this thing on a sort of chance, just as dad did when he invested in Mr. Peterson's opal mine."

"Do you think anything will come of that, Tom?"

"I don't know. If we get down to Panama, after I have made my big gun, we may take a run over, and see how he is making out. But, as I said, I'm going into this big cannon business on a sort of gamble. I have heard, indirectly, that Uncle Sam intends to use a new type of gun in fortifying the Panama Canal. It's about forty-nine miles long, you know, and it will take many guns to cover the whole route, as well as to protect the two entrances."

"Not so very many if you make a gun that will shoot thirty miles," remarked Ned, with a smile.

"I'm not so sure I can do it," went on Tom. "But, even at that, quite a number of guns will be needed. For if any foreign nation, or any combination of nations, intend to get the canal away from us, they won't make the attack from one point. They'll come at us seven different ways for Sunday, and I've never heard yet of a gun that can shoot seven ways at once. That's why so many will be needed.

"But, as I said, I don't know just what type the Ordnance Department will favor, and I want to get a line. Then, even if I invent a cannon that will outshoot all the others, they may not take mine. Though if they do, and buy a number of them, I'll be more than repaid for my labor, besides having the satisfaction of helping my country."

"Good for you, Tom! I wish it was time to go to Sandy Hook now. I'm anxious to see that big gun. Do you know anything about it?"

"Not very much. I have heard that it is not quite as large as the old sixteen-inch rifle that they had to throw away because of some trouble, I don't know just what. It was impractical, in spite of its size and great range. But this new gun they are going to test is considerably smaller, I understand.

"It was invented by a General Wailer, and is, I think, about twelve inches across at the muzzle. In spite of that comparatively small size, it fires a projectile weighing a thousand pounds, or half a ton, and takes five hundred pounds of powder. Its range, of course, no one knows yet, though I have heard it said that General Wailer claims it will shoot twenty miles."

"Whew! Some shot!"

"I'm going to beat it," declared Tom, "and I want to do it without making such a monstrous gun that it will be difficult to cast it.

"You see, Ned, there is, theoretically, nothing to prevent the casting of a steel rifled cannon that would be fifty inches across at the muzzle, and making it a hundred feet long. I mean it could be done on paper—figured out and all that. But whether you would get a corresponding increase in power or range, and be able to throw a relatively larger projectile, is something no one knows, for there never has been such a gun made. Besides, the strain of the big charge of powder needed would be enormous. So I don't want merely to make a giant cannon. I want one that will do a giant's work, and still be somewhere in the middle-sized class."

"I see. Well, you'll probably get some points at Sandy Hook."

"I think so. We go day after tomorrow."

"Is Mr. Damon going?"

"I think not. If he does I'll have to get another pass, for mine only calls for two persons. I got it through a Captain Badger, a friend of mine, stationed at the Sandy Hook barracks. He doesn't have anything to do with the coast defense guns, but he got the pass to the proving grounds for me."

Tom and his chum talked for some time about the prospects for making a giant cannon, and then the young inventor, with Ned's aid, made some powder tests, using some of the explosive that had so nearly caught fire.

"It isn't just what I want," Tom decided, after he had put small quantities in little steel bombs, and exploded them, at a safe distance, and under a bank of earth, by means of an electric primer.

"Why, Tom, that powder certainly burst the bombs all to pieces," said Ned, picking up a shattered piece of steel.

"I know, but it isn't powerful enough for me. I'm going to send for samples of another kind, and if I can't get what I want I'll make my own powder. But come on now, this stuff gives me a headache. Let's take a little flight in the Humming Bird. We'll go see Mr. Damon," and soon the two lads were in the speedy little monoplane, skimming along like the birds. The fresh air soon blew away their headaches, caused by the fumes from the nitro-glycerine, which was the basis of the powder. Dynamite will often produce a headache in those who work with it.

Two days later Tom and Ned set off for Sandy Hook.

This long, neck-like strip of land on the New Jersey coast is, as most of you know, one of the principal defenses of our country.

Foreign vessels that steam into New York harbor first have to pass the line of terrible guns that, back of the earth and concrete defenses, look frowningly out to sea. It is a wonderful place.

On the Sandy Hook Bay side of the Hook there is a life-saving station. Right across, on the sea side, are the big guns. Between are the barracks where the soldiers live, and part of the land is given over to a proving ground, where many of the big guns are taken to be tested.

Tom and Ned reached New York City without incident of moment, and, after a night spent at a hotel, they went to the Battery, whence the small government steamer leaves every day for Sandy Hook. It is a trip of twenty-one miles, and as the bay was rather rough that day, Tom and Ned had a taste of a real sea voyage. But they were too experienced travelers to mind that, though some other visitors were made quite ill.

A landing was made on the bay side of the Hook, it being too rough to permit of a dock being constructed on the ocean side.

"Now we'll see what luck we have," spoke Tom, as he and Ned, inquiring the way to the proving grounds from a soldier on duty, started for them. On the way they passed some of the fortifications.

"Look at that gun!" exclaimed Ned, pointing to a big cannon which seemed to be crouched down in a sort of concrete pit. "How can they fire that, Tom? The muzzle points directly at the stone wall. Does the wall open when they want to fire?"

No, the gun raises up, peeps over the wall, so speak, shoots out its projectile, and then crouches down again."

"Oh, you mean a disappearing gun."

"That's it, Ned. See, it works by compressed air," and Tom showed his chum how, when the gun was loaded, the projectile in place, and the breech-block screwed fast, the officer in charge of the firing squad would, on getting the range from the soldier detailed to calculate it, make the necessary adjustments, and pull the lever.

The compressed air would fill the cylinders, forcing the gun to rise on toggle-jointed arms, so that the muzzle was above the bomb-proof wall. Then it would be fired, and sink back again, out of sight of the enemy.

The boys looked at several different types of big rifled cannon, and then passed on. They could hear firing in the distance, some of the explosions shaking the ground.

"They're making some tests now," said Tom, hurrying forward.

Ned followed until, passing a sort of machine shop, the lads came to where a sentry paced up and down a concrete walk.

"Are these the proving grounds?" asked Tom. "This is the entrance to them," replied the soldier, bringing his rifle to "port," according to the regulations. "What do you want?"

"To go in and watch the gun tests," replied Tom. "I have a permit," and he held it out so the soldier could see it.

"That permit is no good here;" the sentry exclaimed.

"No good?" faltered Tom.

"No, it has to be countersigned by General Wailer. And, as he's on the proving grounds now, you can't see him. He's getting ready for the test of his new cannon."

"But that's just what we want to see!" cried Tom. "We want to get in there purposely for that. Can't you send word to General Wailer?"

"I can't leave my post," replied the sentry, shortly. "You'll have to come another time, when the General isn't busy. You can't get in unless he countersigns that permit."

"Then it may be too late to witness the test," objected the young inventor. "Isn't there some way I can get word to him?"

"I don't think so," replied the sentry. "And I'll have to ask you to leave this vicinity. No strangers are allowed on the proving grounds without a proper pass."

TESTING THE WALLER GUN

Tom looked at Ned in dismay. After all their work and planning, to be thus thwarted, and by a mere technicality! As they stood there, hardly knowing what to do, the sound of a tremendous explosion came to their ears from behind the big pile of earth and concrete that formed the bomb-proof around the testing ground.

"What's that?" cried Ned, as the earth shook.

"Just trying some of the big guns," explained the sentry, who was not a bad-natured chap. He had to do his duty. "You'd better move on," he suggested. "If anything happens the government isn't responsible, you know."

"I wish there was some way of getting in there," murmured Tom.

"You can see General Waller after the test, and he will probably countersign the permit," explained the sentry.

"And we won't see the test of the gun I'm most interested in," objected Tom. "If I could only—"

He stopped as he noticed the sentry salute someone coming up from the rear. Tom and Ned turned to behold a pleasant-faced officer, who, at the sight of the young inventor, exclaimed:

"Well, well! If it isn't my old friend Tom Swift! So you got here on my permit after all?"

"Yes, Captain Badger," replied the lad, and then with a rueful face he added: "But it doesn't seem to be doing me much good. I can't get into the proving grounds."

"You can't? Why not?" and he looked sharply at the sentry.

"Very sorry, sir," spoke the man on guard, "but General Wailer has left orders, Captain Badger, that no outsiders can enter the proving grounds when his new gun is being tested unless he countersigns the permits. And he's engaged just now. I'm sorry, but—"

"Oh, that's all right, Flynn," said Captain Badger. "It isn't your fault, of course. I suppose there is no rule against my going in there?" and he smiled.

"Certainly not, sir. Any officer may go in," and the guard stepped to one side.

"Let me have that pass, Tom, and wait here for me," said the Captain. "I'll see what I can do for you," and the young officer, whose acquaintance Tom had made at the tests when the government was purchasing some aeroplanes for the army, hurried off.

He came back presently, and by his face the lads knew he had been successful.

"It's all right," he said with a smile. "General Waller countersigned the pass without even looking at it. He's so excited over the coming test of his gun that he hardly knows what he is doing. Come on in, boys. I'll go with you."

"Then they haven't tested his gun yet?" Asked Tom, eagerly, anxious to know whether he had missed anything.

"No, they're going to do so in about half an hour. You'll have time to look around a bit. Come on," and showing the sentinel the counter-signed pass, Captain Badger led the two youths into the proving grounds.

Tom and Ned saw so much to interest them that they did not know at which to look first. In some places officers and firing squads were testing small-calibre machine guns, which shot off a round with a noise like a string of firecrackers on the Chinese New Year's. On other barbettes larger guns were being tested, the noise being almost deafening.

"Stand on your tiptoes, and open your mouth when you see a big cannon about to be fired," advised Captain Badger, as he walked alongside the boys.

"What good does that do?" inquired Ned.

"It makes your contact with the earth as small as possible— standing on your toes," the officer explained, "and so reduces the tremor. Opening your mouth, in a measure, equalizes the changed air pressure, caused by the vacuum made when the powder explodes. In other words, you get the same sort of pressure down inside your throat, and in the tubes leading to the ear—the same pressure inside, as outside.

"Often the firing of big guns will burst the ear drums of the officers near the cannon, and this may often be prevented by opening the mouth. It's just like going through a deep tunnel, or sometimes when an elevator descends quickly from a great height. There is too much outside air pressure on the ear drums. By opening your mouth and swallowing rapidly, the pressure is nearly equaled, and you feel no discomfort."

The boys tried this when the next big gun was fired, and they found it true. They noticed quite a crowd of officers and men about a certain large barbette, and Captain Badger led them in that direction.

"Is that General Wailer's gun?" asked Tom.

"That's where they are going to test it," was the answer.

Eagerly Tom and Ned pressed forward. No one of the many officers and soldiers grouped about the new cannon seemed to notice them. A tall man, who seemed very nervous and excited, was hurrying here and there, giving orders rapidly.

"How is that range now?" he asked. "Let me take a look! Are you sure the patrol vessels are far enough out? I think this projectile is going farther than any of you gentlemen have calculated."

"I believe we have correctly estimated the distance," answered someone, and the two entered into a discussion.

"That excited officer is General Wailer," explained Captain Badger, in a low voice, to Tom and Ned.

"I guessed as much," replied the young inventor. Then he went closer to get a better look at the big cannon.

I say big cannon, and yet it was not the largest the government had. In fact, Tom estimated the calibre to be less than twelve inches, but the cannon was very long—much longer in proportion than guns of greater muzzle diameter. Then, too, the breech, or rear part, was very thick and heavy.

"He must be going to use a tremendous lot of powder," said Tom.

"He is," answered Captain Badger. "Some of us think he is going to use too much, but he says it is impossible to burst his gun. He wants to make a long-range record shot, and maybe he will."

"That's a new kind of breech block," commented Tom, as he watched the mechanism being operated.

"Yes, that's General Waller's patent, too. They're going to fire soon."

I might explain, briefly, for the benefit of you boys who have never seen a big, modern cannon, that it consists of a central core of cast steel. This is rifled, just as a small rifle is bored, with twisted grooves throughout its length. The grooves, or rifling, impart a twisting motion to the projectiles, and keep them in a straighter line.

After the central core is made and rifled, thick jackets of steel are "shrunk" on over the rear part of the gun. Sometimes several jackets are put on, one over the other, to make the gun stronger.

If you have ever seen a blacksmith put a tire on a wheel you will understand what I mean. The tire is heated, and this expands it, or makes it larger. It is put on hot, and when it cools it shrinks, getting smaller, and gripping the rim of the wheel in a strong embrace. That is what the jackets of steel do to the big guns.

A big rifled cannon is loaded from the rear, or breech, just as is a breech-loading shotgun or rifle. That is, the cannon is opened at the back and the projectile is put in by means of a derrick, for often the projectiles weigh a thousand pounds or more. Next comes the powder—hundreds of pounds of it—and then it is necessary to close the breech.

The breech block does this. That block is a ponderous piece of steel, quite complicated, and it swings on a hinge fastened to one side of the rear of the gun. Once it is swung back into place, it is made fast by means of screw threads, wedges or in whatever way the inventor of the gun deems best.

The breech block must be very strong, and held firmly in place, or the terrific force of the powder would blow it out, wreck the gun and kill those behind it. You see, the breech block really stands a great part of the strain. The powder is between it and the projectile, and there is a sort of warfare to see which will give way—the projectile or the block. In most cases the projectile gracefully bows, so to speak, and skips out of the muzzle of the gun, though sometimes the big breech block will be shattered.

With eager eyes Tom and Ned watched the preparations for firing the big gun. The charge of powder was hoisted out of the bomb-proof chamber below the barbette, and then the great projectile was brought up in slings. At the sight of that Tom realized that the gun was no ordinary one, for the great piece of steel was nearly three feet long, and must have weighed nearly a thousand pounds. Truly, much powder would be needed to send that on its way.

"I'm afraid, General, that you are using too much of that strong powder," Tom heard one officer say to the inventor of the gun. "It may burst the breech."

"Nonsense, Colonel Washburn. I tell you it is impossible to burst my gun—impossible, sir! I have allowed for every emergency, and calculated every strain. I have a margin of safety equal to fifty per cent."

"Very well, I hope it proves a success."

"Of course it will. It is impossible to burst my gun! Now, are we ready for the test."

The gun was rather crude in form, not having received its final polish, and it was mounted on a temporary carriage. But even with that Tom could see that it was a wonderful weapon, though he thought he would have put on another jacket toward the muzzle, to further strengthen that portion.

"I'm going to make a gun bigger than that," said Tom to Ned. He spoke rather louder than he intended, and, as it was at a moment when there was a period of silence, the words carried to General Waller, who was at that moment near Tom.

"What's that?" inquired the rather fiery-tempered officer, as he looked sharply at our hero.

"I said I was going to make a larger gun than that," repeated Tom, modestly.

"Sir! Do you know what you are saying? How did you come in here, anyhow? I thought no civilians were to be admitted today! Explain how you got here!"

Tom felt an angry flush mounting to his cheeks.

"I came in here on a pass countersigned by you," he replied.

"A pass countersigned by me? Let me it."

Tom passed it over.

"Humph, it doesn't seem to be forged," went on the pompous officer. "Who are you, anyhow?"

"Tom Swift."

"Hum!"

"General Waller, permit me to introduce Tom Swift to you," spoke Captain Badger, stepping forward, and trying not to smile. "He is one of our foremost inventors. It is his type of monoplane that the government has adopted for the coming maneuvers at Panama, you may recall, and he was very helpful to Uncle Sam in stopping that swindling on the border last year—Tom and his big searchlight. Mr. Swift, General Waller," and Captain Badger bowed as he completed the introduction.

"What's that. Tom Swift here? Let me meet him!" exclaimed an elderly officer coming through the crowd. The others parted to make way for him, as he seemed to be a person of some importance, to judge by his uniform, and the medals he wore.

"Tom Swift here!" he went on. "I want to shake hands with you, Tom! I haven't seen you since I negotiated with you for the purchase of those submarines you invented, and which have done such splendid service for the government. Tom, I'm glad to see you here today."

The face of General Waller was a study in blank amazement.

The Impossible Occurs

There were murmurs throughout the throng about the big gun, as the officer approached Tom Swift and shook hands with him.

"What have you in mind now, Tom, that you come to Sandy Hook?" the much-medaled officer asked.

"Nothing much, Admiral," answered our hero.

"Oh, yes, you have!" returned Admiral Woodburn, head of the naval forces of Uncle Sam. "You've got some idea in your head, or you wouldn't come to see this test of my friend's gun. Well, if you can invent anything as good for coast defense, or even interior defense, as your submarines, it will be in keeping with what you have done in the past. I congratulate you, General Waller, on having Tom Swift here to give you the benefit of some of his ideas."

"I—I haven't had the pleasure of meeting Mr. Swift before," said the gun inventor, stiffly. "I did not recognize his name when I countersigned his pass."

It was plain that the greeting of Tom by Admiral Woodburn had had a marked effect in changing sentiment toward our hero. Captain Badger smiled as he noticed with what different eyes the gun inventor now regarded the lad.

"Well, if Tom Swift gives you any points about your gun, you want to adopt them," went on the Admiral. "I thought I knew something about submarines, but Tom taught me some things, too; didn't you, Tom?"

"Oh, it was just a simple matter, Admiral," said Tom, modestly. "Just that little point about the intake valves and the ballast tanks."

"But they changed the whole matter. Yes, General, you take Tom's advice—if he gives you any."

"I don't know that I will need any—as yet," replied General Waller. "I am confident my gun will be a success as it is at present constructed. Later, however, if I should decide to make any changes, I will gladly avail myself of Mr. Swift's counsel," and he bowed stiffly to Tom. "We will now proceed with the test," he went on. "Kindly send a wireless to the patrol ships that we are about to fire, and ask them to note carefully where the projectile falls."

"Very good, sir," spoke the officer in immediate charge of the matter, as he saluted. Soon from the aerials snapped the vicious sparks that told of the wireless telegraph being worked.

I might explain that near the spot where the projectile was expected to fall into the sea—about fifteen miles from Sandy Hook—several war vessels were stationed to warn shipping to give the place a wide berth. This was easy, since the big gun had been aimed at a spot outside of the steamship lanes. Aiming the rifle in a certain direction, and giving it a definite angle of inclination, made it practically certain just where the shot would fall. This is called "getting the range," and while, of course, the exact limit of fire of the new gun was not known, it had been computed as nearly as possible.

"Is everything ready now?" asked General Waller, while Tom was conversing with his friends, Captain Badger and Admiral Woodburn, Ned taking part in the conversation from time to time.

"All ready, sir," was the assurance. The inventor was plainly nervous as the crucial moment of the test approached. He went here and there upon the barbette, testing the various levers and gear wheels of the gun.

The projectile and powder had been put in, the breech-block screwed into place, the primer had been inserted, and all that remained was to press the button that would make the electrical connection, and explode the charge. This act of firing the gun had been intrusted to one of the soldiers, for General Waller and his brother officers were to retire to a bomb-proof, whence they would watch the effect of the fire, and note the course of the projectile.

"It seems to me," remarked Ned, "that the soldier who is going to fire the gun is in the most danger."

"He would be—if it exploded," spoke Tom, for his officer friends had joined their colleagues, most of whom were now walking toward the shelter. "But I think there is little danger.

"You see, the electric wires are long enough to enable him to stand some distance from the gun. And, if he likes, he can crouch behind that concrete wall of the next barbette. Still, there is some chance of an accident, for, no matter how carefully you calculate the strain of a bursting charge of powder, and how strongly you construct the breech-block to stand the strain, there is always the possibility of a flaw in the metal. So, Ned, I think we'll just go to the bombÄproof ourselves, when we see General Waller making for the same place."

"I suppose," remarked Ned, "that in actual warfare anyone who fired one of the big guns would have to stand close to it—closer than that soldier is now."

"Oh, yes—much," replied Tom, as he watched General Waller giving the last instructions to the private who was to press the button. "Only, of course, in war the guns will have been tested, and this one has not. Here he comes; I guess we'd better be moving."

General Waller, having assured himself that everything was as right as possible, had given the last word to the private and was now making his way toward the bomb-proof, within which were gathered his fellow-officers and friends.

"You had better retire from the immediate vicinity of the gun," said its inventor to Tom and Ned, as he passed them. "For, while I have absolute confidence in my cannon, and I know that it is impossible to burst it, the concussion may be unpleasant at such close range."

"Thank you," said Tom. "We are going to get in a safe place."

He could not refrain from contrasting the general's manner now with what it had been at first.

As for Ned, he could not help wondering why, if the inventor had such absolute faith in his weapon, he did not fire it himself, even at the risk of a "concussion."

How it happened was never accurately known, as the soldier declared positively—after he came out of the hospital—that he had not pressed the button. The theory was that the wires had become crossed, making a short circuit, which caused the gun to go off prematurely.

But suddenly, while Tom, Ned and General Waller were still some distance away from the bomb-proof, there was a terrific explosion. It seemed as if the very foundations of the fortifications would be shattered There was a roaring in the air —a hot burst of flame, and instantly such a vacuum was created that Tom and Ned found themselves gasping for breath.

Dazed, shaken in every bone, with their muscles sore, they picked themselves up from the ground, along which they had been blown with great force in the direction of the bomb-proof. Even as Tom struggled to his feet, intending to run to safety in fear of other explosions, he realized what had happened.

"What—what was it?" cried Ned, as he, too, arose.

"The gun burst!" yelled Tom.

He looked to the left and saw General Waller picking himself up, his uniform torn, and blood streaming from a cut on his face. At the same instant Tom was aware of the body of a man flying through the air toward a distant grass plot, and the young inventor recognized it as that of the soldier who had been detailed to fire the great cannon.

Almost instantaneously as everything happened, Tom was aware of noticing several things, as though they took place in sequence. He looked toward where the gun had stood. It was in ruins. The young inventor saw something, which he took to be the projectile, skimming across the sea waves, and he had a fleeting glimpse of the greater portion of the immense weapon itself sinking into the depths of the ocean.

Then, coming down from a great height in the air, he saw a dark object. It was another piece of the cannon that had been hurled skyward.

"Look out!" Tom yelled, instinctively, as he staggered toward the bomb-proof, Ned following.

He saw a number of officers running out to assist General Waller, who seemed too dazed to move. Many of them had torn uniforms, and not a few were bleeding from their injuries. Then the air seemed filled with a rain of small missilesÄstones, dirt, gravel and pieces of metal.

A Big Problem

"Are you much hurt, Ned?"

Tom Swift bent anxiously over the prostrate form of his chum. A big piece of the burst gun had fallen close to Ned—so close, in fact, that Tom, who saw it as he neared the entrance to the bomb-proof, shuddered as he raced back. But there was no sign of injury on his chum.

"Are you much hurt, Ned?"

The lad's eyes opened. He seemed dazed.

"No—no, I guess not," he answered, slowly. "I—I guess I'm as much scared as hurt, Tom. It was the wind from that big piece that knocked me down. It didn't actually hit me."

"No, I should say not," put in Captain Badger, who had run out toward the two lads. "If it had hit you there wouldn't have been much of you left to tell the tale," and he nodded toward the big piece of metal Tom had seen coming down from the sky. That part of the cannon forming a portion of the breech had buried itself deep in the earth. It had landed close to Ned—so close that, as he said, the wind of it, as well as the concussion, perhaps, had thrown him with enough force to send the breath from him.

"Glad to hear that, old man!" exclaimed Tom, with a sigh of relief. "If you'd been hurt I should have blamed myself."

"That would have been foolish. I took the same chance that you did," answered Ned, as he arose, and limped off between the captain and Tom.

A great silence seemed to have followed the terrific report. And now the officers and soldiers began to recover from the stupor into which the accident had thrown them. Sentries began pouring into the proving grounds from other portions of the barracks, and an ambulance call was sent in.

General Waller's comrades had hurried out to him, and were now leading him away. He did not seem to be much hurt, though, like many others, he had received numerous cuts and scratches from bits of stone and gravel scattered by the explosion, as well as from small bits of metal that were thrown in all directions.

"Are you hurt, General?" asked Admiral Woodburn, as he put his arm about the shoulder of the inventor.

"No—that is to say, I don't think so. But what happened? Did they fire some other gun in our direction by mistake?"

For a moment they all hesitated. Then the Admiral said, gently:

"No, General. It was your own gun—it burst."

"My gun! My gun burst?"

"That was it. Fortunately, no one was killed."

"My gun burst! How could that happen? I drew every plan for that gun myself. I made every allowance. I tell you it was impossible for it to burst!"

"But it did burst, General," went on the Admiral. "You can see for yourself," and he turned around and waved his hand toward the barbette where the gun had been mounted. All that remained of it now was part of the temporary carriage, and a small under-portion of the muzzle. The entire breech, with the great block, had been blown into fragments, so powerful was the powder used. The projectile one watcher reported, had gone about three hundred yards over the top of the barbette and then dropped into the sea, very little of the force of the explosive having been expended on that. A large piece of the gun had also been lost in the water off shore.

"My gun burst! My gun burst!" murmured General Waller, as if unable to comprehend it. "My gun burst—it is impossible!"

"But it did," spoke Admiral Woodburn, softly. "Come, you had better see the surgeon. You may be more seriously injured than you think."

"Was anyone else hurt?" asked the inventor, listlessly. He seemed to have lost all interest, for the time being.

"No one seriously, as far as we can learn," was the answer.

"What of the man who fired the gun?" inquired the General.

"He was blown high into the air," said Tom. "I saw him."

"But he is not injured beyond some bruises," put in one of the ambulance surgeons. "We have taken him to the hospital. He fell on a pile of bags that had held concrete, and they saved him. It was a miraculous escape."

"I am glad of it," said General Waller. "It is bad enough to feel that I made some mistake, causing the gun to burst; but I would never cease to reproach myself if I felt that the man who fired it was killed, or even hurt."

His friends led him away, and Tom and Ned went over to look at what remained of the great gun. Truly, the powder, expending its force in a direction not meant for it, had done terrific havoc. Even part of the solid concrete bed of the barbette had been torn up.

An official inquiry was at once started, and, while it would take some time to complete it (for the parts of the gun remaining were to be subjected to an exhaustive test to determine the cause of the weakness), it was found that there was some defect in the wiring and battery that was used to fire the charge.

The soldier who was to press the button was sure he had not done so, as he had been ordered to wait until General Waller gave the signal from the bomb-proof. But the gun went off before its inventor reached that place of safety. Just what had caused the premature discharge could never be learned, as part of the firing apparatus had been blown to atoms.

"Well, Tom, what do you think of it?" asked Ned, who had now fully recovered from the shock. The two were about to leave the proving grounds, having seen all that they cared to.

"I don't know just what to think," was the answer. "It sure was a big explosion, and it goes to prove that, no matter how many calculations you make, when you try a new powder in a new gun you don't know what's going to happen, until after it has happened— and then it's too late. It's a big problem, Ned."

"Do you think you can solve it? Are you still going on with your plan to build the biggest cannon ever made?"

"I sure am, Ned, though I don't know that I'll make out any better than General Waller did. It's too bad his was a failure; but I think I see where he made some mistakes."

"Oh, you do; eh?" suddenly exclaimed a voice, and from a nearby parapet, where he had gone to look at one of the pieces of his gun, stepped General Waller. "So you think I made some mistakes, Tom Swift? Where, pray?"

"In making the breech. The steel jackets were of uneven thickness, making the strain unequal. Then, too, I do not think the powder was sufficiently tested. It was probably of uneven strength. That is only my opinion, sir."

"Well, you are rather young to give opinions to men who have devoted almost all their lives to the study of high explosives."

"I realize that, sir; but you asked me for my opinion. I shall hope to profit by your mistakes, too. That is one reason I wanted to see this test."

"Then you are seriously determined to make a gun that you think will rival mine."

"I am, General Wailer."

"For what purpose—to sell to some foreign government?"

"No, sir!" cried Tom, with flashing eyes. "If I am successful in making a cannon that will fire the longest shots on record, I shall offer it to Uncle Sam first of all. If he does not want it, I shall not dispose of it to any foreign country!"

"Hum! Well, I don't believe you'll succeed. I intend to rebuild my gun at once, though I may make some changes in it. I am sure I shall succeed the next time. But as for you—a mere youth—to hope to rival men who have made this problem a life-study—it is preposterous, sir! Utterly preposterous!" and he uttered these words much as he had declared that it was impossible for his gun to burst, even after it was in fragments."

"Come on, Ned," said Tom, in a low voice. "We'll go back home."

THE NEW POWDER

"Bless my cartridge belt, Tom, you don't really mean to say that stuff is powder!" exclaimed Mr. Damon.

"That's what I hope it will prove to be—and powerful powder at that."

"Why, it looks more like excelsior than anything else," went on the odd man, gingerly taking up some yellowish shreds in his fingers.

"And it will burn as harmlessly as excelsior in the open air," went on Tom. "But I hope to prove, when it is confined in a chamber, that it will be highly explosive. I'm going to make a test of it soon."

"Give me good notice, so I can get over in the next State!" exclaimed Ned Newton, with a laugh.

This was several days after our friends had returned from the disastrous gun test at Sandy Hook. Tom had at once gotten to work on the problem that confronted him—a problem of his own making— to build a giant cannon that would make the longest shots on record. And he had first turned his attention to the powder, or explosive, to be used.

"For," he said, "there is no use having a big gun unless you can fire it. And the gun I am planning will need something more powerful in the powder line than any I've ever heard of."

"Stronger than the kind General Wailer used?" inquired Ned.

"Yes, but I'll make my cannon correspondingly stronger, too, so there will be no danger."

"Bless my shoe buttons!" exclaimed Mr. Damon. "You boys must have had your nerve with you to stay around Sandy Hook after that gun went up in the air."

"Oh, the danger was all over soon after it began," spoke Tom, with a smile. "But now I'm going to test some of this powder. If you want to run away, Mr. Damon, I'll have Koku take you up in one of the airships, and you'll certainly be safe a mile or so in the air," for Tom had instructed his giant servant how to run one of the simpler biplanes.

"No—no, Tom, I'll stick!" exclaimed the eccentric man. "I'll not promise not to hide behind the fence, or something like that, though, Tom; but I'll stick."

"So will I," added Ned. "How are you going to make the test, Tom?"

"I'll tell you in a minute. I want to do a little figuring first."

Tom had, before going to Sandy Hook, made some experiments in powder manufacturing, but they had not been very satisfactory. He had not been able to get power enough. On his return he had undertaken rather a daring innovation. He had mingled two varieties of powder, and the resulting combination would, he hoped, prove just what he wanted.

The powder was in gelatin form, being made with nitro-glycerine as a base. It looked, as Mr. Damon had said, like a bunch of excelsior, only it was yellow instead of white, and it felt not unlike pieces of dry macaroni.

"I have shredded the powder in this manner," Tom explained, "so that it will explode more evenly and quickly. I want it to burn as nearly instantaneously as possible, and I think it will in this form."

"But how are you going to tell how powerful it is unless you fire it in a cannon?" asked Ned. "And you haven't even started your big gun yet."

"Oh, I'll show you," declared Tom. "There are several ways of making a test, but I have one of my own. I am going to take a solid block of steel, of known weight—say about a hundred pounds. This I will put into a sort of square cylinder, or well, closed at the bottom somewhat like the breech of a gun. The block of steel fits so closely in the square well that no air or powder gas can pass it.

"In the bottom of this well, which may be a foot square, I will put a small charge of this new powder. On top of that will come the steel block. Then by means of electric wires I can fire the charge.

"Attached to the steel well, or chamber, will be a gauge, a pressure recorder and other apparatus. When the powder, of which I will use only a pinch, carefully weighing it, goes off, it will raise the hundred-pound weight a certain distance. This will be noted on the scale. There will also be shown the amount of pressure released in the gas given off by the powder. In that way I can make some calculations."

"How?" asked Ned, who was much interested.

"Well, for instance, if one ounce of powder raises the weight three feet, and gives a muzzle pressure of, say, five hundred pounds, I can easily compute what a thousand pounds of powder, acting on a projectile weighing two tons and a half, would do, and how far it would shoot it."

"Bless my differential gear!" cried Mr. Damon. "A projectile weighing two and a half, tons! Tom, it's impossible!"

"That's what General Waller said about his gun; but it burst, just the same," declared Ned. "Poor man, I felt sorry for him. He seemed rather put out at you, Tom."

"I guess he was—a bit—though I didn't mean anything disrespectful in what I said. But now we'll have this test. Koku, take the rest of this powder back. I'll only keep a small quantity."

The giant, who, being more active than Eradicate, had rather supplanted the aged colored man, did as he was bid, and soon Tom, with Ned and Mr. Damon to help him, was preparing for the test.

They went some distance away from any of the buildings, for, though Tom was only going to use a small quantity of the explosive, he did not just know what the result would be, and he wanted to take no chances.

"I know from personal experience what the two kinds of powder from which I made this sample will do," he said; "but it is like taking two known quantities and getting a third unknown one from them. There is an unequal force between the two samples that may make an entirely new compound."

The steel chamber that was to receive the hundred-pound steel block had been prepared in advance, as had the various gauges and registering apparatus.

"Well, I guess we'll start things moving now," went on Tom, as he looked over the things he had brought from his shops to the deserted meadow. The fact of the test had been kept a secret, so there were no spectators. "Ned, give me a hand with this block" Tom went on. "It's a little too heavy to lift alone." He was straining and tugging at the heavy piece of steel.

"Me do!" exclaimed Koku the giant, gently pushing Tom to one side. Then the big man, with one hand, raised the hundred-pound weight as easily as if it were a loaf of bread, and deposited it where Tom wanted it.

"Thanks!" exclaimed our hero, with a laugh. "I didn't make any mistake when I brought you home with me, Koku."

"Huh! I could hab lifted dat weight when I was a young feller!" exclaimed Eradicate, who was, it is needless to say, jealous of the giant.

The powder had been put in the firing chamber. The steel socket had been firmly fixed in the earth, so that if the force of the explosion was in a lateral direction, instead of straight up, no damage would result. The weight, even if it shot from the muzzle of the improvised "cannon," would only go harmlessly up in the air, and then drop back. The firing wires were so long that Tom and his friends could stand some distance away.

"Are you all ready?" cried Tom, as he looked to see that the wiring was clear.

"As ready as we ever shall be," replied Mr. Damon, who, with Ned and the others, had taken refuge behind a low hill.

"Oh, this isn't going to be much of an explosion," laughed Tom. "It won't be any worse than a Fourth of July cannon. Here she goes!"

He pressed the electric button, there was a flash, a dull, muffled report and, for a moment, something black showed at the top of the steel chamber. Then it dropped back inside again.

"Pshaw!" cried Tom, in disappointed tones. "It didn't even blow the weight out of the tube. That powder's no good! It's a failure!"

Followed by the others, the young inventor started toward the small square "cannon." Tom wanted to read the records made by the gases.

Suddenly Koku cried:

"There him be, master! There him be!" and he pointed toward a distant path that traversed the meadow.

"He? Whom do you mean?" asked Tom, startled the giant's excited manner.

"That man what come and look at Master's new powder," was the unexpected answer. "Him say he want to surprise you, and he come today, but no speak. He run away. Look—him go!" and he pointed toward a figure of distinctly military bearing hurrying along the road that led to Shopton.

SOMETHING WRONG

"Bless my buttons!" cried Mr. Damon.

"Let's chase after him!" yelled Ned.

"Koku kin run de fastest oh any oh us," put in Eradicate. "Let him go."

"Hold on—wait a minute!" exclaimed Tom. "We want to know who that man is—and why we're going to chase after him. Koku, I guess it's up to you. Something has been going on here that I don't know anything about. Explain!"

"Well, it's no use to chase after him now," said Ned. "There he goes on his motor-cycle."

As he spoke the man, who, even from a rear view, presented all the characteristics of an army man, so straight was his carriage, leaped upon a motor-cycle that he pulled from the roadside bushes, and soon disappeared in a cloud of dust.

"No, he's gone," spoke Tom, half-regretfully. "But who was he, Koku? You seemed to know him. What was he doing out here, watching my test?"

"Me tell," said the giant, simply. "Little while after Master come back from where him say big gun all go smash, man come to shop when Master out one day. Him very nice man, and him say him know you, and want to help you make big cannon. I say, 'Master no be at home.' Man say him want to give master a little present of powder for use in new cannon. Master be much pleased, man say. Make powder better. I take, and I want Master to be pleased. I put stuff what man gave me in new powder. Man go away—he laugh— he say he be here today see what happen —I tell him you go to make test today. Man say Master be much surprised. That all I know."

Silence followed Koku's statement. To Ned and Mr. Damon it was not exactly clear, but Tom better understood his giant servant's queer talk.

"Is that what you mean, Koku?" asked the young inventor, after a pause. "Did some stranger come here one day when I was out, after I had made my new powder, and did he give you some 'dope' to put in it?"

"What you mean by 'dope'?"

"I mean any sort of stuff."

"Yes, man give me something like sugar, and I sprinkle it on new powder for to surprise Master."

"Well, you've done it, all right," said Tom, grimly. "Have you any of the stuff left?"

"I put all in iron box where Master keep new powder."

"Well, then some of it must be there yet. Probably it sifted through the excelsior-like grains of my new explosive, and we'll find it on the bottom of the powder-case. But enough stuck to the strands to spoil my test. I'll just take a reading of the gauges, and then we'll make an investigation."

Tom, with Ned to help him, made notes of how far the weight had risen in the tube, and took data of other points in the experiment.

"Pshaw!" exclaimed Tom. "There wasn't much more force to my new powder, doped as it apparently has been, than to the stuff I can buy in the open market. But I'm glad I know what the trouble is, for I can remedy it. Come on back to the shop. Koku, don't you ever do anything like this again," and Tom spoke severely.

"No, Master," answered the giant, humbly.

"Did you ever see this man before, Koku?"

"No, Master."

"What kind of a fellow was he?" asked Ned.

"Oh, him got whiskers on him face, and stand very straight, like stick bending backwards. Him look like a soldier, and him blink one eye more than the other."

Tom and Ned started and looked at one another.

"That description fits General Waller," said Ned, in a low voice to his chum.

"Yes, in a way; but it would be out of the question for the General to do such a thing. Besides, the man who ran away, and escaped on his motor-cycle, was larger than General Waller."

"It was hard to tell just what size he was at the distance," spoke Ned. "It doesn't seem as though he would try to spoil your experiments. though."

"Maybe he hoped to spoil my cannon," remarked Tom, with a laugh that had no mirth in it. "My cannon that isn't cast yet. He probably misunderstood Koku's story of the test, and had no idea it was only a miniature, experimental, gun.

"This will have to be looked into. I can't have strangers prowling about here, now that I am going to get to work on a new invention. Koku, I expect you, after this, not to let strangers approach unless I give the word. Eradicate, the same thing applies to you. You didn't see anything of this mysterious man; did you?"

"No, Massa 'Tom. De only s'picious man I see was mab own cousin sneakin' around mah chicken coop de odder night. I tooks mah ole shot gun, an' sa'ntered out dat way. Den in a little while dere wasn't no s'picious man any mo'."

"You didn't shoot him; did you, Rad?" cried Tom, quickly.

"No, Massa Tom—dat is, I didn't shoot on puppose laik. De gun jest natchelly went off by itself accidental-laik, an' it peppered him good an' proper."

"Why, Rad!" cried Ned. "You didn't tell us about this."

"Well, I were 'shamed ob mah cousin, so I was. Anyhow, I only had salt an' pepper in de gun—'stid ob shot. I 'spect mah cousin am pretty well seasoned now. But dat's de only s'picious folks I see, 'ceptin' maybe a peddler what wanted t' gib me a dish pan fo' a pair ob ole shoes; only I didn't hab any."

"There are altogether too many strangers coming about here," went on Tom. "It must be stopped, if I have to string charged electric wires about the shops as I once did."

They hurried back to the shop where the new powder was kept, and Tom at once investigated it. Taking the steel box from where it was stored he carefully removed the several handfuls of excelsior-like explosive. On the bottom of the box, and with some of it clinging to some of the powder threads, was a sort of white powder. It had a peculiar odor.

"Ha!" cried Tom, as soon as he saw it. "I know what that is. It's a new form of gun-cotton, very powerful. Whoever gave it to Koku to put on my powder hoped to blow to atoms any cannon in which it might be used. There's enough here to do a lot of damage."

"How is it that it didn't blow your test cylinder to bits?" asked Ned.

"For the reason that the stuff I use in my powder and this new gun-cotton neutralized one another," the young inventor explained. "One weakened the other, instead of making a stronger combination. A chemical change took place, and lucky for us it did. It was just like a man taking an over-dose of poison—it defeated itself. That's why my experiment was a failure. Now to put this stuff where it can do no harm. Is this what that man gave you, Koku?"

"That's it, Master."

There came a tap on the door of the private room, and instinctively everyone started. Then came the voice of Eradicate, saying:

"Dere's a army gen'men out here to see you. Massa Tom; but I ain't gwine t' let him in lessen as how you says so."

"An army gentleman!" repeated Tom.

"Yais, sah! He say he General Waller, an' he come on a motor-cycle."

"General Waller!" exclaimed Tom. "What can he want out here?"

"And on a motor-cycle, too!" added Ned. "Tom, what's going on, anyhow?"

The young inventor shook his head.

"I don't know," he replied; "but I suppose I had better see him. Here. Koku, put this powder away, and then go outside. Mr. Damon, you'll stay; won't you?"

"If you need me, Tom. Bless my finger nails! But there seems to be something wrong here."

"Show him in, Rad!" called Tom.

"Massa Gen'l Herodotus Waller!" exclaimed the colored man in pompous tones, as he opened the door for the officer, clad in khaki, whom Tom had last seen at Sandy Hook.

"Ah, how do you do, Mr. Swift!" exclaimed General Waller, extending his hand. "I got your letter inviting me to a test of your new explosive. I hope I am not too late."

Tom stared at him in amazement.

FAILURE AND SUCCESS

"You—you got my letter!" stammered Tom, holding out his hand for a missive which the General extended. "I—I don't exactly understand. My letter?"

"Yes, certainly," went on the officer. "It was very kind of you to remember me after—well, to be perfectly frank with you, I did resent, a little, your remarks about my unfortunate gun. But I see you are of a forgiving spirit."

"But I didn't write you any letter!" exclaimed Tom, feeling more and more puzzled.

"You did not? What is this?" and the General unfolded a paper. Tom glanced over it. Plainly it was a request for the General to be present at the test on that day, and it was signed with Tom Swift's name.

But as soon as the young inventor saw it, he knew that it was a forgery.

"I never sent that letter!" he exclaimed. "Look, it is not at all like my handwriting," and he took up some papers from a near-by table and quickly compared some of his writing with that in the letter. The difference was obvious.

"Then who did send it?" asked General Waller. "If someone has been playing a joke on me it will not be well for him!" and he drew himself up pompously.

"If a joke has been played—and it certainly seems so," spoke Tom, "I had no hand in it. And did you come all the way from Sandy Hook because of this letter?"

"No, I am visiting friends in Waterford," said the officer, naming the town where Mr. Damon lived. "My cousin is Mr. Pierce Watkins."

"Bless my doorbell!" exclaimed Mr. Damon, "I know him! He lives just around the corner from me. Bless my very thumb prints!"

General Waller stared at Mr. Damon in some amazement, and resumed:

"Owing to the unfortunate accident to my gun, and to some slight injuries I sustained, I found my health somewhat impaired. I obtained a furlough, and came to visit my cousin. The doctor recommended open air exercise, and so I brought with me my motor-cycle, as I am fond of that means of locomotion."

"I used to be," murmured Mr. Damon; "but I gave it up."

"After his machine climbed a tree," Tom explained, with a smile, remembering how he had originally met Mr. Damon, and bought the damaged machine from him, as told in the first volume of this series.

"So, when I got your letter," continued the General, "I naturally jumped on my machine and came over. Now I find that it is all a hoax."

"I am very sorry, I assure you," said Tom. "We did have a sort of test today; but it was a failure, owing to the fact that someone tampered with my powder. From what you tell me, I am inclined to the belief that the same person may have sent you that letter. Let me look at it again," he requested.

Carefully he scanned it.

"I should say that was written in a sort of German hand; would you not also?" he asked of Mr. Damon.

"I would, Tom."

"A German!" exclaimed General Waller.

At the mention of the word "German" Koku, the giant, who had entered the room, to be stared at in amazement by the officer, exclaimed:

"That he, Master! That he!"

"What do you mean?" inquired Tom.

"German man give me stuff for to put in your powder. I 'member now, he talk like Hans who make our garden here; and he say 'yah' just the same like. That man German sure."

"What does this mean?" inquired the officer.

Quickly Tom told of the visit of an unknown man who had prevailed on the simple-minded giant to "dope" Tom's new powder under the impression that he was doing his master a favor. Then the flight of the spy on a motor-cycle, just as the experiment failed, was related.

"We have a German gardener," went on Tom, "and Koku now recalls that our mysterious visitor had the same sort of speech. This ought to give us a clue."

"Let me see," murmured General Waller. "In the first place your test fails—you learn, then, that your powder has been tampered with—you see a man riding away in haste after having, in all likelihood, spied on your work—your giant servant recalls the visit of a mysterious man, and, when the word 'German' is pronounced in his hearing he recalls that his visitor was of that nationality. So far so good.

"I come to this vicinity for my health. That fact, as are all such regarding officers, was doubtless published in the Army and Navy Journal, so it might easily become known to almost anyone. I receive a letter which I think is from Tom Swift, asking me to attend the test. As the distance is short I go, only to find that the letter has been forged, presumably by a German.

"Question: Can the same German be the agent in both cases?"

"Bless my arithmetic! how concisely you put it!" exclaimed Mr. Damon.

"It is part of my training, I suppose," remarked the officer. "But it strikes me that if we find your German spy, Tom, we will find the man who played the joke on me. And if I do find him— well, I think I shall know how to deal with him," and General Waller assumed his characteristic haughty attitude.

"I believe you are right, General," spoke Tom. "Though why any German would want to prevent my experiments, or even damage my property, and possibly injure my friends, I cannot understand."

"Nor can I," spoke the officer.

"I am sorry you have had your trouble for nothing," went on Tom. "And, if you are in this vicinity when I conduct my next test, I shall be glad to have you come. I will send word by Mr. Damon, and then there will be no chance of a mistake."

"Thank you, Tom, I shall be glad to come I do not know how long I shall remain in this vicinity. If I knew where to look for the German I would make a careful search. As it is, I shall turn this letter over to the United States Secret Service, and see what its agents can do. And, Tom, if you are annoyed again, let me know. You are a sort of rival, so to speak, but, after all, we are both working to serve Uncle Sam. I'll do my best to protect you."

"Thank you, sir," replied Tom. "On my part, I shall keep a good lookout. It will be a bold spy who gets near my shop after this. I'm going to put up my highly-charged protecting electric wires again. We were just talking about them when you came in. Would you like to look about here, General?"

"I would, indeed, Tom. Have you made your big gun yet?"

"No, but I am working on the plans. I want first to decide on the kind of explosive I am to use, so I can make my gun strong enough to stand it."

"A wise idea. I think there is where I made my mistake. I did not figure carefully enough on the strength of material. The internal pressure of the powder I used, as well as the muzzle velocity of my projectile, were both greater than they should have been. Take a lesson from my failure. But I am going to start on another gun soon, and—Tom Swift—I am going to try to beat you!"

"All right, General," answered Tom, genially. "May the best gun win!"

"Bless my powder box!" cried Mr. Damon. "That's the way to talk."

General Waller was much interested in going about Tom's shop, and expressed his surprise at the many inventions he saw. While ordnance matters, big guns and high explosives were his hobby, nevertheless the airships were a source of wonder to him.

"How do you do it, Tom?" he asked.

"Oh, by keeping at it," was the modest answer. "Then my good friends here—Ned and Mr. Damon—help me."

"Bless my check book!" exclaimed the odd gentleman. "It is very little help I give, Tom."

General Waller soon took his departure, promising to call again, to see Tom's test if one were held. He also repeated his determination to set the Secret Service men at work to discover the mysterious German.

"I can't imagine who would want to injure you or me, Tom Swift," he said.

"Do you think they wanted to injure you, General?" asked Mr. Damon.

"It would seem so," remarked Ned. "That man doped Tom's powder, hoping to make it so powerful that it would blow up everything. Then he sends word to the General to be present. If there had been a blow-up he would have gone with it."

"Bless my gaiters, yes!" exclaimed Mr. Damon.

"Well, we'll see if we can ferret him out!" spoke the officer as he took his leave.

Tom, Ned and the others talked the matter over at some length.

"I wonder if we could trace that man who rode away on the motor-cycle?" said Ned.

"We'll try," decided Tom, energetically, and in the electric runabout, that had once performed such a service to his father's bank, the young inventor and his chum were soon traversing the road taken by the spy. They got some traces of him—that is, several persons had seen him pass—but that was all. So they had to record one failure at least.

"I wonder if the General himself could have sent that letter?" mused Ned, as they returned home.

"What! To himself?" cried Tom, in amazement.

"He might have," went on Ned, coolly. "You see, Tom, he admits that he was jealous of you. Now what is there to prevent him from hiring someone to dope your powder, and then, to divert suspicion from himself, faking up a letter and inviting himself to the blowout."

"But if he did that—which I don't believe—why would he come when there was danger, in case his trick worked, of the whole place being blown to kingdom come

"Ah, but you notice he didn't arrive until after danger of an explosion had passed," commented Ned.

"Oh, pshaw!" cried Tom. "I don't take any stock in that theory."

"Well, maybe not," replied Ned. "But it's worth thinking about. I believe if General Waller could prevent you from inventing your big gun, he would."

The days that followed were busy ones for Tom. He worked on the powder problem from morning to night, scoring many failures and only a few successes. But he did not give up, and in the meanwhile drew tentative plans for the big gun.

One evening, after a hard day's work, he went to the library where his father was reading.

"Tom," said Mr. Swift, "do you remember that old fortune hunter, Alec Peterson, who wanted me to go into that opal mine scheme?"

"Yes, Dad. What about him? Has he found it?"

"No, he writes to say he reached the island safely, and has been working some time. He hasn't had any success yet in locating the mine; but he hopes to find it in a week or so."

"That's just like him," murmured Tom. "Well, Dad, if you lose the ten thousand dollars I guess I'll have to make it up to you, for it was on my account that you made the investment."

"Well, you're worth it, Tom," replied his father, with a smile.

A POWERFUL BLAST

"Look out with that box, Koku! Handle it as though it contained a dozen eggs of the extinct great auk, worth about a thousand dollars apiece.

"Eradicate! Don't you dare stumble while you're carrying that tube. If you do, you'll never do it again!"

"By golly, Massa Tom! I—I's gwine t' walk on mah tiptoes all de way!"

Thus Eradicate answered the young inventor, while the giant, Koku, who was carrying a heavy case, nodded his head to show that he understood the danger of his task.

"So you think you've got the right stuff this time, Tom?" asked Ned Newton.

"I'm allowing myself to hope so, Ned."

"Bless my woodpile!" cried Mr. Damon. "I—I really think I'm getting nervous."

It was one afternoon, about two weeks after Tom had made his first test of the new powder. Now, after much hard work, and following many other tests, some of which were more or less successful, he had reached the point where he believed he was on the threshold of success. He had succeeded in making a new explosive that, in the preliminary tests, in which only a small quantity was used, gave promise of being more powerful than any Tom had ever experimented with—his own or the product of some other inventor.

And his experiments had not always been harmless. Once he came within a narrow margin of blowing up the shop and himself with it, and on another occasion some of the slow-burning powder, failing to explode, had set ablaze a shack in which he was working.

Only for the prompt action of Koku, Tom might have been seriously injured. As it was he lost some valuable patterns and papers.

But he had gone on his way, surmounting failure after failure, until now he was ready for the supreme test. This was to be the explosion of a large quantity of the powder in a specially prepared steel tube of great thickness. It was like a miniature cannon, but, unlike the first small one, where the test had failed, this one would carry a special projectile, that would be aimed at an armor plate set up on a big hill.

Tom's hope was that this big blast would show such pressure in foot-tons, and give such muzzle velocity to the projectile, and at the same time such penetrating power, that he would be justified in taking it as the basis of his explosive, and using it in the big gun he intended to make.

The preliminaries had been completed. The special steel tube had been constructed, and mounted on a heavy carriage in a distant part of the Swift grounds. A section of armor plate, a foot and a half in thickness, had been set up at the proper distance. A new projectile, with a hard, penetrating point, had been made—a sort of miniature of the one Tom hoped to use in his giant cannon.

Now the young inventor and his friends were on their way to the scene of the test, taking the powder and other necessaries, including the primers, with them. Tom, Ned and Mr. Damon had some of the gauges to register the energy expended by the improvised cannon. There were charts to be filled in, and other details to be looked after.

"So General Waller won't be here?" remarked Ned, as they walked along, Tom keeping a watchful eye on Koku.

"No," was the reply. "He has gone back to Sandy Hook. He wrote that his health was better, and that he wanted to resume work on a new type of gun."

"I guess he's afraid you'll beat him out, Tom," laughed Ned. "You take my advice, and look out for General Waller."

"Nonsense! I say, Rad! Look out with those primers!"

"I'se lookin' out, Massa Tom. Golly, I don't laik dis yeah job at all! I—I guess I'd better be gittin' at dat whitewashin', Massa Tom. Dat back fence suah needs a coat mighty bad."

"Never you mind about the whitewashing, Rad. You just stick around here for a while. I may need you to sit on the cannon to hold it down."

"Sit on a cannon, Massa Tom! Say, looky heah now! You jest take dese primary things from dish yeah coon. I—I'se got t' go!"

"Why, what's the matter, Rad? Surely you're not afraid; are you?" and Tom winked at Ned.

"No, Massa Tom, I'se not prezactly 'skeered, but I done jest 'membered dat I didn't gib mah mule Boomerang any oats t'day, an' he's suahly gwine t' be desprit mad at me fo' forgettin' dat. I— I'd better go!"

"Nonsense, Rad! I was only fooling. You can go as soon as we get to my private proving grounds, if you like. But you'll have to carry those primers, for all the rest of us have our hands full. Only be careful of 'em!"

"I—I will, Massa Tom."

They kept on, and it was noticed that Mr. Damon gave nervous glances from time to time in the direction of Koku, who was carrying the box of powder. The giant himself, however, did not seem to know the meaning of fear. He carried the box, which contained enough explosive to blow them all into fragments, with as much composure as though it contained loaves of bread.

"Now you can go, Rad," announced Tom, when they reached the lonely field where, pointing toward a big hill, was the little cannon.

"Good, Massa Tom!" cried the colored man, and from the way in which he hurried off no one would ever suspect him of having rheumatic joints.

"Say, that stuff looks just like Swiss cheese," remarked Ned, as Tom opened the box of explosive. It would be incorrect to call it powder, for it had no more the appearance of gunpowder, or any other "powder," than, as Ned said, swiss cheese.

And, indeed, the powerful stuff bore a decided resemblance to that peculiar product of the dairy. It was in thin sheets, with holes pierced through it here and there, irregularly.

"The idea is," Tom explained, "to make a quick-burning explosive. I want the concussion to be scattered through it all at once. It is set off by concussion, you see," he went on. "A sort of cartridge is buried in the middle of it, after it has been inserted in the cannon breech. The cartridge is exploded by a primer, which responds to an electric current. The thin plates, with holes corresponding to the centre hole in a big grain of the hexagonal powder, will, I hope, cause the stuff to burn quickly, and give a tremendous pressure. Now we'll put some in the steel tube, and see what happens."

Even Tom was a little nervous as he prepared for this latest test. But he was not nervous enough to drop any of those queer, cheese-like slabs. For, though he knew that a considerable percussion was needed to set them off, it would not do to take chances. High explosives do not always act alike, even under the same given conditions. What might with perfect safety be done at one time, could not be repeated at another. Tom knew this, and was very careful.

The powder, as I shall occasionally call it for the sake of convenience, though it was not such in the strict sense of the word—the powder was put in the small cannon, together with the primer. Then the wires were attached to it, and extended off for some distance.

"But we won't attach the battery until the last moment," Tom said. "I don't want a premature explosion."

The projectile was also put in, and Tom once more looked to see that the armor plate was in place. Then he adjusted the various gauges to get readings of the power and energy created by his new explosive.

"Well, I guess we're all ready," he announced to his friends. "I'll hook on the battery now, and we'll get off behind that other hill. I had Koku make a sort of cave there—a miniature bomb-proof, that will shelter us."

"Do you think the blast will be powerful enough to make it necessary?" asked Mr. Damon.

"It will, if this larger quantity of explosive acts anything like the small samples I set off," replied the young inventor.

The electric wires were carried behind the protecting hill, whither they all retired.

"Here she goes!" exclaimed Tom, after a pause.

His thumb pressed the electric button, and instantly the ground shook with the tremor of a mighty blast, while a deafening sound reared about them. The earth trembled, and there was a big sheet of flame, seen even in the powerful sunlight.

"Something happened, anyhow!" yelled Tom above the reverberating echoes.

CASTING THE CANNON

"Come on!" yelled Ned. "We'll see how this experiment came out!" and he started to run from beneath the shelter of the hill.

"Hold on!" shouted Tom, laying a restraining hand on his chum's shoulder.

"Why, what's the matter?" asked Ned in surprise.

"Some of that powder may not have exploded," went on the young inventor. "From the sound made I should say the gun burst, and, if it did, that gelatin is bound to be scattered about. There may be a mass of it burning loose somewhere, and it may go off. It ought not to, if my theory about it being harmless in the open is correct, but the trouble is that it's only a theory. Wait a few seconds."

Anxiously they lingered, the echoes of the blast still in their ears, and a peculiar smell in their nostrils.

"But there's no smoke," said Mr. Damon. "Bless my spyglass! I always thought there was smoke at an explosion."

"This is a sort of smokeless powder," explained Tom. "It throws off a slight vapor when it is ignited, but not much. I guess it's safe to go out now. Come on!"

He dropped the pushbutton connected with the igniting battery, and, followed by the others, raced to the scene of the experiment. A curious sight met their eyes.

A great hole had been torn in the hillside, and another where the improvised gun had stood. The gun itself seemed to have disappeared.

"Why—why—where is it?" asked Ned.

"Burst to pieces I guess," replied Tom. "I was afraid that charge was a bit too heavy."

"No, here it is!" shouted Mr. Damon, circling off to one side. "It's been torn from the carriage, and partly buried in the ground," and he indicated a third excavation in the earth.

It was as he had said. The terrific blast had sheared the gun from its temporary carriage, thrown it into the air, and it had come down to bury itself in the soft ground. The carriage had torn loose from the concrete base, and was tossed off in another direction.

"Is the gun shattered?" asked Tom, anxious to know how the weapon had fared. It was, in a sense, a sort of small model of the giant cannon he intended to have cast.

"The breech is cracked a little," answered Mr. Damon, who was examining it; "but otherwise it doesn't seem to be much damaged."

"Good cried Tom. "Another steel jacket will remedy that defect. I guess I'm on the right road at last. But now to see what became of that armor plate."

"Dinner plate not here," spoke Koku, who could not understand how there could be two kind of plates in the world. "Dinner plate gone, but big hole here, and he indicated one in the side of the hill.

"I expect that is where the armor plate is," said Tom, trying not to laugh at the mistake of his giant servant. "Take a look in there, Koku, and, if you can get hold of it, pull it out for us. I'm afraid the piece of nickel-steel armor proved too much for my projectile. But we'll have a look."

Koku disappeared into the miniature cave that had been torn in the side of the bill. It was barely large enough to allow him to go in. But Tom knew none other of them could hope to loosen the piece of steel, imbedded as it must be in the solid earth.

Presently they heard Koku grunting and groaning. He seemed to be having quite a struggle.

"Can you get it, Koku?" asked Torn. "Or shall I send for picks and shovels."

"Me get, Master," was the muffled answer.

Then came a shout, as though in anger Koku had dared the buried plate to defy him. There was a shower of earth at the mouth of the cave, and the giant staggered out with the heavy piece of armor plate. At the sight of it Tom uttered a cry.

"Look!" he shouted. "My projectile went part way through and then carried the plate with it into the side of the hill. Talk about a powerful explosive! I've struck it, all right!"

It was as he had said. The projectile, driven with almost irresistible force, had bitten its way through the armor plate, but a projection at the base of the shell had prevented it from completely passing through. Then, with the energy almost unabated, the projectile had torn the plate loose and hurled it, together with its own body, into the solid earth of the hillside. There, as Koku held them up, they could all see the shell imbedded in the plate, the point sticking out on the other side, as a boy might spear an apple with a sharp stick.

"Bless my spectacle case!" cried Mr. Damon. "This is the greatest ever!"

"It sure is," agreed Ned. "Tom, my boy, I guess you can now make the longest shots on record."

"I can as soon as I get my giant cannon, perhaps," admitted the young inventor. "I think I have solved the problem of the explosive. Now to work on the cannon."

An examination of the gauges, which, being attached to the cannon and plate by electric wires, were not damaged when the blast came, showed that Tom's wildest hopes had been confirmed. He had the most powerful explosive ever made—or at least as far as he had any knowledge, and he had had samples of all the best makes.

Concerning Tom's powder, or explosive, I will only say that he kept the formula of it secret from all save his father. All that he would admit, when the government experts asked him about it, later, was that the base was not nitro-glycerine, but that this entered into it. He agreed, however, in case his gun was accepted by the government, to disclose the secret to the ordnance officers.

But Tom's work was only half done. It was one thing to have a powerful explosive, but there must be some means of utilizing it safely—some cannon in which it could be fired to send a projectile farther than any cannon had ever sent one. And to do this much work was necessary.

Tom figured and planned, far into the night, for many weeks after that. He had to begin all over again, working from the basis of the power of his new explosive. And he had many new problems to figure out.

But finally he had constructed—on paper—a gun that was to his liking. The most exhaustive figuring proved that it had a margin of safety that would obviate all danger of its bursting, even with an accidental over-charge.

"And the next thing is to get the gun cast," said Tom to Ned one day.

"Are you going to do it in your shops?" his chum asked.

"No; it would be out of the question for me. I haven't the facilities. I'm going to give the contract to the Universal Steel Company. We'll pay them a visit in a day or two."

But even the great facilities of the steel corporation proved almost inadequate for Tom's giant cannon. When he showed the drawings, on which he had already secured a patent, the manager balked.

"We can't cast that gun here!" he said.

"Oh, yes, you can!" declared Tom, who had inspected the plant. "I'll show you how."

"Why, we haven't a mould big enough for the central core," was another objection.

"Then we'll make one," declared Tom "We'll dig a pit in the earth, and after it is properly lined we can make the cast there."

"I never thought of that!" exclaimed the manager. "Perhaps it can be done."

"Of course it can!" cried Tom. "Do you think you can shrink on the jackets, and rifle the central tube?"

"Oh, yes, we can do that. The initial cast was what stumped me. But we'll go ahead now."

"And you can wind the breech with wire, and braze it on; can't you?" persisted Tom.

"Yes, I think so. Are you going to have a wire-wound gun?"

"That, in combination with a steel-jacketed one. I'm going to take no chances with 'Swiftite'!" laughed Tom, for so he had named his new explosive, in honor of his father, who had helped him with the formula.

"It must be mighty powerful," exclaimed the manager.

"It is," said Tom, simply.

I am not going to tire my readers with the details leading up to the casting of Tom's big cannon. Sufficient to say that the general plan, in brief, was this: A hole would be dug in the earth, in the center of the largest casting shop—a hole as deep as the gun was to be long. This was about one hundred feet, though the gun, when finished, would be somewhat shorter than this. An allowance was to be made for cutting.

In the center of this hole would be a small "core" made of asbestos and concrete mixed. Around this would be poured the molten steel from great caldrons. It would flow into the hole. The sides of earth—lined with fire-clay—would hold it in, and the middle core would make a hole throughout the length of the central part of the gun. Afterward this hole would be bored and rifled to the proper calibre.

After this central part was done, steel jackets or sleeves would be put on, red-hot, and allowed to shrink. Then would come a winding of wire, to further strengthen the tube, and then more sleeves or jackets. In this way the gun would be made very strong.

As the greatest pressure would come at the breech, or in the powder chamber there, the gun would be thickest at this point, decreasing in size to the muzzle.

It took many weary weeks to get ready for the first cast, but finally Tom received word that it was to be made, and with Ned, and Mr. Damon, he proceeded to the plant of the steel concern.

There was some delay, but finally the manager gave the word. Tom and his friends, standing on a high gallery, watched the tapping of the combined furnaces that were to let the molten steel into the caldrons. There were several of these, and their melted contents were to be poured into the mould at the same time.

Out gushed the liquid steel, giving off a myriad of sparks. The workers, as well as the visitors, had to wear violet-tinted glasses to protect their eyes from the glare.

"Hoist away!" cried the manager, and the electric cranes started off with the caldrons of liquid fire, weighing many tons.

"Pour!" came the command, and into the pit in the earth splashed the melted steel that was to form the big cannon. From each caldron there issued a stream of liquid metal of intense heat. There were numerous explosions as the air bubbles burst— explosions almost like a battery in action.

"So far so good!" exclaimed the manager, with a sigh of relief as the last of the melted stuff ran into the mould. "Now, when it cools, which won't be for some days, we'll see what we have."

"I hope it contains no flaws," spoke Tom, "That is the worst of big guns—you never can tell when a flaw will develop. But I hope—"

Tom was interrupted by the sound of a dispute at one of the outer doors of the shop.

"But I tell you I must go in—I belong here in!" a voice cried. It had a German accent, and at the sound of it Tom and Ned looked at each other.

"Who is there?" asked the manager sharply of the foreman..

"Oh, a crazy German. He belongs in one of the other shops, and I guess he's mixed up. He thinks he belongs here. I sent him about his business."

"That is right," remarked the manager. "I gave orders, at your request," he said to Tom, "that no one but the men in this part of the plant were to be present at the casting. I cant understand what that fellow wanted."

"I think I can," murmured Tom, to himself.

A NIGHT INTRUDER

"Tom, aren't you going to try to get a look at that German?" whispered Ned, as he and his chum came down from the elevated gallery at the conclusion of the cast. "I mean the one who tried to get in!"

"I'd like to, Ned, but I don't want to arouse any suspicion," replied Tom. "I've got to stay here a while yet, and arrange about shrinking on the jackets, after the core is rifled. I don't see how—"

"I'll slip out and see if I can get a peep at him," went on Ned. "If it's like the one Koku described, we'll know that he's still after you."

"All right, Ned. Do as you like, only be cautious."

"I will," promised Tom's chum. So, while the young inventor was busy arranging details with the steel manager, Ned slipped out of a side door of the casting shop, and looked about the yard. He saw a little group of workmen surrounding a man who appeared to be angry.

"I dell you dot is my shop!" one of the men was heard to exclaim—a man whom the others appeared to dragging away with main force.

"And I tell you, Baudermann, that you're mistaken!" insisted one, evidently a foreman. "I told you to work in the brazing department. What do you want to try to force your way into the heavy casting department for? Especially when we're doing one of the biggest jobs that we ever handled—making the new Swift cannon."

"Oh, iss dot vot vas going on in dere?" asked the man addressed as Baudermann. "Shure den, I makes a misdake. I ask your pardon, Herr Blackwell. I to mine own apartment will go. But I dinks my foreman sends me to dot place," and he indicated the casting shop from which he had just been barred.

"All right!" exclaimed the foreman. "Don't make that mistake again, or I'll dock you for lost time."

"Only just a twisted German employee, I guess," thought Ned, as he was about to turn back. "I was mistaken. He probably didn't understand where he was sent."

He passed by the group of men, who, laughing and jeering at the German, were showing him where to go. He seemed to be a new hand in the works.

But as Ned passed he got one look at the man's face. Instead of a stupid countenance, for one instant he had a glimpse of the sharpest, brightest eyes he had ever looked into. And they were hard, cruel eyes, too, with a glint of daring in them. And, as Ned glanced at his figure, he thought he detected a trace of military stiffness—none of the stoop-shouldered slouch that is always the mark of a moulder. The fellow's hands, too, though black and grimy, showed evidences of care under the dirt, and Ned was sure his uncouth language was assumed.

"I'd like to know more about you," murmured Ned, but the man, with one sharp glance at him, passed on, seemingly to his own department of the works.

"Well, what was it?" asked Tom, as his chum rejoined him.

"Nothing very definite, but I'm sure there was something back of it all, Tom. I wouldn't be surprised but what that fellow— whoever he was—whatever his object was—hoped to get in to see the casting; either to get some idea about your new gun, or to do some desperate deed to spoil it."

"Do you think that, Ned?"

"I sure do. You've got to be on your guard, Tom."

"I will. But I wonder what object anyone could have in spoiling my gun?"

"So as to make his own cannon stand in a better light."

"Still thinking of General Waller, are you?"

"I am, Tom."

There was nothing more to be done at present, and, as it would take several days for the big mass of metal to properly cool, Tom, Ned and Mr. Damon returned to Shopton.

There Tom busied himself over many things. Ned helping him, and Mr. Damon lending an occasional hand. Koku was very useful, for often his great strength did what the combined efforts of Tom and his friends could not accomplish.

As for Eradicate, he "puttered around," doing all he could, which was not much, for he was getting old. Still Tom would not think of discharging him, and it was pitiful to see the old colored man try to do things for the young inventor—tasks that were beyond his strength. But if Koku offered to help, Eradicate would draw himself up, and exclaim:

"Git away fom heah! I guess dish yeah coon ain't forgot how t' wait on Massa Tom. Go 'way, giant. I ain't so big as yo'-all, but I know de English language, which is mo' 'n yo' all does. Go on an' lemme be!"

Koku, good naturedly, gave place, for he, too, felt for Eradicate.

"Well, Ned," remarked Tom one day, after the visit of the postman, "I have a letter from the steel people. They are going to take the gun out of the mould tomorrow, and start to rifle it. We'll take a run down in the airship, and see how it looks. I must take those drawings, too, that show the new plan of shrinking on the jackets. I guess I'll keep them in my room, so I won't forget them."

Tom and Ned occupied adjoining and connecting apartments, for, of late, Ned had taken up his residence with his chum. It was shortly after midnight that Ned was awakened by hearing someone prowling about his room. At first he thought it was Tom, for the shorter way to the bath lay through Ned's apartment, but when the lad caught the flash of a pocket electric torch he knew it could not be Tom.

"Who's there?" cried Ned sharply, sitting up in bed.

Instantly the light went out, and there was silence.

"Who's there?" cried Ned again.

This time he thought he heard a stealthy footstep.

"What is it?" called Tom from his chamber.

"Someone is in here!" exclaimed Ned. "Look out, Tom!"

READY FOR THE TEST

Tom Swift acted promptly, for he realized the necessity. The events that had hedged him about since he had begun work on his giant cannon made him suspicious. He did not quite know whom to suspect, nor the reasons for their actions, but he had been on the alert for several days, and was now ready to act.

The instant Ned answered as he did, and warned Tom, the young inventor slid his hand under his pillow and pressed an auxiliary electric switch he had concealed there. In a moment the rooms were flooded with a bright light, and the two lads had a momentary glimpse of an intruder making a dive for the window.

"There he is, Tom!" cried Ned.

"What do you want?" demanded Tom, instinctively. But the intruder did not stay to answer.

Instead, he made a dive for the casement. It was one story above the ground, but this did not cause him any hesitation. It was summer, and the window was open, though a wire mosquito net barred the aperture. This was no hindrance to the man, however.

As Ned and Tom leaped from their beds, Ned catching up the heavy, empty water pitcher as a weapon, and Tom an old Indian war club that served as one of the ornaments of his room, the fellow, with one kick, burst the screen.

Then, clambering out on the sill, he dropped from sight, the boys hearing him land with a thud on the turf below. It was no great leap, though the fall must have jarred him considerably, for the boys heard him grunt, and then groan as if in pain.

"Quick!" cried Ned. "Ring the bell for Koku, Ned. I want to capture this fellow if possible."

"Who is he?" asked Ned.

"I don't know, but we'll see if we can size him up. Signal for the giant!"

There was an electric bell from Tom's room to the apartment of his big servant, and a speaking tube as well. While Ned was pressing the button, and hastily telling the giant what had happened, urging him to get in pursuit of the intruder, Tom had taken from his bureau a powerful, portable, electric flash lamp, of the same variety as that used by the would-be thief. Only Tom's was provided with a tungsten filament, which gave a glaring white pencil of light, increased by reflectors.

And in this glare the young inventor saw, speeding away over the lawn, the form of a big man.

"There he goes, Ned!" he shouted.

"So I see. Koku will be right on the job. I told him not to dress. Can you make out who the fellow is?"

"No, his back is toward us. But he's limping, all right. I guess that jump jarred him up a bit. Where is Koku?"

"There he goes now!" exclaimed Ned, as a figure leaped from the side door of the house—a gigantic figure, scantily clad.

"Get to him, Koku!" cried Tom.

"Me git, Master!" was the reply, and the giant sped on.

"Let's go out and lend a hand!" suggested Ned, looking at the water pitcher as though wondering what he had intended to do with it.

"I'm with you," agreed Tom. "Only I want to get into something a little more substantial than my pajamas."

As the two lads hurriedly slipped on some clothing they heard the voice of Mr. Swift calling:

"What is it, Tom? Has anything happened?"

"Nothing much," was the reassuring answer. "It was a near-happening, only Ned woke up in time. Someone was in our rooms—a burglar, I guess."

"A burglar! Good land a massy!" cried Eradicate, who had also gotten up to see what the excitement was about. "Did you cotch him, Massa Tom?"

"No, Rad; but Koku is after him."

"Koku? Huh, he nebber cotch anybody. I'se got t' git out dere mahse'f! Koku? Hu! I s'pects it's dat no-'count cousin ob mine, arter mah chickens ag'in! I'll lambaste dat coon when I gits him, so I will. I'll cotch him for yo'-all, Massa Tom," and, muttering to himself, the aged colored man endeavored to assume the activity of former years.

"Hark!" exclaimed Ned, as he and Tom were about ready to take part in the chase. "What's that noise, Tom?"

"Sounds like a motor-cycle."

"It is. That fellow—"

"It's the same chap!" interrupted Tom. "No use trying to chase him on that speedy machine. He's a mile away from here by now. He must have had it in waiting, ready for use. But come on, anyhow."

"Where are you going?"

"Out to the shop. I want to see if he got in there."

"But the charged wires?"

"He may have cut them. Come on."

It was as Tom had suspected. The deadly, charged wires, that formed a protecting cordon about his shops, had been cut, and that by an experienced hand, probably by someone wearing rubber gloves, who must have come prepared for that very purpose. During the night the current was supplied to the wires from a storage battery, through an intensifying coil, so that the charge was only a little less deadly than when coming direct from a dynamo.

"This looks bad, Tom," said Ned.

"It does, but wait until we get inside and look around. I'm glad I took my gun-plans to the house with me."

But a quick survey of the shop did not reveal any damage done, nor had anything been taken, as far as Tom could tell. The office of his main shop was pretty well upset, and it looked as though the intruder had made a search for something, and, not finding it, had entered the house.

"It was the gun-plans he was after, all right," decided Tom. "And I believe it was the same fellow who has been making trouble for me right along."

"You mean General Waller?"

"No, that German—the one who was at the machine shop."

"But who is he—what is his object?"

"I don't know who he is, but he evidently wants my plans. Probably he's a disappointed inventor, who has been trying to make a gun himself, and can't. He wants some of my ideas, but he isn't going to get them. Well, we may as well get back to bed, after I connect these wires again. I must think up a plan to conceal them, so they can't be cut."

While Tom and Ned were engaged on this, Koku came back, much out of breath, to report:

"Me not git, Master. He git on bang-bang machine and go off— puff!"

"So we heard, Koku. Never mind, we'll get him yet."

"Hu! Ef I had de fust chanst at him, I'd a cotched dat coon suab!" declared Eradicate, following the giant. "Koku he done git in mah way!" and he glared indignantly at the big man.

"That's all right, Rad," consoled Tom. "You did your best. Now we'll all get to bed. I don't believe he'll come back." Nor did he.

Tom and Ned were up at the first sign of daylight, for they wanted to go to the steel works, some miles away, in time to see the cannon taken out of the mould, and preparations made for boring the rifle channels. They found the manager, anxiously waiting for them.

"Some of my men are as interested in this as you are," he said to the young inventor. "A number of them declare that the cast will be a failure, while some think it will be a success."

"I think it will be all right, if my plans were followed," said Tom. "However, we'll see. By the way, what became of that German who made such a disturbance the day we cast the core?"

"Oh, you mean Baudermann?"

"Yes."

"Why, it's rather queer about him. The foreman of the shop where he was detailed, saw that he was an experienced man, in spite of his seemingly stupid ways, and he was going to promote him, only he never came back."

"Never came back? What do you mean?"

"I mean the day after the cast of the gun was made he disappeared, and never came back."

"Oh!" exclaimed Tom. He said nothing more, but he believed that he understood the man's actions. Failing to obtain the desired information, or perhaps failing to spoil the cast, he realized that his chances were at an end for the present.

With great care the gun was hoisted from the mould. More eyes than Tom's anxiously regarded it as it came up out of the casting pit.

"Bless my buttonhook!" cried Mr. Damon, who had gone with the lads. "It's a monster; isn't it?"

"Oh, wait until you see it with the jackets on exclaimed Ned, who had viewed the completed drawings. "Then you'll open your eyes."

The great piece of hollow steel tubing was lifted to the boring lathe. Then Tom and the manager examined it for superficial flaws.

"Not one!" cried the manager in delight.

"Not that I can see," added Tom.. "It's a success—so far."

"And that was the hardest part of the work," went on the manager of the steel plant. "I can almost guarantee you success from now on."

And, as far as the rifling was concerned, this was true. I will not weary you with the details of how the great core of Tom Swift's giant cannon was bored. Sufficient to say that, after some annoying delays, caused by breaks in the machinery, which had never before been used on such a gigantic piece of work, the rifling was done. After the jackets had been shrunk on, it would be rifled again, to make it true in case of any shrinkage.

Then came the almost Herculean task of shrinking on the great red-hot steel jackets and wire-windings, that would add strength to the great cannon. To do this the central core was set up on end, and the jackets, having been heated in an immense furnace, were hoisted by a great crane over the core, and lowered on it as one would lower his napkin ring over the rolled up napkin.

It took weeks of hard work to do this, and Tom and Ned, with Mr. Damon occasionally for company, remained almost constantly at the plant. But finally the cannon was completed, the rifling was done over again to correct any imperfections, and the manager said:

"You cannon is completed, Mr. Swift. I want to congratulate you on it. Never have we done such a stupendous piece of work. Only for your plans we could not have finished it. It was too big a problem for us. Your cannon is completed, but, of course, it will have to be mounted. What about the carriage?"

"I have plans for that," replied Tom; "but for the present I am going to put it on a temporary one. I want to test the gun now. It looks all right, but whether it will shoot accurately, and for a greater distance than any cannon has ever sent a projectile before, is yet to be seen."

"Where will you test it?"

"That is what we must decide. I don't want to take it too far from here. Perhaps you can select a place where it would be safe to fire it, say with a range of about thirty miles."

"Thirty miles! why, my dear sir—"

"Oh, I'm not altogether sure that it will go that distance," interrupted Tom, with a smile; "but I'm going to try for it, and I want to be on the safe side. Is there such a place near here?"

"Yes, I guess we can pick one out. I'll let you know."

"Then I must get back and arrange for my powder supply," went on the young inventor. "We'll soon test my giant cannon!"

"Bless my ear-drums!" cried Mr. Damon. "I hope nothing bursts. For if that goes up, Tom Swift—"

"I'm not making it to burst," put in Tom, with a smile. "Don't worry. Now, Ned, back to Shopton to get ready for the test."

A WARNING

"Whew, how it rains!" exclaimed Ned, as he looked out of the window.

"And it doesn't seem to show any signs of letting up," remarked Tom. "It's been at it nearly a week now, and it is likely to last a week longer."

"It's beastly," declared his chum. "How can you test your gun in this weather?"

"I can't. I've got to wait for it to clear."

"Bless my rubber boots! it's just got to stop some time," declared Mr. Damon. "Don't worry, Tom."

"But I don't like this delay. I have heard that General Waller has perfected a new gun—and it's a fine one, from all accounts. He has the proving grounds at Sandy Hook to test his on, and I'm handicapped here. He may beat me out."

"Oh, I hope not, Tom!" exclaimed Ned. "I'm going to see what the weather reports say," and he went to hunt up a paper.

It was several weeks after the completion of Tom's giant cannon. In the meanwhile the gun had been moved by the steel company to a little-inhabited part of New York State, some miles from the plant. The gun had been mounted on an improvised carriage, and now Tom and his friends were waiting anxiously for a chance to try it.

The work was not complete, for the steel company employees had been hampered by the rain. Never before, it seemed, had there been so much water coming down from the clouds. Nearly every day was misty, with gradations from mere drizzles to heavy downpours. There were occasional clear stretches, however, and during them the men worked.

A few more days of clear weather would be needed before the gun could be fastened securely to the carriage, and then Tom could fire one of the great projectiles that had been cast for it. Not until then would he know whether or not his cannon was going to be a success.

Meanwhile nothing more had been heard or seen of the spy. He appeared to have given up his attempts to steal Tom's secret, or to spoil his plans, if such was his object.

The place of the test, as I have said, was in a deserted spot. On one side of a great valley the gun was being set up. Its muzzle pointed up the valley, toward the side of a mountain, into which the gigantic projectile could plow its way without doing any damage. Tom was going to fire two kinds of cannon balls—a solid one, and one containing an explosive.

The gun was so mounted that the muzzle could be elevated or depressed, or swung from side to side. In this way the range could be varied. Tom estimated that the greatest possible range would be thirty miles. It could not be more than that, he decided, and he hoped it would not be much less. This extreme range could be attained by elevating the gun to exactly the proper pitch. Of course, any shorter range could, within certain limits, also be reached.

The gun was pointed slantingly up the valley, and there was ample room to attain the thirty-mile range without doing any damage.

At the head of the valley, some miles from where the giant cannon was mounted, was an immense dam, built recently by a water company for impounding a stream and furnishing a supply of drinking water for a distant city. At the other end of the valley was the thriving village of Preston. A railroad ran there, and it was to Preston station that Tom's big gun had been sent, to be transported afterward, on specially made trucks, drawn by powerful autos, to the place where it was now mounted.

Tom had been obliged to buy a piece of land on which to build the temporary carriage, and also contract for a large slice of the opposite mountain, as a target against which to fire his projectiles.

The valley, as I have said, was desolate. It was thickly wooded in spots, and in the centre, near the big dam, which held back the waters of an immense artificial lake, was a great hill, evidently a relic of some glacial epoch. This hill was a sort of division between two valleys.

Tom, Ned, Mr. Damon, with Koku, and some of the employees of the steel company, had hired a deserted farmhouse not far from the place where the gun was being mounted. In this they lived, while Tom directed operations.

"The paper says 'clear' tomorrow," read Ned, on his return. "'Clear, with freshening winds.'"

"That means rain, with no wind at all," declared Tom, with a sigh. "Well, it can't be helped. As Mr. Damon says, it will clear some time."

"Bless my overshoes!" exclaimed the odd gentleman. "It always has cleared; hasn't it?"

No one could deny this.

There came a slackening in the showers, and Tom and Ned, donning raincoats, went out to see how the work was progressing. They found the men from the steel concern busy at the great piece of engineering.

"How are you coming on?" asked Tom of the foreman.

"We could finish it in two days if this rain would only let up," replied the man.

"Well, let's hope that it will," observed Tom.

"If it doesn't, there's likely to be trouble up above," went on the foreman, nodding in the direction of the great dam.

"What do you mean?"

"I mean that the water is getting too high. The dam is weakening, I heard."

"Is that so? Why, I thought they had made it to stand any sort of a flood."

"They evidently didn't count on one like this. They've got the engineer who built it up there, and they're doing their best to strengthen it. I also heard that they're preparing to dynamite it to open breeches here and there in it, in case it is likely to give way suddenly."

"You don't mean it! Say, if it does go out with a rush it will wipe out the village."

"Yes, but it can't hurt us," went on the foreman. "We're too high up on the side of the hill. Even if the dam did burst, if the course of the water could be changed, to send it down that other valley, it would do no harm, for there are no settlements over there," and he pointed to the distant hill.

It was near this hill that Tom intended to direct his projectiles, and on the other side of it was another valley, running at right angles to the one crossed by the dam.

As the foreman had said, if the waters (in case the dam burst) could be turned into this transverse valley, the town could be saved.

"But it would take considerable digging to open a way through that side of the mountain, into the other valley," went on the man.

"Yes," said Tom, and then he gave the matter no further thought, for something came up that needed his attention.

"Have you your explosive here?" asked the foreman of the young inventor the next day, when the weather showed signs of clearing.

"Yes, some of it," said Tom. "I have another supply in a safe place in the village. I didn't want to bring too much here until the gun was to be fired. I can easily get it if we need it. Jove! I wish it would clear. I want to get out in my Humming Bird, but I can't if this keeps up." Tom had brought one of his speedy little airships with him to Preston.

The following day the clouds broke a little, and on the next the sun shone. Then the work on the gun went on apace. Tom and his friends were delighted.

"Well, I think we can try a shot tomorrow!" announced Tom with delight on the evening of the first clear day, when all hands had worked at double time.

"Bless my powder-horn!" exclaimed Mr. Damon. "You don't mean it!"

"Yes, the gun is all in place," went on the young inventor. "Of course, it's only a temporary carriage, and not the disappearing one I shall eventually use. But it will do. I'm going to try a shot tomorrow. Everything is in readiness."

There came a knock on the door of the room Tom had fitted up as an office in the old farmhouse.

"Who is it?" he asked.

"Me—Koku," was the answer.

"Well, what do you want, Koku?"

"Man here say him must see Master."

Tom and Ned looked at each other, suspicion in their eyes.

"Maybe it's that spy again," whispered Ned.

"If it is, we'll be ready for him," murmured his chum. "Show him in, Koku, and you come in too."

But the man who entered at once disarmed suspicion. He was evidently a workman from the dam above, and his manner was strangely excited.

"You folks had better get out of here!" he exclaimed.

"Why?" asked Tom, wondering what was going to happen.

"Why? Because our dam is going to burst within a few hours. I've been sent to warn the folks in town in time to let them take to the hills. You'd better move your outfit. The dam can't last twenty-four hours longer!"

THE BURSTING DAM

"Bless my fountain pen!" exclaimed Mr. Damon. "You don't mean it!"

"I sure do!" went on the man who had brought the startling news. "And the folks down below aren't going to have any more time than they need to get out of the way. They'll have to lose some of their goods, I reckon. But I thought I'd stop on my way down and warn you. You'd better be getting a hustle on."

"It's very kind of you," spoke Torn; "but I don't fancy we are in any danger."

"No danger!" cried the man. "Say, when that water begins to sweep-down here nothing on earth can stop it. That big gun of yours, heavy as it is, will be swept away like a straw, I know—I saw the Johnstown flood!"

"But we're so high up on the side of the hill, that the water won't come here," put in Ned. "We had that all figured out when we heard the dam was weak. We're not in any danger; do you think so, Tom?"

"Well, I hardly do, or I would not have set the gun where I did. Tell me," he went on to the man, "is there any way of opening the dam, to let the water out gradually?"

"There is, but the openings are not enough with such a flood as this. The engineers never counted on so much rain. It's beyond any they ever had here. You see, there was a small creek that we dammed up to make our lake. Some of the water from the spillway flows into that now, but its channel won't hold a hundredth part of the flood if the dam goes out.

"You'd better move, I tell you. The dam is slowly weakening. We've done all we can to save it, but that's out of the question. The only thing to do is to run while there's time. We've tried to make additional openings, but we daren't make any more, or the wall will be so weakened that it will go out in less than twenty-four hours.

"You've had your warning, now profit by it!" he added. "I'm going to tell those poor souls down in the valley below. It will be tough on them; but it can't be helped."

"If the dam bursts and the water could only be turned over into the transverse valley, this one would be safe," said Tom, in a low voice.

"Yes, but it can't be done!" the messenger exclaimed. "Our engineers thought of that, but it would take a week to open a channel, and there isn't time. It can't be done!"

"Maybe it can," spoke Tom, softly, but no one asked him what he meant.

"Well, I must be off," the man went on. "I've done my duty in warning you."

"Yes, you have," agreed Tom, "and if any damage comes to us it will be our own fault. But I don't believe there will."

The man hastened out, murmuring something about "rash and foolhardy people."

"What are you going to do, Tom?" asked Ned.

"Stay right here."

"But if the dam bursts?"

"It may not, but, if it does, we'll be safe. I have had a look at the water, and there's no chance for it to rise here, even if the whole dam went out at once, which is not likely. Don't worry. We'll be all right."

"Bless my checkbook!" cried Mr. Damon. "But what about those poor people in the valley?"

"They will have time to flee, and save their lives," spoke the young inventor; "but they may lose their homes. They can sue the water company for damages, though. Now don't do any more worrying, but get to bed, and be ready for the test tomorrow. And the first thing I do I'm going to have a little flight in the Humming Bird to get my nerves in trim. This long rain has gotten me in poor shape. Koku, you must be on the alert tonight. I don't want anything to happen to my gun at the last minute."

"Me watch!" exclaimed the giant, significantly, as he picked up a heavy club.

"Do you anticipate any trouble?" asked Ned, anxiously.

"No, but it's best to be on the safe side," answered Tom. "Now let's turn in."

Certainly the next day, bright and sunshiny as it broke, had in it little of impending disaster. The weather was fine after the long-continued rains, and the whole valley seemed peaceful and quiet. At the far end could be seen the great dam, with water pouring over it in a thin sheet, forming a small stream that trickled down the centre of the valley, and to the town below.

But, through great pipes that led to the drinking system, though they were unseen, thundered immense streams of solid water, reducing by as much as the engineers were able the pressure on the concrete wall.

Tom and Ned, in the Humming Bird, took a flight out to the dam shortly after breakfast, when the steel men were putting a few finishing touches to the gun carriage, ready for the test that was to take place about noon.

"It doesn't look as though it would burst," observed Ned, as the aircraft hovered over the big artificial lake.

"No," agreed Tom. "But I suppose the engineers want to be on the safe side in case of damage suits. I want to take a look at the place where the other valley comes up to this at right angles."

He steered his powerful little craft in that direction, and circled low over the spot.

"A bursting projectile, about where that big white stone is, would do the trick," murmured Tom.

"What trick?" asked Ned, curiously.

"Oh, I guess I was talking to myself," admitted Tom, with a laugh. "I may not have to do it, Ned."

"Well, you're talking in riddles today, all right, Tom. When you get ready to put me wise, please do."

"I will. Now we'll get back, and fire our first long shot. I do hope I make a record."

There was much to be done, in spite of the fact that the foreman of the steel workers assured Tom that all was in readiness. It was some time that afternoon when word was given for those who wished to retire to an improvised bomb-proof. Word had previously been sent down the valley so that no one, unless he was looking for trouble, need be in the vicinity of the gun, nor near where the shots were to land.

Through powerful glasses Tom and Ned surveyed the distant mountain that was to be the target. Several great squares of white cloth had been put at different bare spots to make the finding of the range easy.

"I guess we're ready now," announced the young inventor, a bit nervously. "Bring up the powder, Koku."

"Me bring," exclaimed the giant, calmly, as he went to the bomb-proof where the powerful explosive was kept.

The great projectile was in readiness to be slung into the breech by means of the hoisting apparatus, for it weighed close to two tons. It was carefully inserted under Tom's supervision. It carried no bursting charge, for Tom's first shot was merely to establish the extreme range that his cannon would shoot.

"Now the powder," called the young inventor. To avoid accidents Koku handled this himself, the hoisting apparatus being dispensed with. Tom figured out that five hundred pounds of his new, powerful explosive would be about the right amount to use, and this quantity, divided into several packages to make the handling easier, was quickly inserted in the breech of the gun by Koku.

"Bless my doormat!" cried Mr. Damon, who stood near, looking nervously on. "Don't drop any of that."

"Me no drop," was the answer.

Tom was busily engaged in figuring on a bit of paper, and Ned, who looked over his shoulder, saw a complicated compilation that looked to he a combination of geometry, algebra, differential calculus and other higher mathematics.

"What are you doing, Tom?" he asked.

"I'm trying to confirm my own theories by means of figures, to see if I can really reach that farthest target."

"What, not the one thirty miles away.

"That's it, Ned. I want to get a thirty-mile range if I can."

"It isn't possible, Tom."

"Bless my tape measure! I should say not!" cried Mr. Damon.

"We'll see," replied Tom, quietly. "Put in the primer, Ned; and, Koku, close the breech and slot it home."

In a few seconds the great gun was ready for firing.

"Now," said Tom, "this thing may be all right, and it may not. The only thing that can cause an accident will be a flaw in the steel. No one can guard against that. So, in order to be on the safe side, we will all go into the bomb-proof, and I will fire the gun from there. The wires are long enough."

They all agreed that this was good advice, and soon the steel men and Tom's friends were gathered in a sort of cave that had been hollowed out in the side of the hill, and at an angle from the big gun.

"If it does burst—which I hope it won't," said Tom, "the pieces will fly in straight lines, so we will be safe enough here. Ned, are you are ready at the instruments?"

"Yes, Tom."

"I want you to note the registered muzzle velocity. Mr. Damon, you will please read the pressure gauge. After I press the button I'm going to watch the landing of the projectile through the telescope."

The gun had been pointed, as I have said, at the farthest target—one thirty miles away, telescope sights on the giant cannon making this possible.

"All ready!" cried Tom.

"All ready," answered Ned.

There was a tense moment; Tom's thumb pressed home the electric button, and then came the explosion.

It seemed for a moment as if everyone was lifted from his feet. They had all stood on their tiptoes, and opened their mouths to lessen the shock, but even then it was terrific. The very ground shook—from the roof of their cave small stones and gravel rattled down on their heads. Their ear-drums were numbed from the shock. And the noise that filled the valley seemed like a thousand thunderbolts merged into one.

Tom rushed from the bombproof, dropping the electric button. He caught sight of his gun, resting undisturbed on the improvised carriage.

"Hurray!" he cried in delight. "She stood the charge all right. And look! look!" he cried, as he pointed the glasses toward the distant hillside. "There goes my projectile as straight as an arrow. There! By Caesar, Ned! It landed within three feet of the target! Oh, you beauty!" he yelled at his giant cannon. "You did all I hoped you would! Thirty miles, Ned! Think of that! A two-ton projectile being shot thirty miles!"

"It's great, Tom!" yelled his chum, clapping him on the back, and capering about. "It's the longest shot on record."

"It certainly is," declared the foreman of the steel workers, who had helped in casting many big guns. "No cannon ever made can equal it. You win, Tom Swift!"

"Bless my armor plate!" gasped Mr. Damon. "What attacking ship against the Panama Canal could float after a shot like that."

"Not one," declared Tom; "especially after I put a bursting charge into the projectile. We'll try that next."

By means of compressed air the gases and some particles of the unexploded powder were blown out of the big cannon. Then it was loaded again, the projectile this time carrying a bursting charge of another explosive that would be set off by concussion.

Once more they retired to the bombproof, and again the great gun was fired. Once more the ground shook, and they were nearly deafened by the shock.

Then, as they looked toward the distant hillside, they saw a shower of earth and great rocks rise up. It was like a sand geyser. Then, when this settled back again, there was left a gaping hole in the side of the mountain.

"That does the business!" cried Tom. "My cannon is a success!"

The last shot did not go quite as far as the first, but it was because a different kind of projectile was used. Tom was perfectly satisfied, however. Several more trials were given the gun, and each one confirmed the young inventor in his belief that he had made a wonderful weapon.

"If that doesn't fortify the Panama Canal nothing will," declared Ned.

"Well, I hope I can convince Uncle Sam of that," spoke Tom, simply.

The muzzle velocity and the pressure were equal to Tom's highest hopes. He knew, now, that he had hit on just the right mixture of powder, and that his gun was correctly proportioned. It showed not the slightest strain.

"Now we'll try another bursting shell," he said, after a rest, during which some records were made. "Then we'll call it a day's work. Koku, bring up some more powder. I'll use a little heavier charge this time."

It was while the gun was being loaded that a horseman was seen riding wildly down the valley. He was waving a red flag in his hand.

"Bless my watch chain!" cried Mr. Damon. "What's that?"

"It looks as though he was coming to give us a warning," suggested the steel foreman.

"Maybe someone has kicked about our shooting," remarked Ned.

"I hope not," murmured Tom.

He looked at the horseman anxiously. The rider came nearer and nearer, wildly waving his flag. He seemed to be shouting something, but his words could not be made out. Finally he came near enough to be heard.

"The dam! The dam!" he cried. "It's bursting. Your shots have hastened it. The cracks are widening. You'd better get away!" And he galloped on.

"Bless my toilet soap!" gasped Mr. Damon.

"I was afraid of this!" murmured Tom. "But, since our shots have hastened the disaster, maybe we can avert it."

"How?" demanded Ned.

"I'll show you. All hands come here and we'll shift this gun. I want it to point at that big white stone!" and he indicated an immense boulder, well up the valley, near the place where the two great gulches joined.

THE DOPED POWDER

"What are you going to do, Tom?" cried Ned, as he, with the others, worked the hand gear that shifted the big gun. When it was permanently mounted electricity would accomplish this work. "What's your game, Tom?"

"Don't you remember, Ned? When we were talking about the chance of the dam bursting, I said if the current of suddenly released water could be turned into the other valley, the people below us would be saved."

"Yes."

"Well, that's what I'm going to do. I'm going to fire a bursting shell at the point where the two valleys come together. I'll break down the barrier of rock and stone between them."

"Bless my shovel and hoe!" cried Mr. Damon.

"If we can turn enough of the water into the other valley, where no one lives, and where it can escape into the big river there, the amount that will flow down this valley will be so small that only a little damage will be done."

"That's right!" declared the steel foreman, as he caught Tom's idea. "It's the only way it could be done, too, for there won't be time to make the necessary excavation any other way. Is the gun swung around far enough, Mr. Swift?"

"No, a little more toward me," answered Tom, as he peered through the telescope sights. "There, that will do. Now to get the proper elevation," and he began to work the other apparatus, having estimated the range as well as he could.

In a few seconds the giant cannon was properly trained on the white rock. Meanwhile the horseman, with his red flag, had continued on down the valley. In spite of his warning of the night before, it developed that a number had disregarded it, and had remained in their homes. Most of the inhabitants, however, had fled to the hills, to stay in tents, or with such neighbors as could accommodate them. Some lingered to move their household goods, while others fled with what they could carry.

It was to see that the town was deserted by these late-stayers that the messenger rode, crying his warning as did the messenger at the bursting of the Johnstown dam twenty-odd years ago.

"The projectile!" cried Tom, as he saw that all was in readiness. "Lively now! I can see the top of the dam beginning to crumble," and he laid aside the telescope he had been using.

The projectile, with a heavy charge of bursting powder, was slung into the breech of the gun.

"Now the powder, Koku!" called Tom. "Be quick; but not so fast that you drop any of it."

"Me fetch," responded the giant, as he hastened toward the small cave where the explosive was kept. As the big man brought the first lot, and Ned was about to insert it in the breech of the gun, behind the projectile, Tom exclaimed:

"Just let me have a look at that. It's some that I first made, and I want to be sure it hasn't gone stale."

Critically he looked at the powerful explosive. As he did so a change came over his face.

"Here, Koku!" the young inventor said. "Where did you get this?"

"In cave, Master."

"Is there any more left?"

"Only enough for this one shoot."

"By Jove!" muttered Tom. "There's been some trick played here!" and he set off on a run toward the bomb-proof.

"What's the matter?" cried Ned, as he noticed the agitation of his chum.

"The powder has been doped!" yelled Tom. "Something has been put in it to make it nonexplosive. It's no good. It wouldn't send that shell a thousand yards, and it's got to go five miles to do any good. My plan won't work."

"Doped the powder?" gasped Ned. "Who could have done it?"

"I don't know. There must have been some spy at work. Quick, run and ask the foreman if any of his men are missing. I'll see if there's enough of the good powder left to break down the barrier!"

Ned was away like a shot, while the others, not knowing what to make of the strange conduct of the two lads, looked on in wonder. Tom raced toward the cave where the powder was stored, Koku following him.

"Bless my shoe laces!" cried Mr. Damon. "Look at the dam now

They gazed to where he pointed. In several places the concrete spillway had crumbled down to a ragged edge, showing that the solid wall was giving way. The amount of water flowing over the dam was greater now. The creek was steadily rising. Down the valley the horseman with the red flag was but a speck in the distance.

"What can I do? What can I do?" murmured Tom. "If all the powder there is left has been doped, I can't save the town! What can I do? What can I do?"

Ned had reached the foreman, who, with his helpers, was standing about the big gun.

"Have any of your men left recently?" yelled Ned.

"Any of my men left? What do you mean?

"Schlichter went yesterday," said the timekeeper. "I thought he was in quite a hurry to get his money, too."

"Schlichter gone!" exclaimed the foreman. "He was no good anyhow. I think he was a sort of Anarchist; always against the government, the way he talked. So he has left; eh? But what's the matter, Ned?"

"Something wrong with the powder. Tom can't shoot the cannon and turn aside the water to save the town. Some of his enemies have been at work. Schlichter leaving at this time, and in such hurry, makes it look suspicious."

"It sure does! And, now I recall it, I saw him yesterday near your powder magazine. I called him down for it, for I knew Tom Swift had given orders that only his own party was to go near it. So the powder is doped; eh?"

"Yes! It's all off now."

He turned to see Tom approaching on the run.

"Any good powder left?" asked Ned.

"Not a pound. Did you hear anything?"

"Yes, one man has disappeared. Oh, Tom, we've got to fail after all! We can't save the town!"

"Yes, we can, Ned. If that dam will only hold for half an hour more."

"What do you mean

"I mean that I have another supply of good powder in the village. I secreted some there, you remember I told you. If I can go get that, and get back here in time, I can break down the barrier with one shot, and save Preston."

"But you never can make the trip there and back in time, with the powder, Tom. It's impossible. The dam may hold half an hour, or it may not. But, if it does, you can't do anything!"

"I can't? Well, I'm going to make a big try, Ned. You stay on the job here. Have everything ready so that when I get back with the new explosive, which I hope hasn't been tampered with, I can shove it into the breech, and set it off. Have the wires, primers and button all ready for me."

Then Tom set off on the run.

"Where are you going?" gasped his chum. "You can never run to Preston and back in time."

"I don't intend to. I'm going in my airship. Koku, never mind bringing the rest of the powder from the cave. It's no good. Run out the Humming Bird. I'm going to drive her to the limit. I've just got to get that powder here on time!"

"Bless my timetable!" gasped Mr. Damon. "That's the only way it can be done. Lucky Tom brought the airship along!"

The young inventor, pausing only to get some cans for the explosive, and some straps with which to fasten them in the monoplane, leaped into the speedy craft.

The motor was adjusted; Koku whirled the propeller blades. There was a staccato succession of explosions, a rushing, roaring sound, and then the craft rose like a bird, and Tom circled about, making a straight course for the distant town, while below him the creek rose higher and higher as the dam continued to crumble away.

BLOWING DOWN THE BARRIER

"Can you see anything of him, Ned?"

"Not a thing, Mr. Damon. Wait—hold on—no! It's only a bird," and the lad lowered the glasses with which he had been sweeping the sky. looking for his chum returning in his airship with the powder.

"He'd better hurry," murmured the foreman. "That dam can't last much longer. The water is rising fast. When it does go out it will go with a rush. Then good-bye to the village of Preston."

"Bless my insurance policy!" cried Mr. Damon. "Don't say such things, my friend."

"But they're true!" insisted the man. "You can see for yourself that the cracks in the dam are getting larger. It will be a big flood when it does come. And I'm not altogether sure that we're safe up here," he added, as he looked down the sides of the hill to where the creek was now rapidly becoming a raging torrent.

"Bless my hat-band!" gasped Mr. Damon. "You—you are getting on my nerves

"I don't want to be a calamity howler," went on the foreman; "but we've got to face this thing. We'd better get ready to vamoose if Tom Swift doesn't reach here in time to fire that shot—and he doesn't seem to be in sight."

Once more Ned swept the sky with his glasses. The roar of the water below them could be plainly heard now.

"I wish I could get hold of that rascally German," muttered the foreman. "I'd give him more than a piece of my mind. It will be his fault if the town is destroyed, for Tom's plan would have saved it. I wonder who he can be, anyhow?"

"Some spy," declared Ned. "We've been having trouble right along, you know, and this is part of the game. I have some suspicions, but Tom doesn't agree with me. Certainly the fellow, whatever his object, has made trouble enough this time."

"I should say so," agreed the foreman.

"Look, Ned!" cried Mr. Damon. "Is that a bird; or is it Tom?" and he pointed to a speck in the sky. Ned quickly focused his glasses on it.

"It's Tom!" he cried a second later. "It's Tom in the Humming Bird!"

"Thank Heaven for that!" exclaimed Mr. Damon, fervently, forgetting to bless anything on this occasion. "If only he can get here in time!"

"He's driving her to the limit!" cried Ned, still watching his chum through the glass. "He's coming!"

"He'll need to," murmured the foreman, grimly. "That dam can't last ten minutes more. Look at the people fleeing from the valley!"

He pointed to the north, and a confused mass of small black objects—men, women and children, doubtless, who had lingered in spite of the other warning—could be seen clambering up the sides of the valley.

"Is everything ready at the gun?" asked Mr. Damon.

"Everything," answered Ned, whom Tom had instructed in all the essentials. "As soon as he lands we'll jam in the powder, and fire the shot."

"I hope he doesn't land too hard, with all that explosive on board," murmured the foreman.

"Bless my checkerboard!" cried Mr. Damon. "Don't suggest such a thing."

"I guess we can trust Tom," spoke Ned.

They looked up. The distant throb of the monoplane's motor could now be heard above the roar of the swollen waters. Tom could be seen in his seat, and beside him, in the other, was a large package.

Nearer and nearer came the monoplane. It began to descend, very gently, for well Tom Swift knew the danger of hitting the ground too hard with the cargo he carried.

He described a circle in the air to check his speed. Then, gently as a bird, he made a landing not far from the gun, the craft running easily over one of the few level places on the side of the hill. Tom yanked on the brake, and the iron-shod pieces of wood dug into the ground, checking the progress of the monoplane on its bicycle wheels.

"Have you got it, Tom?" yelled Ned.

"I have," was the answer of the young inventor as he leaped from his seat.

"Is it good powder?" asked the foreman, anxiously.

"I don't know," spoke Tom. "I didn't have time to look. I just rushed up to where I had stored it, got some out and came back with the motor at full speed. Ran into an airpocket, too, and I thought it was all up with me when I began to fall. But I managed to get out of it. Say, we're going to have it nip and tuck here to save the village."

"That's what!" agreed the foreman, as he helped Koku take the cans of explosive.

"Wait until I look at it," suggested Tom, as he opened one. His trained eye and touch soon told him that this explosive had not been tampered with.

"It's all right!" he shouted. "Into the gun with it, and we'll see what happens."

It was the work of only a few moments to put in the charge. Then, once more, the breech-block was slotted home, and the trailing electric wires unreeled to lead to the bomb-proof.

Tom Swift took one last look through the telescope sights of his giant cannon. He changed the range slightly by means of the hand and worm-screw gear, and then, with the others, ran to the shelter of the cave. For, though the gun had stood the previous tests well, Tom had used a heavier charge this time, both in the firing chamber and in the projectile, and he wanted to take no chances.

"All ready?" asked the young inventor, as he looked around at his friends gathered in the cave.

"I—I guess so," answered Ned, somewhat doubtfully.

Tom hesitated a moment, then, as his fingers stiffened to press the electric button there sounded to the ears of all a dull, booming sound.

"The dam! It has given way!" cried Ned.

"That's it!" shouted the foreman. "Fire!"

Tom pressed the button. Once again was that awful tremor of the earth—the racking shake—the terrific explosion and a shock that knocked a couple of the men down.

"All right!" shouted Tom. "The gun held together. It's safe to go out. We'll see what happened!"

They all rushed from the shelter of the cave. Before them was an awe-inspiring sight. A great wall of water was coming down the valley, from a large opening in the centre of the dam. It seemed to leap forward like a race horse.

Tom declared afterward that he saw his projectile strike the barrier that separated one valley from the other, but none of the others had eyes-sight as keen as this—and perhaps Tom was in error.

But there was no doubt that they all saw what followed. They heard a distant report as the great projectile burst. Then a wall of earth seemed to rise up in front of the advancing wall of water. High into the air great stones and masses of dirt were thrown.

"A good shot!" cried the foreman. "Just in the right place, Tom Swift!"

For a moment it was as though that wall of water hesitated, not deciding whether to continue on down the populated valley, or to swing over into the other gash where it could do comparatively little harm. It was a moment of suspense.

Then, as Tom's great shot had, by means of the exploding projectile, torn down the barrier, the water chose the more direct and shorter path. With a mighty roar, like a distant Niagara, it swept into the new channel the young inventor had made. Into the transverse valley it tumbled and tossed in muddy billows of foam, and only a small portion of the flood added itself to the already swollen creek.

The village of Preston had been saved by the shot from Tom's giant cannon.

THE GOVERNMENT ACCEPTS

"Whew! Let me sit down somewhere and get my breath!" gasped Tom, when it was all over.

"I should think you would want a bit of quiet," replied Ned. "You've been on the jump since early morning."

"Bless my dining-room table!" cried Mr. Damon. "I should say so! I'll go tell the cook to get us all a good meal—we need it," for a competent cook had been installed in the old farmhouse where Tom and his party had their headquarters.

"But you did the trick, Tom, old man!" exclaimed Ned, fervently, as he looked down the valley and saw the receding water. For, with the opening of the channel into the other valley the flood, at no time particularly dangerous near Preston, was subsiding rapidly.

"He sure did," declared the foreman. "No one else could have done it, either."

"Oh, I don't know," spoke Tom, modestly. "It just happened so. There was one minute, though, after I got to the place in Preston where I had stored the powder, that I didn't know whether I would succeed or not."

"How was that?" asked Mr. Damon.

"Why, in my hurry and excitement I forgot the key to the underground storeroom where I had put the explosive. I knew there was no time to get another, so I took a chance and burst in the door with an axe I found in the freight depot."

"I should say you did take a chance!" declared Ned, who knew how "freaky" the high explosive was, and how likely it was, at times, to be set off by the least concussion.

"But it came out all right," went on Tom. "I bundled it into the other seat of my Humming Bird, and started back."

"Had most of the folks left town?" asked the foreman.

"Nearly all," replied Tom. "The last of them were hurrying away as I left. And it shows how scared they were, they didn't pay any attention to me and my flying machine, though I'll wager some of them never saw one before."

"Well, they don't need to be scared any more," put in Mr. Damon "You saved their homes for them, Tom."

"I'd like to get hold of the fellow who doped my powder; that's what I'd like to do," murmured the young inventor. "Ned, we'll have to be doubly watchful from now on. But I must take a look at my gun. That last charge may have strained it."

But the giant cannon was as perfect as the day it was turned out of the shop. Not even the extra charge of the powerful explosive had injured it.

"That's fine!" cried Tom, as he looked at every part. "As soon as this flood is over we'll try some more practice shots. But we're all entitled to a rest now"

The great gun was covered with tarpaulins to protect it from the weather, and then all retired to the house for a bountiful meal. Late that afternoon nearly all signs of the flood had disappeared, save that along the edges of the creek was much driftwood, showing the height to which the creek had risen. But it would have gone much higher had it not been for Tom's timely shot.

The water from the impounded lake continued to pour down into the cross valley, and did some damage, but nothing like what would have followed its advent into Preston. The few inhabitants of the gulch into which the young inventor had directed the flood had had warning, and had fled in time. In Preston, some few houses nearest the banks of the rising creek were flooded, but were not carried away.

The following day some of the officers of the water company paid a visit to Tom, to thank him for what he had done. But for him they would have been responsible for great property damage, and loss of life might have followed.

They intended to rebuild the dam, they said, on a new principle, making it much stronger.

"And," said the president, "we will have an emergency outlet gate into that valley you so providentially opened for us, Mr. Swift. Then, in time of great rain, we can let the water out slowly as we need to."

Tom's chief anxiety, now, was to bring his perfected gun to the notice of the United States Government officials. To have them accept it, he knew he must give it a test before the ordnance board, and before the officers of the army and navy. Accordingly he prepared for this.

He ordered several new projectiles, some of a different type from those heretofore used, and leaving Koku and Ned in charge of the gun, went back to Shopton to superintend the manufacture of an additional supply of his explosive. He took care, too, that no spies gained access to it.

Then, with a plentiful supply of ammunition and projectiles, Tom resumed his practice in the lonely valley. He had, in the meanwhile, sent requests to the proper government officials to come and witness the tests.

At first he met with no success, and he learned, incidentally, that General Waller had built a new gun, the merits of which he was also anxious to show.

"It's a sort of rivalry between us," said Tom to Ned.

But, in a way, fortune favored our hero. For when General Waller tested his new gun, though it did not burst, it did not come up to expectations, and its range was not as great as some of the weapons already in use.

Then, too, Captain Badger acted as Tom's friend at court. He "pulled wires" to good advantage, and at last the government sent word that one of the ordnance officers would be present on a certain day to witness the tests.

"I wish the whole board had come," said Tom. "Probably they have only sent a young fellow, just out of West Point, who will turn me down.

"But I'm going to give him the surprise of his life; and if he doesn't report favorably, and insist on the whole board coming out here, I'll be much disappointed."

Tom made his preparations carefully, and certainly Captain Waydell, the young officer who came to represent Uncle Sam, was impressed. Tom sent shell after shell, heavily charged, against the side of the mountain. Great holes and gashes were torn in the earth. The gun even exceeded the range of thirty miles. And the heaviest armor plate that could be procured was to the projectiles of the giant cannon like cheese to a revolver bullet.

"It's great, Mr. Swift! Great!" declared the young captain. "I shall strongly recommend that the entire board see this test." And when Tom let him fire the gun himself the young man was more than delighted.

He was as good as his word, and a week later the entire ordnance board, from the youngest member to the grave and grizzled veterans, were present to witness the test of Tom's giant cannon.

It is needless to say that it was successful. Tom and Ned, not to mention Mr. Damon, Koku and every loyal member of the steel working gang, saw to it that there was no hitch. The solid shots were regarded with wonder, and when the explosive one was sent against the hillside, making a geyser of earth, the enthusiasm was unbounded.

"We shall certainly recommend your gun, Mr. Swift," declared the Chief of Staff. "It does just what we want it to do, and we have no doubt that Congress will appropriate the money for several with which to fortify the Panama Canal."

"The gun is most wonderful," spoke a voice with a German accent. "It is surprising!"

Tom and Ned both started. They saw an officer, evidently a foreigner, resplendent in gold trimmings, and with many medals, standing near the secretary of the ordnance board.

"Yes, General von Brunderger," agreed the chief, "it is a most timely invention. Mr. Swift, allow me to present you to General von Brunderger, of the German army, who is here learning how Uncle Sam does things."

Tom bowed and shook hands. He glanced sharply at the German, but was sure he had never seen him before. Then all the board, and General von Brunderger, who, it appeared, was present as an invited guest, examined the big cannon critically, while Tom explained the various details.

When the board members left, the chief promised to let Tom know the result of the formal report as soon as possible.

The young inventor did not have long to wait. In about two weeks, during which time he and Ned perfected several little matters about the cannon, there came an official-looking document.

"Well, we'll soon know the verdict," spoke Tom, somewhat nervously, as he opened the envelope. Quickly he read the enclosure.

"What is it!" cried Ned.

"The government accepts my gun!" exclaimed the young inventor. "It will purchase a number as soon as they can be made. We are to take one to Panama, where it will be set up. Hurray, Ned, my boy! Now for Panama!"

OFF FOR PANAMA

"WELL," Tom, it doesn't seem possible; does it, old man?"

"You're right, Ned—in a way. And yet, after all the hard work we've done, almost anything is possible."

"Hard work! We? Oh, pshaw! You've done most of it, Tom. I only helped here and there."

"Indeed, and you did more than that. If it hadn't been for you, Mr. Damon and Koku we'd never have gotten off as soon as we did. The government is the limit for doing things, sometimes."

"Bless my timetable! but I agree with you," put in Mr. Damon. "But at last we are on the way, in spite of delays."

This conversation took place on board one of Uncle Sam's warships, which the President had designated to take Tom's giant cannon to the Panama Canal.

The big gun had been lashed to the deck of the vessel, and was well protected from the weather. In the hold the parts of the disappearing carriage, which Tom had at last succeeded in having made, were securely stowed. In another part of the warship were the big projectiles, some arranged to be fired as solid shots, and others with a bursting charge. There was also a good supply of the powerful explosive, and Tom had taken extraordinary precautions so that it could not be tampered with. Koku had been detailed as a sort of guard over it, and to relieve him was a trustworthy sergeant of marines.

"If anyone tries to dope that powder now, and spoil my test at Panama," declared Tom, "he'll wish he'd never tried it."

"Especially if Koku gets hold of him," added Ned, grimly.

"But I don't believe there is any danger," went on the young inventor. "I spoke about what had happened, and the ordnance board took extra precautions to see that none but men and officers who could be implicitly trusted had anything to do with this expedition."

"You don't really believe anything like treachery would be attempted; do you, Tom?"

"I don't know what to say. Certainly I can't see why anyone connected with Uncle Sam would want to throw cold water on a plan to fortify the canal, even if an outsider has invented the gun—I mean someone like myself, not connected with the army or navy."

"If it's anything it's jealousy," declared Ned, "That General Waller—"

"There you go again, Ned. Let's not talk about it. Come on forward and see what progress we are making."

It must not be supposed that to get the big gun aboard the vessel, arrange for a new supply of the explosive, and for many of the great projectiles, had been easy work. It was a task that taxed the skill and strength of Tom and his friends to the utmost.

There had been wearying delays, especially in the matter of making the disappearing carriage. At times it seemed as if the required projectiles would never be finished. The powder, too, gave trouble, for sometimes batches would be turned out that were utterly worthless.

But Tom never gave up, even when it seemed that some of the failures were purposely made. Ned declared that there was a conspiracy against his chum, but Tom could not see it that way. It was due to a combination of circumstances, he insisted.

But finally the gun had been put aboard the ship, having been transported from the proving ground in the valley, and they were now en route to Panama. There the giant cannon was to be set up, and tried again. If it came up to expectations it was to be finally adopted as the official gun for the protection of the big canal, and Tom would receive a substantial reward.

"And I'm confident that it will make good," said the young inventor to his chum, as they paced the deck of the vessel. "In fact, I'm so sure I have practically engaged the Universal Steel Company to hold itself in readiness to make several more of the guns."

"But suppose Uncle Sam decides against the cannon on this second test?"

"Well, then I've lost out, that's all," declared Tom, philosophically. "But I don't believe they will."

"It certainly is a giant cannon," remarked Ned, as he paused to look at the prostrate monster, lashed to the deck, with its wrappings of tarpaulins. "It looks bigger here than it did when you fired the shot that saved the town, Tom."

"Yes, I suppose it does, by contrast. But let's go down and see how the powder and shells are standing the trip. I told the captain to have them securely lashed, so if we struck rough weather, and the vessel rolled, they wouldn't carry away."

"Especially the powder," put in Ned. "If that starts to banging around—well, I'd rather be somewhere else."

"Bless my rain gauge!" cried Mr. Damon. "Please don't say such things. You make me nervous. You're as bad as that steel foreman."

"All right, I'll be better," promised Ned, with a laugh.

The two chums found that every precaution had been taken in regard to the projectiles and powder. Koku was on guard, the giant regarding the boxes of explosive with a calm but determined eye. It would not be well for any unauthorized hand to tamper with them.

"Am dere anyt'ing I kin do fo' yo'-all, Massa Tom?" inquired Eradicate, as the young inventor and Ned prepared to go on deck again. The aged colored man had insisted on coming as a sort of personal bodyguard to Tom, and the latter had not the heart to refuse him. Eradicate was desperately jealous of the giant.

"Huh!" Eradicate had said, "anybody kin sit an' look at a lot ob dem powder boxes; but 'tain't everybody what kin wait on Massa Tom. I kin, an' I'se gwine t' do it." And so he had.

It was planned to proceed directly to Colon, the eastern terminus of the canal, from New York, stopping at Santiago to transact some government business there. The big gun was to be mounted on a barbette near the Gatun locks, pointing out to sea, and the trial shots would be fired over the water.

Eventually the gun would be so mounted as to swing in a circle,, so as to command the land as well as the water; and, in fact, if the government decided to adopt Tom's giant cannon as the official protective arm of the canal, they would all be so mounted. For, of course, it might be possible for land as well as sea forces to attack and try to capture the big ditch.

The first few days of the voyage were pleasant enough. The weather was fine, and Tom was kept busy explaining to many of the officers aboard the ship the principles of his gun, powder and projectiles. Members of the ordnance board, who had been detailed to witness the test, were also much interested as Tom modestly described his work on the giant cannon.

At Santiago de Cuba, when Tom and Ned were standing near the gangway, watching the officers returning from shore leave, for the ship was to proceed soon, after a two days' stay, the young inventor started as he noticed a military man walking aboard.

"Look, Ned!" he exclaimed, in a low voice.

"Where?"

"At that man—an officer in civilian dress, I should judge— haven't you seen him before?"

"I have, Tom. Now, where was it? I seem to remember his face; and yet he wasn't dressed like this the last time I saw him."

"I guess not, Ned. He had on a uniform then."

"By jinks! I have it. That German officer—von Brunderger! That's he!"

"You're right, Ned. And he's got his servant with him, I guess," and Tom nodded toward a stolid German who was carrying the other's suitcase.

"I wonder what he's doing aboard here?" went on our hero's chum.

"We'll soon know," spoke Tom. "He's seen us and is nodding. We might as well go meet him."

"Ah, my good friend, Tom Swift!" exclaimed General von Brunderger, genially, as he grasped the hands of Tom and Ned. "I am glad to see you both again." He seemed to mean it, though he had not been especially cordial to them at the first gun test. "Take my grip below," he said in German to the man, "and, Rudolph, find Lieutenant Blake and inform him that I am on board. I have been invited to go to Panama by Lieutenant Blake," he added to Tom. "I have never seen the big ditch that you wonderful Americans have so nearly finished."

"It is going to be a big thing," spoke Tom. "I am proud that my gun is going to help protect it."

"Ah, so you were successful, then?" and his voice expressed surprise. "I had not heard. And the big gun; is he here?" Though speaking very good English, von Brunderger occasionally lapsed into the idioms of his Fatherland.

"Yes, it's on board," said Tom. "Are you going to Panama for any special purpose?"

Ned declared afterward that the German started as Tom asked this question, but if he did the young inventor scarcely noticed it. In an instant, however, von Brunderger was composed again.

"I go but to see the big ditch before the water is let in," he replied. "And since your gun is to have a test I shall be glad to witness that. You see, I am commissioned by my Kaiser to learn all that you Americans will allow me to in reference to your ways of doing things—in the army, the navy and in the pursuit of peace. After all, preparation for war is the best means of securing peace. Your officers have been more than kind and I have taken advantage of the offer to go to Panama. Lieutenant Blake said the ship would stop here, and, as I had business in Cuba, I came and waited. I am delighted to see you both again."

He went below, leaving Tom and Ned staring at one another.

"Well, what do you think of it?" asked Ned.

"I don't see anything to be worried about," declared Tom. "It's true that a German once tried to make trouble for me, but this von Brunderger is all right, as far as I can learn. He has the highest references, and is an accredited representative of the Kaiser. You are too suspicious, Ned, just as you were in the case of General Waller."

"Maybe so."

From Santiago, swinging around the island of Jamaica, the warship took her way, with the big gun, to Colon. When half way across the Caribbean Sea they encountered rough weather.

The storm broke without any unusual preliminaries, but quickly increased to a hurricane, and when night fell it saw the big ship rolling and tossing in a tempestuous sea. Torn was anxious about his big gun, but the captain assured him that double lashings would make it perfectly safe.

Tom and Ned had seen little of the German officer that day, nor, in fact, since he came aboard. He kept much in the quarters of the other officers, and the report was current that he was a "jolly good fellow."

Rather anxious as to the outcome of the storm, Tom turned in late that night, not expecting to sleep much, for there were many unusual noises. But he did drop off into a doze, only to be awakened about an hour later by a commotion on deck.

"What's up, Ned?" he called to his chum, who had an adjoining stateroom.

"I don't know, Tom. Something is going on, though. Hear that thumping and pounding!"

As Ned spoke there came a tremendous noise from the deck.

"By Jove!" yelled Tom, jumping from his berth. "It's my big gun! It has torn loose from the lashings and may roll overboard!"

At Gatun Locks

"Steady there now, men! Pass forward those lashings! Careful! Look out, or you'll be caught by it when she rolls! Another turn around the bitts!"

It was the officer of the deck giving orders to a number of marines and sailors as Tom hastily clad, leaped on deck, followed by his chum. The warship was pitching and tossing worse than ever in the heaving billows, and the men were engaged in making fast the giant cannon, which, as Tom had surmised, had torn loose from the steel cables holding it down on deck.

"Come on, Ned!" cried Tom. "We've got to help here!"

"That's right. Look at her swing, would you? If she hits anything it's a goner!"

The breech of the gun appeared to be the end that had come loose, while the muzzle still held fast. And this immense mass of steel was swinging about, eluding the efforts of the ship's officers and crew to capture it. And it seemed only a question of time when the muzzle would tear loose, too. Then, free on deck, the giant cannon would roll through the frail bulwarks, and plunge. into the depths of the sea.

"Look out for yourselves, boys!" cried the officer, as he saw Tom and Ned. "This is no plaything!"

"I know it!" gasped Tom. "But we've got to fasten it down."

"That's what we're trying to do," answered the other. "We did get the bight of a cable over the breech, but the men could not hold it, even though they took a couple of turns around the bitts."

"Ned, go call Koku!" cried Tom. "We need him up here."

"That's right!" declared his chum. "If anyone can hold the cable with the weight of the big gun straining on it, the giant can. I'll get him!"

"On deck, Koku, quick!" gasped Ned. "Master's cannon may fall into the sea."

"But the powder!" asked the big man, simply. "Master told me to guard the powder. I stay here."

"No, I'll stay!" insisted Ned. "You are needed on deck, I'll take your place here."

Koku stared uncomprehendingly for a moment, while the loosened gun continued to thump and pound on the deck as though it would burst through. Then it filtered through the dull brain of honest Koku what was wanted.

"I go," he said, and he hurried up the companionway, while Ned, eager to be with Tom, took up the less exciting work of guarding the powder.

Once more, with the giant strength of Koku to aid in the work, the task of lashing the gun again to the deck was undertaken. A bight of steel cable was gotten around the breech, and then passed to a big bitt, or stanchion, bolted to the deck. Koku, working on the heaving deck, amid the hurricane, took a turn around the brace.

There came a roll of the ship that threatened to send the gun sliding against the stanchion, but Koku braced himself. His arms, great bunches of muscles, strained and fairly cracked with the strain. The wire rope seemed to give. Then, as the ship rolled the other way, the strain eased. Koku, aided by the cable, and by the leverage given by the several turns about the bitts, had held the big gun.

"Quick!" cried Tom. "Now another rope so it can't roll the opposite way, and we'll have her."

For a moment the ship was on a level keel, and taking advantage of this, when the weight of the gun would be neutral, another cable was passed around it. Then it was a comparatively easy matter to put on more lashings until the giant cannon was once more fast.

"Whew! But that was tough work!" exclaimed Tom, as he once more entered the stateroom with Ned.

"It must have been," agreed his chum, who had been relieved at the powder station by the giant.

"I thought it would surely go overboard," went on Tom. "Only for Koku it would have. Those fellows couldn't hold it when the ship rolled."

"How did it happen to get loose?" asked Ned.

"Oh, the cables frayed, I suppose. I'll take a look in the morning. Say, but this is some storm!"

"Is the gun all right now?"

"Yes, it's fastened down like a mummy. It can't get loose unless the whole deck comes with it. We can sleep in peace."

"Not much sleep in this blow, I guess," responded Ned.

But they did manage to get some rest by morning, at which time the hurricane seemed to have blown itself out. The day saw the sea gradually calm down, and the big cannon was made additionally secure against a possible recurrence of the accident. But a few days more and it would be safe at Colon.

Tom and Ned had gone on deck soon after breakfast to look at the cannon. All about were pieces of the broken cables, that had been cast aside when the new lashings were put on. Ned picked up one end, remarking:

"These seem mighty strong. It's queer how they broke."

"Well, there was quite a weight upon them," spoke Tom.

Ned did not reply for a moment. Then, as he looked at another piece of a severed cable, he exclaimed:

"Tom, the weight of your gun never broke these."

"What do you mean, Ned?"

"I mean that they were partly filed, or cut through—then the storm and the pressure of the gun did the rest. Look!"

He held out the piece of wire rope. There, on the end, could be seen several strands cleanly severed, as though a file or a hack-saw had been used.

"By Jove!" murmured Tom. He looked about the deck. There was no one near the big gun. "Ned," whispered his chum, "there's something wrong here.

It's more of that conspiracy to defeat my aims. Don't say anything about this, and we'll keep our eyes open. We'll do a bit of detective work."

"The scoundrels!" exclaimed Ned. "I wish we knew who they were. General Waller isn't aboard, and what other of the officers has a gun of his own that he would rather see accepted by the government than yours?"

"None that I know of," replied Tom.

"General Waller might have hired someone to—"

"Don't go making any unwarranted charges," warned the young inventor.

"Or perhaps that German, Tom, might—"

"Hush!" cautioned Tom. "Here he comes now," and, as he spoke, General von Brunderger came strolling along the deck.

"I am glad to see that the accident of last night had no serious effects," he said, smiling.

"It was no accident!" burst out Ned.

"No accident? You surprise me. I thought—"

"Oh, Ned means that some of the cables look as though they had been cut," hastily put in Tom, nudging his chum in the ribs as a signal for him to keep quiet.

"The cables cut!" exclaimed the German, and his voice indicated anxious solicitude.

"Or else filed," went on Tom easily, with a warning glance at Ned. "But I dare say they were old cables, that had been used on other work, and may have become frayed. Everything is safe now, though. New cables were lashed on this morning."

"I am glad to hear it. It would be a—er—ah, a national calamity to lose so valuable a gun, and the opening of the canal so near at hand. I am glad that your invention is safe, Herr Swift," and he smiled genially at Tom and Ned.

"What did you shut me off for?" asked Ned, when he and his chum were alone in their stateroom again.

"Because I didn't want you to make any breaks before him," answered Tom.

"Then you suspect—"

"I suspect many things, Ned, but I'm not going to show my hand until I'm ready. I'm going to watch and listen."

"And I'll be with you."

But no further accidents occurred. There were no more storms, no attempt was made to meddle with Tom's powder, and in due season the ship arrived at Colon, and after much labor the great gun, its carriage, the shells and the powder were taken to the barbette at the Gatun locks, designed to admit vessels from the Caribbean Sea into Gatun Lake.

"And now for some more hard work," remarked Tom, as all the needful stores were landed.

NEWS OF THE MINE

"Just a little farther over this way, Ned. That's better. Now mark it there, and we'll have it clamped down."

"But can you get enough elevation here, Tom?"

"Oh, yes, I think so. Besides, I've added a few more inches to the lift of the disappearing carriage, and it will send the gun so much farther in the air. I think this will do. Where is Koku?"

"Here I be, Master."

"Just get hold of that small derrick, Koku, and lift up one of the projectiles. I want to see if they come in the right place for the breech before I set the hoisting apparatus permanently."

The giant was soon engaged in winding up the rope of an improvised hoist that stood about in the position the permanent one was to go. From the interior of the barbette, which was, in effect, a bomb-proof structure, there was lifted one of the big projectiles destined to be hurled from Tom Swift's giant cannon.

"Yes, I think that will do," decided the young inventor, as he watched Koku. "Now, Mr. Damon, if you will kindly oversee this part of the work, I'll see if we can't get that motor in better shape. It didn't work worth a cent this morning."

"Bless my rubber coat, Tom, I'll do all I can to help you!" declared the odd man.

"Massa Tom! Massa Tom!" called Eradicate.

"Yes, Rad. What is it?"

"Heah am dem chicken sandwiches, an' some hot coffee fo' yo' all. I done knowed yo' alt wouldn't hab no time t' stop fo' dinnah, so I done made yo' all up a snack."

"That's mighty good of you, Rad," spoke Tom, with a laugh. "I was getting pretty hungry; but I didn't want to stop until I had things moving in better shape. Come on, Ned, let's knock off for a few minutes and take a bite. You, too, Mr. Damon."

As they sat about the place where the gun was being mounted, munching sandwiches and drinking the coffee which the aged colored man had so thoughtfully provided, Eradicate said, with a chuckle:

"By gar! Dey can't git erlong wifout dish yeah coon, arter all! Ha! ha! Dat cocoanut giant he mighty good when it comes t' fastening big guns down so dey won't blow away, but when it comes t' eatin' dey has t' depend on ole Eradicate! Ha! ha! I'se got dat cocoanut giant beat all right!"

"He sure is jealous of Koku," remarked Ned, as Tom and Mr. Damon smiled at the colored man.

"He certainly hit me in the right spot," declared Tom, as he reached for another sandwich.

They had landed from the warship several days before, and from then on there had been hard work and plenty of it. Tom was here, there and everywhere, directing matters so that his gun would be favorably placed.

Some preliminary work had been done before they arrived in the way of preparing a place to mount the gun, and this work was now proceeding. The officers of the ordnance department were in actual charge, but they always deferred to Tom, since he had most at stake.

"It will be some days before you can actually fire your gun; will it not?" asked Ned of his chum, as they finished the lunch, and prepared to resume work.

"Yes—a week at least, I expect. It is taking longer to set up the carriage than I thought. But it will be an improvement over the solid one we formerly used. That was fine, Rad," he concluded as the colored man went back to the shack of which he had taken possession for himself and his cooking operations. It adjoined the quarters to which Tom, Ned, Mr. Damon and Koku had been assigned.

"Golly! I ain't so old yit but what I knows de stuff Massa Tom laiks!" exclaimed the colored man, moving off with a chuckle.

Tom, though he had many suspicions about the cut cables that had nearly been the cause of his gun sliding into the sea, had learned nothing definite—nor had Ned.

The German officer, with his body servant, who seldom spoke, had landed at Colon, and was proceeding to make himself at home with the officers and men who were building the canal. Occasionally he paid a visit to Tom and Ned, where they were engaged about the big gun. He always seemed pleasant, and interested in their labors, asking many question, but that was all, and our hero began to feel that perhaps he was wrong in his suspicions.

As for Ned, he veered uncertainly from one suspicion to another. At one time he declared that von Brunderger and General Waller were in a conspiracy to upset Tom's plans. Again he would accuse the German alone, until Tom laughingly bade him attend more to work and less to theories.

Slowly the work progressed. The gun was mounted after much labor, and then arrangements began to be made for the test. A series of shots were to be fired out to sea, and the proper precautions were to be taken to prevent any ships from being struck.

"Though if you intend to send a projectile thirty miles," said one of the officers, "I'm afraid there may be some danger, after all. Are you sure you have a range of thirty miles, Mr. Swift?"

"I have," answered Tom, calmly, "and with the increased elevation that I am able to get here, it may exceed that."

The officer said nothing, but he looked at Tom in what our hero thought was a peculiar manner.

A few days before the date set for the test one of the sentinels, who had been detailed to keep curiosity-seekers away from the giant cannon, approached Tom and said:

"There is a gentleman asking to see you, Mr. Swift."

"Who is it?" asked Tom, laying aside a pressure gauge he intended attaching to the gun.

"He says his name is Peterson—Alec Peterson. Do you want to see him?"

"Yes, let him come up," directed the young inventor. "Do you hear that, Ned?" he called. "Our fortune-hunting friend is here."

"Maybe he's found that lost opal mine," suggested Ned.

"I hope he has, for dad's sake," went on Tom. "Hello, Mr. Peterson!" he called, as he noticed the old prospector coming along. "Have you had any luck?"

"I heard you were down here," said the many not answering the question directly, "and as I had to run over from my island for some supplies I thought I'd stop and see you. How are you?" and he shook hands.

"Fine!" answered Tom. "Have you found the lost mine yet?"

Alec Peterson paused a moment. Then he said slowly:

"No, Tom, I haven't succeeded in locating the mine yet. But I— I expect to any day now!" he added, hastily.

THE LONGEST SHOT

"Well, Mr. Peterson," remarked Tom, after a pause, "I'm sure I hope you will succeed in your quest. You must have met disappointment so far."

"I have, Tom. But I'm not going to give up. Can't you come over and see me before you go back North?"

"I'll try. Just where is your island?"

"Off in that direction," responded the fortune-hunter, pointing to the northeast. "It's a little farther from here than I thought it was at first—about thirty miles. But I have a little second-hand steam launch that my pardners and I use. I'll come for you, take you over and bring you back any time you say."

"After my gun has been tested," said Tom, with a smile. "Better stay and see it."

"No, I must get back to the island. I have some new information that I am sure will enable me to locate the lost mine."

"Well, good-bye, and good luck to you," called Tom, as the fortune-hunter started away.

"Do you think he'll ever find the opals, Tom?" asked Ned.

His chum shook his head.

"I don't believe so," he answered. "Alec has always been that way—always visionary—always just about to be successful; but never quite getting there."

"Then your father's ten thousand dollars will be lost?"

"Yes, I suppose so; but, in a way, dad can stand it. And if I make good on this gun test, ten thousand dollars won't look very big to me. I guess dad gave it to Alec from a sort of sentimental feeling, anyhow."

"You mean because he saved you from the live wire?"

"That's it, Ned. It was a sort of reward, in a way, and I guess dad won't be broken-hearted if Alec doesn't succeed. Only, of course, he'll feel badly for Alec himself. Poor old man! he won't be able to do much more prospecting. Well, Ned, let's get to work on that ammunition hoist. It still jams a little on the ways, and I want it to work smoothly. There's no use having a hitch—even a small one—when the big bugs assemble to see how my cannon shoots."

"That's right, Tom. Well, start off, I'm with you."

The two youths labored for some time, being helped, of course, by the workmen provided by the government, and some from the steel concern.

There were many little details to look after, not the least of which was the patrolling of the stretch of ocean over which the great projectiles would soar in reaching the far-off targets at which Tom had planned to shoot. No ships were to be allowed to cross the thirty-mile mark while the firing was in progress. So, also, the zone where the shots were expected to fall was to be cleared.

But at last all seemed in readiness. The gun had been tried again and again on its carriage. The projectiles were all in readiness, and the terribly powerful ammunition had been stored below the gun in a bomb-proof chamber, ready to be hoisted out as needed.

Because the gun had been fired so many times with a charge of powder heavier than was ordinarily called for, and had stood the strain well, Tom had no fear of standing reasonably close to it to press the button of the battery. There would be no retreating to the bombproof this time.

The German officer was occasionally seen about the place where the gun was mounted, but he appeared to take only an ordinary interest in it. Tom began to feel more than ever that perhaps his suspicions were unfounded.

Some officials high in government affairs had arrived at Colon in anticipation of the test, which, to Tom's delight, had attracted more attention than he anticipated. At the same time he was a bit nervous.

"Suppose it fails, Ned?" he said.

"Oh, it can't!" cried his chum. "Don't think about such a thing."

Plans had been made for a ship to be stationed near the zone of fire, to report by wireless the character of each shot, the distance it traveled, and how near it came to the target. The messages would be received at a station near the barbette, and at once reported to Tom, so that he would know how the test was progressing.

"Well, today tells the tale!" exclaimed the young inventor, as he got up one morning. "How's the weather, Ned?"

"Couldn't be better—clear as a bell, Tom."

"That's good. Well, let's have grub, and then go out and see how my pet is."

"Oh, I guess nothing could happen, with Koku on guard."

"No, hardly. I'm going to keep him in the ammunition room until after the test, too. I'm going to take no chances."

"That's the ticket!"

The gun was found all right, in its great tarpaulin cover, and Tom had the latter taken off that he might go over every bit of mechanism. He made a few slight changes, and then got ready for the final trials.

On an improvised platform, not too near the giant cannon, had gathered the ordnance board, the specially invited guests, a number of officers and workers in the canal zone, and one or two representatives of foreign governments. Von Brunderger was there, but his "familiar," as Ned had come to call the stolid German servant, was not present.

Tom took some little time to explain, modestly enough, the working of his gun. A number of questions were asked, and then it was announced that the first shot, with only a practice charge of powder, would be fired.

"Careful with that projectile now. That's it, slip it in carefully. A little farther forward. That's better. Now the powder—Koku, are you down there?" and Tom called down the tube into the ammunition chamber.

"Me here, Master," was the reply.

"All right, send up a practice load."

Slowly the powerful explosive came up on the electric hoist. It was placed in the firing chamber and the breech closed.

"Now, gentlemen," said Tom, "this is not a shot for distance. It is merely to try the gun and get it warmed up, so to speak, for the real tests that will follow. All ready?"

"All ready!" answered Ned, who was acting as chief assistant.

"Here she goes!" cried Tom, and he pressed the button.

Many were astonished by the great report, but Tom and the others, who were used to the service charges, hardly noticed this one. Yet when the wireless report came in, giving the range as over fourteen thousand yards, there was a gasp of surprise.

"Over eight miles!" declared one grizzled officer; "and that with only a practice charge. What will happen when he puts in a full one?'

"I don't know," answered a friend.

Tom soon showed them. Quickly he called for another projectile, and it was inserted in the gun. Then the powder began to come up the hoist. Meanwhile the young inventor had assured himself that the gun was all right. Not a part had been strained.

This time, when Tom pressed the button there was such a tremendous concussion that several, who were not prepared for it, were knocked back against their neighbors or sent toppling off their chairs or benches. And as for the report, it was so deafening that for a long time after it many could not hear well.

But Tom, and those who knew the awful power of the big cannon, wore specially prepared eardrum protectors, that served to reduce the shock.

"What is it?" called Tom to the wireless operator, who was receiving the range distance from the marking ship.

"A little less than twenty-nine miles."

"We must do better than that," said Tom. "I'll use more powder, and try one of the newer shells. I'll elevate the gun a trifle, too."

Again came that terrific report, that trembling of the ground, that concussion, that blast of air as it rushed in to fill the vacuum caused, and then the vibrating echoes.

"I think you must have gone the limit this time, Tom!" yelled Ned, as he turned on the compressed air to blow the powder fumes and unconsumed bits of explosive from the gun tube.

"Possibly," admitted Tom. "Here comes the report." The wireless operator waved a slip of paper.

"Thirty-one miles!" he announced.

"Hurray!" cried Mr. Damon. "Bless my telescope! The longest shot on record!"

"I believe it is," admitted the chief of the ordnance department. "I congratulate you, Mr. Swift."

"I think I can do better than that," declared Tom, after looking at the various recording gauges, and noting the elevation of the gun. "I think I can get a little flatter trajectory, and that will give a greater distance. I'm going to try."

"Does that mean more powder, Tom?" asked Ned.

"Yes, and the heaviest shell we have—the one with the bursting charge. I'll fire that, and see what happens. Tell the zone-ship to be on the lookout," he said to the wireless operator, giving a brief statement of what he was about to attempt.

"Isn't it a risk, Tom?" his chum asked.

"Well, not so much. I'm sure my cannon will stand it. Come on now, help me depress the muzzle just a trifle," and by means of the electric current the big gun was raised at the breech a few inches.

As is well known, cannon shots do not go in straight lines. They leave the muzzle, curve upward and come down on another curve. It is this curve described by the projectile that is called the trajectory. The upward curve, as you all know, is caused by the force of the powder, and the downward by the force of gravitation acting on the shot as soon as it reaches its zenith. Were it not for this force the projectiles could be fired in straight lines. But, as it is, the cannon has to be elevated to send the shot up a bit, or it would fall short of its mark.

Consequently, the flatter the trajectory the farther it will go. Tom's object, then, was to flatten the trajectory, by lowering the muzzle of the gun, in order to attain greater distance.

"If this doesn't do the trick, we'll try it with the muzzle a bit lower, and with a trifle more powder," he said to Ned, as he was about to fire.

The young inventor was not a little nervous as he prepared to press the button this time. It was a heavier charge than any used that day, though the same quantity had been fired on other occasions with safety. But he was not going to hesitate.

Coincident with the pressure of Tom's fingers there seemed to be a veritable earthquake. The ground swayed and rocked, and a number of the spectators staggered back. It was like the blast of a hundred thunderbolts. The gun shook as it recoiled from the shock, but the wonderful disappearing carriage, fitted with coiled, pneumatic and hydrostatic buffers, stood the strain.

Following the awful report, the terrific recoil and the howl of the wind as it rushed into the vacuum created, there was an intense silence. The projectile had been seen by some as a dark speck, rushing through the air like a meteor. Then the wireless operator could be seen writing down a message, the telephone-like receivers clamped over his ears.

"Something happened, all right!" he called aloud. "That shot hit something."

"Not one of the ships!" cried Tom, aghast.

"I don't know. There seems to be some difficulty in transmitting. Wait—I'm getting it: now."

As he ceased speaking there came from underneath the great gun the sound of confused shouts. Tom and Ned recognized Koku's voice protesting:

"No—no—you can't come in here! Master said no one was to come in."

"What is it, Koku?" yelled Tom, springing to the speaking tube connecting with the powder magazine, at the same time keeping an eye on the wireless operator. Tom was torn between two anxieties.

"Someone here, Master!" cried the giant. "Him try to fix powder. Ah, I fix you!" and with a savage snarl the giant, in the concrete chamber below, could be heard to attack someone who cried out gutturally in German:

"Help! Help! Help!"

"Come on, Ned!" cried Tom, making a dash for the stairs that led into the magazine. There was confusion all about, but through it all the wireless operator continued to write down the message coming to him through space.

"What is it, Koku? What is it?" cried Tom, plunging down into the little chamber.

As he reached it, a door leading to the outer air flew open, and out rushed a man, badly torn as to his clothes, and scratched and bleeding as to his face. On he ran, across the space back of the barbette, toward the lower tier of seats that had been erected for the spectators.

"It's von Brunderger's servant!" gasped Ned, recognizing the fellow.

"What did he do, Koku?" demanded the young inventor.

"Him sneak in here—have some of that stuff you call 'dope.' I sent up powder, and I come back here to see him try to put some dope in Master's ammunition."

"The scoundrel!" cried Tom. "They're trying to break me, even at the last minute! Come on, Ned."

They raced outside to behold a curious sight. Straight toward von Brunderger rushed the man as if in a frenzy of fear. He called out something in German to his master, and the latter's face went first red, then white. He was observed to look about quickly, as though in alarm, and then, with a shout at his servant, the German officer rushed from the stand, and the two disappeared in the direction of the barracks.

"What does it mean?" cried Ned.

"Give it up," answered Tom, "except that Koku spoiled their trick, whatever it was. It looks as if this was the end of it, and that the mystery has been cleared up."

"Mr. Swift! Where's Mr. Swift?" shouted the wireless operator. "Where are you?"

"Yes; what is it?" demanded Tom, so excited that he hardly knew what he was doing.

"The longest shot on record!" cried the man. "Thirty-three miles, and it struck, exploded, and blew the top off a mountain on an island out there!" and he pointed across the sun-lit sea.

THE LONG-LOST MINE

There was a silence after the inspiring words of the operator, and then it seemed that everyone began to talk at once. The record-breaking shot, the effect of it and the struggle that had taken place in the powder room, together with the flight of von Brunderger and his servant, gave many subjects for excited conversation.

"I've got to get at the bottom of this!" cried Tom, making his way through the press of officials to where the wireless operator stood. "Just repeat that," requested Tom, and they all gave place for him, waiting for the answer.

The operator read the message again.

"Thirty-three miles!" murmured Tom. "That is better than I dared to hope. But what's that about blowing the top off an island?"

"That's what you did, with that explosive shell, Mr. Swift. The operator on the firing-zone ship saw the top fly off when the shell struck. The ship was about half a mile away, and when they heard that shell coming the officers thought it was all up with them. But, instead, it passed over them and demolished the top of the mountain.

"Anybody hurt?" asked Tom, anxiously.

"No, it was an uninhabited island. But you have made the record shot, all right. It went farther than any of the others."

"Then I suppose I ought to be satisfied," remarked Tom, with a smile.

"What was that disturbance, Mr. Swift?" asked the chief ordnance officer, coming forward.

"I don't understand it myself," replied the young inventor. "It appeared that someone went into the ammunition room, and Koku, my giant servant, attacked him."

"As he had a right to do. But who was the intruder?"

"Herr von Brunderger's man."

"Ha! That German officer's! Where is he, he must explain this."

But Herr von Brunderger was not to be found, nor was his man in evidence. They had fled, and when a search was made of their rooms, damaging evidence was found. Before a board of investigating officers Koku told his story, after the gun tests had been declared off for the day, they having been most satisfactory.

The German officer's servant, it appeared, had managed to gain entrance to the ammunition chamber by means of a false key to the outer door. There were two entrances, the other being from the top of the platform where the cannon rested. Koku had seen him about to throw something into one of the ammunition cases, and had grappled with him. There was a fight, and, in spite of the giant's strength, the man had slipped away, leaving part of his garments in the grasp of Koku.

An investigation of some of the powder showed that it had been covered with a chemical that would have made it explode prematurely when placed in the gun. It would probably have wrecked the cannon by blowing out the breech block, and might have done serious damage to life as well as property.

"But what was the object?" asked Ned.

"To destroy Tom's gun," declared Mr. Damon.

"Why should von Brunderger want to do that?"

They found the answer among his papers. He had been a German officer of high rank, but had been dismissed from the secret service of his country for bad conduct. Then, it appeared, he thought of the plan of doing some damage to a foreign country in order to get back in the good graces of his Fatherland.

He forged documents of introduction and authority, and was received with courtesy by the United States officials. In some way he heard of Tom's gun, and that it was likely to be so successful that it would be adopted by the United States government. This he wanted to prevent, and he went to great lengths to accomplish this. It was he, or an agent of his, who forged the letter of invitation to General Waller, and who first tried to spoil Tom's test by doping the powder through Koku.

Later he tried other means, sending a midnight visitor to Tom's house and even going to the length of filing the cables in the storm, so the gun would roll off the warship into the sea. All this was found set down in his papers, for he kept a record of what he had done in order to prove his case to his own government. It was his servant who tried to get near the gun while it was being cast.

That he would be restored to favor had he succeeded, was an open question, though with Germany's friendliness toward the United States it is probable that his acts would have been repudiated. But he was desperate.

Failing in many attempts he resolved on a last one. He sent his servant to the ammunition room to "dope" the powder, hoping that, at the next shot, the gun would be mined. Perhaps he hoped to disable Tom. But the plot failed, and the conspirators escaped. They were never heard of again, probably leaving Panama under assumed names and in disguise.

"Well, that explains the mystery," said Tom to Ned a few days later. "I guess we won't have to worry any more."

"No, and I'm sorry I suspected General Waller."

"Oh, well, he'll never know it, so no harm is done. Oh, but I'm glad this is over. It has gotten on my nerves."

"I should say so," agreed Ned.

"Bless my pillow sham!" cried Mr. Damon. "I think I can get a good night's sleep now. So they have formally accepted your giant cannon, Tom?"

"Yes. The last tests I gave them, showing how easily it could be manipulated, convinced them. It will be one of the official defense guns of the Panama Canal."

"Good! I congratulate you, my boy!" cried the odd man. "And now, bless my postage stamp, let's get back to the United States."

"Before we go," suggested Ned, "let's go take a look at that island from which Tom blew the top. It must be quite a sight—and thirty-three miles away! We can get a launch and go out."

But there was no need. That same day Alec Peterson came to Colon inquiring for Tom. His face showed a new delight.

"Why," cried Tom, "you look as though you had found your opal mine."

"I have!" exclaimed the fortune-hunter. "Or, rather, Tom, I think I have you to thank for finding it for me."

"Me find it?"

"Yes. Did you hear about the top of the island-mountain you blew to pieces?"

"We did, but—"

"That was my island!" exclaimed Mr. Peterson. "The mine was in that mountain, but an earthquake had covered it. I should never have found it but for you. That shot you accidentally fired ripped the mountain apart. My men and I were fortunately at the base of it then, but we sure thought our time had come when that shell struck. It went right over our heads. But it did the business, all right, and opened up the old mine. Tom, your father won't lose his money, we'll all be rich. Oh, that was a lucky shot! I knew it was your cannon that did it."

"I'm glad of it!" answered the young inventor, heartily. "Glad for your sake, Mr. Peterson."

"You must come and see the mine—your mine, Tom, for it never would have been rediscovered had it not been for your giant cannon, that made the longest shot on record, so I'm told."

"We will come, Mr. Peterson, just as soon as I close up matters here."

It did not take Tom long to do this. His type of cannon was formally accepted as a defense for the Panama Canal, and he received a fine contract to allow that type to be used by the government. His powder and projectiles, too, were adopted.

Then, one day, he and Ned, with Koku and Mr. Damon, visited the scene of the great shot. As Mr. Peterson had said, the whole top of the mountain had been blown off by the explosive shell, opening up the old mine. While it was not quite as rich as Mr. Peterson had glowingly painted, still there was a fortune in it, and Mr. Swift got back a substantial sum for his investment.

"And now for the good old U. S. A.!" cried Tom, as they got ready to go back home. "I'm going to take a long rest, and the only thing I'm going to invent for the next six months is a new potato slicer." But whether Tom kept his words can be learned by reading the next volume of this series.

"Bless my hand towel!" cried Mr. Damon. "I think you are entitled to a rest, Tom."

"That's what I say," agreed Ned.

"I'll take care ob him—I'll take care ob Massa Tom," put in Eradicate, as he cast a quick look at Koku. "Giants am all right fo' cannon wuk, but when it comes t' comforts Massa Tom gwine t' 'pend on ole 'Radicate; ain't yo' all, Massa Tom?"

"I guess so, Rad!" exclaimed the young inventor, with a laugh. "Is dinner ready?"

"It suah am, Massa Tom, an' I 'specially made some oh dat fricasseed chicken yo' all does admire so much. Plenty of it, too, Massa Tom."

"That's good, Rad," put in Ned. "For we'll all be hungry after that trip to the island. That sure was a great shot Tom—thirty-three miles!"

"Yes, it went farther than I thought it would," replied Tom. And now, as they are taking a closing meal at Panama, ready to return to the United States, we will take leave of Tom Swift and his friends.

Tom Swift and His Photo Telephone
Or the Picture That Saved a Fortune

TABLE OF CONTENTS:

A Man on the Roof

"Tom, I don't believe it can be done!"

"But, Dad, I'm sure it can!"

Tom Swift looked over at his father, who was seated in an easy chair in the library. The elderly gentleman—his hair was quite white now—slowly shook his head, as he murmured again:

"It can't be done, Tom! It can't be done! I admit that you've made a lot of wonderful things—things I never dreamed of—but this is too much. To transmit pictures over a telephone wire, so that persons cannot only see to whom they are talking, as well as hear them—well, to be frank with you, Tom, I should be sorry to see you waste your time trying to invent such a thing."

"I don't agree with you. Not only do I think it can be done, but I'm going to do it. In fact, I've already started on it. As for wasting my time, well, I haven't anything in particular to do, now that my giant cannon has been perfected, so I might as well be working on my new photo telephone instead of sitting around idle."

"Yes, Tom, I agree with you there," said Mr. Swift. "Sitting around idle isn't good for anyone—man or boy, young or old. So don't think I'm finding fault because you're busy."

"It's only that I don't want to see you throw away your efforts, only to be disappointed in the end. It can't be done, Tom, it can't be done," and the aged inventor shook his head in pitying doubt.

Tom only smiled confidently, and went on:

"Well, Dad, all you'll have to do will be to wait and see. It isn't going to be easy—I grant that. In fact, I've run up against more snags, the little way I've gone so far, than I like to admit. But I'm going to stick at it, and before this year is out I'll guarantee, Father, that you can be at one end of the telephone wire, talking to me, at the other, and I'll see you and you'll see me—if not as plainly as we see each other now, at least plainly enough to make sure of each other."

Mr. Swift chuckled silently, gradually breaking into a louder laugh. Instead of being angry, Tom only regarded his father with an indulgent smile, and continued:

"All right, Dad. Go ahead, laugh!"

"Well, Tom, I'm not exactly laughing at YOU—it's more at the idea than anything else. The idea of talking over a wire and, at the same time, having light waves, as well as electrical waves passing on the same conductor!"

"All right, Dad, go ahead and laugh. I don't mind," said Tom, good-naturedly. "Folks laughed at Bell, when he said he could send a human voice over a copper spring; but Bell went ahead and today we can talk over a thousand miles by wire. That was the telephone."

"Folks laughed at Morse when he said he could send a message over the wire. He let 'em laugh, but we have the telegraph. Folks laughed at Edison, when he said he could take the human voice—or any other sound—and fix it on a wax cylinder or a hard-rubber plate—but he did it, and we have the phonograph. And folks laughed at Santos Dumont, at the Wrights, and at all the other fellows, who said they could take a heavier-than-air machine, and skim above the clouds like a bird; but we do it—I've done it— you've done it."

"Hold on, Tom!" protested Mr. Swift. "I give up! Don't rub it in on your old dad. I admit that folks did laugh at those inventors, with their seemingly impossible schemes, but they made good. And you've made good lots of times where I thought you wouldn't. But just stop to consider for a moment. This thing of sending a picture over a telephone wire is totally out of the question, and entirely opposed to all the principles of science."

"What do I care for principles of science?" cried Tom, and he strode about the room so rapidly that Eradicate, the old colored servant, who came in with the mail, skipped out of the library with the remark:

"Deed, an' Massa Tom must be pow'fully preragitated dis mawnin'!"

"Some of the scientists said it was totally opposed to all natural laws when I planned my electric rifle," went on Tom. "But I made it, and it shot. They said my air glider would never stay up, but she did."

"But, Tom, this is different. You are talking of sending light waves—one of the most delicate forms of motion in the world—over a material wire. It can't be done!"

"Look here, Dad!" exclaimed Tom, coming to a halt in front of his parent. "What is light, anyhow? Merely another form of motion; isn't it?"

"Well, yes, Tom, I suppose it is."

"Of course it is," said Tom. "With vibrations of a certain length and rapidity we get sound—the faster the vibration per second the higher the sound note. Now, then, we have sound waves, or vibrations, traveling at the rate of a mile in a little less than five seconds; that is, with the air at a temperature of sixty degrees. With each increase of a degree of temperature we get an increase of about a foot per second in the rapidity with which sound travels."

"Now, then, light shoots along at the rate of 186,000,000 miles a second. That is more than many times around the earth in a second of time. So we have sound, one kind of wave motion, or energy; we have light, a higher degree of vibration or wave motion, and then we come to electricity—and nobody has ever yet exactly measured the intensity or speed of the electric vibrations."

"But what I'm getting at is this—that electricity must travel pretty nearly as fast as light—if not faster. So I believe that electricity and light have about the same kind of vibrations, or wave motion."

"Now, then, if they do have—and I admit it's up to me to prove it," went on Tom, earnestly—"why can't I send light-waves over a wire, as well as electrical waves?"

Mr. Swift was silent for a moment. Then he said, slowly:

"Well, Tom, I never heard it argued just that way before. Maybe there's something in your photo telephone after all. But it never has been done. You can't deny that!"

He looked at his son triumphantly. It was not because he wanted to get the better of him in argument, that Mr. Swift held to his own views; but he wanted to bring out the best that was in his offspring. Tom accepted the challenge instantly.

"Yes, Dad, it has been done, in a way!" he said, earnestly. "No one has sent a picture over a telephone wire, as far as I know, but during the recent hydroplane tests at Monte Carlo, photographs taken of some of the events in the morning, and afternoon, were developed in the evening, and transmitted over five hundred miles of wire to Paris, and those same photographs were published in the Paris newspapers the next morning."

"Is that right, Tom?"

"It certainly is. The photographs weren't so very clear, but you could make out what they were. Of course that is a different system than the one I'm thinking of. In that case they took a photograph, and made a copper plate of it, as they would for a half-tone illustration. This gave them a picture with ridges and depressions in copper, little hills and valleys, so to speak, according to whether there were light or dark tints in the picture. The dark places meant that the copper lines stood up higher there than where there were light colors."

"Now, by putting this copper plate on a wooden drum, and revolving this drum, with an electrical needle pressing lightly on the ridges of copper, they got a varying degree of electrical current. Where the needle touched a high place in the copper plate the contact was good, and there was a strong current. When the needle got to a light place in the copper—a depression, so to speak—the contact was not so good, and there was only a weak current."

"At the receiving end of the apparatus there was a sensitized film placed on a similar wooden drum. This was to receive the image that came over the five hundred miles of wire. Now then, as the electrical needle, moving across the copper plate, made electrical contacts of different degrees of strength, it worked a delicate galvanometer on the receiving end. The galvanometer caused a beam of light to vary—to grow brighter or dimmer, according as the electrical current was stronger or weaker. And this light, falling on the sensitive plate, made a picture, just like the one on the copper plate in Monte Carlo."

"In other words, where the copper plate was black, showing that considerable printing ink was needed, the negative on the other end was made light. Then when that negative was printed it would come out black, because more light comes through the light places on a photograph negative than through the dark places. And so, with the galvanometer making light flashes on the sensitive plate, the galvanometer being governed by the electrical contacts five hundred miles away, they transmitted a photograph by wire."

"But not a telephone wire, Tom."

"That doesn't make any difference, Dad. It was a wire just the same. But I'm not going into that just now, though later I may want to send photographs by wire. What I'm aiming at is to make an apparatus so that when you go into a telephone booth to talk to a friend, you can see him and he can see you, on a specially prepared plate that will be attached to the telephone."

"You mean see him as in a looking-glass, Tom?"

"Somewhat, yes. Though I shall probably use a metal plate instead of glass. It will be just as if you were talking over a telephone in an open field, where you could see the other party and he could see you."

"But how are you going to do it, Tom?"

"Well, I haven't quite decided. I shall probably have to use the metal called selenium, which is very sensitive to light, and which makes a good or a poor electrical conductor according as more or less light falls on it. After all, a photograph is only lights and shadows, fixed on sensitive paper or films."

"Well, Tom, maybe you can do it, and maybe you can't. I admit you've used some good arguments," said Mr. Swift. "But then, it all comes down to this: What good will it be if you can succeed in sending a picture over a telephone wire?"

"What good, Dad? Why, lots of good. Just think how important it will be in business, if you can make sure that you are talking to the party you think you are. As it is now, unless you know the person's voice, you can't tell that the man on the other end of the wire is the person he says he is. And even a voice can be imitated."

"But if you know the person yourself, he can't be imitated. If you see him, as well as hear his voice, you are sure of what you are doing. Why, think of the big business deals that could be made over the telephone if the two parties could not only hear but see each other. It would be a dead sure thing then. And Mr. Brown wouldn't have to take Mr. Smith's word that it was he who was talking. He could even get witnesses to look at the wire-image if he wanted to, and so clinch the thing. It will prevent a lot of frauds."

"Well, Tom, maybe you're right. Go ahead. I'll say no more against your plans. I wish you all success, and if I can help you, call on me."

"Thanks, Dad. I knew you'd feel that way when you understood. Now I'm going—"

But what Tom Swift was going to do he did not say just then, for above the heads of father and son sounded a rattling, crashing noise, and the whole house seemed to shake Then the voice of Eradicate was heard yelling:

"Good land! Good land ob massy! Come out yeah, Massa Tom! Come right out yeah! Dere's a man on de roof an' he am all tangled up suthin' scandalous! Come right out yeah befo' he falls and translocates his neck! Come on!"

BAD NEWS

With startled glances at each other, Tom and his father rushed from the library to the side of the house, whence came the cries of Eradicate.

"What is it, Rad! what is it?" questioned Tom.

"Is someone hurt?" Mr. Swift wanted to know.

"He mighty soon will be!" exclaimed the colored man. "Look where he am holdin' on! Lucky fo' him he grabbed dat chimbley!"

Tom and his father looked to where Eradicate pointed, and saw a strange sight. A small biplane-airship had become entangled in some of the aerials of Tom's wireless apparatus, and the craft had turned turtle, being held from falling by some of the wire braces.

The birdman had fallen out, but had managed to cling to the chimney, so that he had not reached the ground, and there he clung, while the motor of his airship was banging away, and revolving the propeller blades dangerously close to his head.

"Are you hurt?" cried Tom, to the unknown birdman.

"No, but I'm likely to be unless I get out of here!" was the gasped-out answer.

"Hold fast!" cried Tom. "We'll have you down in a jiffy. Here, Rad, you get the long ladder. Where's Koku? That giant is never around when he's wanted. Find Koku, Rad, and send him here."

"Yas, sah, Massa Tom; directly, sah!" and the colored man hastened off as fast as his aged legs would take him.

And while preparations are thus under way to rescue the birdman from the roof, I will take just a few minutes to tell you a little something more about Tom Swift and his numerous inventions, as set forth in the previous books of this series.

"Tom Swift and His Motor Cycle" was the first book, and in that I related how Tom made the acquaintance of a Mr. Wakefield Damon, of the neighboring town of Waterford, and how Tom bought that gentleman's motor cycle, after it had tried to climb a tree with its rider in the saddle. Mr. Wakefield Damon was an odd man, whose favorite expression was "Bless my shoelaces!" or something equally absurd. Waterford was not far from Shopton, where Tom and his father made their home.

Mr. Swift was also an inventor of note, and Tom soon followed in his father's footsteps. They lived in a large house, with many shops about it, for their work at times required much machinery.

Mrs. Baggert was the housekeeper who looked after Tom and his father, and got their meals, when they consented to take enough time from their inventive work to eat. Another member of the household was Eradicate Sampson, a genial old colored man, who said he was named Eradicate because he used to eradicate the dirt about the place.

Koku, just referred to by Tom, was an immense man, a veritable giant, whom Tom had brought back with him from one of his trips, after escaping from captivity. The young inventor really brought two giants, brothers they were, but one had gone to a museum, and the other took service with our hero, making himself very useful when it came to lifting heavy machinery.

Tom had a close friend in Ned Newton, who was employed in the Shopton bank. Another friend was Miss Mary Nestor, a young lady whose life Tom had once saved. He had many other friends, and some enemies, whom you will meet from time to time in this story.

After Tom had had many adventures on his motor cycle he acquired a motor boat, and in that he and Ned went through some strenuous times on Lake Carlopa, near Tom's home. Then followed an airship, for Tom got that craze, and in the book concerning that machine I related some of the things that happened to him. He had even more wonderful adventures in his submarine, and with his electric runabout our hero was instrumental in saving a bank from ruin by making a trip in the speediest car on the road.

After Tom Swift had sent his wireless message, and saved the castaways of Earthquake Island, he thought he would give up his inventive work for a time, and settle down to a life of ease and quiet.

But the call of the spirit of adventure was still too strong for him to resist. That was why he sought out the diamond makers, and learned the secret of Phantom Mountain. And when he went to the Caves of Ice, and there saw his airship wrecked, Tom was well-nigh discouraged, But he managed to get back to civilization, and later undertook a journey to elephant land, with his powerful electric rifle.

Marvelous adventures underground did Tom Swift have when he went to the City of Gold, and I have set down some of them in the book bearing the latter title. Later on he sought the platinum treasure in his air glider. And when Tom was taken captive, in giant land, only his speedy airship saved him from a hard fate.

By this time moving pictures were beginning to occupy a large place in the scientific, as well as the amusement world, and Tom invented a Wizard Camera which did excellent work. Then came the need of a powerful light, to enable Uncle Sam's custom officers on the border to detect the smugglers, and Tom was successful in making his apparatus.

He thought he would take a rest after that, but with the opening of the Panama Canal came the need of powerful guns to protect that important waterway, and Tom made a Giant Cannon, which enabled the longest shots on record to be fired.

Now, some months had passed, after the successful trial of the big weapon, and Tom longed for new activities. He found them in the idea of a photo telephone, and he and his father were just talking of this when interrupted by the accident to the birdman on the roof of the Swift home.

"Have you got that ladder, Rad?" cried the young inventor, anxiously, as he saw the dangerous position of the man from the airship.

"Yas, sah, Massa Tom! I'se a-camin' wif it!"

"And where's Koku? We'll need him!"

"He's a-camin', too!"

"Here Koku!" exclaimed a deep voice, and a big man came running around the corner of the house. "What is it, Master?"

"We must get him down, Koku!" said Tom, simply. "I will go up on the roof. You had better come, too. Rad, go in the house and get a mattress from the bed. Put it down on the ground where he's likely to fall. Lively now!"

"Yas, sah, Massa Tom!"

"Me git my own ladder—dat one not strong 'nuff!" grunted Koku, who did not speak very good English. He had a very strong ladder, of his own make, built to hold his enormous bulk, and this he soon brought and placed against the side of the house.

Meanwhile Tom and his father had raised the one Eradicate had brought, though Tom did most of the lifting, for his father was elderly, and had once suffered from heart trouble.

"We're coming for you!" cried the young inventor as he began to ascend the ladder, at the same time observing that the giant was coming with his. "Can you hold on a little longer?"

"Yes, I guess so. But I dare not move for fear the propellers will strike me."

"I see. I'll soon shut off the motor," said Tom. "What happened, anyhow?"

"Well, I was flying over your house. I was on my way to pay you a visit, but I didn't intend to do it in just this way," and the birdman smiled grimly. "I didn't see your wireless aerials until I was plumb into them, and then it was too late. I hope I haven't damaged them any."

"Oh, they are easily fixed," said Tom. "I hope you and your biplane are not damaged. This way, Koku!" he called to the giant.

"Say, is—is he real, or am I seeing things?" asked the aviator, as he looked at the big man.

"Oh, he's real, all right," laughed Tom. "Now, then, I'm going to shut off your motor, and then you can quit hugging that chimney, and come down."

"I'll be real glad to," said the birdman.

Making his way cautiously along the gutters of the roof, Tom managed to reach the motor controls. He pulled out the electrical switch, and with a sort of cough and groan the motor stopped. The big propellers ceased revolving, and the aviator could leave his perch in safety.

This he did, edging along until he could climb down and meet Tom, who stood near the ladder.

"Much obliged," said the birdman, as he shook hands with Tom. "My name is Grant Halling. I'm a newcomer in Mansburg," he added, naming a town not far from Shopton. "I know you by reputation, so you don't need to introduce yourself."

"Glad to meet you," said the young inventor, cordially. "Rather a queer place to meet a friend," he went on with a laugh and a glance down to the ground. "Can you climb?"

"Oh, yes, I'm used to that. The next thing will be to get my machine down."

"Oh, we can manage that with Koku's help," spoke Tom. "Koku, get some ropes, and see what you and Rad can do toward getting the aeroplane down," he added to the giant. "Let me know if you need any help."

"Me can do!" exclaimed the big man. "Me fix him!"

Tom and Mr. Halling made their way down the ladder, while the giant proceeded to study out a plan for getting the airship off the roof.

"You say you were coming over to see me, when you ran into my wireless aerials?" asked Tom, curiously, when he had introduced his father to the birdman.

"Yes," went on Mr. Halling. "I have been having some trouble with my motor, and I thought perhaps you could tell me what was wrong. My friend, Mr. Wakefield Damon, sent me to you."

"What! Do you know Mr. Damon?" cried Tom.

"I've known' him for some years. I met him in the West, but I hadn't seen him lately, until I came East. He sent me to see you, and said you would help me."

"Well, any friend of Mr. Damon's is a friend of mine!" exclaimed Tom, genially. "I'll have a look at your machine as soon as Koku gets it down. How is Mr. Damon, anyhow? I haven't seen him in over two weeks."

"I'm sorry to say he isn't very well, Mr. Swift."

"Is he ill? What is the trouble?"

"He isn't exactly ill," went on Mr. Halling, "but he is fretting himself into a sickness, worrying over his lost fortune."

"His lost fortune!" cried Tom, in surprise at the bad news concerning his friend. "I didn't know he had lost his money!"

"He hasn't yet, but he's in a fair way to, he says. It's something about bad investments, and he did speak of the trickery of one man, I didn't get the particulars. But he certainly feels very badly over it."

"I should think he would," put in Mr. Swift. "Tom, we must look into this. If we can help Mr. Damon—"

"We certainly will," interrupted Tom. "Now come in the house, Mr. Halling. I'm sure you must be quite shaken up by your upset."

"I am, to tell you the truth, though it isn't the first accident I've had in my airship."

They were proceeding toward the house, when there came a cry from Koku, who had fastened a rope about the airship to lower it.

"Master! Master!" cried the giant. "The rope am slippin'. Grab the end of it!"

Tom's Failure

"Come on!" cried Tom, quickly, as, turning', he saw the accident about to happen. "Your craft will surely be smashed if she slips to the ground, Mr. Halling!"

"You're right! This seems to be my unlucky day!" The birdman, limping slightly from his fall, hurried with Tom to where a rope trailed on the ground. Koku had fastened one end to the airship, and had taken a turn of the cable about the chimney. He had been lowering the biplane to the ground, but he had not allowed for its great weight, and the rope had slipped from his big hands.

But Tom and Mr. Halling were just in time. They grabbed the slipping hempen strands, and thus checked the falling craft until Koku could get a better grip.

"All right now," said the giant, when he had made fast the rope. "Me fix now. Master can go."

"Think he can lower it?" asked Mr. Halling, doubtfully.

"Oh, surely," said Tom. "Koku's as strong as a horse. You needn't worry. He'll get it down all right. But you are limping."

"Yes, I jammed my leg a little."

"Don't you want a doctor?"

"Oh, no, not for a little thing like that."

But Tom insisted on looking at his new friend's wound, and found quite a cut on the thigh, which the young inventor insisted on binding up.

"That feels better," said the birdman, as he stretched out on a couch. "Now if you can look my machine over, and tell me what's the matter with it, I'll be much obliged to you, and I'll get on my way."

"Not quite so fast as that!" laughed Tom. "I wouldn't want to see you start off with your lame leg, and certainly I would not want to see you use your aircraft after what she's gone through, until we've given her a test. You can't tell what part you might have strained."

"Well, I suppose you are right. But I think I'd better go to a hotel, or send for an auto and go home."

"Now you needn't do anything of the kind," spoke Tom, hospitably. "We've got lots of room here, and for that matter we have plenty of autos and airships, too, as well as a motor boat. You just rest yourself here. Later we'll look over your craft."

After dinner, when Mr. Halling said he felt much better, Tom agreed to go out with him and look at the airship. As he feared, he found several things the matter with it, in addition to the motor trouble which had been the cause for Mr. Halling's call on the young inventor.

"Can she be fixed?" asked the birdman, who explained that, as yet, he was only an amateur in the practice of flying.

"Oh, yes, we can fix her up for you," said Tom. "But it will take several days. You'll have to leave it here."

"Well, I'll be glad to do that, for I know she will be all the better when you get through with her. But I think I am able to go on home now, and I really ought to. There is some business I must attend to."

"Speaking of business," remarked Tom, "can you tell me anything more of Mr. Damon's financial troubles?"

"No, not much. All I know is that when I called on him the other day I found him with his check book out, and he was doing a lot of figuring. He looked pretty blue and downcast, I can tell you."

"I'm sorry about that," spoke Tom, musingly. "Mr. Damon is a very good friend of mine, and I'd do anything to help him. I certainly wouldn't like to see him lose his fortune. Bad investments, you say it was?"

"Partly so, and yet I'm inclined to think if he does lose his money it will be due to some trickery. Mr. Damon is not the man to make bad investments by himself."

"Indeed he is not," agreed Tom. "You say he spoke of some man?"

"Yes, but not definitely. He did not mention any name. But Mr. Damon was certainly quite blue."

"That's unlike him," remarked Tom. "He is usually very jolly. He must be feeling quite badly. I'll go over and have a talk with him, as soon as I can."

"Do. I think he would appreciate it. And now I must see about getting home."

"I'll take you in one of my cars," said Tom, who had several automobiles. "I don't want to see you strain that injured leg of yours."

"You're very good—especially after I tangled up your wireless aerials; but I didn't see them until I was right into them," apologized Mr. Halling.

"They're a new kind of wire," said Tom, "and are not very plain to see. I must put up some warning signs. But don't worry about damaging them. They were only up temporarily anyhow, and I was going to take them down to arrange for my photo telephone."

"Photo telephone, eh? Is that something new?"

"It will be—if I can get it working," said Tom, with a smile.

A little later Tom had taken Mr. Halling home, and then he set about making arrangements for repairing the damaged airship. This took him the better part of a week, but he did not regret the time, for while he was working he was busy making plans for his newest invention—the photo telephone.

One afternoon, when Tom had completed the repairs to the airship, and had spent some time setting up an experimental telephone line, the young inventor received a call from his chum, Ned Newton.

"Well, well, what are you up to now?" asked Ned, as he saw his chum seated in a booth, with a telephone receiver to his ear, meanwhile looking steadily at a polished metal plate in front of him. "Trying to hypnotize yourself, Tom?"

"Not exactly. Quiet, Ned, please. I'm trying to listen."

Ned was too familiar with his chum's work to take offense at this. The young banker took a seat on a box, and silently watched Tom. The inventor shifted several switches, pressed one button after another, and tilted the polished metal plate at different angles. Then he closed the door of the little telephone booth, and Ned, through the ground glass door, saw a light shining.

"I wonder what new game Tom is up to?" Ned mused.

Presently the door opened, and Tom stuck out his head.

"Ned, come here," he invited. "Look at that metal plate and see if you can notice anything on it. I've been staring at it so steadily that my eyes are full of sticks. See what you can make out."

"What is this?" asked Ned. "No trick; is it? I won't be blown up, or get my eyes full of pepper; will I?"

"Nonsense! Of course not. I'm trying to make a photo telephone. I have the telephone part down pat, but I can't see anything of the photo image. See if you can."

Ned stared at the polished plate, while Tom did things to it, making electrical connections, and tilting it at various angles.

"See anything, Ned?" asked Tom.

The other shook his head.

"Whom am I supposed to see?" he asked.

"Why, Koku is at the other end of the wire. I'm having him help me."

Ned gazed from the polished plate out of a side window of the shop, into the yard.

"Well, that Koku is certainly a wonderful giant," said Ned, with a laugh.

"How so?" asked Tom.

"Why he can not be in two places at once. You say he ought to be at the other end of this wire, and there he is out there, spading up the garden."

Tom stared for a second and then exclaimed:

"Well, if that isn't the limit! I put him in the telephone booth in the machine shop, and told him to stay there until I was through. What in the world is he doing out there?"

"Koku!" he called to the giant, "why didn't you stay at the telephone where I put you? Why did you run away?"

"Ha!" exclaimed the giant, who, for all his great size was a simple chap, "little thing go 'tick-tick' and then 'clap-clap!' Koku no like—Koku t'ink bad spirit in telumfoam—Koku come out!"

"Well, no wonder I couldn't see any image on the plate!" exclaimed Tom. "There was nobody there. Now, Ned, you try it; will you, please?"

"Sure. Anything to oblige!"

"Then go in the other telephone booth. You can talk to me on the wire. Say anything you like—the telephone part is all right. Then you just stand so that the light in the booth shines on your face. The machine will do the rest—if it works."

Ned hurried off and was soon talking to his chum over the wire from the branch telephone in the machine shop. Ned stood in the glare of an electric light, and looked at a polished plate similar to the one in the other booth.

"Are you there, Ned?" asked Tom.

"Yes, I'm here."

"Is the light on?"

"Yes."

"And you're looking at the plate?"

"Sure. Can you see any reflection in your plate?"

"No, not a thing," answered Tom, and there was great discouragement in his voice. "The thing is a failure, Ned. Come on back," and the young banker could hear his chum hang up the telephone receiver at the other end.

"That's too bad," murmured Ned, knowing how Tom must feel. "I'll have to cheer him up a bit."

Run Down

When Ned Newton got back to where Tom sat in the small telephone booth, the young banker found his chum staring rather moodily at the polished metal plate on the shelf that held the talking instrument.

"So it was no go; eh, Tom?"

"No go at all, Ned, and I thought sure I had it right this time."

"Then this isn't your first experiment?"

"Land no! I've been at it, off and on, for over a month, and I can't seem to get any farther. I'm up against a snag now, good and hard."

"Then there wasn't any image on your plate?"

"Not a thing, Ned. I don't suppose you caught any glimpse of me in your plate?" asked Tom, half hopefully.

"No. I couldn't see a thing. So you are going to try and make this thing work both ways, are you?"

"That's my intention, But I can fix it so that a person can control the apparatus at his end, and only see the person he is talking to, not being seen himself, unless he wishes it. That is, I hope to do that. Just now nobody can see anybody," and Tom sighed.

"Give it up," advised Ned. "It's too hard a nut to crack, Tom!"

"Indeed, I'll not give it up, Ned! I'm going to work along a new line. I must try a different solution of selenium on the metal plate. Perhaps I may have to try using a sensitized plate, and develop it later, though I do want to get the machine down so you can see a perfect image without the need of developing. And I will, too!" cried Tom. "I'll get some new selenium."

Eradicate, who came into the shop just then, heard the end of Tom's remarks. A strange look came over his honest black face, and he exclaimed:

"What all am dat, Massa Tom? Yo'ah gwine t' bring de new millenium heah? Dat's de end of de world, ain't it-dat millenium? Golly! Dish yeah coon neber 'spected t' lib t' see dat. De millenium! Oh mah landy!"

"No, Rad!" laughed Tom. "I was speaking about selenium, a sort of metallic combination that is a peculiar conductor of electricity. The more light that shines on it the better conductor it is, and the less light, the poorer."

"It must be queer stuff," said Ned.

"It is," declared Tom. "I think it is the only thing to use in this photo telephone experiment, though I might try the metal plate method, as they did between Monte Carlo and Paris. But I am not trying to make newspaper pictures."

"What is selenium, anyhow?" asked Ned. "Remember, Tom, I'm not up on this scientific stuff as you are."

"Selenium," went on Tom, "was discovered in 1817, by J. J. Berzelius, and he gave it that name from the Greek word for moon, on account of selenium being so similar, in some ways, to tellurium. That last is named after the Latin word tellus, the earth."

"Do they dig it?" Ned wanted to know.

"Well, sometimes selenium is found in combination with metals, in the form of selenides, the more important minerals of that kind being eucharite, crooksite, clausthalite, naumannite and zorgite—"

"Good night!" interrupted Ned, with a laugh, holding up his hands. "Stop it, Tom!" he pleaded. "You'll give me a headache with all those big words."

"Oh, they're easy, once you get used to them," said the young inventor, with a smile. "Perhaps it will be easier if I say that sometimes selenium is found in native sulphur. Selenium is usually obtained from the flue-dust or chamber deposits of some factory where sulphuric acid is made. They take this dust and treat it with acids until they get the pure selenium. Sometimes selenium comes in crystal forms, and again it is combined with various metals for different uses."

"There's one good thing about it. There are several varieties, and I'll try them all before I give up."

"That's the way to talk!" cried Ned. "Never say die! Don't give up the ship, and all that. But, Tom, what you need now is a little fun. You've been poking away at this too long. Come on out on the lake, and have a ride in the motor boat. It will do you good. It will do me good. I'm a bit rusty myself—been working hard lately. Come on—let's go out on the lake."

"I believe I will!" exclaimed Tom, after thinking it over for a moment. "I need a little fresh air. Sitting in that telephone booth, trying to get an image on a plate, and not succeeding, has gotten on my nerves. I want to write out an order for Koku to take to town, though. I want to get some fresh selenium, and then I'm going to make new plates."

Tom made some memoranda, and then, giving Koku the order for the chemist, the young inventor closed up his shop, and went with Ned down to Lake Carlopa, where the motor boat was moored.

This was not the same boat Tom had first purchased, some years ago, but a comparatively new and powerful craft.

"It sure is one grand little day for a ride," remarked Ned, as he got in the craft, while Tom looked over the engine.

"Yes, I'm glad you came over, and routed me out," said the young inventor. "When I get going on a thing I don't know enough to stop. Oh, I forgot something!"

"What?" asked Ned.

"I forgot to leave word about Mr. Railing's airship. It's all fixed and ready for him, but I put on a new control, and I wanted to explain to him about it. He might not know how to work it. I left word with father, though, that if he came for it he must not try it until he had seen me. I guess it will be all right. I don't want to go back to the house now."

"No, it's too far," agreed Ned.

"I have it!" exclaimed Tom. "I'll telephone to dad from here, not to let Halling go up until I come back. He may not come for his machine; but, if he does, it's best to be on the safe side Ned."

"Oh, sure."

Accordingly, Tom 'phoned from his boat-house, and Mr. Swift promised to see the bird-man if he called. Then Ned and Tom gave themselves up to the delights of a trip on the water.

The Kilo, which name Tom had selected for his new craft, was a powerful boat, and comfortable. It swept on down the lake, and many other persons, in their pleasure craft, turned to look at Tom's fine one.

"Lots of folks out today," observed Ned, as they went around a point of the shore.

"Yes, quite a number," agreed Tom, leaning forward to adjust the motor. "I wonder what's got into her?" he said, in some annoyance, as he made various adjustments. "One of the cylinders is missing."

"Maybe it needs a new spark plug," suggested Ned.

"Maybe. Guess I'll stop and put one in."

Tom slowed down the motor, and headed his boat over toward shore, intending to tie up there for a while.

As he shifted the wheel he heard a cry behind him, and at the same time a hoarse, domineering voice called out:

"Here, what do you mean, changing your course that way? Look out, or I'll run you down! Get out of my way, you land-lubber, you!"

Startled, Ned and Tom turned. They saw, rushing up on them from astern, a powerful red motor boat, at the wheel of which sat a stout man, with a very florid face and a commanding air.

"Get out of my way!" he cried. "I can't stop so short! Look out, or I'll run you down!"

Tom, with a fierce feeling of resentment at the fellow, was about to shift the course of the Kilo, but he was too late.

A moment later there came a smashing blow on the stern port quarter and the Kilo heeled over at a dangerous angle, while, with a rending, splintering sound of wood, the big red motorboat swept on past Tom and Ned, her rubstreak grinding along the side of the Kilo.

Sharp Words

"Great Scott, Tom! What happened?"

"I know as much as you, Ned. That fellow ran us down, that's all."

"Are we leaking?" and with this question Ned sprang from his place near the bow, and looked toward the stern, where the heaviest blow had been struck.

The Kilo had swung back to an even keel again, but was still bobbing about on the water.

"Any hole there?" cried Tom, as he swung the wheel over to point his craft toward shore, in case she showed a tendency to sink.

"I can't see any hole," answered Ned. "But water is coming in here."

"Then there's a leak all right! Probably some of the seams are opened, or it may be coming in around the shaft stuffing-box. Here, Ned, take the wheel, and I'll start up the engine again," for with the blow the motor had stopped.

"What are you going to do?" asked Ned, as he again made his way forward.

"Take her to shore, of course. It's deep out here and I don't want her to go down at this point."

"Say, what do you think of that fellow, anyhow, Tom?"

"I wouldn't like to tell you. Look, he's coming back."

This was so, for, as the boys watched, the big red motor boat had swung about in a circle and was headed for them.

"I'll tell him what I think of him, at any rate," murmured Tom, as he bent over his motor. "And, later on, I'll let the lawyers talk to him."

"You mean you'll sue him, Tom?"

"Well, I'm certainly not going to let him run into me and spring a leak, for nothing. That won't go with me!"

By this time Tom had the motor started, but he throttled it down so that it just turned the propeller. With it running at full speed there was considerable vibration, and this would further open the leaking seams. So much water might thus be let in that the craft could not be gotten ashore.

"Head her over, Ned," cried Tom, when he found he had sufficient headway. "Steer for Ramsey's dock. There's a marine railway next to him, and I can haul her out for repairs."

"That's the talk, Tom!" cried his chum.

By this time the big, red motor boat was close beside Tom's craft.

The man at the wheel, a stout-bodied and stout-faced man, with a complexion nearly the color of his boat, glared at the two young men.

"What do you fellows mean?" called out the man, in deep booming tones—tones that he tried to make imposing, but which, to the trained ears of Tom and Ned, sounded only like the enraged bellow of some bully. "What do you mean, I say? Getting on my course like that!"

Ned could see Tom biting his lips, and clenching his hands to keep down his temper. But it was too much. To be run into, and then insulted, was more than Tom could stand.

"Look here!" he cried, standing up and facing the red-faced man, "I don't know who you are, and I don't care. But I'll tell you one thing—you'll pay for the damage you did to my boat!"

"I'll pay for it? Come, that's pretty good! Ha! Ha!" laughed the self-important man. "Why, I was thinking of making a complaint against you for crossing my course that way. If I find my boat is damaged I shall certainly do so anyhow. Have we suffered any damage, Snuffin?" and he looked back at a grimy-faced mechinician who was oiling the big, throbbing motor, which was now running with the clutch out.

"No, sir, I don't think we're damaged, sir," answered the man, deferentially.

"Well, it's a lucky thing for these land-lubbers that we aren't. I should certainly sue them. The idea of crossing my course the way they did. Weren't they in the wrong, Snuffin?"

The man hesitated for a moment, and glanced at Tom and Ned, as though asking their indulgence.

"Well, I asked you a question, Snuffin!" exclaimed the red-faced man sharply.

"Yes—yes, sir, they shouldn't have turned the way they did," answered the man, in a low voice.

"Well, of all the nerve!" murmured Tom, and stopped his motor. Then, stepping to the side of his disabled and leaking boat, he exclaimed:

"Look here! Either you folks don't know anything about navigation rules, or you aren't heeding them. I had a perfect right to turn and go ashore when I did, for I found my engine was out of order, and I wanted to fix it. I blew the usual signal on the whistle, showing my intention to turn off my course, and if you had been listening you would have heard it."

"If you had even been watching you would have seen me shift, and then, coming on at the speed you did, it was your place to warn me by a whistle, so that I could keep straight on until you had passed me."

"But you did not. You kept right on and ran into me, and the only wonder is that you didn't sink me. Talk about me getting in your way! Why, you deliberately ran me down after I had given the right signal. I'll make a complaint against you, that's what I will."

If possible the red-faced man got even more rosy than usual. He fairly puffed up, he was so angry.

"Listen to that, will you, Snuffin!" he cried. "Listen to that! He says he blew his whistle to tell us he was going to turn in."

"That's what I did!" said Tom, calmly.

"Preposterous! Did you hear it, Snuffin?" puffed the important man.

"Yes—yes, I think I did, sir," answered the machinist, in a hesitating voice.

"You did? What! You mean to tell me you heard their whistle?"

"Yes—yes, sir!"

"Why—why—er—I—" the big man puffed and blew, but seemed to find no words in which to express himself. "Snuffin, I'll have a talk with you when we get home," he finally said. most significantly. "The idea of saying you heard a whistle blown! There was nothing of the kind! I shall make a complaint against these land-lubbers myself. Do you know who they are, Snuffin?"

"Yes—yes, sir," was the answer, as the man glanced at Tom. "At least I know one of them, sir."

"Very good. Give me his name. I'll attend to the rest."

Tom looked at the big man sharply. He had never seen him before, as far as he could recall. As for the machinist, the young inventor had a dim recollection that once the man might have worked in his shop.

"Go ahead, Snuffin!" said the big man, mopping his face with a large silk handkerchief, which, even at that distance, gave out a powerful perfume. "Go ahead, Snuffin, and we will settle this matter later," and, adjusting a large rose in his buttonhole, the self-important individual took his place on the cushioned seat at the wheel, while the big red motor boat drew off down the river.

"Well, of all the nerve!" gasped Ned. "Isn't he the limit?"

"Never mind," spoke Tom, with a little laugh. "I'm sorry I lost my temper, and even bothered to answer him. We'll let the lawyers do the rest of the talking. Take the wheel, Ned."

"But are you going to let him get away like this, Tom? Without asking him to pay for the damage to your boat, when he was clearly in the wrong?"

"Oh, I'll ask him to pay all right; but I'll do it the proper way. Now come on. If we stay here chinning much longer the Kilo will go down. I must find out who he is. I think I know Snuffin—he used to work for me, I now recall."

"Don't you know who that big man is?" asked Ned, as he took the wheel, while Tom again started the motor. The water was now almost up to the lower rim of the fly wheel.

"No; who is he?" asked Tom.

"Shallock Peters."

"Well, I know as much as I did before," laughed Tom. "That doesn't tell me anything."

"Why, I thought everybody in the town knew Shallock Peters," went on Ned. "He tried to do some business with our bank, but was turned down. I hear he's gone to the other one, though. He's what we call a get-rich-quick schemer, Tom—a promoter."

"I thought he acted like that sort of a character."

"Well, that's what he is. He's got half a dozen schemes under way, and he hasn't been in town over a month. I wonder you haven't seen or heard of him."

"I've been too busy over my photo telephone."

"I suppose so. Well, this fellow Peters struck Shopton about a month ago. He bought the old Wardell homestead, and began to show off at once. He's got two autos, and this big motor boat. He always goes around with a silk hat and a flower in his buttonhole. A big bluff—that's what he is."

"He acted so to me," was Tom's comment. "Well, he isn't going to scare me. The idea! Why, he seemed to think we were in the wrong; whereas he was, and his man knew it, too."

"Yes, but the poor fellow was afraid to say so. I felt sorry for him."

"So did I," added Tom. "Well, Kilo is out of commission for the present. Guess we'll have to finish our outing by walking, Ned."

"Oh, I don't mind. But it makes me mad to have a fellow act the way he did."

"Well, there's no good in getting mad," was Tom's smiling rejoinder. "We'll take it out of him legally. That's the best way in the end. But I can't help saying I don't like Mr. Shallock Peters."

"And I don't either," added Ned.

A WARNING

"There, she's about right now, Ned. Hold her there!"

"Aye, aye, Captain Tom!"

"Jove, she's leaking like a sieve! We only got her here just in time!"

"That's right," agreed Ned.

Tom and his chum had managed to get the Kilo to Ramsey's dock, and over the ways of the inclined marine railway that led from the shop on shore down into the river. Then, poling the craft along, until she was in the "cradle," Ned held her there while Tom went on shore to wind up the windlass that pulled the car, containing the boat, up the incline.

"I'll give you a hand, as soon as I find she sets level," called Ned, from his place in the boat.

"All right—don't worry. There are good gears on this windlass, and she works easy," replied Tom.

In a short time the boat was out of the water, but, as Tom grimly remarked, "the water was not out of her," for a stream poured from the stuffing-box, through which the propeller shaft entered, and water also ran out through the seams that had been opened by the collision.

"Quite a smash, Tom," observed the boat repairer, when he had come out to look over the Kilo. "How'd it happen?"

"Oh, Shallock Peters, with his big red boat, ran into us!" said Ned, sharply.

"Ha, Peters; eh?" exclaimed the boatman. "That's the second craft he's damaged inside a week with his speed mania. There's Bert Johnson's little speeder over there," and he pointed to one over which some men were working. "Had to put a whole new stern in her, and what do you think that man Peters did?"

"What?" asked Tom, as he bent down to see how much damage his craft had sustained.

"He wouldn't pay young Johnson a cent of money for the repairs," went on Mr. Houston, the boatman. "It was all Peters's fault, too."

"Couldn't he make him pay?" asked Tom.

"Well, young Johnson asked for it—no more than right, too; but Peters only sneered and laughed at him."

"Why didn't he sue?" asked Ned.

"Costs too much money to hire lawyers, I reckon. So he played you the same trick; eh. Tom?"

"Pretty much, yes. But he won't get off so easily, I can tell you that!" and there was a grim and determined look on the face of the young inventor. "How long will it take to fix my boat, Mr. Houston?"

"Nigh onto two weeks, Tom. I'm terrible rushed now."

Tom whistled ruefully.

"I could do it myself quicker, if I could get her back to my shop," he said. "But she'd sink on the home trip. All right, do the best you can, Mr. Houston."

"I will that, Tom."

The two chums walked out of the boat-repair place.

"What are you going to do, Tom?" asked Ned, as they strolled along.

"Well, since we can't go motor boating, I guess I may as well go back and see if that new supply of selenium has come. I do want to get my photo telephone working, Ned."

"And that's all the outing you're going to take—less than an hour!" exclaimed Ned, reproachfully.

"Oh, well, all you wanted to do was to get me out of a rut, as you called it," laughed Tom. "And you've done it—you and Mr. Peters together. It jolted up my brain, and I guess I can think better now. Come on back and watch me tinker away, Ned."

"Not much! I'm going to stay out and get some fresh air while I can. You'd better, too."

"I will, later."

So Tom turned back to his workshop, and Ned strolled on into the country, for his day's work at the bank was over. And for some time after that—until far into the night—Tom Swift worked at the knotty problem of the photo telephone.

But the young inventor was baffled. Try as he might, he could not get the image to show on the metal plate, nor could he get any results by using a regular photographic plate, and developing it afterward.

"There is something wrong with the transmission of the light waves over the wire," Tom confessed to his father.

"You'll never do it, Tom," said the aged inventor. "You are only wasting a whole lot of time."

"Well, as I haven't anything else to do now, it isn't much loss," spoke Tom, ruefully. "But I'm going to make this work, Dad!"

"All right, son. It's up to you. Only I tell you it can't be done."

Tom, himself, was almost ready to admit this, when, a week later, he seemed to be no nearer a solution of the problem than he was at first. He had tried everything he could think of, and he had Eradicate and Koku, the giant, almost distracted, by making them stay in small telephone booths for hours at a time, while the young inventor tried to get some reflection of one face or the other to come over the wire.

Koku finally got so nervous over the matter, that he flatly refused to "pose" any longer, so Tom was forced to use Eradicate. As for that elderly man of all work, after many trials, all unsuccessful, he remarked:

"Massa Tom, I reckon I knows what's wrong."

"Yes, Rad? Well, what is it?"

"Mah face am too black—dat's de trouble. You done want a white-complected gen'man to stand in dat booth an' look at dat lookin' glass plate. I'se too black! I suah is!"

"No, that isn't it, Rad," laughed Tom, hopelessly. "If the thing works at all it will send a black man's face over the wire as well as a white man's. I guess the truth of it is that you're like Koku. You're getting tired. I don't know as I blame you. I'm getting a bit weary myself. I'm going to take a rest. I'll send for another kind of selenium crystals I've heard of, and we'll try them. In the meanwhile—I'll take a little vacation."

"Get out my small airship, Rad, and I'll take a little flight."

"Dat's de way to talk, Massa Tom," was the glad rejoinder.

"I'm going over to see Mr. Damon, Father," announced Tom to Mr. Swift a little later, when his speedy monoplane was waiting for him. "I haven't seen him in some time, and I'd like to get at the truth of what Mr. Halling said about Mr. Damon's fortune being in danger. I'll be back soon."

"All right, Tom. And say—"

"Yes, Dad, what is it?" asked Tom, as he paused in the act of getting in the seat.

"If he wants any ready cash, you know we've got plenty."

"Oh, sure. I was going to tell him we'd help him out."

Then, as Koku spun the propeller blades, Tom grasped the steering wheel, and, tilting the elevating rudder, he was soon soaring into the air, he and his craft becoming smaller and smaller as they were lost to sight in the distance, while the rattle and roar of the powerful motor became fainter.

In a comparatively short time Tom had made a successful landing in the big yard in front of Mr. Damon's house, and, walking up the path, kept a lookout for his friend.

"I wonder why he didn't come out to meet me?" mused Tom, for usually when the eccentric man heard the throbbing of Tom's motor, he was out waiting for the young inventor. But this time it was not the case.

"Is Mr. Damon in?" Tom asked of the maid who answered his ring.

"Yes, Mr. Swift. You'll find him in the library," and she ushered him in.

"Oh, hello, Tom," greeted Mr. Damon, but the tone was so listless, and his friend's manner so gloomy that the young inventor was quite embarrassed.

"Have a chair," went on Mr. Damon. "I'll talk to you in a minute, Tom. I've got to finish this letter, and it's a hard one to write, let me tell you."

Now Tom was more astonished than ever. Not once had Mr. Damon "blessed," anything, and when this did not happen Tom was sure something was wrong. He waited until his friend had sealed the letter, and turned to him with a sigh. Then Tom said boldly:

"Mr. Damon, is it true that you're having hard luck—in money matters?"

"Why, yes, Tom, I'm afraid I am," was the quick answer. "But who told you?"

"Grant Halling. He was over to get me to fix his airship," and Tom briefly related what had happened.

"Oh, yes, I did mention the matter to him," went on Mr. Damon, and his tone was still listless. "So he told you; did he? Well, matters aren't any better, Tom. In fact, they're worse. I just had to write to a man who was asking for help, and I had to refuse him, though he needs it very much. The truth is I hadn't the money. Tom, I'm afraid I'm going to be a very poor man soon."

"Impossible, Mr. Damon! Why, I thought your investments—"

"I've made some bad ones of late, Tom. I've been pretty foolish, I'm afraid. I drew out some money I had in government bonds, and invested in certain stocks sold by a Mr. Shallock Peters."

"Shallock Peters!" cried Tom, almost jumping out of his chair. "Why, I know him—I mean I've met him."

"Have you, Tom? Well, then, all I've got to say is to steer clear of him, my boy. Don't have anything to do with him," and, with something of a return of his usual energy Mr. Damon banged his fist down on his desk. "Give him a wide berth, Tom, and if you see him coming, turn your back. He'd talk a miser into giving him his last cent. Keep away from Shallock Peters, Tom. Bless my necktie, he's a scoundrel, that's what he is!" and again Mr. Damon banged his desk forcibly.

Soft Words

"Well, I'm glad of one thing!" exclaimed Tom, when the ink bottle and the paper cutter on Mr. Damon's desk had ceased rattling, because of the violence of the blow. "I'm glad of one thing."

"What's that, Tom?" asked his friend.

"I heard you bless something at last—the first time since I came in."

"Oh!" and Mr. Damon laughed. "Well, Tom, I haven't been blessing things lately—that's a fact. I haven't had the heart for it. There are too many business complications. I wish I'd never met this Peters."

"So do I," said Tom. "My motor boat would not have been damaged then."

"Did he do that, Tom?"

"He certainly did, and then he accused me of being at fault."

"That would be just like him. Tell me about it, Tom."

When the young inventor finished the story of the collision Mr. Damon sat silent for a moment. Then he remarked slowly:

"That's just like Peters. A big bluff—that's what he is. I wish I'd discovered that fact sooner—I'd be money in pocket. But I allowed myself to be deceived by his talk about big profits. At first he seemed like a smart business man, and he certainly had fine recommendations. But I am inclined to believe, now, that the recommendations were forged."

"What did he do to you, Mr. Damon?" asked Tom, with ready sympathy.

"It's too complicated to go into details over, Tom, but to make a long story short, he got me to invest nearly all my fortune in some enterprises that, I fear, are doomed to failure. And if they do fail, I'll be a ruined man."

"No, you won't!" exclaimed Tom. "That's one reason why I came here today. Father told me to offer you all the ready money you needed to get out of your trouble. How much do you need, Mr. Damon?"

"Bless my collar button! That's like your father, Tom," and now Mr. Damon seemed more like his old self. "Bless my shoes, a man never knows who his real friends are until trouble comes. I can't say how I thank you and your father, Tom. But I'm not going to take advantage of him."

"It wouldn't be taking any advantage of him, Mr. Damon. He has money lying idle, and he'd like to have you use it."

"Well, Tom, I might use it, if I had only myself to think about. But there's no use in throwing good money after bad. If I took yours now this fellow Peters would only get it, and that would be the last of it."

"No, Tom, thank you and your father just the same, but I'll try to weather the storm a bit longer myself. Then, if I do go down I won't drag anybody else with me. I'll hang on to the wreck a bit longer. The storm may blow over, or—or something may happen to this fellow Peters."

"Has he really got you in his grip, Mr. Damon?"

"He has, and, to a certain extent, it's my own fault. I should have been suspicious of him. And now, Tom, let me give you a further word of warning. You heard me say to steer clear of this Peters?"

"Yes, and I'm going to. But I'm going to make him pay for damaging my boat, if I possibly can."

"Maybe it would be wiser not to try that, Tom. I tell you he's a tricky man. And one thing more. I have heard that this man Peters makes a specialty of organizing companies to take up new inventions."

"Is that so?" asked Tom, interestedly.

"Yes, but that's as far as it goes. Peters gets the invention, and the man, out of whose brain it came, gets nothing."

"In other words, he swindles them?"

"That's it, Tom. If not in one way, then in another. He cheats them out of the profits of their inventions. So I want to warn you to be on the lookout."

"Don't worry," said Tom. "Peters will get nothing from my father or me. We'll be on our guard. Not that I think he will try it, but it's just as well to be warned. I didn't like him from the moment he ran into me, and, now that I know what he has done to you, I like him still less. He won't get anything from me!"

"I'm glad to hear you say so, Tom. I wish he'd gotten nothing out of me."

"Are you sure you won't let my father help you, financially, Mr. Damon?"

"No, Tom, at least not for the present. I'm going to make another fight to hold on to my fortune. If I find I can't do it alone, then I'll call on you. I'm real glad you called. Bless my shoestring! I feel better now."

"I'm glad of it," laughed Tom, and he saw that his friend was in a better state of mind, as his "blessings" showed.

Tom remained for a little longer, talking to Mr. Damon, and then took his leave, flying back home in the airship.

"Gen'man t' see yo', Massa Tom," announced Eradicate, as he helped Tom wheel the monoplane back into the shed.

"Is that so, Rad? Where is he?"

"Settin' in th' library. Yo' father am out, so I asted him in dere."

"That's right, Rad. Who is he, do you know?"

"No, sah, Massa Tom, I doan't. He shore does use a pow'ful nice perfume on his pocket hanky, though. Yum-yum!"

"Perfume!" exclaimed Tom, his mind going back to the day he had had the trouble with Mr. Peters. "Is he a big, red-faced man, Rad?"

"No, sah, Massa Tom. He's a white-faced, skinny man."

"Then it can't be Peters," mused Tom. "I guess perhaps it's that lawyer I wrote to about bringing suit to get back what it cost me to have the Kilo fixed. I'll see him at once. Oh, by the way, it isn't Mr. Grant Halling; is it? The gentleman who got tangled up in our aerials with his airship? Is it he?"

"No, sah, Massa Tom. 'Tain't him."

"I thought perhaps he had gotten into more trouble," mused Tom, as he took off his airship "togs," and started for the house. For Mr. Halling had called for his repaired airship some time ago, and had promised to pay Tom another and more conventional visit, some future day.

Tom did not know the visitor whom he greeted in the library a little later. The man, as Eradicate had said, was rather pale of face, and certainly he was not very fleshy.

"Mr. Tom Swift, I think?" said the man, rising and holding out his hand.

"That's my name. I don't believe I know you, though."

"No, I haven't your reputation," said the man, with a laugh that Tom did not like. "We can't all be great inventors like you," and, somehow, Tom liked the man less than before, for he detected an undertone of sneering patronage in the words. Tom disliked praise, and he felt that this was not sincere.

"I have called on a little matter of business," went on the man. "My name is Harrison Boylan, and I represent Mr. Shallock Peters."

Instinctively Tom stiffened. Receiving a call from a representative of the man against whom Mr. Damon had warned him only a short time before was a strange coincidence, Tom thought.

"You had some little accident, when your motor boat and that of Mr. Peters collided, a brief time ago; did you not?" went on Mr. Boylan.

"I did," said Tom, and, as he motioned the caller to be seated Tom saw, with a start, that some of the drawings of his photo telephone were lying on a desk in plain sight. They were within easy reach of the man, and Tom thought the sheets looked as though they had been recently handled. They were not in the orderly array Tom had made of them before going out.

"If he is a spy, and has been looking at them," mused Tom, "he may steal my invention." Then he calmed himself, as he realized that he, himself, had not yet perfected his latest idea. "I guess he couldn't make much of the drawings," Tom thought.

"Yes, the collision was most unfortunate," went on Mr. Boylan, "and Mr. Peters has instructed me to say—"

"If he's told you to say that it was my fault, you may as well save your time," cut in Tom. "I don't want to be impolite, but I have my own opinion of the affair. And I might add that I have instructed a lawyer to begin a suit against Mr. Peters—"

"No necessity for that at all!" interrupted the man, in soft accents. "No necessity at all. I am sorry you did that, for there was no need. Mr. Peters has instructed me to say that he realizes the accident was entirely his own fault, and he is very willing— nay, anxious, to pay all damages. In fact, that is why I am here, and I am empowered, my dear Mr. Swift, to offer you five hundred dollars, to pay for the repairs to your motor boat. If that is not enough—"

The man paused, and drew a thick wallet front his pocket. Tom felt a little embarrassed over what he had said.

"Oh," spoke the young inventor, "the repair bill is only about three hundred dollars. I'm sorry—"

"Now that's all right, Mr. Swift! It's all right," and the man, with his soft words, raised a white, restraining hand. "Not another word. Mr. Peters did not know who you were that day he so unfortunately ran into you. If he had, he would not have spoken as he did. He supposed you were some amateur motor-boatist, and he was—well, he admits it—he was provoked."

"Since then he has made inquiries, and, learning who you were, he at once authorized me to make a settlement in full. So if five hundred dollars—"

"The repair bill," said Tom, and his voice was not very cordial, in spite of the other's persuasive smile, "the bill came to three hundred forty-seven dollars. Here is the receipted bill. I paid it, and, to be frank with you, I intended bringing suit against Mr. Peters for that sum."

"No need, no need at all, I assure you!" interrupted Mr. Boylan, as he counted off some bills. "There you are, and I regret that you and Mr. Peters had such a misunderstanding. It was all his fault, and he wants to apologize to you."

"The apology is accepted," said Tom, and he smiled a trifle. "Also the money. I take it merely as a matter of justice, for I assure you that Mr. Peters's own machinist will say the accident was his employer's fault."

"No doubt of it, not the least in the world," said the caller. "And now that I have this disagreeable business over, let me speak of something more pleasant."

Instinctively Tom felt that now the real object of the man's call would be made plain—that the matter of paying the damages was only a blind. Tom steeled himself for what was to come.

"You know, I suppose," went on Mr. Boylan, smiling at Tom, "that Mr. Peters is a man of many and large interests."

"I have heard something like that," said Tom, cautiously.

"Yes. Well, he is an organizer—a promoter, if you like. He supplies the money for large enterprises, and is, therefore, a benefactor of the human race. Where persons have no cash with which to exploit their—well, say their inventions. Mr. Peters takes them, and makes money out of them."

"No doubt," thought Tom, grimly.

"In other cases, where an inventor is working at a handicap, say with too many interests, Mr. Peters takes hold of one of his ideas, and makes it pay much better than the inventor has been able to do."

"Now, Mr. Peters has heard of you, and he would like to do you good."

"Yes, I guess he would," thought Tom. "He would like to do me—and do me good and brown. Here's where I've got to play a game myself."

"And so," went on Mr. Boylan, "Mr. Peters has sent me to you to ask you to allow him to exploit one, or several, of your inventions. He will form a large stock company, put one of your inventions on the market, and make you a rich man. Now what do you say?" and he looked at Tom and smiled—smiled, the young inventor could not help thinking, like a cat looking at a mouse. "What do you say, Mr. Swift?"

For a moment Tom did not answer. Then getting up and opening the library door, to indicate that the interview was at an end, the young inventor smiled, and said:

"Tell Mr. Peters that I thank him, but that I have nothing for him to exploit, or with which to form a company to market."

"Wha—what!" faltered the visitor. "Do you mean to say you will not take advantage of his remarkable offer?"

"That's just what I mean to say," replied Tom, with a smile.

"You won't do business with Mr. Peters? You won't let him do you good?"

"No," said Tom, quietly.

"Why—why, that's the strangest—the most preposterous thing I ever heard of!" protested Mr. Boylan. "What—what shall I say to Mr. Peters?"

"Tell him," said Tom, "tell him, from me, and excuse the slang, if you like, but tell him there is—nothing doing!"

TOM IS BAFFLED

Amazement held Mr. Boylan silent for a moment, and then, staring at Tom, as though he could not believe what he had heard the young inventor say, the representative of Mr. Peters exclaimed:

"Nothing doing?"

"That's what I said," repeated Tom, calmly.

"But—but you don't understand, I'm afraid."

"Oh, but indeed I do."

"Then you refuse to let my friend, Mr. Peters, exploit some of your inventions?"

"I refuse absolutely."

"Oh, come now. Take an invention that hasn't been very successful."

"Well, I don't like to boast," said Tom with a smile, "but all of my inventions have been successful. They don't need any aid from Mr. Peters, thank you."

"But this one!" went on the visitor eagerly, "this one about some new kind of telephone," and he motioned to the drawings on the table. "Has that been a success? Excuse me for having looked at the plans, but I did not think you would mind. Has that telephone been a success? If it has not perhaps Mr. Peters could form a company to—"

"How did you know those drawings referred to a telephone?" asked Tom, suspiciously, for the papers did not make it clear just what the invention was.

"Why, I understood—I heard, in fact, that you were working on a new photo telephone, and—"

"Who told you?" asked Tom quickly.

"Oh, no one in particular. The colored man who sent me here mentioned—"

"Eradicate!" thought Tom. "He must have been talking. That isn't like him. I must look into this."

Then to his caller he said:

"Really, you must excuse me, Mr. Boylan, but I don't care to do any business with Mr. Peters. Tell him, with my thanks, that there is really nothing doing in his line. I prefer to exploit my own inventions."

"That is your last word?"

"Yes," returned Tom, as he gathered up the drawings.

"Well," said Mr. Boylan, and Tom could not help thinking there was a veiled threat in his tones, "you will regret this. You will be sorry for not having accepted this offer."

"I think not," replied Tom, confidently. "Good-day."

The young inventor sat for some time thinking deeply, when his visitor had gone. He called Eradicate to him, and gently questioned the old colored man, for Eradicate was ageing fast of late, and Tom did not want him to feel badly.

It developed that the servant had been closely cross-questioned by Mr. Boylan, while he was waiting for Tom, and it was small wonder that the old colored man had let slip a reference to the photo telephone. But he really knew nothing of the details of the invention, so he could have given out no secrets.

"But at the same time," mused Tom, "I must be on guard against these fellows. That Boylan seems a pretty slick sort of a chap. As for Peters, he's a big 'bluff,' to be perfectly frank. I'm glad I had Mr. Damon's warning in mind, or I might have been tempted to do business with him."

"Now to get busy at this photo telephone again. I'm going to try a totally different system of transmission. I'll use an alternating current on the third wire, and see if that makes it any better. And I'll put in the most sensitive selenium plate I can make. I'm going to have this thing a success."

Tom carefully examined the drawings of his invention, at which papers Mr. Boylan had confessed to looking. As far as the young inventor could tell none was missing, and as they were not completed it would be hard work for anyone not familiar with them to have gotten any of Tom's ideas.

"But at the same time I'm going to be on my guard," mused Tom. "And now for another trial."

Tom Swift worked hard during the following week, and so closely did he stick to his home and workshop that he did not even pay a visit to Mr. Damon, so he did not learn in what condition that gentleman's affairs were. Tom even denied himself to his chum Ned, so taken up was the young inventor with working out the telephone problem, until Ned fairly forced himself into the shop one day, and insisted on Tom coming out.

"You need some fresh air!" exclaimed Ned. "Come on out in the motor boat again. She's all fixed now; isn't she?"

"Yes," answered Tom, "but—"

"Oh, 'but me no buts,' as Mr. Shakespeare would say. Come on, Tom. It will do you good. I want a spin myself."

"All right, I will go for a little while," agreed Tom. "I am feeling a bit rusty, and my head seems filled with cobwebs."

"Can't get the old thing to come out properly; eh?"

"No. I guess dad was more than half right when he said it couldn't be done. But I haven't given up. Maybe I'll think of some new plan if I take a little run. Come along."

They went down to the boat house, and soon were out on the lake in the Kilo.

"She runs better since you had her fixed," remarked Ned.

"Yes, they did a good job."

"Did you sue Peters?"

"Didn't have to. He sent the money," and Tom told of his interview with Mr. Boylan. This was news to Ned, as was also the financial trouble of Mr. Damon.

"Well," said the young banker, "that bears out what I had heard of Peters—that he was a get-rich-quick chap, and a good one to steer clear of."

"Speaking of steering clear," laughed Tom, "there he is now, in his big boat," and he pointed to a red blur coming up the lake. "I'll give him a wide enough berth this time."

But though Mr. Peters, in his powerful motor boat, passed close to Tom's more modest craft, the big man did not glance toward our hero and his chum. Nor did Mr. Boylan, who was with his friend, look over.

"I guess they've had enough of you," chuckled Ned.

"Probably he wishes he hadn't paid me that money," said Tom. "Very likely he thought, after he handed it over, that I'd be only too willing to let him manage one of my inventions. But he has another guess coming."

Tom and Ned rode on for some distance, thoroughly enjoying the spin on the lake that fine Summer day. They stopped for lunch at a picnic resort, and coming back in the cool of the evening they found themselves in the midst of a little flotilla of pleasure craft, all decorated with Japanese lanterns.

"Better slow down a bit," Ned advised Tom, for many of the pleasure craft were canoes and light row boats. "Our wash may upset some of them."

"Guess you're right, old man," agreed Tom, as he closed the gasoline throttle, to reduce speed. Hardly had he done so than there broke in upon the merry shouts and singing of the pleasure-seekers the staccato exhaust of a powerful motor boat, coming directly behind Tom's craft.

Then came the shrill warning of an electrical siren horn.

"Somebody's in a hurry," observed Tom.

"Yes," answered Ned. "It sound's like Peters's boat, too."

"It is!" exclaimed Tom. "Here he comes. He ought to know better than to cut through this raft of boats at that speed."

"Is he headed toward us?"

"No, I guess he's had enough of that. But look at him!"

With undiminished speed the burly promoter was driving his boat on. The big vibrating horn kept up its clamor, and a powerful searchlight in front dazzled the eyes.

"Look out! Look out!" cried several.

Many of the rowers and paddlers made haste to clear a lane for the big, speedy motor craft, and Peters and his friends (for there were several men in his boat now) seemed to accept this as a matter of course, and their right.

"Somebody'll be swamped!" exclaimed Ned.

Hardly had he spoken than, as the big red boat dashed past in a smother of foam, there came a startled cry in girls' voices.

"Look!" cried Tom. "That canoe's upset! Speed her up, Ned! We've got to get 'em!"

A GLEAM OF HOPE

"Where are they?"

"Who are they?"

"Over this way! There's their canoe!"

"Look out for that motor boat!"

"Who was it ran them down? They ought to be arrested!"

These were only a few of the cries that followed the upsetting of the frail canoe by the wash from the powerful red boat. On Tom's Kilo there was a small, electrical searchlight which he had not yet switched on. But, with his call to Ned Newton to speed up the motor, that had been slowed down, Tom, with one turn of his fingers, set the lamp aglow, while, with the other hand, he whirled the wheel over to head his craft for the spot where he saw two figures struggling in the water.

Fortunately the lanterns on the various canoes and row-boats, as well as the light on the bow of Tom's Kilo, made an illumination that gave the rescuers a good chance to work. Many other boats besides Tom's had headed for the scene, but his was the more practical, since the others—all quite small ones—were pretty well filled.

"There they are, Ned!" Tom suddenly cried. "Throw out the clutch! I'll get 'em!"

"Want any help?"

"No, you stay at the engine, and mind what I say. Reverse now! We're going to pass them!"

Ned threw in the backing gear, and the screw churned the water to foam under the stern of the Kilo.

Tom leaned over the bow, and made a grab for the gasping, struggling figure of a girl in the water. At the same time he had tossed overboard a cork life ring, attached to a rope which, in turn, was made fast to the forward deck-cleat. "Grab that!" cried Tom. "Hold on, and I'll have you out in a second! That's enough, Ned! Shut her off!"

The Kilo came to a standstill, and, a second later, Tom had pulled into his boat one of the girls. She would have collapsed, and fallen in a heap on the bottom boards, had not Ned, who had come forward from the engine, caught her.

Then Tom, again leaning over the side, pulled in the other girl, who was clinging to the life ring.

"You're all right," Tom assured her, as she came up, gasping, choking and crying hysterically. "You're all right!"

"Is—is Minnie saved?" she sobbed.

"Yes, Grace! I'm here," answered the one Ned was supporting.

"Oh, wasn't it terrible!" cried the second girl Tom had saved.

"I thought we would be drowned, even though we can swim."

"Yes, it—it was so—so sudden!" gasped her companion. "What happened?"

"The wash from that big boat upset you," explained Tom. "That fellow ought to be ashamed of himself, rushing along the way he did. Now, can I take you girls anywhere? Your canoe seems to have drifted off."

"I have it!" someone called. "It's turned over, but I can tow it to shore."

"And I'll take the girls home," offered a gentleman in a large rowboat. "My wife will look after them. They live near us," and he mentioned his own name and the names of the two girls Tom had saved. The young inventor did not know them, but he introduced himself and Ned.

"This is the annual moonlight outing of our little boat club," explained the man who had offered to look after the girls, "and it is the first time we ever had an accident. This was not our fault, though."

"Indeed it was not," agreed Tom, after he had helped the two dripping young ladies into the rowboat. "It was due to Mr. Peters's speed mania."

"I shall make a complaint against him to the navigation authorities," said Mr. Ralston, who was looking after the girls. "He must think he, alone, has any rights on this lake."

With renewed thanks to Tom and Ned, the rescued girls were rowed off to their homes, while the interrupted water carnival was continued.

"Some little excitement; eh, Tom?" remarked Ned, when they were once more under way.

"Yes. We seem to run into that fellow Peters, or some of his doings, quite often lately."

"And it isn't a good sign, either," murmured Ned.

For some minutes after that Tom did not speak. In fact he was so silent that Ned at last inquired:

"What's the matter, Tom—in love?"

"Far from it. But, Ned, I've got an idea."

"And I've got a wet suit of clothes where that nice young lady fainted in my arms. I'm soaked."

"That's what gave me the idea—the water, I mean. I noticed how everything was reflected in it, and, do you know, Ned, I believe I have been working on the wrong principle for my photo telephone."

"Wrong, Tom, how is that?"

"Why, I've been using a dry plate, and I think I should have used a wet one. You know how even in a little puddle of water on the sidewalk you can see yourself reflected?"

"Yes, I've often seen that."

"Well then, 'bless my watch chain!' as Mr. Damon would say, I think I've got just what I want. I'm going to try a wet plate now, and I think it will work. Come on now. Speed up! I'm in a great big hurry to get home and try it!"

"Well, Tom, I sure will be glad if you've got the right idea," laughed Ned. "It will be worth getting wet through for, if you strike something. Good luck!"

Tom could hardly wait to fasten up his boat for the night, so eager was he to get to his shop laboratory and try the new idea. A gleam of hope had come to him.

It was still early evening, and Tom, when enticed out by Ned, had left his photo telephone apparatus in readiness to go on with his trials as soon as he should have come back.

"Now for it, Ned!" exclaimed the young inventor, as he took off his coat. "First I'll sensitize a selenium plate, and then I'll wet it. Water is always a good conductor of electricity, and it's a wonder that I forgot that when I was planning this photo telephone. But seeing the sparkle of lights, and the reflection of ourselves in the lake to-night, brought it back to me. Now then, you haven't anything special to do; have you?"

"Not a thing, Tom."

"That's good. Then you get in this other telephone closet—the one in the casting shop. I'll put a prepared plate in there, and one in the booth where I'm to sit. Then I'll switch on the current, and we'll see if I can make you out, and you notice whether my image appears on your plate."

It took some little time to make ready for this new test. Tom was filled with enthusiasm, and he was sure it was going to be successful this time. Ned watched him prepare the selenium plates —plates that were so sensitive to illumination that, in the dark, the metal would hardly transmit a current of electricity, but in the light would do so readily, its conductivity depending on the amount of light it received.

"There, I guess we're all ready, Ned," announced Tom, at last. "Now you go to your little coop, and I'll shut myself up in mine. We can talk over the telephone."

Seated in the little booth in one of the smaller of Tom's shops, Ned proceeded with his part in the new experiment. A small shelf had been fitted up in the booth, or closet, and on this was the apparatus, consisting of a portable telephone set, and a small box, in which was set a selenium plate. This plate had been wet by a spray of water in order to test Tom's new theory.

In a similar booth, several hundred feet away, and in another building, Tom took his place. The two booths were connected by wires, and in each one was an electric light.

"All ready, Ned?" asked Tom, through the telephone.

"All ready," came the answer.

"Now then, turn on your switch—the one I showed you—and look right at the sensitized plate. Then turn out your light, and slowly turn it on. It's a new kind, and the light comes up gradually, like gas or an oil lamp. Turn it on easily."

"I get you, Tom."

Ned did as requested. Slowly the illumination in the booth increased.

"Do you get anything, Tom?" asked Ned, over the wire.

"Not yet," was the somewhat discouraged answer. "Go ahead, turn on more light, and keep your face close to the plate."

Ned did so.

"How about it now?" he asked, a moment later.

"Nothing—yet," was the answer. And then suddenly Tom's voice rose to a scream over the wire.

"Ned—Ned! Quick!" he called. "Come here—I—I—"

The voice died off into a meaningless gurgle.

MIDNIGHT VISITORS

Ned Newton never knew exactly how he got out of the telephone booth. He seemed to give but one jump, tearing the clamped receiver from his ear, and almost upsetting the photo apparatus in his mad rush to help Tom. Certain it is, however, that he did get out, and a few seconds later he was speeding toward the shop where Tom had taken his position in a booth.

Ned burst in, crying out:

"Tom! What is it? What happened? What's the matter?"

There was no answer. Fearing the worst, Ned hurried to the small booth, in one corner of the big, dimly lighted shop. He could see Tom's lamp burning in the telephone compartment,

"Tom! Tom!" called the young banker.

Still there was no answer, and Ned, springing forward, threw open the double, sound-proof door of the booth. Then he saw Tom lying unconscious, with his head and arms on the table in front of him, while the low buzzing of the electrical apparatus in the transmitting box told that the current had not been shut off.

"Tom! Tom!" cried Ned in his chum's ear He shook him by the shoulder,

"Are you hurt? What is the matter?"

The young inventor seemed unconscious, and for a moment Ned had a wild idea that Tom had been shocked to death, possibly by some crossed live wire coming in contact with the telephone circuit.

"But that couldn't have happened, or I'd have been shocked myself," mused Ned.

Then he became aware of a curious, sweet, sickish odor in the booth. It was overpowering. Ned felt himself growing dizzy.

"I have it—chloroform!" he gasped. "In some way Tom has been overcome by chloroform. I've got to get him to the fresh air."

Once he had solved the puzzle of Tom's unconsciousness, Ned was quick to act. He caught Tom under the arms, and dragged him out of the booth, and to the outer door of the shop. Almost before Ned had reached there with his limp burden, Tom began to revive, and soon the fresh, cool night air completed the work.

"I—I," began the young inventor. "Ned, I—I—"

"take it easy, Tom," advised his chum. "You'll be all right in a few minutes. What happened? Shall I call your father, or Koku?"

"No—don't. It would only—only alarm dad," faltered Tom. "I'm getting all right now. But he—he nearly had me, Ned!"

"He had you? What do you mean, Tom? Who had you?"

"I don't know who it was, but when I was talking to you over the wire, all of a sudden I felt a hand behind me. It slipped over my mouth and nose, and

I smelled chloroform. I knew right away something was wrong, and I called to you. That's all I remember. I guess I must have gone off."

"You did," spoke Ned. "You were unconscious when I got to you. I couldn't imagine what had happened. First I thought it was an electrical shock. Then I smelled that chloroform. But who could it have been, Tom?"

"Give it up, Ned! I haven't the slightest idea."

"Could they have been going to rob you?"

"I haven't a thing but a nickel watch on me," went on Tom. "I left all my cash in the house. If it was robbery, it wasn't me, personally, they were after."

"What then? Some of your inventions?"

"That's my idea now, Ned. You remember some years ago Jake Burke and his gang held me up and took one of dad's patents away from me?"

"Yes, I've heard you mention that. It was when you first got your motor cycle; wasn't it?"

"That's right. Well, what I was going to say was that they used chloroform on me then, and—"

"You think this is the same crowd? Why, I thought they were captured."

"No, they got away, but I haven't heard anything of them in years. Now it may be they have come back for revenge, for you know we got back the stolen property."

"That's right. Say, Tom, it might be so. What are you going to do about it?"

"I hardly know. If it was Jake Burke, alias Happy Harry, and his crowd, including Appleson, Morse and Featherton, they're a bad lot. I wouldn't want father to know they were around, for he'd be sure to worry himself sick. He never really got over the time they attacked me, and got the patent away. Dad sure thought he was ruined then."

"Now if I tell him I was chloroformed again to-night, and that I think it was Burke and his crowd, he'd be sure to get ill over it. So I'm just going to keep mum."

"Well, perhaps it's the best plan. But you ought to do something."

"Oh, I will, Ned, don't worry about that. I feel much better now."

"How did it happen?" asked Ned, his curiosity not yet satisfied.

"I don't know, exactly. I was in the booth, talking to you, and not paying much attention to anything else. I was adjusting and readjusting the current, trying to get that image to appear on the plate. All at once, I felt someone back of me, and, before I could turn, that hand, with the chloroform sponge, was over my mouth and nose. I struggled, and called out, but it wasn't much use."

"But they didn't do anything else—they didn't take anything; did they, Tom?"

"I don't know, Ned. We'll have to look around. They must have sneaked into the shop. I left the door open, you see. It would have been easy enough."

"How many were there?"

"I couldn't tell. I only felt one fellow at me; but he may have had others with him."

"What particular invention were they after, Tom?"

"I'm sure I don't know. There are several models in here that would be valuable. I know one thing, though, they couldn't have been after my photo telephone," and Tom laughed grimly.

"Why not?" Ned wanted to know.

"Because it's a failure—that's what! It's a dead, sure failure, Ned, and I'm going to give it up!" and Tom spoke bitterly.

"Oh, don't say that!" urged his chum. "You may be right on the verge of perfecting it, Tom. Didn't you see any image at all on the plate?"

"Not a shadow. I must be on the wrong track. Well, never mind about that now. I'm going to look around, and see if those fellows took anything."

Tom was feeling more like himself again, the effects of the chloroform having passed away. He had breathed the fumes of it for only a little while, so no harm had been done. He and Ned made an examination of the shop, but found nothing missing.

There were no traces of the intruders, however, though the two chums looked carefully about outside the building.

"You were too quick for them, Ned," said Tom. "You came as soon as I called. They heard me speaking, and must have known that I had given the alarm."

"Yes, I didn't lose any time," admitted Ned, "but I didn't see a sign of anyone as I ran up."

"They must have been pretty quick at getting away. Well, now to decide what's best to do to-night."

After some consultation and consideration it was decided to set the burglar alarms in every building of the Swift plant. Some time previous, when he had been working on a number of valuable inventions, unscrupulous men had tried to steal his ideas and models. To prevent this Tom had arranged a system of burglar alarms, and had also fitted up a wizard camera that would take moving pictures of anyone coming within its focus. The camera could be set to work at night, in connection with the burglar alarms.

The apparatus was effective, and thus an end was put to the efforts of the criminals. But now it seemed Tom would have to take new precautionary measures. His camera, however, was not available, as he had loaned it to a scientific society for exhibition.

"But we'll attach the burglar wires," decided Tom, "and see what happens."

"It might be a good plan to have Koku on guard," said Tom's chum. "That giant could handle four or five of the chaps as easily as you and I could tackle one."

"That's right," agreed Tom. "I'll put him on guard. Whew! That chloroform is giving me a headache. Guess I'll go to bed. I wish you'd stay over tonight, Ned, if you haven't anything else to do. I may need you."

"Then of course I'll stay, Tom. I'll telephone home that I won't be in."

A little later Tom had put away his new photo telephone apparatus, and had prepared for the warm reception of any unbidden callers.

"I wish I hadn't started on this new invention," said Tom, half bitterly, as he locked up the main parts of his machine, "I know it will never work."

"Oh, yes it will," spoke Ned, cheerfully. "You never failed yet, Tom Swift, in anything you undertook, and you're not going to now."

"Well, that's good of you to say, Ned, but I think you're wrong this time. But I'm not going to think any more about it tonight, anyhow. Now to find Koku and put him on watch."

The giant listened carefully to Tom's simple instructions.

"If any bad men come in the night, Koku," said the young inventor, "you catch them!"

"Yes, master, me catch!" said Koku, grimly. "Me catch!" and he stretched out his powerful arms, and clenched his big hands in a way that boded no good to evildoers.

Nothing was said to Mr. Swift, to Mrs. Baggert, or to Eradicate about what had happened, for Tom did not want to worry them. The burglar alarms were set, Koku took his place where he could watch the signals, and at the same time be ready to rush out, for, somehow, Tom had an idea that the men who had attacked him would come back.

Tom and Ned occupied adjoining rooms, and soon were ready for bed. But, somehow, Tom could not sleep. He lay awake, tossing from side to side, and, in spite of his resolution not to think about his photo telephone invention, his mind ran on nothing but that.

"I can't see what next to do to make it work," he told himself, over and over again. "Something is wrong—but what?"

At length he fell into a fitful doze, and he had a wild dream that he was sliding down hill on a big mirror in which all sorts of reflections were seen—reflections that he could not get to show in the selenium plates.

Then Tom felt the mirror bobbing up and down like a motor boat in a storm. He felt the vibration, and he heard a voice calling in his ear:

"Get up, Tom! Get up!"

"Yes! What is it?" he sleepily exclaimed,

"Hush!" was the caution he heard, and then he realized that his dream had been caused by Ned shaking him.

"Well?" whispered Tom, in tense tones.

"Midnight visitors!" answered his chum "The burglar alarm has just gone off! The airship hangar drop fell. Koku has gone out. Come on!"

THE AIRSHIP IS TAKEN

Tom leaped silently out of bed, and stood for a moment half dazed, so soundly had he been sleeping.

"Come on!" urged Ned softly, realizing that his chum had not fully comprehended. "Koku will hold them until we get there. I haven't roused anyone else."

"That's right," whispered Tom, as he began putting on his clothes. "I don't want father to know. When did it happen?"

"Just a little while ago. I couldn't sleep very well, but I fell into a doze, and then I heard the buzzer of the alarm go off. I saw that the drop, showing that the hangar had been entered, had fallen. I got to the window in time to see Koku going toward the shed from his little coop. Then I came to you."

"Glad you did," answered Tom. "I didn't think I was sleeping so soundly."

Together the two chums made their way from their rooms down the dimly-lighted hall to a side door, whence they could reach the airship hangar, or shed.

"Won't we need something—a gun or—" began Ned.

"Clubs are better—especially at night when you can't see to aim very well," whispered back Tom. "I've got a couple of good ones downstairs. I could use my electric rifle, and set it merely to disable temporarily whoever the charge hit, but it's a little too risky. Koku has a habit of getting in the way at the most unexpected times. He's so big, you know. I think clubs will be best."

"All right, Tom, just as you say," agreed Ned. "But who do you think it can be?"

"I haven't the least idea. Probably the same fellows who were after me before, though. This time I'll find out what their game is, and what they're after."

The chums reached the lower hall, and there Tom picked out two African war clubs which he had brought back with him from one of his many trips into wild lands.

"These are just the thing!" exclaimed Ned, swinging his about.

"Careful," cautioned Tom, "If you hit something you'll rouse the house, and I don't want my father and Mrs. Baggert, to say nothing of Eradicate, awakened."

"Excuse me," murmured Ned. "But we'd better be getting a move on."

"That's right," agreed Tom. He dropped into a side pocket a small but powerful electric flash lamp, and then he and Ned let themselves out.

There had been a bright moon, but it was now overcast by clouds. However, there was sufficient light to enable the two lads to see objects quite clearly. All about them were the various buildings that made up the manufacturing and experimental plant of Tom Swift and his father. Farthest away from the house was the big shed where once Tom had kept a balloon, but which was now given over to his several airships. In front of it was a big, level grassy space, needed to enable the aircraft to get a "running start" before they could mount into the clouds.

"See anything of Koku?" whispered Ned.

"No," answered Tom, in the same cautious voice. "I guess he must be hiding—"

"There he goes now!" hissed Ned, pointing to a big figure that was approaching the hangar. It was undoubtedly that of the giant, and he could be seen, in the dim light, stalking cautiously along.

"I wonder where the uninvited guests are?" asked Tom.

"Probably in the airship shed," answered Ned. "Koku was after them as soon as the alarm went off, and they couldn't have gotten away. They must be inside there yet. But what can their game be?"

"It's hard to say," admitted Tom. "They may be trying to get something belonging to me, or they may imagine they can pick up some valuable secrets. Or they may—" He stopped suddenly, and then exclaimed:

"Come on, Ned! They're after one of the airships! That's it! My big biplane is all ready to start, and they can get it in motion inside of a few seconds. Oh, why didn't I hurry?" he added, bitterly.

But the hangar was still some distance away, and it would take two or three minutes of running to reach it.

Meanwhile, and at the instant Tom had his thought of the possible theft of his biggest aircraft, something happened.

The doors of the shed were suddenly thrown open, and the two boys could see the large airship being wheeled out. The hazy light of the moon behind the clouds shone on the expanse of white planes, and on the fish-tail rudder, one of Tom's latest ideas.

"Hey, there!" cried Tom, warningly.

"Leave that alone!" yelled Ned.

"Koku! Koku!" shouted Tom, shrilly. "Get after those fellows!"

"Me get!" boomed out the giant, in his deep voice.

He had been standing near the entrance to the hangar, probably waiting for developments, and watching for the arrival of Tom and Ned. The big form was seen to leap forward, and then several dark shadows swarmed from around the airship, and were seen to fling themselves upon the giant.

"That's a fight!" cried Ned. "They're attacking him!"

"Koku can take care of himself!" murmured Tom. "But come on. I don't see what their game is."

He understood a moment later, however, for while several of the midnight visitors were engaged in a hand-to-hand tussle with the giant there came a sharp, throbbing roar of the airship motor in motion. The propellers were being whirled rapidly about.

"Koku! Koku!" cried Tom, for he was still some distance off. "Never mind them! Don't let the airship be taken!"

But Koku could only grunt. Big and strong as he was, half a dozen men attacking him at once hampered him. He threw them from him, one after another, and was gradually making his way toward the now slowly-moving airship. But would he be in time?

Tom and Ned could not hope to reach the machine before Koku, though they were running at top speed.

"Koku! Koku!" yelled Tom. "Don't let them get away!"

But Koku could only grunt—harder this time—for he fell heavily, being tripped by a stick thrust between his legs. He lay for a moment stunned.

"They're going to get away!" panted Tom, making an effort to increase his speed.

"That's what!" agreed Ned.

Even as they spoke the roar of the airship motor increased. Several of the dark forms which had been engaged in the struggle with Koku were seen to pick themselves up, and run toward the airship, that was now in motion, moving on the bicycle wheels over the grass plot, preparatory to mounting upward in the sky.

"Stop! Stop!" commanded Tom. But it was all in vain.

The men leaped aboard the airship, which could carry six persons, and a moment later, with a deafening roar, as the engine opened up full, the big craft shot upward, taking away all but two of the midnight visitors. These, who had seemingly been stunned by Koku, now arose from the ground, and staggered off in the darkness.

"Get them!" cried Tom.

"We must see to Koku!" added Ned, "Look, there goes your airship, Tom!"

"Yes, I know. But we can't stop that now. Let's see if we can get a clue in these fellows!"

He pointed toward the two who had run off in the dark underbrush surrounding the hangar plaza, and he and Ned trailed them as well as they could. But from the first they knew it would be useless, for there were many hiding places, and, a little way beyond, was a clump of trees.

After a short search Tom gave up reluctantly, and came back to where Koku was now sitting on the ground.

"Are you hurt?" he asked of the giant.

"My mind hurt—that all," said the big man.

"I guess he means his feelings are hurt," Tom explained. "Do you know who they were, Koku?"

"No, master."

"But we must do something!" cried Ned. "They've got your airship, Tom."

"I know it," said the young inventor, calmly. "But we can't do anything now. You can hardly hear her, let alone see her. She's moving fast!"

He pointed upward to the darkness. Like some black bird of prey the airship was already lost to sight, though it would have seemed as if her white planes might render her visible. But she had moved so swiftly that, during the short search, she had already disappeared.

"Aren't you going to do anything?" asked Ned.

"Certainly," spoke Tom. "I'm going to telephone an alarm to all the nearby towns. This is certainly a queer game, Ned."

A Strange Disappearance

Disappointed and puzzled, Tom and Ned went to where Koku was standing in rather a dazed attitude. The giant, like all large bodies, moved slowly, not only bodily but mentally. He could understand exactly what had happened, except that he had not prevailed over the "pygmies" who had attacked him. They had been too many for him.

"Let's take a look inside," suggested Tom, when, by another glance upward, he had made sure that all trace of his big airship was gone. "Maybe we can get a clue. Then, Koku, you tell us what happened."

"It all happened to me," said the giant, simply. "Me no make anything happen to them."

"That's about right," laughed Tom, ruefully. "It all happened to us."

The lights in the hangar were switched on, but a careful search revealed little. The men, half a dozen or more, had come evidently well prepared for the taking away of Tom Swift's airship, and they had done so.

Entrance had been effected by forcing a small side door. True, the burglar alarm had given notice of the presence of the men, but Tom and Ned had not acted quite quickly enough. Koku had been at the hangar almost as soon as the men themselves, but he had watched and waited for orders, instead of going in at once, and this had given the intruders time to wheel out the craft and start the motor.

"Why didn't you jump right in on them when you saw what they were up to, Koku?" asked Tom.

"Me wait for master. Me think master want to see who men were. Me go in—they run."

"Well, of course that's so, in a way," admitted Tom. "They probably would have run, but they'd have run *without* my airship instead of *with* it, if they hadn't had time to get it outside the hangar. However, there's no use in crying over lost biplanes. The next thing is how to get her back. Did you know any of the men, Koku?"

"No, master."

"Then we haven't any clue that way. They laid their plans well. They just let you tangle yourself up with them, Koku, while the head ones got the motor going; an easy matter, since it was all ready to start. Then they tripped you, Koku, and as many of them as could, made a jump for the machine. Then they were off."

"Well, what's the next thing to do?" asked Ned, when another look about the shed had shown that not the slightest clue was available.

"I'm going to do some telephoning," Tom stated. "A big airship like mine can't go scooting around the country without being noticed. And those fellows can't go on forever. They've got to have gasoline and oil, and to get them they'll have to come down. I'll get it back, sooner or later; but the question is: Why did they take her?"

"To sell," suggested Ned.

"I think not," Tom said. "A big airship like mine isn't easy to sell. People who would buy it would ask questions that might not easily be answered. I'm inclined to think that some other reason made them take her, and it's up to us to find out what it was. Let's go into the house."

"Hark!" suddenly exclaimed Ned, holding up his hand for silence. They all heard footsteps outside the hangar.

Tom sprang to the door, flashing his electric light, and a voice exclaimed: "Golly! Chicken thieves!"

"Oh, is it you, Eradicate?" asked the young inventor, with a laugh. "No, it isn't chicken thieves—they were after bigger game this time."

"Suffin happen?" asked the colored man. "Massa Swift he heah a noise, an' see a light, an' he sent me out yeah t' see what all am gwine on."

"Yes, something happened," admitted Tom. "They got the Eagle, Rad."

"What! Yo' big airship?"

"Yes."

"Huh! Dat's too bad, Massa Tom. I suah am sorry t' heah dat. Who done it?"

"We don't know, Rad."

"Maybe it was dat low-down cousin ob mine what tried t' git mah chickens, onct!"

"No, Rad, it wasn't your cousin. But I'll telephone the alarm to the police. They may be able to help me get the Eagle back."

Within the next hour several messages were sent to the authorities of nearby towns, asking them to be on the watch for the stolen airship. This was about all that could be done, and after Mr. Swift had been told the story of the night's happenings, everyone went back to bed again.

Further search the next morning brought forth no clues, though Tom, Ned and the others beat about in the bushes where the men had disappeared.

One or two reports were heard from surrounding towns, to the effect that several persons had heard a strange throbbing sound in the night, that, possibly, was caused by the passage of the airship overhead. One such report came from Waterford, the home town of Mr. Damon.

"Let's go over there," suggested Ned, to his chum. "I'd like to see our friend, and maybe we can get some other clues by circulating around there."

"Oh, I don't know," spoke Tom, rather listlessly.

"Why not?" Ned wanted to know.

"Well, I ought to be working on my photo telephone," was the answer. "I've got a new idea now. I'm going to try a different kind of current, and use a more sensitive plate. And I'll use a tungsten filament lamp in the sending booth."

"Oh, let your experiments go for a little while, Tom," suggested Ned. "Come on over to Mr. Damon's. The trouble with you is that you keep too long at a thing, once you start."

"That's the only way to succeed," remarked Tom. "Really, Ned, while I feel sorry about the airship, of course, I ought to be working on my telephone. I'll get the Eagle back sooner or later."

"That's not the way to talk, Tom. Let's follow up this clue."

"Well, if you insist on it I suppose I may as well go. We'll take the little monoplane. I've fixed her up to carry double. I guess— "

Tom Swift broke off suddenly, as the telephone at his elbow rang.

"Hello," he said, taking off the receiver. "Yes, this is Tom Swift. Oh, good morning, Mrs. Damon! Eh! What's that? Mr. Damon has disappeared? You don't tell me! Disappeared! Yes, yes, I can come right over. Be there in a few minutes. Eh? You don't know what to make of it? Oh, well, maybe it can easily be explained. Yes, Ned Newton and I will be right over. Don't worry."

Tom hung up the receiver and turned to his chum.

"What do you think of that?" he asked.

"What is it?"

"Why, Mr. Damon mysteriously vanished last night, and this morning word came from his bankers that every cent of his fortune had disappeared! He's lost everything!"

"Maybe—maybe—" hesitated Ned.

"No, Mr. Damon isn't that kind of a man," said Tom, stoutly. "He hasn't made away with himself."

"But something is wrong!"

"Evidently, and it's up to us to find out what it is. I shouldn't be surprised but that he knew of this coming trouble and started out to prevent it if he could."

"But he wouldn't disappear and make his wife worry."

"No, that's so. Well, we'll have to go over there and find out all about it."

"Say, Tom!" exclaimed Ned, as they were getting the small, but swift monoplane ready for the flight, "could there be any connection with the disappearance of Mr. Damon and the taking of the Eagle?"

Tom started in surprise.

"How could there be?" he asked.

"Oh, I don't know," answered Ned. "It was only an idea."

"Well, we'll see what Mrs. Damon has to say," spoke the young inventor, as he took his seat beside Ned, and motioned to Koku to twirl the propeller.

THE TELEPHONE PICTURE

"Oh, Tom Swift! I'm so glad to see you!"

Mrs. Damon clasped her arms, in motherly fashion, about the young inventor. He held her close, and his own eyes were not free from tears as he witnessed the grief of his best friend's wife.

"Now, don't worry, Mrs. Damon," said Tom, sympathetically. "Everything will be all right," and he led her to a chair.

"All right, Tom! How can it be?" and the lady raised a tear-stained face. "My husband has disappeared, without a word! It's just as if the earth had opened and swallowed him up! I can't find a trace of him! How can it be all right?"

"Well, we'll find him, Mrs. Damon. Don't worry. Ned and I will get right to work, and I'll have all the police and detectives within fifty miles on the search—if we have to go that far."

"Oh, it's awfully good of you, Tom. I—I didn't know who else to turn to in my trouble but you."

"And why shouldn't you come to me? I'd do anything for you and Mr. Damon. Now tell me all about it."

Tom and Ned had just arrived at the Damon home in the airship, to find the wife of the eccentric man almost distracted over her husband's strange disappearance.

"It happened last night," Mrs. Damon said, when she was somewhat composed. "Last night about twelve o'clock."

"Twelve o'clock!" cried Tom, in surprise "Why that's about the time—"
He stopped suddenly.

"What were you going to say?" asked Mrs. Damon.

"Oh—nothing," answered Tom. "I—I'll tell you later. Go on, please."

"It is all so confusing," proceeded Mrs. Damon. "You know my husband has been in trouble of late—financial trouble?"

"Yes," responded Tom, "he mentioned it to me."

"I don't know any of the details," sighed Mrs. Damon, "but I know he was mixed up with a man named Peters."

"I know him, too," spoke Tom, grimly.

"My husband has been very gloomy of late," went on Mrs. Damon. "He foolishly entrusted almost his entire fortune to that man, and last night he told me it was probably all gone. He said he saw only the barest chance to save it, but that he was going to take that chance."

"Did he go into details?" asked Tom.

"No, that was all he said. That was about ten o'clock. He didn't want to go to bed. He just sat about, and he kept saying over and over again: 'Bless my tombstone!' 'Bless the cemetery!' and all such stuff as that. You know how he was," and she smiled through her tears.

"Yes," said Tom. "I know. Only it wasn't like him to bless such grewsome things. He was more jolly."

"He hasn't been, of late," sighed his wife. "Well, he sat about all the evening, and he kept figuring away, trying, I suppose, to find some way out of his trouble."

"Why didn't he come to my father?" cried Tom. "I told him he could have all the money he needed to tide him over."

"Well, Mr. Damon was queer that way," said his wife. "He wanted to be independent. I urged him to call you up, but he said he'd fight it out alone."

"As I said, we sat there, and he kept feeling more and more blue, and blessing his funeral, and the hearse and all such things as that. He kept looking at the clock, too, and I wondered at that."

"'Are you expecting someone?' I asked him. He said he wasn't, exactly, but I made sure he was, and finally, about half-past eleven, he put on his hat and went out."

"'Where are you going?' I asked him."

"'Oh, just to get a breath of air. I can't sleep,' he said. I didn't think much of that, as he often used to go out and walk about a bit before going to bed. So he went out, and I began to see about locking up, for I never trust the servants."

"It must have been about an hour later when I heard voices out in front. I looked, and I saw Mr. Damon talking to a man."

"Who was he?" asked Tom, eagerly, on the alert for the slightest clue.

"I thought at the time," said Mrs. Damon, "that it was one of the neighbors. I have learned since, however, that it was not. Anyhow, this man and Mr. Damon stood talking for a little while, and then they went off together. I didn't think it strange at the time, supposing he was merely strolling up and down in front with Mr. Blackson, who lives next door, He often had done that before."

"Well, I saw that the house was locked up, and then I sat down in a chair to wait for Mr. Damon to come back. I was getting sleepy, for we don't usually stay up so late. I suppose I must have dozed off, but I was suddenly awakened by hearing a peculiar noise. I sat up in alarm, and then I realized that Mr. Damon had not come in."

"I was frightened then, and I called my maid. It was nearly one o'clock, and my husband never stays out as late as that. We went next door, and found that Mr. Blackson had not been out of his house that evening. So it could not have been he to whom Mr. Damon was speaking."

"We roused up other neighbors, and they searched all about the grounds, thinking he might have been overcome by a sudden faint. But we could not find him. My husband had disappeared— mysteriously disappeared!" and the lady broke into sobs.

"Now don't worry," said Tom, soothingly, as he put his arms about her as he would have done to his own mother, had she been alive, "We'll get him back!"

"But how can you? No one knows where he is."

"Oh, yes!" said Tom, confidently, "Mr. Damon himself knows where he is, and unless he has gone away voluntarily, I think you will soon hear from him."

"What do you mean by—voluntarily?" asked the wife.

"First let me ask you a question," came from Tom. "You said you were awakened by a peculiar noise. What sort of a sound was it?"

"Why, a whirring, throbbing noise, like—like—"

She paused for a comparison.

"Like an airship?" asked Tom, with a good deal of eagerness.

"That was it!" cried Mrs. Damon. "I was trying to think where I had heard the sound before. It was just like the noise your airship makes, Tom!"

"That settles it!" exclaimed the young inventor.

"Settles what?" asked Ned.

"The manner of Mr. Damon's disappearance. He was taken away—or went away—in my airship—the airship that was stolen from my shed last night!"

Mrs. Damon stared at Tom in amazement.

"Why—why—how could that be?" she asked.

Quickly Tom told of what had happened at his place.

"I begin to see through it," he said. "There is some plot here, and we've got to get to the bottom of it. Mr. Damon either went with these men in the airship willingly, or he was taken away by force. I'm inclined to think he went of his own accord, or you would have heard some outcry, Mrs. Damon."

"Well, perhaps so," she admitted. "But would he go away in that manner without telling me?"

"He might," said Tom, willing to test his theory on all sides. "He might not have wanted you to worry, for you know you dislike him to go up an airships."

"Yes, I do. Oh, if I only thought he did go away of his own accord, I could understand it. He went, if he did, to try and save his fortune."

"It does look as though he had an appointment with someone, Tom," suggested Ned. "His looking at the clock, and then going out, and all that."

"Yes," admitted the young inventor, "and now I'm inclined to change my theory a bit. It may have been some other airship than mine that was used."

"How so?" asked Ned.

"Because the men who took mine were unprincipled fellows. Mr. Damon would not have gone away with men who would steal an airship."

"Not if he knew it," admitted Ned. "Well, then, let's consider two airships—yours and the other that came to keep the appointment with Mr. Damon. If the last is true, why should he want to go away in an airship at midnight? Why couldn't he take a train, or an auto?"

"Well, we don't know all the ins and outs," admitted Tom. "Taking a midnight airship ride is rather strange, but that may have been the only course open. We'll have to let the explanation go until later. At any rate, Mrs. Damon, I feel sure that your husband did go off through the air—either in my Eagle or in some other craft."

"Well, I'm glad to hear you say so, Tom Swift, though it sounds a dreadful thing to say. But if he did go off of his own accord, I know he did it for the best. And he may not have told me, for fear I would worry. I can understand that. But why isn't he back now?"

Tom had been rather dreading that question. It was one he had asked himself, and he had found no good answer for it. If there had been such need of haste, that an airship had to be used. why had not Mr. Damon come back ere this? Unless, as Tom feared to admit, even to himself, there had been some accident.

Half a dozen theories flashed through his mind, but he could not select a good, working one,—particularly as there were no clues. Disappearing in an airship was the one best means of not leaving a trace behind. An auto, a motor boat, a train, a horse and carriage—all these could be more or less easily traced. But an airship—

If Mr. Damon wanted to cover up his tracks, or if he had been taken away, and his captors wanted to baffle pursuit, the best means had been adopted.

"Now don't you worry," advised Tom to Mrs. Damon. "I know it looks funny, but I think it will come out all right. Ned and I will do all we can. Mr. Damon must have known what he was about. But, to be on the safe side, we'll send out a general alarm through the police."

"Oh, I don't know what I'd done if you hadn't come to help me!" exclaimed Mrs. Damon.

"Just you leave it to me!" said the young inventor, cheerfully. "I'll find Mr. Damon!"

But, though he spoke thus confidently, Tom Swift had not the slightest notion, just then, of how to set about his difficult task. He had had hard problems to solve before, so he was not going to give up this one. First he wanted to think matters out, and arrange a plan of action.

He and Ned made a careful examination of the grounds of the Damon homestead. There was little they could learn, though they did find where an airship had landed in a meadow, not far away, and where it had made a flying start off again.

Carefully Tom looked at the marks made by the wheels of the airship.

"They're the same distance apart as those on the Eagle," he said to his chum, "and the tires are the same. But that isn't saying anything, as lots of airships have the same equipment. So we won't jump to any conclusions that way."

Tom and Ned interviewed several of the neighbors, but beyond learning that some of them had heard the throbbing of the midnight airship, that was as far as they got on that line.

There was nothing more they could do in Waterford, and, leaving Mrs. Damon, who had summoned a relative to stay with her, the two chums made a quick trip back through the air to Shopton. As Eradicate came out to help put away the monoplane Tom noticed that the colored man was holding one hand as though it hurt him.

"What's the matter, Rad?" asked the young investor.

"Oh, nuffin—jest natcherly nuffin, Massa Tom."

But Eradicate spoke evasively and in a manner that roused Tom's suspicions.

"Boomerang, your mule, didn't kick you; did he?"

"No, sah, Massa Tom, no sah. 'Twern't nuffin laik dat."

"But what was it? Your hand is hurt!"

"Well, Massa Tom, I s'pose I done bettah tell yo' all. I'se had a shock!"

"A shock?"

"Yas, sah. A shock. A lickrish shock."

"Oh, you mean an electrical shock. That's too bad. I suppose you must have touched a live wire."

"No, sah. 'Twern't dat way."

"How was it, then?"

"Well, yo' see, Massa Tom, I were playin' a joke on Koku."

"Oh, you were; eh? Then I suppose Koku shocked you," laughed Tom.

"No, sah. I—I'll tell you. Dat giant man he were in de telefoam boof in de pattern shop—you know—de one where yo' all been tryin' to make pishures."

"Yes, I know. Go on!" exclaimed Tom, impatiently.

"Well, he were in dere, Massa Tom, an' I slipped into de boof in de next shop—de odder place where yo' all been 'speermentin'. I called out on de telefoam, loud laik de Angel Gabriel gwine t' holler at de last trump: 'Look out, yo' ole sinnah!' I yell it jest t' scare Koku."

"I see," said Tom, a bit severely, for he did not like Eradicate interfering with the instruments. "And did you scare Koku?"

"Oh, yas, sah, Massa Tom. I skeered him all right; but suffin else done happen. When I put down de telefoam I got a terrible shock. It hurts yit!"

"Well," remarked Tom, "I suppose I ought to feel sorry for you, but I can't. You should let things alone. Now I've got to see if you did any damage. Come along, Ned."

Tom was the first to enter the telephone booth where Eradicate had played the part of the Angel Gabriel. He looked at the wires and apparatus, but could see nothing wrong.

Then he glanced at the selenium plate, on which he hoped, some day, to imprint an image from over the wire. And, as he saw the smooth surface he started, and cried.

"Ned! Ned, come here quick!"

"What is it?" asked his chum, Crowding into the booth.

"Look at that plate! Tell me what you see!"

Ned looked.

"Why—why it's Koku's picture!" he gasped.

"Exactly!" cried Tom. "In some way my experiment has succeeded when I was away. Eradicate must have made some new connection by his monkeying. Ned, it's a success! I've got my first photo telephone picture! Hurray!"

Making Improvements

Tom Swift was so overjoyed and excited that for a few moments he capered about, inside the booth, and outside, knocking against his chum Ned, clapping him on the back, and doing all manner of boyish "stunts."

"It's a success, Ned! I've struck it!" cried Tom, in delight.

"Ouch! You struck *me*, you mean!" replied Ned, rubbing his shoulder, where the young inventor had imparted a resounding blow of joy.

"What of it?" exclaimed Tom. "My apparatus works! I can send a picture by telephone! It's great, Ned!"

"But I don't exactly understand how it happened," said Ned, in some bewilderment, as he gazed at the selenium plate.

"Neither do I," admitted Tom, when he had somewhat calmed down. "That is, I don't exactly understand what made the thing succeed now, when it wouldn't work for me a little while ago. But I've got to go into that. I'll have to interview that rascal Eradicate, and learn what he did when he played that trick on Koku. Yes, and I'll have to see Koku, too. We've got to get at the bottom of this, Ned."

"I suppose so. You've got your hands full, Tom, with your photo telephone, and the disappearance of Mr. Damon."

"Yes, and my own airship, too. I must get after that. Whew! A lot of things to do! But I like work, Ned. The more the better."

"Yes, that's like you, Tom. But what are you going to get at first?"

"Let me see; the telephone, I think. I'll have Rad and Koku in here and talk to them. I say, you Eradicate!" he called out of the door of the shop, as he saw the colored man going past, holding his shocked arm tenderly.

"Yas, sah, Massa Tom, I'se comin'! What is it yo' all wants, Massa Tom?"

"I want you to show me exactly what you did to the wires, and other things in here, when you played that Angel Gabriel trick on your partner Koku."

"Partner! He ain't mah partner!" exclaimed Eradicate with a scowl, for there was not the best of feeling between the two. Eradicate had served in the Swift family many years, and he rather resented the coming of the giant, who performed many services formerly the province of the colored man.

"Well, never mind what he is, Rad," laughed Tom. "You just show me what you did. Come now, something happened in here, and I want to find out what it was."

"Oh, suffin done happened all right, Massa Tom. Yas, sah! Suffin done happened!" cried Eradicate, with such odd emphasis that Tom and Ned both laughed.

"An' suffin happened to me," went on the colored man, rubbing his shocked arm.

"Well, tell us about it," suggested Tom.

"It was dish yeah way," proceeded Eradicate. And he told more in detail how, seeing Koku cleaning and sweeping out the other telephone booth, he had thought of the trick to play on him. Both telephones had what are called "amplifiers" attached, that could be switched on when needed. These amplifiers were somewhat like the horn of a phonograph—they increased, or magnified the sound, so that one could hear a voice from any part of the shop, and need not necessarily have the telephone receiver at his ear.

Seeing Koku near the instrument, Eradicate had switched on the amplifier, and had called into his instrument, trying to scare the giant. And he did startle Koku, for the loud voice, coming so suddenly, sent the giant out of the booth on the run.

"But you must have done something else," insisted Tom. "Look here, Rad," and the young inventor pointed to the picture on the plate.

"Mah gracious sakes!" gasped the colored man. "Why dat's Koku hisse'f!" and he looked in awe at the likeness.

"That's what you did, Rad!"

"Me? I done dat? No, sah, Massa Tom. I neber did! No, sah!" Eradicate spoke emphatically.

"Yes you did, Rad. You took that picture of Koku over my photo telephone, and I want you to show me exactly what you did—what wires and switches you touched and changed, and all that."

"Yo—yo' done say I tuck dat pishure, Massa Tom?"

"You sure did, Rad."

"Well—well, good land o' massy! An' I done dat!"

Eradicate stared in wonder at the image of the giant on the plate, and shook his head doubtingly.

"I—I didn't know I could do it. I never knowed I had it in me!" he murmured.

Tom and Ned laughed long and loud, and then the young inventor said:

"Now look here, Rad. You've done me a mighty big service, though you didn't know it, and I want to thank you. I'm sorry about your arm, and I'll have the doctor look at it. But now I want you to show me all the things you touched when you played that joke on Koku. In some way you did what I haven't been able to do, You took the picture. There's probably just one little thing I've overlooked, and you stumbled on it by accident. Now go ahead and show me."

Eradicate thought for a moment, and then said:

"Well, I done turned on de current, laik I seen you done, Massa Tom."

"Yes, go on. You connected the telephone."

"Yas, sah. Den I switched on that flyer thing yo' all has rigged up."

"You switched on the amplifier, yes. Go on."

"An'—an' den I plugged in dish year wire," and the colored man pointed to one near the top of the booth.

"You switched on that wire, Rad! Why, great Scott, man! That's connected to the arc light circuit—it carries over a thousand volts. And you switched that into the telephone circuit?"

"Dat's what I done did, Massa Tom; yas, Bah!"

"What for?"

"Why, I done want t' make mah voice good an' loud t' skeer dat rascal Koku!"

Tom stared at the colored man in amazement.

"No wonder you got a shock!" exclaimed the young inventor. "You didn't get all the thousand volts, for part of it was shunted off; but you got a good charge, all right. So that's what did the business; eh? It was the combination of the two electrical circuits that sent the photograph over the wire."

"I understand it now, Rad; but you did more than I've been able to do. I never, in a hundred years, would have thought of switching on that current. It never occurred to me. But you, doing it by accident, brought out the truth. It's often that way in discoveries. And Koku was standing in the other telephone booth, near the plate there, when you switched in this current, Rad?"

"Yas, sah, Massa Tom. He were. An' yo' ought t' see him hop when he heard mah voice yellin' at him. Ha! ha! ha!"

Eradicate chuckled at the thought. Then a pain in his shocked arm made him wince. A wry look passed over his face.

"Yas, sah, Koku done jump about ten feet," he said. "An'—an' den I jump too. Ain't no use in denyin' dat fact. I done jump when I got dat shock!"

"All right, Rad. You may go now. I think I'm on the right track!" exclaimed Tom. "Come on, Ned, we'll try some experiments, and we'll see what we can do."

"No shocks though—cut out the shocks, Tom," stipulated his chum.

"Oh, sure! No shocks! Now let's bet busy and improve on Eradicate's Angel Gabriel system."

Tom made a quick examination of the apparatus.

"I understand it, I think," he said. "Koku was near the plate in the other booth when Rad put on the double current. There was a light there, and in an instant his likeness was sent over the wire, and imprinted on this plate. Now let's see what we can do. You go to that other booth, Ned. I'll see if I can get your picture, and send you mine. Here, take some extra selenium plates along. You know how to connect them."

"I think so," answered Ned.

"This image is really too faint to be of much use," went on Tom, as he looked at the one of Koku. "I think I can improve on it. But we're on the right track."

A little later Ned stood in the other booth, while Tom arranged the wires, and made the connections in the way accidently discovered by Eradicate. The young inventor had put in a new plate, carefully putting away the one with the picture of the giant, This plate could be used again, when the film, into which the image was imprinted, had been washed off.

"All ready, Ned," called Tom, over the wire, when he was about to turn the switch. "Stand still, and I'll get you."

The connection was made, and Tom uttered a cry of joy. For there, staring at him from the plate in front of him was the face of Ned.

It was somewhat reduced in size, of course, and was not extra clear, but anyone who knew Ned could have told he was at the other end of the wire.

"Do you get me, Tom?" called Ned, over the telephone.

"I sure do! Now see if you can get me."

Tom made other connections, and then looked at the sending plate of his instrument, there being both a sending and receiving plate in each booth, just as there was a receiver and a transmitter to the telephone.

"Hurray! I see you, Tom!" cried Ned, over the wire. "Say, this is great!"

"It isn't as good as I want it," went on Tom. "But it proves that I'm right. The photo telephone is a fact, and now persons using the wire can be sure of the other person they are conversing with. I must tell dad. He wouldn't believe I could do it!"

And indeed Mr. Swift was surprised when Tom proved, by actual demonstration, that a picture could be sent over the wire.

"Tom, I congratulate you!" declared the aged inventor. "It is good news!"

"Yes, but we have bad news of Mr. Damon," said Tom, and he told his father of the disappearance of the eccentric man. Mr. Swift at once telephoned his sympathy to Mrs. Damon, and offered to do anything he could for her.

"But Tom can help you more than I can," he said. "You can depend on Tom."

"I know that," replied Mrs. Damon, over the wire.

And certainly Tom Swift had many things to do now. He hardly knew at what to begin first, but now, since he was on the right road in regard to his photo telephone, he would work at improving it.

And to this end he devoted himself, after he had sent out a general alarm to the police of nearby towns, in regard to the disappearance of Mr. Damon. The airship clue, he believed, as did the police, would be a good one to work on.

For several days after this nothing of moment occurred. Mr. Damon could not be located, and Tom's airship might still be sailing above the clouds as far as getting any trace of it was concerned.

Meanwhile the young inventor, with the help of Ned, who was given a leave of absence from the bank, worked hard to improve the photo telephone.

THE AIRSHIP CLUE

"Now Ned, we'll try again. I'm going to use a still stronger current, and this is the most sensitive selenium plate I've turned out yet. We'll see if we can't get a better likeness of you—one that will be plainer."

It was Tom Swift who was speaking, and he and his chum had just completed some hard work on the new photo telephone. Though the apparatus did what Tom had claimed for it, still he was far from satisfied. He could transmit over the wire the picture of a person talking at the telephone, but the likeness was too faint to make the apparatus commercially profitable.

"It's like the first moving pictures," said Tom. "They moved, but that was about all they did."

"I say," remarked Ned, as he was about to take his place in the booth where the telephone and apparatus were located, "this double-strength electrical current you're speaking of won't shock me; will it? I don't want what happened to Eradicate to happen to me, Tom."

"Don't worry. Nothing will happen. The trouble with Rad was that he didn't have the wires insulated when he turned that arc current switch by mistake—or, rather, to play his joke. But he's all right now."

"Yes, but I'm not going to take any chances," insisted Ned. "I want to be insulated myself."

"I'll see to that," promised Tom. "Now get to your booth."

For the purpose of experiments Tom had strung a new line between two of his shops, They were both within sight, and the line was not very long; but, as I have said, Tom knew that if his apparatus would work over a short distance, it would also be successful over a long one, provided he could maintain the proper force of current, which he was sure could be accomplished.

"And if they can send pictures from Monte Carlo to Paris I can do the same," declared Tom, though his system of photo telephony was different from sending by a telegraph system—a reproduction of a picture on a copper plate. Tom's apparatus transmitted the likeness of the living person.

It took some little time for the young inventor, and Ned working with him, to fix up the new wires and switch on the current. But at last it was complete, and Ned took his place at one telephone, with the two sensitive plates before him. Tom did the same, and they proceeded to talk over the wire, first making sure that the vocal connection was perfect.

"All ready now, Ned! We'll try it," called Tom to his chum, over the wire. "Look straight at the plate. I want to get your image first, and then I'll send mine, if it's a success,"

Ned did as requested, and in a few minutes he could hear Tom exclaim, joyfully:

"It's better, Ned! It's coming out real clear. I can see you almost as plainly as if you were right in the booth with me. But turn on your light a little stronger."

Tom could hear, through the telephone, his chum moving about, and then he caught a startled exclamation.

"What's the matter?" asked Tom anxiously.

"I got a shock!" cried Ned. "I thought you said you had this thing fixed. Great Scott, Tom! It nearly yanked the arm off me! Is this a joke?"

"No, old man. No, of course not! Something must be wrong. I didn't mean that. Wait, I'll take a look. Say, it does seem as if everything was going wrong with this invention. But I'm on the right track, and soon I'll have it all right. Wait a second. I'll be right over."

Tom found that it was only a simple displacement of a wire that had given Ned a shock, and he soon had this remedied.

"Now we'll try again," he said. This time nothing wrong occurred, and soon Tom saw the clearest image he had yet observed on his telephone photo plate.

"Switch me on now, Ned," he called to his chum, and Ned reported that he could see Tom very plainly.

"So far—so good," observed Tom, as he came from the booth. "But there are several things I want yet to do."

"Such as what?" questioned Ned.

"Well, I want to arrange to have two kinds of pictures come over the wire. I want it so that a person can go into a booth, call up a friend, and then switch on the picture plate, so he can see his friend as well as talk to him. I want this plate to be like a mirror, so that any number of images can be made to appear on it. In that way it can be used over and over again. In fact it will be exactly like a mirror, or a telescope. No matter how far two persons may be apart they can both see and talk to one another."

"That's a big contract, Tom."

"Yes, but you've seen that it can be done. Then another thing I want to do is to have it arranged so that I can make a photograph of a person over a wire."

"Meaning what?"

"Meaning that if a certain person talks to me over the wire, I can turn my switch, and get a picture of him here at my apparatus connected with my telephone. To do that I'll merely need a sending apparatus at the other end of the telephone line—not a receiving machine."

"Could you arrange it so that the person who was talking to you would have his picture taken whether he wanted it or not?" asked Ned.

"Yes, it might be done," spoke Tom, thoughtfully. "I could conceal the sending plate somewhere in the telephone booth, and arrange the proper light, I suppose."

"That might be a good way in which to catch a criminal," went on Ned. "Often crooks call up on the telephone, but they know they are safe. The authorities can't see them—they can only hear them. Now if you could get a photograph of them while they were telephoning—"

"I see!" cried Tom, excitedly. "That's a great idea! I'll work on that, Ned."

And, all enthusiasm, Tom began to plan new schemes with his photo telephone.

The young inventor did not forget his promise to help Mrs. Damon. But he could get absolutely no clue to her husband's whereabouts. Mr. Damon had completely and mysteriously disappeared. His fortune, too, seemed to have been swallowed up by the sharpers, though lawyers engaged by Tom could fasten no criminal acts on Mr. Peters, who indignantly denied that he had done anything unlawful.

If he had, he had done it in such a way that he could not be brought to justice. The promoter was still about Shopton, as well groomed as ever, with his rose in his buttonhole, and wearing his silk hat. He still speeded up and down Lake Carlopa in his powerful motor boat. But he gave Tom Swift a wide berth.

Late one night, when Tom and Ned had been working at the new photo telephone, after all the rest of the household had retired, Tom suddenly looked up from his drawings and exclaimed:

"What's that?"

"What's what?" inquired Ned.

"That sound? Don't you hear it? Listen!"

"It's an airship—maybe yours coming back!" cried the young banker.

As he spoke Ned did hear, seemingly in the air above the house, a curious, throbbing, pulsating sound.

"That's so! It is an airship motor!" exclaimed Tom. "Come on out!"

Together they rushed from the house, but, ere they reached the yard, the sound had ceased. They looked up into the sky, but could see nothing, though the night was light from a full moon.

"I certainly heard it," said Tom.

"So did I," asserted Ned. "But where is it now?"

They advanced toward the group of work-buildings. Something showing white in the moonlight, before the hangar, caught Ned's eyes.

"Look!" he exclaimed. "There's an airship, Tom!"

The two rushed over to the level landing place before the big shed. And there, as if she had just been run out for a flight, was the Eagle. She had come back in the night, as mysteriously as she had been taken away.

SUCCESS

"Well, this gets me!" exclaimed Tom.

"It sure is strange," agreed Ned. "How did she come here?"

"She didn't come alone—that's sure," went on Tom. "Someone brought her here, made a landing, and got away before we could get out."

The two chums were standing near the Eagle, which had come back so mysteriously.

"Just a couple of seconds sooner and we'd have seen who brought her here," went on Tom. "But they must have shut off the motor some distance up, and then they volplaned down. That's why we didn't hear them."

Ned went over and put his hand on the motor.

"Ouch!" he cried, jumping back. "It's hot!"

"Showing that she's been running up to within a few minutes ago," said Tom. "Well, as I said before, this sure does get me. First these mysterious men take my airship, and then they bring her back again, without so much as thanking me for the use of her."

"Who in the world can they be?" asked Ned.

"I haven't the least idea. But I'm going to find out, if it's at all possible. We'll look the machine over in the morning, and see if we can get any clues. No use in doing that now. Come on, we'll put her back in the hangar."

"Say!" exclaimed Ned, as a sudden idea came to him. "It couldn't be Mr. Damon who had your airship; could it, Tom?"

"I don't know. Why do you ask that?"

"Well, he might have wanted to get away from his enemies for a while, and he might have taken your Eagle, and—"

"Mr. Damon wouldn't trail along with a crowd like the one that took away my airship," said Tom, decidedly. "You've got another guess coming, Ned. Mr. Damon had nothing to do with this."

"And yet the night he disappeared an airship was heard near his house."

"That's so. Well, I give up. This is sure a mystery. We'll have a look at it in the morning. One thing I'll do, though, I'll telephone over to Mr. Damon's house and see if his wife has heard any news. I've been doing that quite often of late, so she won't think anything of it. In that way we can find out if he had anything to do with my airship. But let's run her into the shed first."

This was done, and Koku, the giant, was sent to sleep in the hangar to guard against another theft. But it was not likely that the mysterious men, once having brought the airship back, would come for it again.

Tom called up Mrs. Damon on the telephone, but there was no news of the missing man. He expressed his sympathy, and said he would come and see her soon. He told Mrs. Damon not to get discouraged, adding that he, and others, were doing all that was possible. But, in spite of this, Mrs. Damon, naturally, did worry.

The next morning the two chums inspected the airship, so mysteriously returned to them. Part after part they went over, and found nothing wrong. The motor ran perfectly, and there was not so much as a bent spoke in the landing wheels. For all that could be told by an inspection of the craft she might never have been out of the hangar.

"Hello, here's something!" cried Tom, as he got up from the operator's seat, where he had taken his place to test the various controls.

"What is it?" asked Ned.

"A button. A queer sort of a button. I never had any like that on my clothes, and I'm sure you didn't. Look!" and Tom held out a large, metal button of curious design.

"It must have come off the coat of one of the men who had your airship, Tom," said his chum. "Save it. You may find that it's a clue."

"I will. No telling what it may lead to. Well, I guess that's all we can find."

And it was. But Tom little realized what a clue the button was going to be. Nothing more could be learned by staring at the returned airship, so he and Ned went back to the house.

Tom Swift had many things to do, but his chief concern was for the photo telephone. Now that he was near the goal of success he worked harder than ever. The idea Ned had given him of being able to take the picture of a person at the instrument—without the knowledge of that person—appealed strongly to Tom.

"That's going to be a valuable invention!" he declared, but little he knew how valuable it would prove to him and to others.

It was about a week later when Tom was ready to try the new apparatus. Meanwhile he had prepared different plates, and had changed his wiring system. In the days that had passed nothing new had been learned concerning the whereabouts of Mr. Damon, nor of the men who had so mysteriously taken away Tom's airship.

All was in readiness for the trial. Tom sent Ned to the booth that he had constructed in the airship hangar, some distance away from the house. The other booth Tom had placed in his library, an entirely new system of wires being used.

"Now Ned," explained Tom, "the idea is this! You go into that booth, just as if it were a public one, and ring me up in the regular way. Of course we haven't a central here, but that doesn't matter. Now while I'm talking to you I want to see you. You don't know that, of course."

"The point is to see if I can get your picture while you're talking to me, and not let you know a thing about it."

"Think you can do it, Tom?"

"I'm going to try. We'll soon know. Go ahead."

A little later Ned was calling up his chum, as casually as he could, under the circumstances.

"All right!" called Tom to his chum. "Start in and talk. Say anything you like—it doesn't matter. I want to see if I can get your picture. Is the light burning in your booth?"

"Yes, Tom."

"All right then. Go ahead."

Ned talked of the weather—of anything. Meanwhile Tom was busy. Concealed in the booth occupied by Ned was a sending plate. It could not be seen unless one knew just where to look for it. In Tom's booth was a receiving plate.

The experiment did not take long. Presently Tom called to Ned that he need stay there no longer.

"Come on to the house," invited the young inventor, "and we'll develope this plate." For in this system it was necessary to develope the receiving plate, as is done with an ordinary photographic one. Tom wanted a permanent record.

Eagerly the chums in the dark room looked down into the tray containing the plate and the developing solution.

"Something's coming out!" cried Ned, eagerly.

"Yes! And it's you!" exclaimed Tom. "See, Ned, I got your picture over the telephone. Success! I've struck it! This is the best yet!"

At that moment, as the picture came out more and more plainly, someone knocked on the door of the dark room.

"Who is it?" asked Tom.

"Gen'man t' see you," said Eradicate. "He say he come from Mistah Peters!"

"Mr. Peters—that rascally promoter!" whispered Tom to his chum. "What does this mean?"

THE MYSTERIOUS MESSAGE

Tom Swift and his chum looked at one another strangely for a moment in the dim, red light of the dark room. Then the young inventor spoke:

"I'm not going to see him. Tell him so, Rad!"

"Hold on a second," suggested Ned. "Maybe you had better see him, Tom. It may have something to with Mr. Damon's lost fortune."

"That's so! I didn't think of that. And I may get a clue to his disappearance, though I don't imagine Peters had anything to do with that. Wait, Rad. Tell the gentleman I'll see him. Did he give any name, Rad?"

"Yas, sah. Him done say him Mistah Boylan."

"The same man who called to see me once before, trying to get me to do some business with Peters," murmured Tom. "Very well, I'll see him as soon as this picture is fixed. Tell him to wait, Rad."

A little later Tom went to where his caller awaited in the library. This time there were no plans to be looked at, the young inventor having made a practice of keeping all his valuable papers locked in a safe.

"You go into the next room, Ned," Tom had said to his chum. "Leave the door open, so you can hear what is said."

"Why, do you think there'll be trouble? Maybe we'd better have Koku on hand to—"

"Oh, no, nothing like that," laughed Tom. "I just want you to listen to what's said so, if need be, you can be a witness later. I don't know what their game is, but I don't trust Peters and his crowd. They may want to get control of some of my patents, and they may try some underhanded work. If they do I want to be in a position to stop them."

"All right," agreed Ned, and he took his place.

But Mr. Boylan's errand was not at all sensational, it would seem. He bowed to Tom, perhaps a little distantly, for they had not parted the best of friends on a former occasion.

"I suppose you are surprised to see me," began Mr. Boylan.

"Well, I am, to tell the truth," Tom said, calmly.

"I am here at the request of my employer, Mr. Peters," went on the caller. "He says he is forming a new and very powerful company to exploit airships, and he wants to know whether you would not reconsider your determination not to let him do some business for you."

"No, I'm afraid I don't care to go into anything like that," said Tom.

"It would be a good thing for you," proceeded Mr. Boylan, eagerly. "Mr. Peters is able to command large capital, and if you would permit the use of your airships—or one of them—as a model, and would supervise the construction of others, we could confidently expect large sales. Thus you would profit, and I am frank to admit that the company, and Mr. Peters, also, would make money. Mr. Peters is perfectly free to confess that he is in business to make money, but he is also willing to let others share with him. Come now, what do you say?"

"I am sorry, but I shall have to say the same thing I said before," replied Tom. "Nothing doing!"

Mr. Boylan glanced rather angrily at the young inventor, and then, with a shrug of his shoulders, remarked:

"Well, you have the say, of course. But I would like to remind you that this is going to be a very large airship company, and if your inventions are not exploited some others will be. And Mr. Peters also desired me to say that this is the last offer he would make you."

"Tell him," said Tom, "that I am much obliged, but that I have no business that I can entrust to him. If he wishes to make some other type of airship, that is his affair. Good-day."

As Mr. Boylan was going out Tom noticed a button dangling from the back of his caller's coat. It hung by a thread, being one of the pair usually sewed on the back of a cutaway garment.

"I think you had better take off that button before it falls," suggested Tom. "You may lose it, and perhaps it would be hard to match."

"That's so. Thank you!" said Mr. Boylan. He tried to reach around and get it, but he was too stout to turn easily, especially as the coat was tight-fitting.

"I'll get it for you," offered Tom, as he pulled it off. "There is one missing, though," he said, as he handed the button to the man. And then Tom started as he saw the pattern of the one in his hand.

"One gone? That's too bad," murmured Mr. Boylan. "Those buttons were imported, and I doubt if I can replace them. They are rather odd."

"Yes," agreed Tom, gazing as if fascinated at the one he still held. "They are rather odd."

And then, as he passed it over, like a flash it came to him where he had seen a button like that before. He had found it in his airship, which had been so mysteriously taken away and returned.

Tom could hardly restrain his impatience until Mr. Boylan had gone. The young inventor had half a notion to produce the other button, matching the one he had just pulled off his visitor's coat, and tell where he had found it. But he held himself back. He wanted to talk first to Ned.

And, when his chum came in, Tom cried:

"Ned, what do you think? I know who had my airship!"

"How?" asked Ned, in wonder.

"By that button clue! Yes, it's the same kind—they're as alike as twins!" and Tom brought out the button which he had put away in his desk. "See, Boylan had one just like this on the back of his coat. The other was missing. Here it is—it was in the seat of my airship, where it was probably pulled off as he moved about. Ned, I think I've got the right clue at last."

Ned said nothing for several seconds. Then he remarked slowly:

"Well, Tom, it proves one thing; but not the other."

"What do you mean?"

"I mean that it may be perfectly true that the button came off Mr. Boylan's coat, but that doesn't prove that he wore it. You can be reasonably sure that the coat was having a ride in your Eagle, but was Boylan in the coat? That's the question."

"In the coat? Of course he was in it!" cried Tom.

"You can't be sure. Someone may have borrowed his coat to take a midnight ride in the airship."

"Mr. Boylan doesn't look to be the kind of a man who would lend his clothes," remarked Tom.

"You never can tell. Someone may have borrowed it without his knowledge. You'd better go a bit slow, Tom."

"Well, maybe I had. But it's a clue, anyhow."

Ned agreed to this.

"And all I've got to do is to find out who was in the coat when it was riding about in my airship," went on Tom.

"Yes," said Ned, "and then maybe you'll have some clue to the disappearance of Mr. Damon."

"Right you are! Come on, let's get busy!"

"As if we hadn't been busy all the while!" laughed Ned. "I'll lose my place at the bank if I don't get back soon."

"Oh, stay a little longer—a few days," urged Tom. "I'm sure that something is going to happen soon. Anyhow my photo telephone is about perfected. But I've just thought of another improvement."

"What is it?"

"I'm going to arrange a sort of dictaphone, or phonograph, so I can get a permanent record of what a person says over the wire, as well as get a picture of him saying it. Then everything will be complete. This last won't be hard to do, as there are several machines on the market now, for preserving a record of telephone conversations. I'll make mine a bit different, though."

"Tom, is there any limit to what you're going to do?" asked Ned, admiringly.

"Oh, yes, I'm going to stop soon, and retire," laughed the young inventor.

After talking the matter over, Tom and his chum decided to wait a day or so before taking any action in regard to the button clue to the takers of the airship. After all, no great harm had been done, and Tom was more anxious to locate Mr. Damon, and try to get back his fortune, as well as to perfect his photo telephone, than he was to discover those who had helped themselves to the Eagle.

Tom and Ned put in some busy days, arranging the phonograph attachment. It was easy, compared to the hard work of sending a picture over the wire. They paid several visits to Mrs. Damon, but she had no news of her missing husband, and, as the days went by, she suffered more and more under the strain.

Finally Tom's new invention was fully completed. It was a great success, and he not only secured pictures of Ned and others over the wire, as he talked to them, but he imprinted on wax cylinders, to be reproduced later, the very things they said.

It was a day or so after he had demonstrated his new attachment for the first time, that Tom received a most urgent message from Mrs. Damon.

"Tom," she said, over the telephone, "I wish you would call. Something very mysterious has happened."

"Mr. Damon hasn't come back; has he?" asked Tom eagerly.

"No—but I wish I could say he had. This concerns him, however. Can you come?"

"I'll be there right away."

In his speedy monoplane Tom soon reached Waterford. Ned did not accompany him this time.

"Now what is it, Mrs. Damon?" asked the young inventor.

"About half an hour before I called you," she said, "I received a mysterious message."

"Who brought it?" asked Tom quickly.

"No one. It came over the telephone. Someone, whose voice I did not know, said to me: 'Sign the land papers, and send them to us, and your husband will be released.'"

"That message came over the wire?" cried Tom, excitedly.

"Yes," answered Mrs. Damon. "Oh, I am so frightened! I don't know what to do!" and the lady burst into tears.

ANOTHER CALL

Tom Swift, for the moment, did not know what to do. It was a strange situation, and one he had never thought of. What did the mysterious message mean? He must think it all out, and plan some line of action. Clearly Mrs. Damon was not able to do so.

"Now let's get at this in some kind of order," suggested the youth, when Mrs. Damon had calmed herself. It was his habit to have a method about doing things. "And don't worry," he advised. "I am certain some good will come of this. It proves one thing, that's sure."

"What is it, Tom?"

"That Mr. Damon is alive and well. Otherwise the message would not have said he would be 'released.' It wasn't from anyone you know; was it?"

"No, I'm sure I never heard the voice before."

Tom paused a moment to think how useful his photo telephone and phonograph arrangement might have been in this case.

"How did the telephone call come in?" inquired the young inventor.

"In the usual way," answered Mrs. Damon. "The bell rang, and, as I happened to be near the instrument, I answered it, as I often do, when the maid is busy. A voice asked if I was Mrs. Damon, and of course I said I was. Then I heard this: 'Sign the land papers, and send them to us, and your husband will be released.'"

"Was that all?" Tom asked.

"I think so—I made a note of it at the time." Mrs. Damon looked into a small red book. "No, that wasn't all," she said, quickly. "I was so astonished, at hearing those strange words about my husband, that I didn't know what to say. Before I could ask any questions the voice went on to say, rather abruptly: 'We will call you again.'"

"That's good!" cried Tom. "I only hope they do it while I am here. Perhaps I can get some clue as to who it was called you. But was this all you heard?"

"Yes, I'm sure that was all. I had forgotten about the last words, but I see I have them written down in my note book."

"Did you ask any questions?" inquired Tom.

"Oh, indeed I did! As soon as I got over being stunned by what I heard, I asked all sorts of questions. I demanded to know who was speaking, what they meant, where they were, and all that. I begged them to tell me something of my husband."

"And what did they say?"

"Not a thing. There wasn't a sound in the telephone. The receiver was hung up, breaking the connection after that message to me— that mysterious message."

"Yes, it was mysterious," agreed Tom, thoughtfully. "I can't understand it. But didn't you try to learn from the central operator where the call had come from?"

"Oh, yes, indeed, Tom! As soon as I found out the person speaking to me had rung off, I got the girl in the exchange."

"And what did she say?"

"That the call came from an automatic pay station in a drug store in town. I have the address. It was one of those telephones where you put your money for the call in a slot."

"I see. Well, the first thing to do is for me to go to that drug store and find out, if I can, who used the telephone about that time. It's a slim chance, but we'll have to take it. Was it a man's voice, or a woman's?"

"Oh, a man's, I'm sure. It was very deep and heavy. No woman could speak like that."

"So much is settled, anyhow. Now about the land papers—what was meant?"

"I'll tell you," said Mrs. Damon. "You know part of our property—considerable land and some buildings—is in my name. Mr. Damon had it fixed so a number of years ago, in order to protect me. No one could get this property, and land, unless I signed the deeds, or agreed to sign them. Now all of Mr. Damon's fortune is tied up in some of Mr. Peters's companies. That is why my husband has disappeared."

"He didn't disappear—he was taken away against his will; I'm positive of that!" exclaimed Tom.

"Perhaps so," agreed Mrs. Damon, sadly. "But those are the papers referred to, I'm sure."

"Probably," assented Tom. "The rascals want to get control of everything—even your possessions. Not satisfied with ruining Mr. Damon, they want to make you a beggar, too. So they are playing on your fears. They promise to release your husband if you will give them the land."

"Yes, that must be it, Tom. What would you advise me to do? I am so frightened over this!"

"Do? Don't you do anything!" cried Tom. "We'll fool these rascals yet. If they got those papers they might release Mr. Damon, or they might not—fearing he would cause their arrest later. But we'll have him released anyhow, and we'll save what is left of your fortune. Put those land papers in a safe-deposit box, and let me do the rest. I'm going to catch those fellows!"

"But how, Tom? You don't know who they are. And a mere message over a telephone won't give you a clue to where they are."

"Perhaps not an ordinary message," agreed Tom. "But I'm going to try some of my new inventions. You said they told you they were going to call again?"

"That's what they said, Tom."

"Well, when they do, I want to be here. I want to listen to that message. If you will allow me, I'll take up my residence here for a while, Mrs. Damon."

"Allow you? I'll be only too glad if you will, Tom. But I thought you were going to try to get some clue from the drug store where the mysterious message came from."

"I'll let Ned Newton do that. I want to stay here."

Tom telephoned to Ned to meet him at Mrs. Damon's house, and also to bring with him certain things from the laboratory. And when Ned arrived in an auto, with various bits of apparatus, Tom put in some busy hours.

Meanwhile Ned was sent to the drug store, to see if any clues could be obtained there as to who had sent the message. As Tom had feared, nothing could be learned. There were several automatic 'phones in the place, and they were used very often during the day by the public. The drug clerks took little or no notice of the persons entering or leaving the booths, since the dropping of a coin in the slot was all that was necessary to be connected with central.

"Well, we've got to wait for the second call here," said Tom, who had been busy during Ned's absence. He had fitted to Mrs. Damon's telephone a recording wax phonograph cylinder, to get a record of the speaker's voice. And he had also put in an extension telephone, so that he could listen while Mrs. Damon talked to the unknown.

"There, I guess we're ready for them," said Tom, late that afternoon. But no queer call came in that day. It was the next morning. about ten o'clock, after Mrs. Damon had passed a restless night, that the telephone bell rang. Tom, who was on the alert, was at his auxiliary instrument in a flash. He motioned to Mrs. Damon to answer on the main wire.

"Hello," she spoke into the transmitter. "Who is this?"

"Are you Mrs. Damon?" Tom heard come over the wire in a deep voice, and by the manner in which Mrs. Damon signalled the young inventor knew that, at the other end of the line, was the mysterious man who had spoken before.

THE BUZZING SOUND

"Are you Mrs. Damon?" came the question again—rather more impatiently this time, Tom thought.

"Yes," answered the lady, glancing over at Tom. The extension telephone was in the same room. Softly Tom switched on the phonograph attachment. The little wax cylinder began to revolve noiselessly, ready to record the faintest word that came over the wire.

"You got a message from me yesterday," went on the hoarse voice. In vain Tom tried to recall whether or not he had heard it before. He could not place it.

"Who are you?" asked Mrs. Damon. She and Tom had previously agreed on a line of talk. "Tell me your name, please."

"There's no need for any names to be used," went on the unknown at the other end of the wire. "You heard what I said yesterday. Are you willing to send me those land title papers, if we release your husband?"

"But where shall I send them?" asked Mrs. Damon, to gain time.

"You'll be told where. And listen—no tricks! You needn't try to find out who I am, nor where I am. Just send those papers if you want to see your husband again."

"Oh, how is he? Tell me about him! You are cruel to keep him a prisoner like this! I demand that you release him!"

Tom had not told Mrs. Damon to say this. It came out of her own heart—she could not prevent the agonized outburst.

"Never mind about that, now," came the gruff voice over the wire. "Are you willing to send the papers?"

Mrs. Damon looked over to Tom for silent instructions. He nodded his head in assent.

"Yes, I—I will send them if you tell me where to get them to you —if you will release Mr. Damon," said the anxious wife. "But tell me who you are—and where you are!" she begged.

"None of that! I'm not looking to be arrested. You get the papers ready, and I'll let you know to-morrow, about this time, where to send them."

"Wait a minute!" called Mrs. Damon, to gain more time. "I must know just what papers you want."

"All right, I'll tell you," and he began to describe the different ones.

It took a little time for the unknown to give this information to Mrs. Damon. The man was very particular about the papers. There were trust deeds, among other things, and he probably thought that once he had possession of them, with Mrs. Damon's signature, even though it had been obtained under a threat, he could claim the property. Later it was learned that such was not the case, for Mrs. Damon, with Tom's aid, could have proved the fraud, had the scoundrels tried to get the remainder of the Damon fortune.

But at the time it seemed to the helpless woman that everything she owned would be taken from her. Though she said she did not care, as long as Mr. Damon was restored to her.

As I have said, the telephoning of the instructions about the papers took some time. Tom had counted on this, and had made his plans accordingly.

As soon as the telephone call had come in, Tom had communicated with a private detective who was in waiting, and this man had gone to the drug store whence the first call had come. He was going to try to make the arrest of the man telephoning.

But for fear the scoundrel would go to a different instrument, Tom took another precaution. This was to have one of the operators in the central exchange on the watch. As soon as Mrs. Damon's house was in connection with another telephone, the location of the latter would be noted, and another private detective would be sent there. Thus Tom hoped to catch the man at the 'phone.

Meanwhile Tom listened to the hoarse voice at the other end of the wire, giving the directions to Mrs. Damon. Tom hoped that soon there would be an arrest made.

Meanwhile the talk was being faithfully recorded on the phonograph cylinder. And, as the man talked on, Tom became aware of a curious undercurrent of sound. It was a buzzing noise, that Tom knew did not come from the instrument itself. It was not the peculiar tapping, singing noise heard in a telephone receiver, caused by induced electrical currents, or by wire trouble.

"This is certainly different," mused Tom. He was trying to recall where he had heard the noise before. Sometimes it was faint, and then it would gradually increase, droning off into faintness once more. Occasionally it was so loud that Mrs. Damon could not hear the talk about the papers, and the man would have to repeat.

But finally he came to an end.

"This is all now," he said, sharply. Tom heard the words above the queer, buzzing, humming sound. "You are keeping me too long. I think you are up to some game, but it won't do you any good, Mrs. Damon. I'll 'phone you to-morrow where to send the papers. And if you don't send them—if you try any tricks—it will be the worse for you and Mr. Damon!"

There was a click, that told of a receiver being placed back on the hook, and the voice ceased. So, also, did the queer, buzzing sound over which Tom puzzled.

"What can it have been?" he asked. "Did you hear it, Mrs. Damon?"

"What, Tom?"

"That buzzing sound."

"Yes, I heard, but I didn't know what it was. Oh, Tom, what shall I do?"

"Don't worry. We'll see if anything happened. They may have caught that fellow. If not I'll plan another scheme."

Tom's first act was to call up the telephone exchange to learn where the second call had come from. He got the information at once. The address was in the suburbs. The man had not gone to the drug store this time.

"Did the detective get out to that address?" asked Tom eagerly of the manager.

"Yes. As soon as we were certain that he was the party you wanted, your man got right after him, Mr. Swift."

"That's good, I hope he catches him!" cried the young inventor. "We'll have to wait and find out."

"He said he'd call up and let you know as soon as he reached the place," the telephone manager informed Tom.

There was nothing to do but wait, and meanwhile Tom did what he could to comfort Mrs. Damon. She was quite nervous and inclined to be hysterical, and the youth thought it wise to have a cousin, who had come to stay with her, summon the doctor.

"But, Tom, what shall I do about those papers?" Mrs. Damon asked him. "Shall I send them?"

"Indeed not!"

"But I want Mr. Damon restored to me," she pleaded. "I don't care about the money. He can make more."

"Well, we'll not give those scoundrels the satisfaction of getting any money out of you. Just wait now, I'll work this thing out, and find a way to catch that fellow. If I could only think what that buzzing sound was—"

Then, in a flash, it came to Tom.

"A sawmill! A planing mill!" he cried. "That's what it was! That fellow was telephoning from some place near a sawmill!"

The telephone rang in the midst of Tom's excited comments.

"Yes—yes!" he called eagerly. "Who is it—what is it?"

"This is Larsen—the private detective you sent."

"Oh, yes, you were at the drug store."

"Yes, Mr. Swift. Well, that party didn't call up from here."

"I know, Larsen. It was from another station. We're after him. Much obliged to you. Come on back."

Tom was sure his theory was right. The man had called up the Damon house from some telephone near a sawmill. And a little later Tom's theory was proved to be true. He got a report from the second detective. Unfortunately the man had not been able to reach the telephone station before the unknown speaker had departed.

"Was the place near a sawmill?" asked Tom, eagerly.

"It was," answered the detective over the wire. "The telephone is right next door to one. It's an automatic pay station and no one seems to have noticed who the man was who telephoned. I couldn't get a single clue. I'm sorry."

"Never mind," said Tom, as cheerfully as he could. "I think I'm on the right track now. I'm going to lay a trap for this fellow."

SETTING THE TRAP

Troublesome problems seemed to be multiplying for Tom Swift. He admitted as much himself after the failure to capture the man who had telephoned to Mrs. Damon. He had hoped that his plan of sending detectives to the location of the telephones would succeed. Since it had not the youth must try other means.

"Now, Ned," he said to his chum, when they were on their way from Mrs. Damon's, it being impossible to do anything further there. "Now, Ned, we've got to think this thing out together."

"I'm willing, Tom. I'll do what I can."

"I know you will. Now the thing to do is to go at this thing systematically. Otherwise we'll be working around in a circle, and won't get anywhere. In the first place, let's set down what we do know. Then we'll put down what we don't know, and go after that."

"Put down what you don't know?" exclaimed Ned. "How are you going to put down a thing when you don't know it?"

"I mean we can put a question mark after it, so to speak. For instance we don't know where Mr. Damon is, but we want to find out."

"Oh, I see. Well, let's start off with the things we do know."

The two friends were at Tom's house by now, having come from Waterford in Tom's airship. After thinking over all the exciting happenings of the past few days, Tom remarked: "Now, Ned, for the things we do know. In the first place Mr. Damon is missing, and his fortune is about gone. There is considerable left to Mrs. Damon, however, but those scoundrels may get that away from her, if we don't watch out. Secondly, my airship was taken and brought back, with a button more than it had when it went away. Said button exactly matched one off Mr. Boylan's coat."

"Thirdly, Mr. Damon was either taken away or went away, in an airship—either in mine or someone else's. Fourthly, Mrs. Damon has received telephonic communications from the man, or men, who have her husband. Fifthly, Mr. Peters, either legally or illegally, is responsible for the loss of Mr. Damon's fortune. Now: there you are—for the things we do know."

"Now for the things we don't know. We don't know who has taken Mr. Damon away, nor where he is, to begin with the most important."

"Hold on, Tom, I think you're wrong," broke in Ned.

"In what way?"

"About not knowing who is responsible for the taking away of Mr. Damon. I think it's as plain as the nose on your face that Peters is responsible."

"I can't see it that way," said Tom, quickly. "I will admit that it looks as though Boylan had been in my airship, but as for Peters taking Mr. Damon away—why, Peters is around town all the while, and if he had a hand in the disappearance of Mr. Damon, do you think he'd stay here, when he knows we are working on the case? And would he send Boylan to see me if Boylan had been one of those who had a hand in it? They wouldn't dare, especially as they know I'm working on the case."

"Peters is a bad lot. I'll grant you, though, he was fair enough to pay for my motor boat. I don't believe he had anything to do with taking Mr. Damon away."

"Do you think he was the person who was talking to Mrs. Damon about the papers?"

"No, Ned. I don't. I listened to that fellow's voice carefully. It wasn't like Peters's. I'm going to put it in the phonograph, too, and let you listen to it. Then see what you say."

Tom did this, a little later. The record of the voice, as it came over the wire, was listened to from the wax cylinder, and Ned had to admit that it was not much like that of the promoter.

"Well, what's next to be done?" asked the young banker.

"I'm going to set a trap," replied Tom, with a grin.

"Set a trap?"

"Yes, a sort of mouse-trap. I'm glad my photo telephone is now perfected, Ned."

"What has that got to do with it?"

"That's going to be my trap, Ned. Here is my game. You know this fellow—this strange unknown—is going to call up Mrs. Damon to-morrow. Well, I'll be ready for him. I'm going to put in the booth where he will telephone from, one of my photo telephones—that is, the sending apparatus. In Mrs. Damon's house, attached to her telephone, will be the receiving plate, as well as the phonograph cylinder."

"When this fellow starts to talk he'll be sending us his picture, though he won't know it, and we'll be getting a record of his voice. Then we'll have him just where we want him."

"Good!" cried Ned. "But, Tom, there's a weak spot in your mouse-trap."

"What is it?"

"How are you going to know which telephone the unknown will call up from? He may go to any of a hundred, more or less."

"He might—yes. But that's a chance we've got to take. It isn't so much of a chance, though when you stop to think that he will probably go to some public telephone in an isolated spot, and, unless I'm much mistaken he will go to a telephone near where he was today. He knows that was safe, since we didn't capture him, and he's very likely to come back."

"But to make the thing as sure as possible, I'm going to attach my apparatus to a number of public telephones in the vicinity of the one near the sawmill. So if the fellow doesn't get caught in one, he will in another. I admit it's taking a chance; but what else can we do?"

"I suppose you're right, Tom. It's like setting a number of traps."

"Exactly. A trapper can't be sure where he is going to get his catch, so he picks out the place, or run-way, where the game has been in the habit of coming. He hides his traps about that place, and trusts to luck that the animal will blunder into one of them."

"Criminals, to my way of thinking, are a good bit like animals. They seem to come back to their old haunts. Nearly any police story proves this. And it's that on which I am counting to capture this criminal. So I'm going to fit up as many telephones with my photo and phonograph outfit, as I can in the time we have. You'll have to help me. Luckily I've got plenty of selenium plates for the sending end. I'll only need one at the receiving end. Now we'll have to go and have a talk with the telephone manager, after which we'll get busy."

"You've overlooked one thing, Tom."

"What's that, Ned?"

"Why, if you know about which telephone this fellow is going to use, why can't you have police stationed near it to capture him as soon as he begins to talk?"

"Well, I did think of that, Ned; but it won't work."

"Why not?"

"Because, in the first place this man, or some of his friends, will be on the watch. When he goes into the place to telephone there'll be a look-out, I'm sure, and he'd either put off talking to Mrs. Damon, or he'd escape before we had any evidence against him."

"You see I've got to get evidence that will stand in the courts to convict this fellow, and if he's scared off before we get that, the game will be up."

"That's what my photo telephone will do—it will get the evidence, just as a dictaphone does. In fact, I'm thinking of working it out on those lines, after I clear up this business."

"Just suppose we had detectives stationed at all the telephones near the sawmill, where this fellow would be likely to go. In the first place no one has seen him, as far as we know, so there's no telling what sort of a chap he is. And you can't go up to a perfect stranger and arrest him because you think he is the man who has spirited away Mr. Damon."

"Another thing. Until this fellow has talked, and made his offer to Mrs. Damon, to restore her husband, in exchange for certain papers, we have no hold over him."

"But he has done that, Tom. You heard him, and you have his voice down on the wax cylinder."

"Yes, but I haven't had a glimpse of his face. That's what I want, and what I'm going to get. Suppose he does go into the telephone booth, and tell Mrs. Damon an address where she is to send the papers. Even if a detective was near at hand he might not catch what was said. Or, if he did, on what ground could he arrest a man who, very likely, would be a perfect stranger to him? The detective couldn't say: 'I take you into custody for telephoning an address to Mrs. Damon.' That, in itself, is no crime."

"No, I suppose not," admitted Ned. "You've got this all thought out, Tom."

"I hope I have. You see it takes quite a combination to get evidence against a criminal—evidence that will convict him. That's why I have to be so careful in setting my trap."

"I see, Tom. Well, it's about time for us to get busy; isn't it?"

"It sure is. There's lots to do. First we'll go see the telephone people."

Tom explained to the 'phone manager the necessity for what he was about to do. The manager at once agreed to let the young inventor have a free hand. He was much interested in the photo telephone, and Tom promised to give his company a chance to use it on their lines, later.

The telephone near the sawmill was easily located. It was in a general store, and the instrument was in a booth. To this instrument Tom attached his sending plate, and he also substituted for the ordinary incandescent light, a powerful tungsten one, that would give illumination enough to cause the likeness to be transmitted over the wire.

The same thing was done to a number of the public telephones in that vicinity, each one being fitted up so that the picture of whoever talked would be transmitted over the wire when Tom turned the switch. To help the plan further the telephone manager marked a number of other 'phones, "Out of Order," for the time being.

"Now, I think we're done!" exclaimed the young inventor, with a sigh, late that night. He and Ned and the line manager had worked hard.

"Yes," answered the young banker, "the traps are set. The question is: Will our rat be caught?"

THE PHOTO TELEPHONE

Tom Swift was taking, as he afterward confessed, "a mighty big chance." But it seemed the only way. He was working against cunning men, and had to be as cunning as they.

True, the man he hoped to capture, through the combination of his photo telephone and the phonograph, might go to some other instrument than one of those Tom had adjusted. But this could not be helped. In all he had put his new attachment on eight 'phones in the vicinity of the sawmill. So he had eight chances in his favor, and as many against him as there were other telephones in use.

"It's a mighty small margin in our favor," sighed Tom.

"It sure is," agreed Ned. They were at Mrs., Damon's house, waiting for the call to come in.

"But we couldn't do anything else," went on Tom.

"No," spoke Ned, "and I have a great deal of hope in the proverbial Swift luck, Tom."

"Well, I only hope it holds good this time!" laughed the young inventor.

"There are a good many things that can go wrong," observed Ned. "The least little slip-up may spoil your traps, Tom."

"I know it, Ned. But I've got to take the chance. We've just got to do something for Mrs. Damon. She's wearing herself out by worrying," he added in a low voice, for indeed the wife of his friend felt the absence of her husband greatly. She had lost flesh, she ate scarcely anything, and her nights were wakeful ones of terror.

"What if this fails?" asked Ned.

"Then I'm going to work that button clue to the limit," replied Tom. "I'll go to Boylan and see what he and Peters have to say."

"If you'd done as I suggested you'd have gone to them first," spoke Ned. "You'll find they're mixed up in this."

"Maybe; but I doubt it. I tell you there isn't a clue leading to Peters—as yet."

"But there will be," insisted Ned. "You'll see that that I'm right this time."

"I can't see it, Ned. As a matter of fact, I would have gone to Boylan about that button I found in my airship only I've been so busy on this photo telephone, and in arranging the trap, that I haven't had time. But if this fails—and I'm hoping it won't—I'll get after him," and there was a grim look on the young inventor's face.

It was wearying and nervous work—this waiting. Tom and Ned felt the strain as they sat there in Mrs. Damon's library, near the telephone. It had been fitted up in readiness. Attached to the receiving wires was a sensitive plate, on which Tom hoped would be imprinted the image of the man at the other end of the wire—the criminal who, in exchange for the valuable land papers, would give Mr. Damon his liberty.

There was also the phonograph cylinder to record the man's voice. Several times, while waiting for the call to come in, Tom got up to test the apparatus. It was in perfect working order.

As before, there was an extension telephone, so that Mrs. Damon could talk to the unknown, while Tom could hear as well. But he planned to take no part in the conversation unless something unforeseen occurred.

Mr. Damon was an enthusiastic photographer, and he had a dark room adjoining his library. It was in this dark room that Tom planned to develop the photo telephone plate.

On this occasion he was not going to use the metal plate in which, ordinarily, the image of the person talking appeared. That record was but a fleeting one, as in a mirror. This time Tom wanted a permanent picture that could, if necessary, be used in a court of justice.

Tom's plan was this: If the person who had demanded the papers came to one of the photo telephones, and spoke to Mrs. Damon, Tom would switch on the receiving apparatus. Thus, while the man was talking, his picture would be taken, though he would not know of the thing being done.

His voice would also be recorded on the wax cylinder, and he would be equally unaware of this.

When Tom had imprinted the fellow's image on the prepared plate, he would go quickly to the dark room and develop it. A wet print could be made, and with this as evidence, and to use in identification, a quick trip could be made to the place whence the man had telephoned. Tom hoped thus to capture him.

To this end he had his airship in waiting, and as soon as he had developed the picture he planned to rush off to the vicinity of the sawmill, and make a prisoner of the man whose features would be revealed to him over the wire.

It was a hazardous plan—a risky one—but it was the best that he could evolve. Tom had instructed Mrs. Damon to keep the man in conversation as long as possible, in order to give the young inventor himself time to rush off in his airship. But of course the man might get suspicious and leave. That was another chance that had to be taken.

"If I had thought of it in time," said Tom, musingly, as he paced up and down in the library waiting for the 'phone to ring, "if I had thought of it in time I would have rigged up two plates—one for a temporary, or looking-glass, picture, and the other for a permanent one. In that way I could rush off as soon as I got a glimpse of the fellow. But it's too late to do that now. I'll have to develop this plate."

Waiting is the most wearisome work there is. Tom and Ned found this to be the case, as they sat there, hoping each moment that the telephone bell would ring, and that the man at the other end of the wire would be the mysterious stranger. Mrs. Damon, too, felt the nervous strain.

"This is about the hour he called up yesterday," said Tom, in a low voice, after coming back from a trip to the window to see that his airship was in readiness. He had brought over to help in starting it, for he was using his most powerful and speedy craft, and the propellers were hard to turn.

"Yes," answered Mrs. Damon. "It was just about this hour, Tom. Oh, I do hope—"

She was interrupted by the jingle of the telephone bell. With a jump Tom was at the auxiliary instrument, while Mrs. Damon lifted off the receiver of her own telephone.

"Yes; what is it?" she asked, in a voice that she tried to make calm.

"Do you know who this is?" Tom heard come over the wire.

"Are you the—er—the person who was to give me an address where I am to send certain papers?"

"Yes. I'm the same one. I'm glad to see that you have acted sensibly. If I get the papers all right, you'll soon have your husband back. Now do as I say. Take down this address."

"Very well," assented Mrs. Damon. She looked over at Tom. He was intently listening, and he, too, would note the address given. The trap was about to be sprung. The game had walked into it. Just which telephone was being used Tom could not as yet tell. It was evidently not the one nearest the planing mill, for Tom could not hear the buzzing sound. It was well he had put his attachment on several instruments.

"One moment, please," said Mrs. Damon, to the unknown at the other end of the wire. This was in accordance with the pre-arranged plan.

"Well, what is it?" asked the man, impatiently. "I have no time to waste."

Tom heard again the same gruff tones, and he tried in vain to recognize them.

"I want you take down a message to Mr. Damon," said his wife. "This is very important. It can do you no harm to give him this message; but I want you to get it exact. If you do not promise to deliver it I shall call all negotiations off."

"Oh, all right I'll take the message; but be quick about it. Then I'll give you the address where you are to send the papers."

"This is the message," went on Mrs. Damon. "Please write it down. It is very important to me. Have you a pencil?"

"Yes, I have one. Wait until I get a bit of paper. It's so dark in this booth—wait until I turn on the light."

Tom could not repress a pleased and joyful exclamation. It was just what he had hoped the man would do—turn on the light in the booth. Indeed, it was necessary for the success of the trap that the light be switched on. Otherwise no picture could be transmitted over the wire. And the plan of having the man write down a message to Mr. Damon was arranged with that end in view. The man would need a light to see to write, and Tom's apparatus must be lighted in order to make it work. The plot was coming along finely.

"There!" exclaimed the man at the other end of the wire. "I have a light now. Go ahead with your message, Mrs. Damon. But make it short. I can't stay here long."

Then Mrs. Damon began dictating the message she and Tom had agreed upon. It was as long as they dared make it, for they wanted to keep the man in the booth to the last second.

"Dear Husband," began Mrs. Damon. What the message was does not matter. It has nothing to do with this story. Sufficient to say that the moment the man began writing it down, as Tom could tell over the sensitive wire, by the scratching of the pencil—at that moment Tom, knowing the light was on in the distant telephone booth, switched on the picture-taking apparatus. His receiving apparatus at once indicated that the image was being made on the sensitive plate.

It took only a few seconds of time, and with the plate in the holder Tom hastened to the dark room to develop it. Ned took his chum's place at the telephone, to see that all worked smoothly. The photo telephone had done it's work. Whose image would be found imprinted on the sensitive plate? Tom's hands trembled so that he could scarcely put it in the developing solution.

THE ESCAPE

Ned Newton, listening at the auxiliary telephone heard the man, to whom Mrs. Damon was dictating her message to her husband, utter an exclamation of impatience.

"I'm afraid I can't take down any more," he called. "That is enough. Now you listen. I want you to send me those papers."

"And I am willing to," went on Mrs. Damon, while Ned listened to the talk, the phonograph faithfully recording it.

"I wonder whose picture Tom will find," mused Ned.

The unknown, at the other end of the wire, began giving Mrs. Damon a description of just what papers he wanted, and how to mail them to him. He gave an address that Ned recognized as that of a cigar store, where many persons received their mail under assumed names. The postal authorities had, for a long time, tried to get evidence against it

"That's going to make it hard to get him, when he comes for the papers," thought Ned. "He's a foxy criminal, all right. But I guess Tom will turn the trick."

Mrs. Damon was carefully noting down the address. She really intended to send the papers, if it proved that there was no other way in which she could secure the release of her husband. But she did not count on all of Tom's plans. "Why doesn't he develop that plate?" thought Ned. "He'll be too late, in spite of his airship. That fellow will skip."

It was at that moment that Tom came into the library. He moved cautiously, for he realized that a loud sound in the room would carry to the man at the other end of the wire. Tom motioned for Ned to come to him. He held out a dripping photographic plate.

"It's Peters!" said Tom, in a hoarse whisper.

"Peters?" gasped Ned. "How could it be? His voice—"

"I know. It didn't sound a bit like Peters over the 'phone, but there's his picture, all right!"

Tom held up the plate. There, imprinted on it by the wonderful power of the young inventor's latest appliance, was the image of the rascally promoter. As plainly as in life he was shown, even to his silk hat and the flower in his button-hole. He was in a telephone booth—that much could be told from the photograph that had been transmitted over the wire, but which booth could not be said—they were nearly all alike.

"Peters!" gasped Ned. "I thought he was the fellow, Tom."

"Yes, I know. You were right, and I was wrong. But I did not recognize his voice. It was very hoarse. He must have a bad cold." Later this was learned to have been the case. "There's no time to lose," whispered Tom, while Mrs. Damon was doing her best to prolong the conversation in order to hold the man at the other end of the wire. "Ned, get central on the other telephone, and see where this call came from. Then we'll get there as fast as the airship will take us."

A second and temporary telephone line had been installed in the Damon home, and on this Ned was soon talking, while Tom, putting the photographic plate away for future use, rushed out to get his airship in shape for a quick flight. He had modified his plans. Instead of having a detective take a print of the photo telephone image, and make the arrest, Tom was going to try to capture Peters himself. He believed he could do it. One look at the wet plate was enough. He knew Peters, though it upset some of his theories to learn that it was the promoter who was responsible for Mr. Damon's disappearance.

The man at the other end of the wire was evidently getting impatient. Possibly he suspected some trick. "I've got to go now," he called to Mrs. Damon. "If I don't get those papers in the morning it will be the worse for Mr. Damon."

"Oh, I'll send you the papers," she said.

By this time Ned had gotten into communication with the manager of the central telephone exchange, and had learned the location of the instrument Peters was using. It was about a mile from the one near the sawmill.

"Come on!" called Tom to his chum, as the latter gave him this information. "The Firefly is tuned up for a hundred miles an hour! We'll be there in ten minutes! We must catch him red-handed, if possible!"

"He's gone!" gasped Mrs. Damon as she came to the outer door, and watched Tom and Ned taking their places in the airship, while Koku prepared to twirl the propellers.

"Gone!" echoed Tom, blankly.

"Yes, he hung up the receiver."

"See if you can't get him back," suggested the young inventor. "Ask Central to ring that number again. We'll be there in a jiffy. Maybe he'll come to the telephone again. Or he may even call up his partners and tell them the game is working his way. Try to get him back, Mrs. Damon."

"I will," she said.

And, as she hurried back to the instrument, Tom and Ned shot up toward the blue sky in an endeavor to capture the man at the other telephone.

"And to think it was Peters!" cried Tom into Ned's ear, shouting to be heard above the roar of the motor exhaust.

"I thought he'd turn out to be mixed up in the affair," said Ned.

"Well, you were right. I was off, that time," admitted Tom, as he guided his powerful craft above the trees. "I was willing to admit that he had something to do with Mr. Damon's financial trouble, but as for kidnapping him—well, you never can tell."

They drove on at a breath-catching pace, and it seemed hardly a minute after leaving Mrs. Damon's house before Tom called:

"There's the building where the telephone is located."

"And now for that rascal Peters!" cried Ned.

The airship swooped down, to the great astonishment of some workmen nearby.

Hardly had the wheels ceased revolving on the ground, as Tom made a quick landing, than he was out of his seat, and running toward the telephone. He knew the place at once from having heard Ned's description, and besides, this was one of the places where he had installed his apparatus.

Into the store Tom burst, and made a rush for the 'phone booth. He threw open the door. The place was empty!

"The man—the man who was telephoning!" Tom called to the proprietor of the place.

"You mean that big man, with the tall hat, who was in there so long?"

"Yes, where is he?"

"Gone. About two minutes ago."

"Which way?"

"Over toward Shopton, and in one of the fastest autos that ever scattered dust in this section."

"He's escaped us!" said Tom to Ned. "But we'll get him yet! Come on!"

"I'm with you. Say, do you know what this looks like to me?"

"What?"

"It looks as if Peters was scared and was going to run away to stay!"

ON THE TRAIL

Such a crowd had quickly gathered about Tom's airship that it was impossible to start it. Men and boys, and even some girls and women, coming from no one knew where, stood about the machine, making wondering remarks about it.

"Stand back, if you please!" cried Tom, good-naturedly. "We've got to get after the fellow in the auto."

"You'll have hard work catching him, friend, in that rig," remarked a man. "He was fracturing all the speed laws ever passed. I reckon he was going nigh onto sixty miles an hour."

"We can make a hundred," spoke Ned, quietly.

"A hundred! Get out!" cried the man. "Nothing can go as fast as that!"

"We'll show you, if we once get started," said Tom. "I guess we'll have to get one of these fellows to twirl the propellers for us, Ned," he added. "I didn't think, or I'd have brought the self-starting machine," for this one of Tom's had to be started by someone turning over the propellers, once or twice, to enable the motor to begin to speed. On some of his aircraft the young inventor had attached a starter, something like the ones on the newest autos.

"What are you going to do?" asked Ned, as Tom looked to the priming of the cylinders.

"I'm going to get on the trail of Peters," he said. "He's at the bottom of the whole business; and it's a surprise to me. I'm going to trail him right down to the ground now, and make him give up Mr. Damon and his fortune,"

"But you don't know where he is, Tom."

"I'll find out. He isn't such an easy man to miss—he's too conspicuous. Besides, if he's just left in his auto we may catch him before he gets to Shopton."

"Do you think he's going there?"

"I think so. And I think, Ned, that he's become suspicious and will light out. Something must have happened, while he was telephoning, and he got frightened, as big a bluff as he is. But we'll get him. Come on! Will you turn over the propellers, please? I'll show you how to do it," Tom went on to a big, strong man standing close to the blades.

"Sure I'll do it," was the answer. "I was a helper once at an airship meet, and I know how."

"Get back out of the way in time," the young inventor warned him. "They start very suddenly, sometimes."

"All right, friend, I'll watch out," was the reply, and with Tom and Ned in their seats, the former at the steering wheel, the craft of the air was soon throbbing and trembling under the first turn, for the cylinders were still warm from the run from Mrs. Damon's house.

The telephone was in an outlying section of Waterford—a section devoted in the main to shops and factories, and the homes of those employed in various lines of manufacture. Peters had chosen his place well, for there were many roads leading to and from this section, and he could easily make his escape.

"But we'll get after him," thought Tom, grimly, as he let the airship run down the straight road a short distance on the bicycle wheels, to give it momentum enough so that it would rise.

Then, with the tilting of the elevation rudder, the craft rose gracefully, amid admiring cheers from the crowd. Tom did not go up very far, as he wanted to hover near the ground, to pick out the speeding auto containing Peters.

But this time luck was not with Tom. He and Ned did sight a number of cars speeding along the highway toward Shopton, but when they got near enough to observe the occupants they were disappointed not to behold the man they sought. Tom circled about for some time, but it was of no use, and then he headed his craft back toward Waterford.

"Where are you going?" asked Ned, yelling the words into the ear of his chum.

"Back to Mrs. Damon's," answered Tom, in equally loud tones.

It was impossible to talk above the roaring and throbbing of the motor, so the two lads kept silent until the airship had landed near Mrs. Damon's home.

"I want to see if Mrs. Damon is all right," Tom explained, as he jumped from the still moving machine. "Then we'll go to Shopton, and cause Peters's arrest. I can make a charge against him now, and the evidence of the photo telephone will convict him, I'm sure. And I also want to see if Mrs. Damon has had any other word."

She had not, however, though she was more nervous and worried than ever.

"Oh, Tom, what shall I do?" she exclaimed. "I am so frightened! What do you suppose they will do to Mr. Damon?"

"Nothing at all!" Tom assured her. "He will be all right. I think matters are coming to a crisis now, and very likely he'll be with you inside of twenty-four hours. The game is up, and I guess Peters knows it. I'm going to have him arrested at once."

"Shall I send those land papers, Tom?"

"Indeed you must not! But I'll talk to you about that later. Just put away that phonograph record of Peters's talk. I'll take along the photo telephone negative, and have some prints made—or, I guess, since we're going in the airship, that I'd better leave it here for the present. We'll use it as evidence against Peters. Come on, Ned."

"Where to now?"

"Peters's house. He's probably there, arranging to cover up his tracks when he lights out."

But Shallock Peters did better than merely cover up his tracks. He covered himself up, so to speak. For when Ned and Tom, after a quick flight in the airship, reached his house, the promoter had left, and the servants, who were quite excited, did not know where he had gone.

"He just packed up a few clothes and ran out," said one of the maids. "He didn't say anything about our wages, either, and he owes me over a month."

"Me too," said another.

"Well, if he doesn't pay me some of my back wages soon, I'll sue him!" declared the gardener. "He owes me more than three months, but he kept putting me off."

And, so it seemed, Peters had done with several of his employes. When the promoter came to Shopton he had taken an elaborate house and engaged a staff of servants. Peters was not married, but he gave a number of entertainments to which the wealthy men of Shopton and their wives came. Later it was found that the bills for these had never been paid. In short, Peters was a "bluff" in more ways than one.

Tom told enough of his story to the servants to get them on his side. Indeed, now that their employer had gone, and under such queer circumstances, they had no sympathy for him. They were only concerned about their own money, and Tom was given admittance to the house.

Tom made a casual search, hoping to find some clue to the whereabouts of Mr. Damon, or to get some papers that would save his fortune. But the search was unsuccessful.

There was a safe in the room Peters used for an office, but when Tom got there the strong box was open, and only some worthless documents remained.

"He smelled a rat, all right," said Tom, grimly. "After he telephoned to Mrs. Damon something happened that gave him an intimation that someone was after him. So he got away as soon as he could."

"But what are you going to do about it, Tom?"

"Get right after him. He can't have gotten very far. I want him and I want Boylan. We're getting close to the end of the trail, Ned."

"Yes, but we haven't found Mr. Damon yet, and his fortune seems to have vanished."

"Well, we'll do the best we can," said Tom, grimly. "Now I'm going to get a warrant for the arrest of Peters, and one for Boylan, and I'm going to get myself appointed a special officer with power to serve them. We've got our work cut out for us, Ned."

"Well, I'm with you to the end."

"I know you are!" cried Tom.

THE LONELY HOUSE

The young inventor had little difficulty in getting the warrants he sought. In the case of Boylan, who seemed to be Peters's right-hand man, when it came to criminal work, Tom made a charge of unlawfully taking the airship. This would be enough to hold the man on until other evidence could be obtained against him.

As for Peters, he was accused of taking certain valuable bonds and stocks belonging to Mr. Damon. Mrs. Damon gave the necessary evidence in this case, and the authorities were told that later, when Peters should have been arrested, other evidence so skillfully gotten by Tom's photo telephone, would be brought before the court.

"It's a new way of convicting a man—by a photo telephone—but I guess it's a good one," said the judge who signed the warrants.

"Well, now that we've got what we want, the next thing to do is to get the men—Peters, and the others," said Tom, as he and Ned sat in Tom's library after several hours of strenuous work.

"How are you going to start?" the young banker wanted to know. "It seems a strange thing that a man like Mr. Damon could be made away with, and kept in hiding so long without something being heard of him. I'm afraid, Tom, that something must have happened to him."

"I think so too, Ned. Nothing serious, though," Tom added, quickly, as he saw the look of alarm on his chum's face. "I think Mr. Damon at first went away of his own accord."

"Of his own accord?"

"Yes. I think Peters induced him to go with him, on the pretense that he could recover his fortune. After getting Mr. Damon in their power they kept him, probably to get the rest of his fortune away from him."

"But you stopped that, Tom," said Ned, proud of his chum's abilities.

"Well, I hope so," admitted the young inventor. "But I've still got plenty to do."

"Have you a starting point?"

"For one thing," Tom answered, "I'm going to have Mrs. Damon mail a fake package to the address Peters gave. If he, or any of his men, call for it, we'll have a detective on the watch, and arrest them."

"Good!"

"Of course it may not work," spoke Tom; "but it's something to try, and we can't miss any chances."

Accordingly, the next day, a package containing only blank paper, made up to represent the documents demanded by Peters as the price of releasing Mr. Damon, was mailed to the address Mrs. Damon had received over the wire from the rascally promoter. Then a private detective was engaged to be on the watch, to take into custody whoever called for the bundle. Tom, though, had not much hope of anything coming of this, as it was evident that Peters had taken the alarm, and left.

"And now," said Tom, when he had safely put away the wax record, containing the incriminating talk of Peters, and had printed several photographs, so wonderfully taken over the wire, "now to get on the trail again."

It was not an easy one to follow. Tom began at the deserted home of the alleged financier. The establishment was broken up, for many tradesmen came with bills that had not been paid, and some of them levied on what little personal property there was to satisfy their claims. The servants left, sorrowful enough over their missing wages. The place was closed up under the sheriff's orders.

But of Peters and his men not a trace could be found. Tom and Ned traveled all over the surrounding country, looking for clues, but in vain. They made several trips in the airship, but finally decided that an automobile was more practical for their work, and kept to that.

They did find some traces of Peters. As Tom had said, the man was too prominent not to be noticed. He might have disguised himself, though it seemed that the promoter was a proud man, and liked to be seen in flashy clothes, a silk hat, and with a buttonhole bouquet.

This made it easy to get the first trace of him. He had been seen to take a train at the Shopton station, though he had not bought a ticket. The promoter had paid his fare to Branchford, a junction point, but there all trace of him was lost. It was not even certain that he went there.

"He may have done that to throw us off," said Tom. "Just because he paid his way to Branchford, doesn't say he went there. He may have gotten off at the next station beyond Shopton."

"Do you think he's still lingering around here?" asked Ned.

"I shouldn't be surprised," was Tom's answer. "He knows that there is still some of the Damon property left, and he is probably hungry for that. We'll get him yet, Ned."

But at the end of several days Tom's hopes did not seem in a fair way to be realized. He and Ned followed one useless clue after another. All the trails seemed blind ones. But Tom never gave up.

He was devoting all his time now to the finding of his friend Mr. Damon, and to the recovery of his fortune. In fact the latter was not so important to Tom as was the former. For Mrs. Damon was on the verge of a nervous collapse on account of the absence of her husband.

"If I could only have some word from him, Tom!" she cried, helplessly.

To Tom the matter was very puzzling. It seemed utterly impossible that Mr. Damon could be kept so close a prisoner that he could not manage to get some word to his friends. It was not as if he was a child. He was a man of more than ordinary abilities. Surely he might find a way to outwit his enemies.

But the days passed, and no word came. A number of detectives had been employed, but they were no more successful than Tom. The latter had given up his inventive work, for the time being, to devote all his time to the solution of the mystery.

Tom and Ned had been away from Shopton for three days, following the most promising clue they had yet received. But it had failed at the end, and one afternoon they found themselves in a small town, about a hundred miles from Shopton. They had been motoring.

"I think I'll call up the house," said Tom. "Dad may have received some news, or Mrs. Damon may have sent him some word. I'll get my father on the wire."

Connection to Tom's house was soon made, and Ned, who was listening to his chum's remarks, was startled to hear him cry out:

"What's that you say? My airship taken again? When did it happen? Yes, I'm listening. Go on, Father!"

Then followed a silence while Tom listened, breaking in now and then with an excited remark, Suddenly he called:

"Good-by, Dad! I'm coming right home!"

Tom hung up the receiver with a bang, and turned to his chum.

"What do you think!" he cried. "The Eagle was taken again last night! The same way as before. Nobody got a glimpse of the thieves, though. Dad has been trying to get in communication with me ever since. I'm glad I called up. Now we'll get right back to Shopton, and see what we can do. This is the limit! Peters and his crowd will be kidnapping us, next."

"That's right," agreed Ned.

He and Tom were soon off again, speeding in the auto toward Shopton. But the roads were bad, after a heavy rain, and they did not make fast time.

The coming of dusk found them with more than thirty miles to go. They were in an almost deserted section of the country when suddenly, as they were running slowly up a hill, there was a sudden crack, the auto gave a lurch to one side of the roadway and then settled heavily. Tom clapped on both brakes quickly, and gave a cry of dismay.

"Broken front axle!" he said. "We're dished, Ned!"

They got out, being no more harmed than by the jolting. The car was out of commission. The two chums looked around Except for a lonely house, that bore every mark of being deserted, not a dwelling was in sight where they might ask for aid or shelter.

And, as they looked, from that lonely house came a strange cry—a cry as though for help!

THE AIRSHIP CAPTURE

"Did you hear that?" cried Ned.

"I certainly did," answered Tom. "What was it."

"Sounded to me like a cry of some sort."

"It was. An animal, I'd say."

The two chums moved away from the broken auto, and looked at each other. Then, by a common impulse, they started toward the lonely house, which was set back some distance from the road.

"Let's see who it was," suggested Tom, "After all, though it looks deserted, there may be someone in the house, and we've got to have some kind of help. I don't want to leave my car on the road all night, though it will have to be repaired before I can use it again."

"It sure is a bad break," agreed Ned.

As they walked toward the deserted House they heard the strange cry again. It was louder this time, and following it the boys heard a sound as if a blow had been struck.

"Someone is being attacked!" cried Tom. "Maybe some poor tramp has taken shelter in there and a dog is after them. Come on, Ned, we've got to help!"

They started on a run for the lonely house, but while still some distance away a curious thing happened.

There was a sudden cry—an appeal for help it seemed—but this time in the open. And, as Tom and Ned looked, they saw several men running from the rear of the old house. Between them they carried an inert form,

"Something's wrong!" exclaimed Tom, "There's crooked work going on here, Ned."

"You're right! It's up to us to stop it! Come on!"

But before the boys had taken half a dozen more steps they heard that which caused them great surprise. For from a shed behind the house came the unmistakable throb and roar of a motor.

"They're going off in an auto!" cried Ned.

"And they're carrying someone with them!" exclaimed Tom.

By this time they had gotten to a point where they could see the shed, and what was their astonishment to see being rolled from it a big biplane. At the sight of it Tom cried:

"It's the Eagle! That's my airship, Ned!"

"You're right! How did it get here?"

"That's for us to find out. I shouldn't wonder, Ned, but what we're at last on the trail of Peters and his crowd!"

The men—there were four or five of them, Ned guessed—now broke into a run, still carrying among them the inert form of another. The cries for help had ceased, and it seemed as if the unfortunate one was unconscious.

A moment later, and before the boys could do anything, had they the power, the men fairly jumped aboard Tom Swift's biggest airship. The unconscious one was carried with them.

Then the motor was speeded up. The roar and throbbing were almost deafening.

"Stop that! Hold on! That's my machine!" yelled Tom.

He might as well have spoken to the wind. With a rush and a roar the big Eagle shot away and upward, carrying the men and their mysterious, unconscious companion. It was getting too dark for Tom and Ned to make out the forms or features of the strangers.

"We're too late!" said Ned, hopelessly.

"Yes, they got away," agreed Tom. "Oh, if only I had my speedy little monoplane!"

"But who can they be? How did your airship get here? And who is that man they carried out of the house?" cried Ned.

"I don't know the last—maybe one of their crowd who was injured in a fight."

"What crowd?"

"The Peters gang, of course. Can't you see it, Ned?"

Unable to do anything, the two youths watched the flight of the Eagle. She did not move at her usual speed, for she was carrying too heavy a load.

Presently from the air overhead, and slightly behind them, the boys heard the sound of another motor. They turned quickly.

"Look!" cried Ned. "Another airship, by all that's wonderful!"

"If we could only stop them!" exclaimed Tom. "That's a big machine, and they could take us aboard. Then we could chase the Eagle. We could catch her, too, for she's overloaded!"

Frantically he and Tom waved their caps at the man who was now almost overhead in his airship. The boys did not call. They well knew, with the noise of the motor, the occupant of the airship could not hear them. But they waved and pointed to the slowly-moving Eagle.

To their surprise and delight the man above them shut off his engine, and seemed about to come down. Then Tom cried, knowing he could be heard:

"Help us capture that airship? It's mine and they've stolen it!"

"All right! Be with you in a minute!" came back the answer from above.

The second biplane came down to earth, ands as it ceased running along on its bicycle wheels, the occupant jumped out.

"Hello, Tom Swift!" he called, as he took off his goggles.

"Why—why it's Mr. Halling!" cried the young inventor, in delight, recognizing the birdman who had brought him the first news of Mr. Damon's trouble, the day the airship became entangled in the aerials of the wireless on Tom's house.

"What are you doing here, Tom?" asked Mr. Hailing. "What has happened?"

"We're looking for Mr. Damon. That's a bad crowd there," and he pointed toward the other aircraft. "They have my Eagle. Can you help me catch them?"

"I certainly can—and will! Get aboard! I can carry four."

"Then you have a new machine?"

"Yes, and a dandy! All the latest improvements—self-starter and all! I'm glad of a chance to show it to you."

"And I'm glad, too!" cried Tom. "It was providential that you happened along. What were you doing here?"

"Just out on a trial spin. But come on, if we're going to catch those fellows!"

Quickly Tom, Ned, and Mr. Halling climbed into the seats of the new airship. It was started from a switch, and in a few seconds it was on the wing, chasing after the Eagle.

Then began a strange race, a race in the air after the unknown strangers who had Tom's machine. Had the Eagle not been so heavily laden it might have escaped, for Tom's craft was a speedy one. But this time it had to give the palm to Mr. Grant Halling's. Faster and faster in pursuit flew the Star, as the new craft was called. Faster and faster, until at last, coming directly over the Eagle, Mr. Halling sent his craft down in such a manner as to "blanket" the other. In an instant she began to sink, and with cries of alarm the men shut off the motor and started to volplane to the earth.

But they made an unskillful landing. The Eagle tilted to one side, and came down with a crash. There were cries of pain, then silence, and a few seconds later two men ran away from the disabled airship. But there were three senseless forms on the ground beside the craft when Tom, Ned and Mr. Halling ran up. In the fading light Tom saw a face he knew—three faces in fact.

"Mr. Damon!" he cried. "We've found him, Ned!"

"But—too late—maybe!" answered Ned, in a low voice, as he, too, recognized the man who had been missing so long.

Mr. Halling was bending over the unconscious form of his friend.

"He's alive!" he cried, joyfully. "And not much hurt, either. But he has been ill, and looks half starved. Who are these men?"

Tom gave a hasty look.

"Shallock Peters and Harrison Boylan!" he cried. "Ned, at last we've caught the scoundrels!"

It was true. Chance had played into the hands of Tom Swift. While Mr. Halling was looking after Mr. Damon, reviving him, the young inventor and Ned quickly bound the hands and feet of the two plotters with pieces of wire from the broken airship.

Presently Mr. Damon opened his eyes.

"Where am I? What happened? Oh, bless my watch chain—it's Tom Swift! Bless my cigar case, I—"

"He's all right!" cried Tom, joyfully. "When Mr. Damon blesses something beside his tombstone he's all right."

Peters and Boylan soon revived, both being merely stunned, as was Mr. Damon. They looked about in wonder, and then, feeling that they were prisoners, resigned themselves to their fate. Both men were shabbily dressed, and Tom would hardly have known the once spick and span Mr. Peters. He had no rose in his buttonhole now.

"Well, you have me, I see," he said, coolly. "I was afraid we were playing for too high a stake."

"Yes, we've got you," replied Tom,

"But you can't prove much against me," went on Peters. "I'll deny everything."

"We'll see about that," added the young inventor, grimly, and thought of the picture in the plate and the record on the wax cylinder.

"We've got to get Mr. Damon to some place where he can be looked after," broke in Mr. Halling. "Then we'll hear the story."

A passing farmer was prevailed on to take the party in his big wagon to the nearest town, Mr. Hailing going on ahead in his airship. Tom's craft could not be moved, being badly damaged.

Once in town Peters and Boylan were put in jail, on the charges for which Tom carried warrants. Mr. Damon was taken to a hotel and a doctor summoned. It was as Mr. Halling had guessed. His friend had been ill, and so weak that he could not get out of bed. It was this that enabled the plotters to so easily keep him a prisoner.

By degrees Mr. Damon told his story. He had rashly allowed Peters to get control of most of his fortune, and, in a vain hope of getting back some of his losses, had, one night—the night he disappeared, in fact—agreed to meet Peters and some of his men to talk matters over. Of this Mr. Damon said nothing to his wife.

He went out that night to meet Peters in the garden, but the plotters had changed their plans. They boldly kidnapped their victim, chloroformed him and took him away in Tom's airship, which Boylan and some of his tools daringly stole a short time previously. Later they returned it, as they had no use for it at the lonely house.

Mr. Damon was taken to the house, and there kept a prisoner. The men hoped to prevail on the fears of his wife to make her give up the valuable property. But we have seen how Tom foiled Peters.

The experience of Mr. Damon, coupled with rough treatment he received, and lack of good food, soon made him ill. He was so weak that he could not help himself, and with that he was kept under guard. So he had no chance to escape or send his wife or friends any word.

"But I'm all right now, Tom, thanks to you!" said he. "Bless my pocketbook, I don't care if my fortune is lost, as long as I'm alive and can get back to my wife."

"But I don't believe your fortune will be lost," said Tom. "I think I have the picture and other evidence that will save it," and he told of his photo telephone, and of what it had accomplished.

"Bless my eyelashes!" cried Mr. Damon. "What a young man you are, Tom Swift!"

Tom smiled gladly. He knew now that his old friend was himself once more.

There is little left to tell. Chance had aided Tom in a most wonderful way—chance and the presence of Mr. Halling with his airship at just the right moment.

Tom made a diligent effort to find out who it was that had chloroformed him in the telephone booth that time, but learned nothing definite. Peters and Boylan were both examined as to this on their trials, but denied it, and the young inventor was forced to conclude that it must have been some of the unscrupulous men who had taken his father's patent some time before.

"They may have heard of your prosperity, and thought it a good chance to rob you," suggested Ned.

"Maybe," agreed Tom. "Well, we'll let it go at that. Only I hope they don't come again."

Mr. Damon was soon home with his wife again, and Peters and Boylan were held in heavy bail. They had secreted most of Mr. Damon's wealth, falsely telling him it was lost, and they were forced to give back his fortune. The evidence against them was clear and conclusive. When Tom went into court with his phonograph record of the talk of Peters, even though the man's voice was hoarse from a cold when he talked, and when his picture was shown, in the telephone booth, the jury at once convicted him.

Boylan, when he learned of the missing button in Tom's possession, confessed that he and some of his men who were birdmen had taken Tom's airship. They wanted a means of getting Mr. Damon to the lonely house without being traced, and they accomplished it.

As Tom had surmised, Peters had become suspicious after his last talk with Mrs. Damon, and had fled. He disguised himself and went into hiding with the others at the lonely house. Then he learned that the authorities of another city. where he had swindled many, were on his trail, and he decided to decamp with his gang, taking Mr. Damon with them. For this purpose Tom's airship was taken the second time, and a wholesale escape, with Mr. Damon a prisoner, was planned.

But fate was against the plotters. Two of them did manage to get away, but they were not really wanted. The big fish were Peters and Boylan, and they were securely caught in the net of the law. Peters was greatly surprised when he learned of Tom's trap, and of the photo telephone. He had no idea he had been incriminating himself when he talked over the wire.

"Well, it's all over," remarked Ned to Tom, one day, when the disabled auto and the airship had been brought home and repaired. "The plotters are in prison for long terms, and Mr. Damon is found, together with his fortune. The photo telephone did it, Tom."

"Not all of it—but a good bit," admitted the young inventor, with a smile.

"What are you going to do next, Tom?"

"I hardly know. I think—"

Before Tom could finish, a voice was heard in the hall outside the library.

"Bless my overshoes! Where's Tom? I want to thank him again for what he did for me," and Mr. Damon, now fully recovered, came in. "Bless my suspender button, but it's good to be alive, Tom!" he cried.

"It certainly is," agreed Tom. "And the next time you go for a conference with such men as Peters, look out for airships."

"I will, Tom, I will!" exclaimed Mr. Damon. "Bless my watch chain, I will!"

And now, for a time, we will say good-bye to Tom Swift, leaving him to perfect his other inventions.

Tom Swift and His Aerial Warship
Or the Naval Terror of the Seas

TABLE OF CONTENTS:

Tom Is Puzzled

"What's the matter, Tom? You look rather blue!"

"Blue! Say, Ned, I'd turn red, green, yellow, or any other color of the rainbow, if I thought it would help matters any."

"Whew!"

Ned Newton, the chum and companion of Tom Swift, gave vent to a whistle of surprise, as he gazed at the young fellow sitting opposite him, near a bench covered with strange-looking tools and machinery, while blueprints and drawings were scattered about.

Ranged on the sides of the room were models of many queer craft, most of them flying machines of one sort or another, while through the open door that led into a large shed could be seen the outlines of a speedy monoplane.

"As bad as that, eh, Tom?" went on Ned. "I thought something was up when I first came in, but, if you'll excuse a second mention of the color scheme, I should say it was blue—decidedly blue. You look as though you had lost your last friend, and I want to assure you that if you do feel that way, it's dead wrong. There's myself, for one, and I'm sure Mr. Damon—"

"Bless my gasoline tank!" exclaimed Tom, with a laugh, in imitation of the gentleman Ned Newton had mentioned, "I know that! I'm not worrying over the loss of any friends."

"And there are Eradicate, and Koku, the giant, just to mention a couple of others," went on Ned, with a smile.

"That's enough!" exclaimed Tom. "It isn't that, I tell you."

"Well, what is it then? Here I go and get a half-holiday off from the bank, and just at the busiest time, too, to come and see you, and I find you in a brown study, looking as blue as indigo, and maybe you're all yellow inside from a bilious attack, for all I know."

"Quite a combination of colors," admitted Tom. "But it isn't what you think. It's just that I'm puzzled, Ned."

"Puzzled?" and Ned raised his eyebrows to indicate how surprised he was that anything should puzzle his friend.

"Yes, genuinely puzzled."

"Has anything gone wrong?" Ned asked. "No one is trying to take any of your pet inventions away from you, is there?"

"No, not exactly that, though it is about one of my inventions I am puzzled. I guess I haven't shown you my very latest; have I, Ned?"

"Well, I don't know, Tom. Time was when I could keep track of you and your inventions, but that was in your early days, when you started with a motorcycle and were glad enough to have a motorboat. But, since you've taken to aerial navigation and submarine work, not to mention one or two other lines of activity, I give up. I don't know where to look next, Tom, for something new."

"Well, this isn't so very new," went on the young inventor, for Tom Swift had designed and patented many new machines of the air, earth and water. "I'm just trying to work out some new problems in aerial navigation, Ned," he went on.

"I thought there weren't any more," spoke Ned, soberly enough.

"Come, now, none of that!" exclaimed Tom, with a laugh. "Why, the surface of aerial navigation has only been scratched. The science is far from being understood, or even made safe, not to say perfected, as water and land travel have been. There's lots of chance yet."

"And you're working on something new?" asked Ned, as he looked around the shop where he and Tom were sitting. As the young bank employee had said, he had come away from the institution that afternoon to have a little holiday with his chum, but Tom, seated in the midst of his inventions, seemed little inclined to jollity.

Through the open windows came the hum of distant machinery, for Tom Swift and his father were the heads of a company founded to manufacture and market their many inventions, and about their home were grouped several buildings. From a small plant the business had grown to be a great tree, under the direction of Tom and his father.

"Yes, I'm working on something new," admitted Tom, after a moment of silence.

"And, Ned," he went on, "there's no reason why you shouldn't see it. I've been keeping it a bit secret, until I had it a little further advanced, but I've got to a point now where I'm stuck, and perhaps it will do me good to talk to someone about it."

"Not to talk to me, though, I'm afraid. What I don't know about machinery, Tom, would fill a great many books. I don't see how I can help you," and Ned laughed.

"Well, perhaps you can, just the same, though you may not know a lot of technical things about machines. It sometimes helps me just to tell my troubles to a disinterested person, and hear him ask questions. I've got dad half distracted trying to solve the problem, so I've had to let up on him for a while. Come on out and see what you make of it."

"Sure, Tom, anything to oblige. If you want me to sit in front of your photo-telephone, and have my picture taken, I'm agreeable, even if you shoot off a flashlight at my ear. Or, if you want me to see how long I can stay under water without breathing I'll try that, too, provided you don't leave me under too long, lead the way—I'm agreeable as far as I'm able, old man."

"Oh, it isn't anything like that," Tom answered with a laugh. "I might as well give you a few hints, so you'll know what I'm driving at. Then I'll take you out and show it to you."

"What is it—air, earth or water?" asked Ned Newton, for he knew his chum's activities led along all three lines.

"This happens to be air."

"A new balloon?"

"Something like that. I call it my aerial warship, though."

"Aerial warship, Tom! That sounds rather dangerous!"

"It will be dangerous, too, if I can get it to work. That's what it's intended for."

"But a warship of the air!" cried Ned. "You can't mean it. A warship carries guns, mortars, bombs, and—"

"Yes, I know," interrupted Tom, "and I appreciate all that when I called my newest craft an aerial warship."

"But," objected Ned, "an aircraft that will carry big guns will be so large that—"

"Oh, mine is large enough," Tom broke in.

"Then it's finished!" cried Ned eagerly, for he was much interested in his chum's inventions.

"Well, not exactly," Tom said. "But what I was going to tell you was that all guns are not necessarily large. You can get big results with small guns and projectiles now, for high-powered explosives come in small packages. So it isn't altogether a question of carrying a certain amount of weight. Of course, an aerial warship will have to be big, for it will have to carry extra machinery to give it extra speed, and it will have to carry a certain armament, and a large crew will be needed. So, as I said, it will need to be large. But that problem isn't worrying me."

"Well, what is it, then?" asked Ned.

"It's the recoil," said Tom, with a gesture of despair.

"The recoil?" questioned Ned, wonderingly.

"Yes, from the guns, you know. I haven't been able to overcome that, and, until I do, I'm afraid my latest invention will be a failure."

Ned shook his head.

"I'm afraid I can't help you any," he said. "The only thing I know about recoils is connected with an old shotgun my father used to own.

"I took that once, when he didn't know it," Ned proceeded. "It was pretty heavily loaded, for the crows had been having fun in our cornfield, and dad had been shooting at them. This time I thought I'd take a chance.

"Well, I fired the gun. But it must have had a double charge in it and been rusted at that. All I know is that after I pulled the trigger I thought the end of the world had come. I heard a clap of thunder, and then I went flying over backward into a blackberry patch."

"That was the recoil," said Tom.

"The what?" asked Ned.

"The recoil. The recoil of the gun knocked you over.

"Oh, yes," observed Ned, rubbing his shoulder in a reflective sort of way. "I always thought it was something like that. But, at the time I put it down to an explosion, and let it go at that."

"No, it wasn't an explosion, properly speaking," said Tom. "You see, when powder explodes, in a gun, or otherwise, its force is exerted in all directions, up, down and every way.

"This went mostly backward—in my direction," said Ned ruefully.

"You only thought so," returned Tom. "Most of the power went out in front, to force out the shot. Part of it, of course, was exerted on the barrel of the gun—that was sideways—but the strength of the steel held it in. And part of the force went backward against your shoulder. That part was the recoil, and it is the recoil of the guns I figure on putting aboard my aerial warship that is giving me such trouble."

"Is that what makes you look so blue?" asked Ned.

"That's it. I can't seem to find a way by which to take up the recoil, and the force of it, from all the guns I want to carry, will just about tear my ship to pieces, I figure."

"Then you haven't actually tried it out yet?" asked Ned.

"Not the guns, no. I have the warship of the air nearly done, but I've worked out on paper the problem of the guns far enough so that I know I'm up against it. It can't be done, and an aerial warship without guns wouldn't be worth much, I'm afraid."

"I suppose not," agreed Ned. "And is it only the recoil that is bothering you?"

"Mostly. But come, take a look at my latest pet," and Tom arose to lead the way to another shed, a large one in the distance, toward which he waved his hand to indicate to his chum that there was housed the wonderful invention.

The two chums crossed the yard, threading their way through the various buildings, until they stood in front of the structure to which Tom had called attention.

"It's in here," he said. "I don't mind admitting that I'm quite proud of it, Ned; that is, proud as far as I've gone. But the gun business sure has me worried. I'm going to talk it off on you. Hello!" cried Tom suddenly, as he put a key in the complicated lock on the door, "someone has been in here. I wonder who it is?"

Ned was a little startled at the look on Tom s face and the sound of alarm in his chum's voice.

A Fire Alarm

Tom Swift quickly opened the door of the big shed. It was built to house a dirigible balloon, or airship of some sort. Ned could easily tell that from his knowledge of Tom's previous inventions.

"Something wrong?" asked the young bank clerk.

"I don't know," returned Tom, and then as he looked inside the place, he breathed a sigh of relief.

"Oh, it's you, is it, Koku?" he asked, as a veritable giant of a man came forward.

"Yes, master, it is only Koku and your father," spoke the big chap, with rather a strange accent.

"Oh, is my father here?" asked Tom. "I was wondering who had opened the door of this shed."

"Yes, Tom," responded the elder Swift, coming up to them, "I had a new idea in regard to some of those side guy wires, and I wanted to try it out. I brought Koku with me to use his strength on some of them."

"That's all right, Dad. Ned and I came out to wrestle with that recoil problem again. I want to try some guns on the craft soon, but—"

"You'd better not, Tom," warned his father. "It will never work, I tell you. You can't expect to take up quick-firing guns and bombs in an airship, and have them work properly. Better give it up."

"I never will. I'll make it work, Dad!"

"I don't believe you will, Tom. This time you have bitten off more than you can chew, to use a homely but expressive statement."

"Well, Dad, we'll see," began Tom easily. "There she is, Ned," he went on. "Now, if you'll come around here

But Tom never finished that sentence, for at that moment there came running into the airship shed an elderly, short, stout, fussy gentleman, followed by an aged colored man. Both of them seemed very much excited.

"Bless my socks, Tom!" cried the short, stout man. "There sure is trouble!"

"I should say So, Massa Tom!" added the colored man. "I done did prognosticate dat some day de combustible material of which dat shed am composed would conflaggrate—"

"What's the matter?" interrupted Tom, jumping forward. "Speak out! Eradicate! Mr. Damon, what is it?"

"The red shed!" cried the short little man. "The red shed, Tom

"It's on fire!" yelled the colored man.

"Great thunderclaps!" cried Tom. "Come on —everybody on the job!" he yelled. "Koku, pull the alarm! If that red shed goes—"

Instantly the place was in confusion. Tom and Ned, looking from a window of the hangar, saw a billow of black smoke roll across the yard. But already the private fire bell was clanging out its warning. And, while the work of

fighting the flames is under way, I will halt the progress of this story long
enough to give my new readers a little idea of who Tom Swift is, so they may
read this book more intelligently. Those of you who have perused the previous
volumes may skip this part.

Tom Swift, though rather young in years, was an inventor of note. His
tastes and talents were developed along the line of machinery and locomotion.
Motorcycles, automobiles, motorboats, submarine craft, and, latest of all, craft
of the air, had occupied the attention of Tom Swift and his father for some
years.

Mr. Swift was a widower, and lived with Tom, his only son, in the village
of Shopton, New York State. Mrs. Baggert kept house for them, and an aged
colored man, Eradicate Sampson, with his mule, Boomerang, did "odd jobs"
about the Shopton home and factories.

Among Tom's friends was a Mr. Wakefield Damon, from a nearby village.
Mr. Damon was always blessing something, from his hat to his shoes, a
harmless sort of habit that seemed to afford him much comfort. Then there
was Ned Newton, a boyhood chum of Tom's, who worked in the Shopton bank.
I will just mention Mary Nestor, a young lady of Shopton, in whom Tom was
more than ordinarily interested. I have spoken of Koku, the giant. He really
was a giant of a man, of enormous strength, and was one of two whom Tom
had brought with him from a strange land where Tom was held captive for a
time. You may read about it in a book devoted to those adventures.

Tom took Koku into his service, somewhat to the dismay of Eradicate, who
was desperately jealous. But poor Eradicate was getting old, and could not do
as much as he thought he could. So, in a great measure, Koku replaced him,
and Tom found much use for the giant's strength.

Tom had begun his inventive work when, some years before this story
opens, he had bargained for Mr. Damon's motorcycle, after that machine had
shot its owner into a tree. Mr. Damon was, naturally, perhaps, much
disgusted, and sold the affair cheap. Tom repaired it, made some
improvements, and, in the first volume of this series, entitled "Tom Swift and
His Motorcycles," you may read of his rather thrilling adventures on his
speedy road-steed.

From then on Tom had passed a busy life, making many machines and
having some thrilling times with them. Just previous to the opening of this
story Tom had made a peculiar instrument, described in the volume entitled
"Tom Swift and His Photo-Telephone." With that a person talking could not
only see the features of the person with whom he was conversing, but, by
means of a selenium plate and a sort of camera, a permanent picture could be
taken of the person at either end of the wire.

By means of this invention Tom had been able to make a picture that had
saved a fortune. But Tom did not stop there. With him to invent was as
natural and necessary as breathing. He simply could not stop it. And so we
find him now about to show to his chum, Ned Newton, his latest patent, an
aerial warship, which, however, was not the success Tom had hoped for.

But just at present other matters than the warship were in Tom's mind. The red shed was on fire.

That mere statement might not mean anything special to the ordinary person, but to Tom, his father, and those who knew about his shops, it meant much.

"The red shed!" Tom cried. "We mustn't let that get the best of us! Everybody at work! Father, not you, though. You mustn't excite yourself!"

Even in the midst of the alarm Tom thought of his father, for the aged man had a weak heart, and had on one occasion nearly expired, being saved just in time by the arrival of a doctor, whom Tom brought to the scene after a wonderful race through the air.

"But, Tom, I can help," objected the aged inventor.

"Now, you just take care of yourself, Father!" Tom cried. "There are enough of us to look after this fire, I think."

"But, Tom, it—it's the red shed!" gasped Mr. Swift.

"I realize that, Dad. But it can't have much of a start yet. Is the alarm ringing, Koku?"

"Yes, Master," replied the giant, in correct but stilted English. "I have set the indicator to signal the alarm in every shop on the premises."

"That's right." Tom sprang toward the door. "Eradicate!" he called.

"Yais, sah! Heah I is!" answered the colored man. "I'll go git mah mule, Boomerang, right away, an' he—"

"Don't you bring Boomerang on the scene!" Tom yelled. "When I want that shed kicked apart I can do it better than by using a mule's heels. And you know you can't do a thing with Boomerang when he sees fire."

"Now dat's so, Massa Tom. But I could put blinkers on him, an'—"

"No, you let Boomerang stay where he is. Come on, Ned. We'll see what we can do. Mr. Damon—"

"Yes, Tom, I'm right here," answered the peculiar man, for he had come over from his home in Waterford to pay a visit to his friends, Tom and Mr. Swift. "I'll do anything I can to help you, Tom, bless my necktie!" he went on. "Only say the word!"

"We've got to get some of the stuff out of the place!" Tom cried. "We may be able to save it, but I can't take a chance on putting out the fire and letting some of the things in there go up in smoke. Come on!"

Those in the shed where was housed what Tom hoped would prove to be a successful aerial warship rushed to the open. From the other shops and buildings nearby were pouring men and boys, for the Swift plant employed a number of hands now.

Above the shouts and yells, above the crackle of flames, could be heard the clanging of the alarm bell, set ringing by Koku, who had pulled the signal in the airship shed. From there it had gone to every building in the plant, being relayed by the telephone operator, whose duty it was to look after that.

"My, you've got a big enough fire-fighting force, Tom!" cried Ned in his chum's ear.

"Yes, I guess we can master it, if it hasn't gotten the best of us. Say, it's going some, though!"

Tom pointed to where a shed, painted red—a sign of danger— could be seen partly enveloped in smoke, amid the black clouds of which shot out red tongues of flame.

"What have you got it painted red for?" Ned asked pantingly, as they ran on.

"Because—" Tom began, but the rest of the sentence was lost in a yell.

Tom had caught sight of Eradicate and the giant, Koku, unreeling from a central standpipe a long line of hose.

"Don't take that!" Tom cried. "Don't use that hose! Drop it!"

"What's the matter? Is it rotten?" Ned wanted to know.

"No, but if they pull it out the water will be turned on automatically."

"Well, isn't that what you want at a fire—water?" Ned demanded.

"Not at this fire," was Tom's answer. "There's a lot of calcium carbide in that red shed—that's why it's red—to warn the men of danger. You know what happens when water gets on carbide—there's an explosion, and there's enough carbide in that shed to send the whole works sky high.

"Drop that hose!" yelled Tom in louder tones. "Drop it, Rad— Koku! Do you want to kill us all!"

A Desperate Battle

Tom's tones and voice were so insistent that the giant and the colored man had no choice but to obey. They dropped the hose which, half unreeled, lay like some twisted snake in the grass. Had it been pulled out all the way the water would have spurted from the nozzle, for it was of the automatic variety, with which Tom had equipped all his plant.

"But what are you going to do, Tom, if you don't use water?" asked Ned, wonderingly.

"I don't know—yet, but I know water is the worst thing you can put on carbide," returned Tom. For all he spoke Slowly his brain was working fast. Already, even now, he was planning how best to give battle to the flames.

It needed but an instant's thought on the part of Ned to make him understand that Tom was right. It would be well-nigh fatal to use water on carbide. Those of you who have bicycle lanterns, in which that not very pleasant-smelling chemical is used, know that if a few drops of water are allowed to drip slowly on the gray crystals acetylene gas is generated, which makes a brilliant light. But, if the water drips too fast, the gas is generated too quickly, and an explosion results. In lamps, of course, and in lighting plants where carbide is used, there are automatic arrangements to prevent the water flowing too freely to the chemical. But Tom knew if the hose were turned on the fire in the red shed a great explosion would result, for some of the tins of carbide would be melted by the heat.

Yet the fire needed to be coped with. Already the flames were coming through the roof, and the windows and door were spouting red fire and volumes of smoke.

Several other employees of Tom's plant had made ready to unreel more hose, but the warning of the young inventor, shouted to Eradicate and Koku, had had its effect. Every man dropped the line he had begun to unreel.

"Ha! Massa Tom say drop de hose, but how yo' gwine t' squirt watah on a fire wifout a hose; answer me dat?" and Eradicate looked at Koku.

"Me no know," was the slow answer. "I guess Koku go pull shed down and stamp out fire."

"Huh! Maybe yo' could do dat in cannibal land, where yo' all come from," spoke Eradicate, "but yo' can't do dat heah! 'Sides, de red shed will blow up soon. Dere's suffin' else in dere except carbide, an' dat's gwine t' go up soon, dat's suah!"

"Maybe you get your strong man-mule, Boomerang," suggested Koku. "Nothing ever hurt him—explosion or nothing. He can kick shed all to pieces, and put out fire."

"Dat's what I wanted t' do, but Massa Tom say I cain't," explained the colored man. "Golly! Look at dat fire!"

Indeed the blaze was now assuming alarming proportions. The red shed, which was not a small structure, was blazing on all sides. About it stood the men from the various shops.

"Tom, you must do something," said Mr. Swift. "If the flames once reach that helmanite—"

"I know, Father. But that explosive is in double vacuum containers, and it will be safe for some time yet. Besides, it's in the cellar. It's the carbide I'm most worried about. We daren't use water."

"But something will have to be done!" exclaimed Mr. Damon. "Bless my red necktie, if we don't—"

"Better get back a way," suggested Tom. "Something may go off!"

His words of warning had their effect, and the whole circle moved back several paces.

"Is there anything of value in the shed?" asked Ned.

"I should say there was!" Tom answered. "I hoped we could get some of them out, but we can't now—until the fire dies down a bit, at any rate."

"Look, Tom! The pattern shop roof is catching!" shouted Mr. Swift, pointing to where a little spurt of flame showed on the roof of a distant building.

"It's from sparks!" Tom said.

"Any danger of using water there?" Ned wanted to know.

"No, use all you like! That's the only thing to do. Come on, you with the hose!" Tom yelled. "Save the other buildings!"

"But are you going to let the red shed burn?" asked Mr. Swift. "You know what it means, Tom."

"Yes, Father, I know. And I'm going to fight that fire in a new way. But we must save the other buildings, too. Play water on all the other sheds and structures!" ordered the young inventor. "I'll tackle this one myself. Oh, Ned!" he called.

"Yes," answered his chum. "What is it?"

"You take charge of protecting the place where the new aerial warship is stored. Will you? I can't afford to lose that."

"I'll look after it, Tom. No harm in using water there, though; is there?"

"Not if you don't use too much. Some of the woodwork isn't varnished yet, and I wouldn't want it to be wet. But do the best you can. Take Koku and Eradicate with you. They can't do any good here."

"Do you mean to say you're going to give up and let this burn?"

"Not a bit of it, Ned. But I have another plan I want to try. Lively now! The wind's changing, and it's blowing over toward my aerial warship shed. If that catches—"

Tom shook his head protestingly, and Ned set off on the run, calling to the colored man and the giant to get out another line of hose.

"I wonder what Tom is going to do?" mused Ned, as he neared the big shed he and the others had left on the alarm of fire.

Tom, himself, seemed in no doubt as to his procedure With one look at the blazing red shed, as if to form an opinion as to how much longer it could burn without getting entirely beyond control, Tom set off on a run toward another large structure. Ned, glancing toward his chum, observed:

"The dirigible shed! I wonder what his game is? Surely that can't be in danger—it's too far off!"

Ned was right as to the last statement. The shed, where was housed a great dirigible balloon Tom had made, but which he seldom used of late, was sufficiently removed from the zone of fire to be out of danger.

Meanwhile several members of the fire-fighting force that had been summoned from the various shops by the alarm, had made an effort to save from the red shed some of the more valuable of the contents. There were some machines in there, as well as explosives and chemicals, in addition to the store of carbide.

But the fire was now too hot to enable much to be done in the way of salvage. One or two small things were carried out from a little addition to the main structure, and then the rescuers were driven back by the heat of the flames, as well as by the rolling clouds of black smoke.

"Keep away!" warned Mr. Swift. "It will explode soon. Keep back!"

"That's right!" added Mr. Damon. "Bless my powder-horn! We may all be going sky-high soon, and without aid from any of Tom Swift's aeroplanes, either."

Warned by the aged inventor, the throng of men began slowly moving away from the immediate neighborhood of the blazing shed. Though it may seem to the reader that some time has elapsed since the first sounding of the alarm, all that I have set down took place in a very short period—hardly three minutes elapsing since Tom and the others came rushing out of the aerial warship building.

Suddenly a cry arose from the crowd of men near the red shed. Ned, who stood ready with several lines of hose, in charge of Koku, Eradicate and others, to turn them on the airship shed, in case of need, looked in the direction of the excited throng.

The young bank clerk saw a strange sight. From the top of the dirigible balloon shed a long, black, cigar-shaped body arose, floating gradually upward. The very roof of the shed slid back out of the way, as Tom pressed the operating lever, and the dirigible was free to rise—as free as though it had been in an open field.

"He's going up!" cried Ned in surprise. "Making an ascent at a time like this, when he ought to stay here to fight the fire! What's gotten into Tom, I'd like to know? I wonder if he can be—"

Ned did not finish his half-formed sentence. A dreadful thought came into his mind. What if the sudden fire, and the threatened danger, as well as the prospective loss that confronted Tom, had affected his mind?

"It certainly looks so," mused Ned, as he saw the big balloon float free from the shed. There was no doubt but that Tom was in it. He could be seen standing within the pilot-house, operating the various wheels and levers that controlled the ship of the air.

"What can he be up to?" marveled Tom. "Is he going to run away from the fire?"

Koku, Eradicate and several others were attracted by the sight of the great dirigible, now a considerable distance up in the air. Certainly it looked as though Tom Swift were running away. Yet Ned knew his chum better than that.

Then, as they watched, Ned and the others saw the direction of the balloon change. She turned around in response to the influence of the rudders and propellers, and was headed straight for the blazing shed, but some distance above it.

"What can he be planning?" wondered Ned.

He did not have long to wait to find out.

An instant later Tom's plan was made clear to his chum. He saw Tom circling over the burning red shed, and then the bank clerk saw what looked like fine rain dropping from the lower part of the balloon straight into the flames.

"He can't be dousing water on from up above there," reasoned Ned. "Pouring water on carbide from a height is just as bad as spurting it on from a hose, though perhaps not so dangerous to the persons doing it. But it can't be—"

"By Jove!" suddenly exclaimed Ned, as he had a better view of what was going on. "It's sand, that's what it is! Tom is giving battle to the flames with sand from the ballast bags of the dirigible! Hurray? That's the ticket! Sand! The only thing safe to use in case of an explosive chemical fire.

"Fine for you. Tom Swift! Fine!"

SUSPICIONS

High up aloft, over the blazing red shed, with its dangerous contents that any moment might explode, Tom Swift continued to hold his big dirigible balloon as near the flames as possible. And as he stood outside on the small deck in front of the pilot-house, where were located the various controls, the young inventor pulled the levers that emptied bag after bag of fine sand on the spouting flames that, already, were beginning to die down as a result of this effectual quenching.

"Tom's done the trick!" yelled Ned, paying little attention now to the big airship shed, since he saw that the danger was about over.

"Dhat's what he suah hab done!" agreed Eradicate. "Mah ole mule Boomerang couldn't 'a' done any better."

"Huh! Your mule afraid of fire," remarked Koku.

"What's dat? Mah mule afraid ob fire?" cried the colored man. "Look heah, yo' great, big, overgrowed specimen ob an equilateral quadruped, I'll hab yo' all understand dat when yo' all speaks dat way about a friend ob mine dat yo'—"

"That'll do, Rad!" broke in Ned, with a laugh. He knew that when Tom's helper grew excited on the subject of his mule there was no Stopping him, and Boomerang was a point on which Eradicate and Koku were always arguing. "The fire is under control now."

"Yes, it seems to have gone visiting," observed Koku.

"Visiting?" queried Ned, in some surprise.

"Yes, that is, it is going out," went on Koku.

"Oh, I understand!" laughed Ned. "Yes, and I hope it doesn't pay us another visit soon. Oh, look at Tom, would you!" he cried, for the young aviator had swung his ship about over the flames, to bring another row of sand bags directly above a place where the fire was hottest.

Down showered more sand from the bags which Tom opened. No fire could long continue to blaze under that treatment. The supply of air was cut off, and without that no fire can exist. Water would have been worse than useless, because of the carbide, but the sand covered it up so that it was made perfectly harmless.

Moving slowly, the airship hovered over every part of the now slowly expiring flames, the burned opening in the roof of the shed making it possible for the sand to reach the spots where it was most needed. The flames died out in section after section, until no more could be seen—only clouds of black smoke.

"How is it now?" came Tom's voice, as he spoke from the deck of the balloon through a megaphone.

"Almost out," answered Mr. Damon. "A little more sand, Tom."

The eccentric man had caught up a piece of paper and, rolling it into a cone, made an improvised megaphone of that.

"Haven't much more sand left," was Tom's comment, as he sent down a last shower. "That will have to do. Hustle that carbide and other explosive stuff out of there now, while you have a chance."

"That's it!" cried Ned, who caught his chums meaning. "Come on, Koku. There's work for you."

"Me like work," answered the giant, stretching out his great arms.

The last of the sand had completely smothered the fire, and Tom, observing from aloft that his work was well done, moved away in the dirigible, sending it to a landing space some little distance away from the shed whence it had arisen. It was impossible to drop it back again through the roof of the hangar, as the balloon was of such bulk that even a little breeze would deflect it so that it could not be accurately anchored. But Tom had it under very good control, and soon it was being held down on the ground by some of his helpers.

As all the sand ballast had been allowed to run out Tom was obliged to open the gas-valves and let some of the lifting vapor escape, or he could not have descended.

"Come on, now!" cried the inventor, as he leaped from the deck of his sky craft. "Let's clean out the red shed. That fire is only smothered, and there may be sparks smoldering under that sand, which will burst into flame, if we're not careful. Let's get the explosives out of the way."

"Bless my insurance policy, yes," exclaimed Mr. Damon. "That was a fine move of yours."

"It was the only way I could think of to put out the fire," Tom replied. "I knew water was out of the question, and sand was the next thing."

"But I didn't know where to get any until I happened to think of the ballast bags of my dirigible. Then I knew, if I could get above the fire, I could do the trick. I had to fly pretty high, though, as the fire was hot, and I was afraid it might explode the gas bag and wreck me."

"You were taking a chance," remarked Ned.

"Oh, well, you have to take chances in this business," observed Tom, with a smile. "Now, then, let's finish this work."

The sand, falling from the ballast bags of the dirigible, had so effectually quenched the fire that it was soon cool enough to permit close approach. Koku, Tom and some of the men who best knew how to handle the explosives, were soon engaged in the work of salvage.

"I wish I could help you, Tom," said his aged father. "I don't seem able to do anything but stand here and look on," and he gazed about him rather sadly.

"Never you mind, Dad!" Tom exclaimed. "We'll get along all right now. You'd better go up to the house. Mr. Damon will go with you."

"Yes, of course!" exclaimed the odd man, catching a wink from Tom, who wanted his father not to get too excited on account of his weak heart. "Come along, Professor Swift. The danger is all over."

"All right," assented the aged inventor, with a look at the still smoking shed.

"And, Dad, when you haven't anything else to do," went on Tom, rather whimsically, "you might be thinking up some plan to take up the recoil of those guns on my aerial warship. I confess I'm clean stumped on that point."

"Your aerial warship will never be a success," declared Mr. Swift. "You might as well give that up, Tom."

"Don't you believe it, Dad!" cried Tom, with more of a jolly air of one chum toward another than as though the talk was between father and son. "You solve the recoil problem for me, and I'll take care of the rest, and make the air warship sail. But we've got something else to do just now. Lively, boys."

While Mr. Swift, taking Mr. Damon's arm, walked toward the house, Tom, Ned, Koku, and some of the workmen began carrying out the explosives which had so narrowly escaped the fire. With long hooks the men pulled the shed apart, where the side walls had partly been burned through. Tom maintained an efficient firefighting force at his works, and the men had the proper tools with which to work.

Soon large openings were made on three sides of the red shed, or rather, what was left of it, and through these the dangerous chemicals and carbide, in sheet-iron cans, were carried out to a place of safety. In a little while nothing remained but a heap of hot sand, some charred embers and certain material that had been burned.

"Much loss, Tom?" asked Ned, as they surveyed the ruins. They were both black and grimy, tired and dirty, but there was a great sense of satisfaction.

"Well, yes, there's more lost than I like to think of," answered Tom slowly, "but it would have been a heap sight worse if the stuff had gone up. Still, I can replace what I've lost, except a few models I kept in this place. I really oughtn't to have stored them here, but since I've been working on my new aerial warship I have sort of let other matters slide. I intended to make the red shed nothing but a storehouse for explosive chemicals, but I still had some of my plans and models in it when it caught."

"Only for the sand the whole place might have gone," said Ned in a low voice.

"Yes. It's lucky I had plenty of ballast aboard the dirigible. You see, I've been running it alone lately, and I had to take on plenty of sand to make up for the weight of the several passengers I usually carry. So I had plenty of stuff to shower down on the fire. I wonder how it started, anyhow? I must investigate this."

"Mr. Damon and Eradicate seem to have seen it first," remarked Ned.

"Yes. At least they gave the alarm. Guess I'll ask Eradicate how he happened to notice. Oh, I say, Rad!" Tom called to the colored man.

"Yais, sah, Massa Tom! I'se comin'!" the darky cried, as he finished piling up, at a safe distance from the fire, a number of cans of carbide.

"How'd you happen to see the red shed ablaze?" Tom asked.

"Why, it was jest dish yeah way, Massa Tom," began the colored man. "I had jest been feedin' mah mule, Boomerang. He were pow'ful hungry, Boomerang were, an', when I give him some oats, wif a carrot sliced up in 'em—no, hole on—did I gib him a carrot t'day, or was it yist'day?—I done fo'got. No, it were yist'day I done gib him de carrot, I 'member now, 'case—"

"Oh, never mind the carrot, or Boomerang, either, Rad!" broke in Tom, "I'm asking you about the fire."

"An' I'se tellin' yo', Massa Tom," declared Eradicate, with a rather reproachful look at his master. "But I wanted t' do it right an' proper. I were comin' from Boomerang's stable, an' I see suffin' red spoutin' up at one corner ob de red shed. I knowed it were fire right away, an' I yelled."

"Yes, I heard you yell," Tom said. "But what I wanted to know is, did you see anyone near the red shed at the time?"

"No, Massa Tom, I done didn't."

"I wonder if Mr. Damon did? I must ask him," went on the young inventor. "Come, on, Ned, we'll go up to the house. Everything is all right here, I think. Whew! But that was some excitement. And I didn't show you my aerial warship after all! Nor have you settled that recoil problem for me."

"Time enough, I guess," responded Ned. "You sure did have a lucky escape, Tom."

"That's right. Well, Koku, what is it?" for the giant had approached, holding out something in his hand.

"Koku found this in red shed," went on the giant, holding out a round, blackened object. "Maybe him powder; go bang-bang!"

"Oh, you think it's something explosive, eh?" asked Tom, as he took the object from the giant.

"Koku no think much," was the answer. "Him look funny."

Tom did not speak for a moment. Then he cried:

"Look funny! I should say it did! See here, Ned, if this isn't suspicious I'll eat my hat!" and Tom beckoned excitedly to his chum, who had walked on a little in advance.

A Queer Stranger

What Tom Swift held in his hand looked like a small cannon ball, but it could not have been solid or the young aviator would not so easily have held it out at arm's length for his friend Ned Newton to look at.

"This puts a different face on it, Ned," Tom went on, as he turned the object over.

"Is that likely to go off?" the bank clerk asked, as he came to a halt a little distance from his friend.

"Go off? No, it's done all the damage it could, I guess."

"Damage? It looks to me as though it had suffered the most damage itself. What is it, one of your models? Looks like a bomb to me."

"And that's what it is, Ned."

"Not one of those you're going to use on your aerial warship, is it, Tom?"

"Not exactly. I never saw this before, but it's what started the fire in the red shed all right; I'm sure of that."

"Do you really mean it?" cried Ned.

"I sure do."

"Well, if that's the case, I wouldn't leave such dangerous things around where there are explosives, Tom."

"I didn't, Ned. I wouldn't have had this within a hundred miles of my shed, if I could have had my way. It's a fire bomb, and it was set to go off at a certain time. Only I think something went wrong, and the bomb started a fire ahead of time.

"If it had worked at night, when we were all asleep, we might not have put the fire out so easily. This sure is suspicious! I'm glad you found this, Koku."

Tom was carefully examining the bomb, as Ned had correctly named it. The bank clerk, now that he was assured by his chum that the, object had done all the harm it could, approached closer.

What he saw was merely a hollow shell of iron, with a small opening in it, as though intended for a place through which to put a charge of explosives and a fuse.

"But there was no explosion, Tom," explained Ned.

"I know it," said Tom quietly. "It wasn't an explosive bomb. Smell that!"

He held the object under Ned's nose so suddenly that the young bank clerk jumped back.

"Oh, don't get nervous," laughed Tom. "It can't hurt you now. But what does that smell like?"

Ned sniffed, sniffed again, thought for a moment, and then sniffed a third time.

"Why," he said slowly, "I don't just know the name of it, but it's that funny stuff you mix up sometimes to put in the oxygen tanks when we go up in the rarefied atmosphere in the balloon or airship."

"Manganese and potash," spoke Tom. "That and two or three other things that form a chemical combination which goes off by itself of spontaneous combustion after a certain time. Only the person who put this bomb together didn't get the chemical mixture just right, and it went off ahead of time; for which we have to be duly thankful."

"Do you really think that, Tom?" cried Ned.

"I'm positive of it," was the quiet answer.

"Why—why—that would mean some one tried to set fire to the red shed, Tom!"

"They not only tried it, but did it," responded Tom, more coolly than seemed natural under the circumstances. "Only for the fact that the mixture went off before it was intended to, and found us all alert and ready—well, I don't like to think what might have happened," and Tom cast a look about at his group of buildings with their valuable contents.

"You mean some one purposely put that bomb in the red shed, Tom?"

"That's exactly what I mean. Some enemy, who wanted to do me an injury, planned this thing deliberately. He filled this steel shell with chemicals which, of themselves, after a certain time, would send out a hot tongue of flame through this hole," and Tom pointed to the opening in the round steel shell.

"He knew the fire would be practically unquenchable by ordinary means, and he counted on its soon eating its way into the carbide and other explosives. Only it didn't."

"Why, Tom!" cried Ned. "It was just like one of those alarm-clock dynamite bombs—set to go off at a certain time."

"Exactly," Tom said, "only this was more delicate, and, if it had worked properly, there wouldn't have been a vestige left to give us a clue. But the fire, thanks to the ballast sand in the dirigible, was put out in time. The fuse burned itself out, but I can tell by the smell that chemicals were in it. That's all, Koku," he went on to the giant who had stood waiting, not understanding all the talk between Tom and Ned. "I'll take care of this now."

"Bad man put it there?" asked the giant, who at least comprehended that something was wrong.

"Well, yes, I guess you could say it was a bad man," replied Tom.

"Ha! If Koku find bad man—bad for that man!" muttered the giant, as he clasped his two enormous hands together, as though they were already on the fellow who had tried to do Tom Swift such an injury.

"I wouldn't like to be that man, if Koku catches him," observed Ned. "Have you any idea who it could be, Tom?"

"Not the least. Of course I know I have enemies, Ned. Every successful inventor has persons who imagine he has stolen their ideas, whether he has ever seen them or not. It may have been one of those persons, or some half-mad crank, who was jealous. It would be impossible to say, Ned."

"It wouldn't be Andy Foger, would it?"

"No; I don't believe Andy has been in this neighborhood for some time. The last lesson we gave him sickened him, I guess."

"How about those diamond-makers, whose secret you discovered? They wouldn't be trying to get back at you, would they?"

Well, it's possible, Ned. But I don't imagine so. They seem to have been pretty well broken up. No, I don't believe it was the diamond-makers who put this fire bomb in the red shed. Their line of activities didn't include this branch. It takes a chemist to know just how to blend the things contained in the bomb, and even a good chemist is likely to fail—as this one did, as far as time went."

"What are you going to do about it?" Ned asked.

"I don't know," and Tom spoke slowly, "I hoped I was done with all that sort of thing," he went on; "fighting enemies whom I have never knowingly injured. But it seems they are still after me. Well, Ned, this gives us something to do, at all events."

"You mean trying to find out who these fellows are?"

"Yes; that is, if you are willing to help."

"Well, I guess I am!" cried the bank clerk with sparkling eyes. "I wouldn't ask anything better. We've been in things like this before, Tom, and we'll go in again—and win! I'll help you all I can. Now, let's see if we can pick up any other clues. This is like old times!" and Ned laughed, for he, like Tom, enjoyed a good "fight," and one in which the odds were against them.

"We sure will have our hands full," declared the young inventor. "Trying to solve the problem of carrying guns on an aerial warship, and finding out who set this fire."

"Then you're not going to give up your aerial warship idea?"

"No, indeed!" Tom cried. "What made you think that?"

"Well, the way your father spoke—"

"Oh, dear old dad!" exclaimed Tom affectionately. "I don't want to argue with him, but he's dead wrong!"

"Then you are going to make a go of it?"

"I sure am, Ned! All I have to solve is the recoil proposition, and, as soon as we get straightened out from this fire, we'll tackle that problem again—you and I. But I sure would like to know who put this in my red shed," and Tom looked in a puzzled manner at the empty fire bomb he still held.

Tom paused, on his way to the house, to put the bomb in one of his offices.

"No use letting dad know about this," he went on. It would only be something else for him to worry about."

"That's right," agreed Ned.

By this time nearly all evidences of the fire, except for the blackened ruins of the shed, had been cleared away. High in the air hung a cloud of black smoke, caused by some chemicals that had burned harmlessly save for that pall. Tom Swift had indeed had a lucky escape.

The young inventor, finding his father quieted down and conversing easily with Mr. Damon, who was blessing everything he could think of, motioned to Ned to follow him out of the house again.

"We'll leave dad here," said Tom, "and do a little investigating on our own account. We'll look for clues while they're fresh."

But, it must be confessed, after Tom and Ned had spent the rest of that day in and about the burned shed, they were little wiser than when they started. They found the place where the fire bomb had evidently been placed, right inside the main entrance to the shed. Tom knew it had been there because there were peculiar marks on the charred wood, and a certain queer smell of chemicals that confirmed his belief.

"They put the bomb there to prevent anyone going in at the first alarm and saving anything," Tom said. "They didn't count on the roof burning through first, giving me a chance to use the sand. I made the roof of the red shed flimsy just on that account, so the force of the explosion if one ever came, would be mostly upward. You know the expanding gases, caused by an explosion or by rapid combustion, always do just as electricity does, seek the shortest and easiest route. In this case I made the roof the easiest route."

"A lucky provision," observed Ned.

That night Tom had to confess himself beaten, as far as finding clues was concerned. The empty fire bomb was the only one, and that seemed valueless.

Close questioning of the workmen failed to disclose anything. Tom was particularly anxious to discover if any mysterious strangers had been seen about the works. There was a strict rule about admitting them to the plant, however, and it could not be learned that this had been violated.

"Well, we'll just have to lay that aside for a while," Tom said the next day, when Ned again came to pay a visit. "Now, what do you say to tackling, with me, that recoil problem on the aerial warship?"

"I'm ready, if you are," Ned agreed, "though I know about as much of those things as a snake does about dancing. But I'm game."

The two friends walked out toward the shed where Tom's new craft was housed. As yet Ned had not seen it. On the way they saw Eradicate walking along, talking to himself, as he often did.

"I wonder what he has on his mind," remarked Ned musingly.

"Something does seem to be worrying him," agreed Tom.

As they neared the colored man, they could hear him saying:

"He suah did hab nerve, dat's what he did! De idea ob askin' me all dem questions, an' den wantin' t' know if I'd sell him!"

"What's that, Eradicate?" asked Tom.

"Oh, it's a man I met when I were comin' back from de ash dump," Eradicate explained. One of the colored man's duties was to cart ashes away from Tom's various shops, and dump them in a certain swampy lot. With an old ramshackle cart, and his mule, Boomerang, Eradicate did this task to perfection.

"A man—what sort of a man?" asked Tom, always ready to be suspicious of anything unusual.

"He were a queer man," went on the aged colored helper. "First he stopped me an' asted me fo' a ride. He was a dressed-up gen'man, too, an' I were suah s'prised at him wantin' t" set in mah ole ash cart," said Eradicate. "But I done was polite t' him, an' fixed a blanket so's he wouldn't git too dirty. Den he asted me ef I didn't wuk fo' yo', Massa Tom, an' of course I says as how I did. Den he asted me about de fire, an' how much damage it done, an' how we put it out. An' he end up by sayin' he'd laik t' buy mah mule, Boomerang, an' he wants t' come heah dis arternoon an' talk t' me about it."

"He does, eh?" cried Tom. "What sort of a man was he, Rad?"

"Well, a gen'man sort ob man, Massa Tom. Stranger t' me. I nebber seed him afo'. He suah was monstrous polite t' ole black Eradicate, an' he gib me a half-dollar, too, jest fo' a little ride. But I aint' gwine t' sell Boomerang, no indeedy, I ain't!" and Eradicate shook his gray, kinky head decidedly.

"Ned, there may be something in this!" said Tom, in an excited whisper to his chum. "I don't like the idea of a mysterious stranger questioning Eradicate!"

THE AERIAL WARSHIP

Ned Newton looked at Tom questioningly. Then he glanced at the unsuspicious colored man, who was industriously polishing the half-dollar the mysterious stranger had given him.

"Rad, just exactly what sort of a man was this one you speak of?" asked Tom.

"Why, he were a gen'man—"

"Yes, I know that much. You've said it before. But was he an Englishman, an American—or—"

Tom paused and waited for an answer.

"I think he were a Frenchman," spoke Eradicate. "I done didn't see him eat no frogs' laigs, but he smoked a cigarette dat had a funny smell, and he suah was monstrous polite. He suah was a Frenchman. I think."

Tom and Ned laughed at Eradicate's description of the man, but Tom's face was soon grave again.

"Tell us more about him, Rad," he suggested. "Did he seem especially interested in the fire?"

"No, sah, Massa Tom, he seemed laik he was more special interested in mah mule, Boomerang. He done asted how long I had him, an' how much I wanted fo' him, an' how old he was."

"But every once in a while he put in some question about the fire, or about our shops, didn't he, Rad?" Tom wanted to know.

The colored man scratched his kinky head, and glanced with a queer look at Tom.

"How yo' all done guess dat?" he asked.

"Answer my question," insisted Tom.

"Yes, sah, he done did ask about yo', and de wuks, ebery now and den," Rad confessed. "But how yo' all knowed dat, Massa Tom, when I were a-tellin' yo' all about him astin' fo' mah mule, done gets me—dat's what it suah does."

"Never mind, Rad. He asked questions about the plant, that's all I want to know. But you didn't tell him much, did you?"

Eradicate looked reproachfully at his master.

"Yo' all done knows me bettah dan dat, Massa Tom," the old colored man said. "Yo' all know yo' done gib orders fo' nobody t' talk about yo' projections."

"Yes, I know I gave those orders," Tom said, with a smile, "but I want to make sure that they have been followed."

"Well, I done follered 'em, Massa Tom."

"Then you didn't tell this queer stranger, Frenchman, or whatever he is, much about my place?"

"I didn't tell him nuffin', sah. I done frowed dust in his eyes."

Ned uttered an exclamation of surprise.

"Eradicate is speaking figuratively," Tom said, with a laugh.

"Dat's what I means," the colored man went on. "I done fooled him. When he asted me about de fire I said it didn't do no damage at all—in fack dat we'd rather hab de fire dan not hab it, 'case it done gib us a chance t' practice our hose drill."

"That's good," laughed Tom. "What else?"

"Well, he done sort ob hinted t' me ef we all knowed how de fire done start. I says as how we did, dat we done start it ourse'ves fo' practice, an dat we done expected it all along, an' were ready fo' it. Course I knows dat were a sort of fairy story, Massa Tom, but den dat cigarette-smokin' Frenchman didn't hab no right t' asted me so many questions, did he?"

"No, indeed, Rad. And I'm glad you didn't give him straight answers. So he's coming here later on, is he?"

"T' see ef I wants t' sell mah mule, Boomerang, yais, sah. I sort ob thought maybe you'd want t' hab a look at dat man, so I tole him t' come on. Course I doan't want t' sell Boomerang, but ef he was t' offer me a big lot ob money fo' him I'd take it."

"Of course," Tom answered. "Very well, Rad. You may go on now, and don't say anything to anyone about what you have told me."

"I won't, Massa Tom," promised the colored man, as he went off muttering to himself.

"Well, what do you make of it, Tom?" asked Ned of his chum, as they walked on toward the shed of the new, big aerial warship.

"I don't know just what to think, Ned. Of course things like this have happened before—persons trying to worm secrets out of Eradicate, or some of the other men."

"They never succeeded in getting much, I'm glad to say, but it always keeps me worried for fear something will happen," Tom concluded.

"But about this Frenchman?"

"Well, he must be a new one. And, now I come to think of it, I did hear some of the men speaking about a foreigner—a stranger— being around town last week. It was just a casual reference, and I paid little attention to it. Now it looks as though there might be something in it."

"Do you think he'll come to bargain with Eradicate about the mule?" Ned asked.

"Hardly. That was only talk to make Eradicate unsuspicious. The stranger, whoever he was, sized Rad up partly right. I surmised, when Rad said he asked a lot of questions about the mule, that was only to divert suspicion. and that he'd come back to the subject of the fire every chance he got."

"And you were right."

"Yes, so it seems. But I don't believe the fellow will come around here. It would be too risky. All the same, we'll be prepared for him. I'll just rig up one of my photo-telephone machines, so that, if he does come to have a talk with Rad, we can both see and hear him."

"That's great, Tom! But do you think this fellow had anything to do with the fire?"

"I don't know. He knew about it, of course. This isn't the first fire we've had in the works, and, though we always fight them ourselves, still news of it will leak out to the town. So he could easily have known about it. And he might be in with those who set it, for I firmly believe the fire was set by someone who has an object in injuring me."

"It's too bad!" declared Ned. "Seems as though they might let you alone, if they haven't gumption enough to invent things for themselves."

"Well, don't worry. Maybe it will come out all right," returned Tom. "Now, let's go and have a look at my aerial warship. I haven't shown it to you yet. Then we'll get ready for that mysterious Frenchman, if he comes—but I don't believe he will."

The young inventor unlocked the door of the shed where he kept his latest "pet," and at the sight which met his eyes Ned Newton uttered an exclamation of surprise.

"Tom, what is it?" he cried in an awed voice.

"My aerial warship!" was the quiet answer.

Ned Newton gave vent to a long whistle, and then began a detailed examination of the wonderful craft he saw before him. That is, he made as detailed an examination as was possible under the circumstances, for it was a long time before the young bank clerk fully appreciated all Tom Swift had accomplished in building the Mars, which was the warlike name painted in red letters on the big gas container that tugged and swayed overhead.

"Tom, however did you do it?" gasped Ned at length.

"By hard work," was the modest reply. "I've been at this for a longer time than you'd suppose, working on it at odd moments. I had a lot of help, too, or I never could have done it. And now it is nearly all finished, as far as the ship itself is concerned. The only thing that bothers me is to provide for the recoil of the guns I want to carry. Maybe you can help me with that. Come on, now, I'll explain how the affair works, and what I hope to accomplish with it."

In brief Tom's aerial warship was a sort of German Zeppelin type of dirigible balloon, rising in the air by means of a gas container, or, rather, several of them, for the section for holding the lifting gas element was divided by bulkheads.

The chief difference between dirigible balloons and ordinary aeroplanes, as you all know, is that the former are lifted from the earth by a gas, such as hydrogen, which is lighter than air, while the aeroplane lifts itself by getting into motion, when broad, flat planes, or surfaces, hold it up, just as a flat stone is held up when you sail it through the air. The moment the stone, or aeroplane, loses its forward motion, it begins to fall.

This is not so with a dirigible balloon. It is held in the air by means of the lifting gas, and once so in the air can be sent in any direction by means of propellers and rudders.

Tom's aerial warship contained many new features. While it was as large as some of the war-type Zeppelins, it differed from them materially. But the details would be of more interest to a scientific builder of such things than to the ordinary reader, so I will not weary you with them.

Sufficient to say that Tom's craft consisted first of a great semi-rigid bag, or envelope, made of specially prepared oiled silk and aluminum, to hold the gas, which was manufactured on board. There were a number of gas-tight compartments, so that if one, or even if a number of them burst, or were shot by an enemy, the craft would still remain afloat.

Below the big gas bag was the ship proper, a light but strong and rigid framework about which were built enclosed cabins. These cabins, or compartments, housed the driving machinery, the gas-generating plant, living, sleeping and dining quarters, and a pilot-house, whence the ship could be controlled.

But this was not all.

Ned, making a tour of the Mars, as she swayed gently in the big shed, saw where several aluminum pedestals were mounted, fore and aft and on either beam of the ship.

"They look just like places where you intend to mount guns," said Ned to Tom.

"And that's exactly what they are," the young inventor replied. "I have the guns nearly ready for mounting, but I can't seem to think of a way of providing for the recoil. And if I don't take care of that, I'm likely to find my ship coming apart under me, after we bombard the enemy with a broadside or two."

"Then you intend to fight with this ship?" asked Ned.

"Well, no; not exactly personally. I was thinking of offering it to the United States Government. Foreign nations are getting ready large fleets of aerial warships, so why shouldn't we? Matters in Europe are mighty uncertain. There may be a great war there in which aerial craft will play a big part. I am conceited enough to think I can build one that will measure up to the foreign ones, and I'll soon be in a position to know."

"What do you mean?"

"I mean I have already communicated with our government experts, and they are soon to come and inspect this craft. I have sent them word that it is about finished. There is only the matter of the guns, and some of the ordnance officers may be able to help me out with a suggestion, for I admit I am stuck!" exclaimed Tom.

"Then you're going to do the same with this aerial warship as you did with your big lantern and that immense gun you perfected?" asked Ned.

"That's right," confirmed Tom. My former readers will know to what Ned Newton referred, and those of you who do not may learn the details of how Tom helped Uncle Sam, by reading the previous volumes, "Tom Swift and His Great Searchlight," and "Tom Swift and His Giant Cannon."

"When do you expect the government experts?," Ned asked.

"Within a few days, now. But I'll have to hustle to get ready for them, as this fire has put me back. There are quite a number of details I need to change. Well, now, let me explain about that gun recoil business. Maybe you can help me."

"Fire away," laughed Ned. "I'll do the best I can."

Tom led the way from the main shed, where the aerial warship was housed, to a small private office. As Ned entered, the door, pulled by a strong spring, swung after him. He held back his hand to prevent it from slamming, but there was no need, for a patent arrangement took up all the force, and the door closed gently. Ned looked around, not much surprised, for the same sort of door-check was in use at his bank. But a sudden idea came to him.

"There you are, Tom!" he cried. "Why not take up the recoil of the guns on your aerial warship by some such device as that?" and Ned pointed to the door-check.

WARNINGS

For a moment or two Tom Swift did not seem to comprehend what Ned had said. He remained staring, first at his chum, who stood pointing, and from him Tom's gaze wandered to the top of the door. It may have been, and probably was, that Tom was thinking of other matters at that instant. But Ned said again:

"Wouldn't that do, Tom? Check the recoil of the gun with whatever stuff is in that arrangement!"

A sudden change came over Tom's face. It was lighted up with a gleam of understanding.

"By Jove, Ned, old man!" he cried. "I believe you've struck it! And to think that has been under my nose, or, rather, over my head, all this while, and I never thought of it. Hurray! That will solve the problem!"

"Do you think it will?" asked Ned, glad that he had contributed something, if only an idea, to Tom's aerial warship.

"I'm almost sure it will. I'll give it a trial right away."

"What's in that door-check?" Ned asked. "I never stopped before to think what useful things they are, though at the bank, with the big, heavy doors, they are mighty useful."

"They are a combination of springs and hydrostatic valves," began Tom.

"Good-night!" laughed Ned. "Excuse the slang, Tom, but what in the world is a hydrostatic valve?"

"A valve through which liquids pass. In this door-check there may be a mixture of water, alcohol and glycerine, the alcohol to prevent freezing in cold weather, and the glycerine to give body to the mixture so it will not flow through the valves too freely."

"And do you think you can put something like that on your guns, so the recoil will be taken up?" Ned wanted to know.

"I think so," spoke Tom. "I'm going to work on it right away, and we'll soon see how it will turn out It's mighty lucky you thought of that, for I sure was up against it, as the boys say."

"It just seemed to come to me," spoke Ned, "seeing how easily the door closed."

"If the thing works I'll give you due credit for it," promised Tom. "Now, I've got to figure out how much force a modified hydrostatic valve check like that will take up, and how much recoil my biggest gun will have."

"Then you're going to put several guns on the Mars?" asked Ned.

"Yes, four quick-firers, at least, two on each side, and heavier guns at the bow and stern, to throw explosive shells in a horizontal or upward direction. For a downward direction we won't need any guns, we can simply drop the bombs, or shells, from a release clutch."

"Drop them on other air craft?" Ned wanted to know.

"Well, if it's necessary, yes. Though I guess there won't be much chance of doing that to a rival aeroplane or dirigible. But in flying over cities or forts, explosive bombs can be dropped very nicely. For use in attacking other air craft I am going to depend on my lateral fire, from the guns mounted on either beam, and in the bow and stern."

"You speak as though you, yourself, were going into a battle of the air," said Ned.

"No, I don't believe I'll go that far," Tom replied. "Though, if the government wants my craft, I may have to go aloft and fire shots at targets for them to show them how things work.

"Please don't think that I am in favor of war, Ned," went on Tom earnestly. "I hate it, and I wish the time would come when all nations would disarm. But if the other countries are laying themselves out to have aerial battleships, it is time the United States did also. We must not be left behind, especially in view of what is taking place in Europe."

"I suppose that's right," agreed Ned. "Have you any of your guns ready?"

"Yes, all but the mounting of them on the supports aboard the Mars. I haven't dared do that yet, and fire them, until I provided some means of taking up the recoil. Now I'm going to get right to work on that problem."

There was considerable detailed figuring and computation work ahead of Tom Swift, and I will not weary you by going into the details of higher mathematics. Even Ned lost interest after the start of the problem, though he was interested when Tom took down the door-check and began measuring the amount of force it would take up, computing it on scales and spring balances.

Once this had been done, and Tom had figured just how much force could be expected to be taken up by a larger check, with stronger hydrostatic valves, the young inventor explained:

"And now to see how much recoil force my guns develop!"

"Are you really going to fire the guns?" asked Ned.

"Surely," answered Tom. "That's the only way to get at real results. I'll have the guns taken out and mounted in a big field. Then we'll fire them, and measure the recoil."

"Well, that may be some fun," spoke Ned, with a grin. "More fun than all these figures," and he looked at the mass of details on Tom's desk.

This was the second or third day after the fire in the red shed, and in the interim Tom had been busy making computations. These were about finished. Meanwhile further investigation bad been made of clues leading to the origin of the blaze in the shed, but nothing had been learned.

A photo-telephone had been installed near Eradicate's quarters, in the hope that the mysterious stranger might keep his promise, and come to see about the mule. In that case something would have been learned about him. But, as Tom feared, the man did not appear.

Ned was much interested in the guns, and, a little later, he helped Tom and Koku mount them in a vacant lot. The giant's strength came in handy in handling the big parts.

Mr. Swift strolled past, as the guns were being mounted for the preliminary test, and inquired what his son was doing

"It will never work, Tom, never!" declared the aged inventor, when informed. "You can't take up those guns in your air craft, and fire them with any degree of safety."

"You wait, Dad," laughed Tom. "You haven't yet seen how the Newton hydrostatic recoil operates."

Ned smiled with pleasure at this.

It took nearly a week to get all the guns mounted, for some of them required considerable work, and it was also necessary to attach gauges to them to register the recoil and pressure. In the meanwhile Tom had been in further communication with government experts who were soon to call on him to inspect the aerial warship, with a view to purchase.

"When are they coming?" asked Ned, as he and Tom went out one morning to make the first test of the guns.

"They will be here any day, now. They didn't set any definite date. I suppose they want to take us unawares, to see that I don't 'frame-up' any game on them. Well, I'll be ready any time they come. Now, Koku, bring along those shells, and don't drop any of them, for that new powder is freakish stuff."

"Me no drop any, Master," spoke the giant, as he lifted the boxes of explosives in his strong arms.

The largest gun was loaded and aimed at a distant hill, for Tom knew that if the recoil apparatus would take care of the excess force of his largest gun, the problem of the smaller ones would be easy to solve.

"Here, Rad, where are you going?" Tom asked, as he noticed the colored man walking away, after having completed a task assigned to him.

"Where's I gwine, Massa Tom?"

"Yes, Rad, that's what I asked you."

"I—I'se gwine t' feed mah mule, Boomerang," said the colored man slowly. "It's his eatin' time. jest now, Massa Tom."

"Nonsense! It isn't anywhere near noon yet."

"Yais, sab, Massa Tom, I knows dat," said Eradicate, as he carefully edged away from the big gun, "but I'se done changed de eatin' hours ob dat mule. He had a little touch ob indigestion de udder day, an' I'se feedin' him diff'rent now. So I guess as how yo'll hab t' 'scuse me now, Massa Tom."

"Oh, well, trot along," laughed the young inventor. "I guess we won't need you. Is everything all right there, Koku?"

"All right, Master."

"Now, Ned, if you'll stand here," went on Tom, "and note the extreme point to which the hand on the pressure gauge goes, I'll be obliged to you. Just jot it down on this pad."

"Here comes someone," remarked the bank clerk, as he saw that his pencil was sharpened. He pointed to the field back of them.

"It's Mr. Damon," observed Tom. "We'll wait until he arrives. He'll be interested in this."

"Bless my collar button, Tom! What's going on?" asked the eccentric man, as he came up. "Has war been declared?"

"Just practicing," replied the young inventor. "Getting ready to put the armament on my aerial warship."

"Well, as long as I'm behind the guns I'm all right, I suppose?"

"Perfectly," Tom replied. "Now then, Ned, I think we'll fire."

There was a moment of inspection, to see that nothing had been forgotten, and then the big gun was discharged. There was a loud report, not as heavy, though, as Ned had expected, but there was no puff of smoke, for Tom was using smokeless powder. Only a little flash of flame was observed.

"Catch the figure, Ned!" Tom cried.

"I have it!" was the answer. "Eighty thousand!"

"Good! And I can build a recoil check that will take up to one hundred and twenty thousand pounds pressure. That ought to be margin of safety enough. Now we'll try another shot."

The echoes of the first had hardly died away before the second gun was ready for the test. That, too, was satisfactory, and then the smaller ones were operated. These were not quite so satisfactory, as the recoil developed was larger, in proportion to their size, than Tom had figured.

"But I can easily put a larger hydrostatic check on them," he said. "Now, we'll fire by batteries, and see what the total is."

Then began a perfect bombardment of the distant hillside, service charges being used v, and explosive shells sent out so that dirt, stones and gravel flew in all directions. Danger signs and flags had been posted, and a cordon of Tom's men kept spectators away from the hill, so no one would be in the danger zone.

The young inventor was busy making some calculations after the last of the firing had been completed. Koku was packing up the unfired shells, and Mr. Damon was blessing his ear-drums, and the pieces of cotton he had stuffed in to protect them, when a tall, erect man was observed strolling over the fields in the direction of the guns.

"Somebody's coming, Tom," warned Ned.

"Yes, and a stranger, too," observed Tom. "I wonder if that can be Eradicate's Frenchman?"

But a look at the stranger's face disproved that surmise. He had a frank and pleasant countenance, obviously American.

"I beg your pardon," he began, addressing everyone in general, "but I am looking for Tom Swift. I was told he was here."

"I am Tom Swift," replied our hero.

"Ah! Well, I am Lieutenant Marbury, with whom you had some correspondence recently about—"

"Oh, yes, Lieutenant Marbury, of the United States Navy," interrupted Tom. "I'm glad to see you," he went on, holding out his hand. "We are just completing some tests with the guns. You called, I presume, in reference to my aerial warship?"

"That is it—yes. Have you it ready for a trial flight?"

"Well, almost. It can be made ready in a few hours. You see, I have been delayed. There was a fire in the plant

"A fire!" exclaimed the officer in surprise. "How was that? We heard nothing of it in Washington."

"No, I kept it rather quiet," Tom explained. "We had reason to suspect that it was a fire purposely set, in a shed where I kept a quantity of explosives."

"Ha!" exclaimed Lieutenant Marbury. "This fits in with what I have heard. And did you not receive warning?" he asked Tom.

"Warning? No. Of what?"

"Of foreign spies!" was the unexpected answer. "I am sorry. Some of our Secret Service men unearthed something of a plot against you, and I presumed you had been told to watch out. If you had, the fire might not have occurred. There must have been some error in Washington. But let me tell you now, Tom Swift—be on your guard!"

A SUSPECTED PLOT

The officer's words were so filled with meaning that Tom started. Ned Newton, too, showed the effect he felt.

"Do you really mean that?" asked the young inventor, looking around to make sure his father was not present. On account of Professor Swift's weak heart, Tom wished to spare him all possible worry.

"I certainly do mean it," insisted Lieutenant Marbury. "And, while I am rather amazed at the news of the fire, for I did not think the plotters would be so bold as that, it is in line with what I expected, and what we suspected in Washington."

"And that was—what?" asked Tom.

"The existence of a well-laid plot, not only against our government, but against you!"

"And why have they singled me out?" Tom demanded.

"I might as well tell it from the beginning," the officer went on. "As long as you have not received any official warning from Washington you had better hear the whole story. But are you sure you had no word?"

"Well, now, I won't be so sure," Tom confessed. "I have been working very hard, the last two days, making some intricate calculations. I have rather neglected my mail, to tell you the truth.

"And, come to think of it, there were several letters received with the Washington postmark. But, I supposed they had to do with some of my patents, and I only casually glanced over them. There was one letter, though, that I couldn't make head or tail of."

"Ha! That was it!" cried the lieutenant. "It was the warning in cipher or code. I didn't think they would neglect to send it to you."

"But what good would it do me if I couldn't read it?" asked Tom.

"You must also have received a method of deciphering the message," the officer said. "Probably you overlooked that. The Secret Service men sent you the warning in code, so it would not be found out by the plotters, and, to make sure you could understand it, a method of translating the cipher was sent in a separate envelope. It is too bad you missed it."

"Yes, for I might have been on my guard," agreed Tom. "The red shed might not have burned, but, as it was, only slight damage was done."

"Owing to the fact that Tom put the fire out with sand ballast from his dirigible!" cried Ned. "You should have seen it!"

"I should have liked to be here," the lieutenant spoke. "But, if I were you, Tom Swift, I would take means to prevent a repetition of such things."

"I shall," Tom decided. "But, if we want to talk, we had better go to my office, where we can be more private. I don't want the workmen to hear too much."

Now that the firing was over, a number of Tom's men from the shops had assembled around the cannon. Most of them, the young inventor felt, could be trusted, but in so large a gathering one could never be sure.

"Did you come on from Washington yesterday?" asked Tom, as he, Ned and the officer strolled toward the shed where was housed the aerial warship.

"Yes, and I spent the night in New York. I arrived in town a short time ago, and came right on out here. At your house I was told you were over in the fields conducting experiments, so I came on here."

"Glad you did," Tom said. "I'll soon have something to show you, I hope. But I am interested in hearing the details of this suspected plot. Are you sure one exists?"

"Perfectly sure," was the answer. "We don't know all the details yet, nor who are concerned in it, but we are working on the case. The Secret Service has several agents in the field.

"We are convinced in Washington," went on Lieutenant Marbury, when he, Tom and Ned were seated in the private office, "that foreign spies are at work against you and against our government."

"Why against me?" asked Tom, in wonder.

"Because of the inventions you have perfected and turned over to Uncle Sam—notably the giant cannon, which rivals anything foreign European powers have, and the great searchlight, which proved so effective against the border smugglers. The success of those two alone, to say nothing of your submarine, has not only made foreign nations jealous, but they fear you—and us," the officer went on.

"Well, if they only take it out in fear—"

"But they won't!" interrupted the officer—" They are seeking to destroy those inventions. More than once, of late, we have nipped a plot just in time."

"Have they really tried to damage the big gun?" asked Tom, referring to one he had built and set up at Panama.

"They have. And now this fire proves that they are taking other measures—they are working directly against you."

"Why, I wonder?"

"Either to prevent you from making further inventions, or to stop you from completing your latest—the aerial warship."

"But I didn't know the foreign governments knew about that," Tom exclaimed. "It was a secret."

"Few secrets are safe from foreign Spies," declared Lieutenant Marbury. "They have a great ferreting-out system on the other side. We are just beginning to appreciate it. But our own men have not been idle."

"Have they really learned anything?" Tom asked. "Nothing definite enough to warrant us in acting," was the answer of the government man. "But we know enough to let us see that the plot is far-reaching."

"Are the French in it?" asked Ned impulsively.

"The French! Why do you ask that?"

"Tell him about Eradicate, and the man who wanted to buy the mule, Tom," suggested Ned,

Thereupon the young inventor mentioned the story told by Eradicate. He also brought out the fire-bomb, and explained his theory as to how it had operated to set the red shed ablaze.

"I think you are right," said Lieutenant Marbury. "And, as regards the French, I might say they are not the only nation banded to obtain our secrets—yours and the government's!"

"But I thought the French and the English were friendly toward us!" Ned exclaimed.

"So they are, in a certain measure," the officer went on. "And Russia is, too. But, in all foreign countries there are two parties, the war party, as it might be called, and the peace element.

"But I might add that it is neither France, England, nor Russia that we must fear. It is a certain other great nation, which at present I will not name."

"And you think spies set this fire?"

"I certainly do."

"But what measures shall I adopt against this plot?" Tom asked.

"We will talk that over," said Lieutenant Marbury. "But, before I go into details, I want to give you another warning. You must be very careful about—"

A sudden knock on the door interrupted the speaker.

THE RECOIL CHECK

"Who is that?" asked Ned Newton, with a quick glance at his chum.

"I don't know," Tom answered. "I left orders we weren't to be disturbed unless it was something important."

"May be something has happened," suggested the navy officer, "another fire, perhaps, or a—"

"It isn't a fire," Tom answered. "The automatic alarm would be ringing before this in that case."

The knock was repeated. Tom went softly to the door and opened it quickly, to disclose, standing in the corridor, one of the messengers employed about the shops.

"Well, what is it?" asked Tom a bit sharply.

"Oh, if you please, Mn Swift," said the boy, a man has applied for work at the main office, and you know you left orders there that if any machinists came along, we were to—"

"Oh, so I did," Tom exclaimed. "I had forgotten about that," he went on to Lieutenant Marbury and Ned. "I am in need of helpers to rush through the finishing touches on my aerial warship, and I left word, if any applied, as they often do, coming here from other cities, that I wanted to see them. How many are there?" Tom asked of the messenger.

"Two, this time. They both say they're good mechanics."

"That's what they all say," interposed Tom, with a smile. "But, though they may be good mechanics in their own line, they need to have special qualifications to work on airships. Tell them to wait, Rodney," Tom went on to the lad, "and I'll see them presently."

As the boy went away, and Tom closed the door, he turned to Lieutenant Marbury.

"You were about to give me another warning when that interruption came. You might complete it now."

"Yes, it was another warning," spoke the officer, "and one I hope you will heed. It concerns yourself, personally."

"Do you mean he is in danger?" asked Ned quickly.

"That's exactly what I do mean," was the prompt reply. "In danger of personal injury, if not something worse."

Tom did not seem as alarmed as he might reasonably have been under the circumstances.

"Danger, eh?" he repeated coolly. "On the part of whom?"

"That's just where I can't warn you," the officer replied. "I can only give you that hint, and beg of you to be careful."

"Do you mean you are not allowed to tell?" asked Ned

"No, indeed; it isn't that!" the lieutenant hastened to assure the young man. "I would gladly tell, if I knew. But this plot, like the other one, directed against the inventions themselves, is so shrouded in mystery that I cannot get to the bottom of it.

"Our Secret Service men have been working on it for some time, not only in order to protect you, because of what you have done for the government, but because Uncle Sam wishes to protect his own property, especially the searchlight and the big cannon. But, though our agents have worked hard, they have not been able to get any clues that would put them on the right trail.

"So we can only warn you to be careful, and this I do in all earnestness. That was part of my errand in coming here, though, of course, I am anxious to inspect the new aerial warship you have constructed. So watch out for two things—your inventions, and, more than all, your life!"

"Do you really think they would do me bodily harm?" Tom asked, a trifle skeptical.

"I certainly do. These foreign spies are desperate. If they cannot secure the use of these inventions to their own country, they are determined not to let this country have the benefit of them."

"Well, I'll be careful," Tom promised. "I'm no more anxious than anyone else to run my head into danger, and I certainly don't want any of my shops or inventions destroyed. The fire in the red shed was as close as I want anything to come."

"That's right!" agreed Ned. "And, if there's anything I can do, Tom, don't hesitate to call on me."

"All right, old man. I won't forget. And now, perhaps, you would like to see the Mars," he said to the lieutenant.

"I certainly would," was the ready answer. "But hadn't you better see those men who are waiting to find out about positions here?"

"There's no hurry about them," Tom said. "We have applicants every day, and it's earlier than the hour when I usually see them. They can wait. Now I want your opinion on my new craft. But, you must remember that it is not yet completed, and only recently did I begin to solve the problem of mounting the guns. So be a little easy with your criticisms."

Followed by Ned and Lieutenant Marbury, Tom led the way into the big airship shed. There, Swaying about at its moorings, was the immense aerial warship. To Ned's eyes it looked complete enough, but, when Tom pointed out the various parts, and explained to the government officer how it was going to work, Ned understood that considerable yet remained to be done on it.

Tom showed his official guest how a new system of elevation and depressing rudders had ben adopted, how a new type of propeller was to be used and indicated several other improvements. The lower, or cabin, part of the aircraft could be entered by mounting a short ladder from the ground, and Tom took Ned and Lieutenant Marbury through the engine-room and other compartments of the Mars.

"It certainly is most complete," the officer observed. "And when you get the guns mounted I shall be glad to make an official test. You understand," he went on, to Tom, "that we are vitally interested in the guns, since we now have many aircraft that can be used purely for scouting purposes. What we want is something for offense, a veritable naval terror of the seas."

"I understand," Tom answered. "And I am going to begin work on mounting the guns at once. I am going to use the Newton recoil check," he added. "Ned, here, is responsible for that."

"Is that so?" asked the lieutenant, as Tom clapped his chum on the back.

"Yes, that's his invention."

"Oh, it isn't anything of the sort," Ned objected. "I just—"

"Yes, he just happened to solve the problem for me!" interrupted Tom, as he told the story of the door-spring.

"A good idea!" commented Lieutenant Marbury.

Tom then briefly described the principle on which his aerial warship would work, explaining how the lifting gas would raise it, with its load of crew, guns and explosives, high into the air; how it could then be sent ahead, backward, to either side, or around in a circle, by means of the propellers and the rudders, and how it could be raised or lowered, either by rudders or by forcing more gas into the lifting bags, or by letting some of the vapor out.

And, while this was being done by the pilot or captain in charge, the crew could be manning the guns with which hostile airships would be attacked, and bombs dropped on the forts or battleships of the enemy.

"It seems very complete," observed the lieutenant. "I shall be glad when I can give it an official test."

"Which ought to be in about a week," Tom said. "Meanwhile I shall be glad if you will be my guest here."

And so that was arranged.

Leaving Ned and the lieutenant to entertain each other, Tom went to see the mechanics who had applied for places. He found them satisfactory and engaged them. One of them had worked for him before. The other was a stranger, but he had been employed in a large aeroplane factory, and brought good recommendations.

There followed busy days at the Swift plant, and work was pushed on the aerial warship. The hardest task was the mounting of the guns, and equipping them with the recoil check, without which it would be impossible to fire them with the craft sailing through the air.

But finally one of the big guns, and two of the smaller ones were in place, with the apparatus designed to reduce the recoil shock, and then Tom decided to have a test of the Mars.

"Up in the air, do you mean?" asked Ned, who was spending all his spare time with his chum.

"Well, a little way up in the air, at least," Tom answered. "I'll make a sort of captive balloon of my craft, and see how she behaves. I don't want to take too many chances with that new recoil check, though it seems to work perfectly in theory."

The day came when, for the first time, the Mars was to come out of the big shed where she had been constructed. The craft was not completed for a flight as yet, but could be made so in a few days, with rush work. The roof of the great shed slid back, and the big envelope containing the buoyant gas rose slowly upward. There was a cry of surprise from the many workmen in the yard, as they saw, most of them for the first time, the wonderful new craft. It did not go up very high, being held in place with anchor ropes.

The sun glistened on the bright brass and nickel parts, and glinted from the gleaming barrels of the quick-firing guns.

"That's enough!" Tom called to the men below, who were paying out the ropes from the windlasses. "Hold her there."

Tom, Ned, Lieutenant Marbury and Mr. Damon were aboard the captive Mars.

Looking about, to see that all was in readiness, Tom gave orders to load the guns, blank charges being used, of course.

The recoil apparatus was in place, and it now remained to see if it would do the work for which it was designed.

"All ready?" asked the young inventor.

"Bless my accident insurance policy!" exclaimed Mr. Damon. "I'm as ready as ever I shall be, Tom. Let 'em go!"

"Hold fast!" cried Tom, as he prepared to press the electrical switch which would set off the guns. Ned and Lieutenant Marbury stood near the indicators to notice how much of the recoil would be neutralized by the check apparatus.

"Here we go!" cried the young inventor, and, at the same moment, from down below on the ground, came a warning cry:

"Don't shoot, Massa Tom. Don't shoot! Mah mule, Boomerang—"

But Eradicate had spoken too late. Tom pressed the switch; there was a deafening crash, a spurt of flame, and then followed wild cries and confused shouts, while the echoes of the reports rolled about the hills surrounding Shopton.

THE NEW MEN

"What was the matter down there?"

"Was anyone hurt?"

"Don't forget to look at those pressure gauges!"

"Bless my ham sandwich!"

Thus came the cries from those aboard the captive Mars. Ned, Lieutenant Marbury and Tom had called out in the order named. And, of course, I do not need to tell you what remark Mr. Damon made. Tom glanced toward where Ned and the government man stood, and saw that they had made notes of the pressure recorded on the recoil checks directly after the guns were fired. Mr. Damon, blessing innumerable objects under his breath, was looking over the side of the rail to discover the cause of the commotion and cries of warning from below.

"I don't believe it was anything serious, Tom," said the odd man. "No one seems to be hurt." "Look at Eradicate!" suddenly exclaimed Ned.

"And his mule! I guess that's what the trouble was, Tom!"

They looked to where the young bank employee pointed, and saw the old colored man, seated on the seat of his ramshackle wagon, doing his best to pull down to a walk the big galloping mule, which was dragging the vehicle around in a circle.

"Whoa, dere!" Eradicate was shouting, as he pulled on the lines. "Whoa, dere! Dat's jest laik yo', Boomerang, t' run when dere ain't no call fo' it, nohow! Ef I done wanted yo' t' git a move on, yo'd lay down 'side de road an' go to sleep. Whoa, now!"

But the noise of the shots had evidently frightened the long-eared animal, and he was in no mood for stopping, now that he had once started. It was not until some of the workmen ran out from the group where they had gathered to watch Tom's test, and got in front of Boomerang, that they succeeded in bringing him to a halt.

Eradicate climbed slowly down from the seat, and limped around until he stood in front of his pet.

"Yo'—yo're a nice one, ain't yo'?" he demanded in sarcastic tones. "Yo' done enough runnin' in a few minutes fo' a week ob Sundays, an' now I won't be able t' git a move out ob ye! I'se ashamed ob yo', dat's what I is! Puffickly ashamed ob yo'. Go 'long, now, an' yo' won't git no oats dish yeah day! No sah!" and, highly indignant, Eradicate led the now slowly-ambling mule off to the stable.

"I won't shoot again until you have him shut up, Rad!" laughed Tom. "I didn't know you were so close when I set off those guns."

"Dat's all right, Massa Tom," was the reply. "I done called t' you t' wait, but yo' didn't heah me, I 'spects. But it doan't mattah, now. Shoot all yo' laik,

Boomerang won't run any mo' dis week. He done runned his laigs off now. Shoot away!"

But Tom was not quite ready to do this. He wanted to see what effect the first shots had had on his aerial warship, and to learn whether or not the newly devised recoil check had done what was expected of it.

"No more shooting right away," called the young inventor. "I want to see how we made out with the first round. How did she check up, Ned?"

"Fine, as far as I can tell."

"Yes, indeed," added Lieutenant Marbury. "The recoil was hardly noticeable, though, of course, with the full battery of guns in use, it might be more so."

"I hope not," answered Tom. "I haven't used the full strength of the recoil check yet. I can tune it up more, and when I do, and when I have it attached to all the guns, big and little, I think we'll do the trick. But now for a harder test."

The rest of that day was spent in trying out the guns, firing them with practice and service charges, though none of the shells used contained projectiles. It would not have been possible to shoot these, with the Mars held in place in the midst of Tom's factory buildings.

"Well, is she a success, Tom?" asked Ned, when the experimenting was over for the time being.

"I think I can say so—yes," was the answer, with a questioning look at the officer.

"Indeed it is—a great success! We must give the Newton shock absorber due credit."

Ned blushed with pleasure.

"It was only my suggestion," he said. "Tom worked it all out."

"But I needed the Suggestion to start with," the young inventor replied.

"Of course something may develop when you take your craft high in the air, and discharge the guns there," said the lieutenant. "In a rarefied atmosphere the recoil check may not be as effective as at the earth's surface. But, in such case doubtless, you can increase the strength of the springs and the hydrostatic valves."

"Yes, I counted on that," Tom explained. "I shall have to work out that formula, though, and be ready for it. But, on the whole, I am pretty well satisfied."

"And indeed you may well feel that way," commented the government official.

The Mars was hauled back into the shed, and the roof slid shut over the craft. Much yet remained to do on it, but now that Tom was sure the important item of armament was taken care of, he could devote his entire time to the finishing touches.

As his plant was working on several other pieces of machinery, some of it for the United States Government, and some designed for his own use, Tom found himself obliged to hire several new hands. An advertisement in a New

York newspaper brought a large number of replies, and for a day or two Tom was kept busy sifting out the least desirable, and arranging to see those whose answers showed they knew something of the business requirements.

Meanwhile Lieutenant Marbury remained as Tom's guest, and was helpful in making suggestions that would enable the young inventor to meet the government's requirements.

"I'd like, also, to get on the track of those spies who, I am sure, wish to do you harm," said the lieutenant, "but clues seem to be scarce around here."

"They are, indeed," agreed Tom. "I guess the way in which we handled that fire in the red shed sort of discouraged them."

Lieutenant Marbury shook his head.

"They're not so easily discouraged as that," he remarked. "And, with the situation in Europe growing more acute every day, I am afraid some of those foreigners will take desperate measures to gain their ends."

"What particular ends do you mean?"

"Well, I think they will either try to so injure you that you will not be able to finish this aerial warship, or they will damage the craft itself, steal your plans, or damage some of your other inventions."

"But what object would they have in doing such a thing?" Tom wanted to know. "How would that help France, Germany or Russia, to do me an injury?"

"They are seeking to strike at the United States through you," was the answer. "They don't want Uncle Sam to have such formidable weapons as your great searchlight, the giant cannon, or this new warship of the clouds."

"But why not, as long as the United States does not intend to go to war with any of the foreign nations?" Tom inquired.

"No, it is true we do not intend to go to war with any of the conflicting European nations," admitted Lieutenant Marbury, "but you have no idea how jealous each of those foreign nations is of all the others. Each one fears that the United States will cease to be neutral, and will aid one or the other."

"Oh, so that's' it?" exclaimed Tom.

"Yes, each nation, which may, at a moments notice, be drawn into a war with one or more rival nations, fears that we may throw in our lot with its enemies."

"And, to prevent that, they want to destroy some of my inventions?" asked Tom.

"That's the way I believe it will work out. So you must be careful, especially since you have taken on so many new men.

"That's so," agreed the young inventor. "I have had to engage more strangers than ever before, for I am anxious to get the Mars finished and give it a good test. And, now that you have mentioned it, there are some of those men of whom I am a bit suspicious."

"Have they done anything to make you feel that way?" asked the lieutenant.

"Well, not exactly; it is more their bearing, and the manner in which they go about the works. I must keep my eye on them, for it takes only a few discontented men to spoil a whole shop full. I will be on my guard."

"And not only about your new airship and other inventions," said the officer, "but about yourself, personally. Will you do that?"

"Yes, though I don't imagine anything like that will happen."

"Well, be on your guard, at all events," warned Lieutenant Marbury.

As Tom had said, he had been obliged to hire a number of new men. Some of these were machinists who had worked for him, or his father, on previous occasions, and, when tasks were few, had been dismissed, to go to other shops. These men, Tom felt sure, could be relied upon.

But there were a number of others, from New York, and other large cities, of whom Tom was not so sure.

"You have more foreigners than I ever knew you to hire before, Tom," his father said to him one day, coming back from a tour of the shops.

"Yes, I have quite a number," Tom admitted. "But they are all good workmen. They stood the test."

"Yes, some of them are too good," observed the older inventor. "I saw one of them making up a small motor the other day, and he was winding the armature a new way. I spoke to him about it, and he tried to prove that his way was an improvement on yours. Why, he'd have had it short-circuited in no time if I hadn't stopped him."

"Is that so?" asked Tom. "That is news to me. I must look into this."

"Are any of the new men employed on the Mars?" Mr. Swift asked.

"No, not yet, but I shall have to shift some there from other work I think, in order to get finished on time."

"Well, they will bear watching I think," his father said.

"Why, have you seen anything—do you—" began the young man, for Mr. Swift had not been told of the suspicions of the lieutenant.

"Oh, it isn't anything special," the older inventor went on. "Only I wouldn't let a man I didn't know much about get too much knowledge of my latest invention."

"I won't, Dad. Thanks for telling me. This latest craft is sure going to be a beauty."

"Then you think it will work, Tom?"

"I'm sure of it, Dad!"

Mr. Swift shook his head in doubt.

A DAY OFF

Tom Swift pondered long and intently over what his father had said to him. He sat for several minutes in his private office, after the aged inventor had passed out, reviewing in his mind the talk just finished.

"I wonder," said Tom slowly, "if any of the new men could have obtained work here for the purpose of furthering that plot the lieutenant suspects? I wonder if that could be true?"

And the more Tom thought of it, the more he was convinced that such a thing was at least possible.

"I must make a close inspection, and weed out any suspicious characters," he decided, "though I need every man I have working now, to get the Mars finished in time. Yes, I must look into this."

Tom had reached a point in his work where he could leave much to his helpers. He had several good foremen, and, with his father to take general supervision over more important details, the young inventor had more time to himself. Of course he did not lay too many burdens on his father's shoulders since Mr. Swift's health was not of the best.

But Tom's latest idea, the aerial warship, was so well on toward completion that his presence was not needed in that shop more than two or three times a day.

"When I'm not there I'll go about in the other shops, and sort of size up the situation," he decided. "I may be able to get a line on some of those plotters, if there are any here."

Lieutenant Marbury had departed for a time, to look after some personal matters, but he was to return inside of a week, when it was hoped to give the aerial warship its first real test in flight, and under some of the conditions that it would meet with in actual warfare.

As Tom was about to leave his office, to put into effect his new resolution to make a casual inspection of the other shops, he met Koku, the giant, coming in. Koku's hands and face were black with oil and machine filings.

"Well, what have you been doing?" Tom wanted to know. "Did you have an accident?" For Koku had no knowledge of machinery, and could not even be trusted to tighten up a simple nut by himself. But if some one stood near him, and directed him how to apply his enormous strength, Koku could do more than several machines.

"No accident, Master," he replied. "I help man lift that hammer-hammer thing that pounds so. It get stuck!"

"What, the hammer of the drop forger?" cried Tom. "Was that out of order again?"

"Him stuck," explained Koku simply.

There was an automatic trip-hammer in one of the shops, used for pounding out drop forgings, and this hammer seemed to take especial delight in getting out of order. Very often it jammed, or "stuck," as Koku described it, and if the hammer could not be forced back on the channel or upright guide-plates, it meant that it must be taken apart, and valuable time lost. Once Koku had been near when the hammer got out of order, and while the workmen were preparing to dismantle it, the giant seized the big block of steel, and with a heave of his mighty shoulders forced it back on the guides.

"And is that what you did this time?" asked Tom.

"Yes, Master. Me fix hammer," Koku answered. "I get dirty, I no care. Man say I no can fix. I show him I can!"

"What man said that?"

"Man who run hammer. Ha! I lift him by one finger! He say he no like to work on hammer. He want to work on airship. I tell him I tell you, maybe you give him job—he baby! Koku can work hammer. Me fix it when it get stuck."

"Well, maybe you know what you're talking about, but I don't," said Tom, with a pleasant smile at his big helper. "Come on, Koku, we'll go see what it all means."

"Koku work hammer, maybe?" asked the giant hope fully.

"Well, I'll see," half promised Tom. "If it's going to get out of gear all the while it might pay me to keep you at it so you could get it back in place whenever it kicked up a fuss, and so save time. I'll see about it."

Koku led the way to the shop where the triphammer was installed. It was working perfectly now, as Tom could tell by the thundering blows it struck. The man operating it looked up as Tom approached, and, at a gesture from the young inventor, shut off the power.

"Been having trouble here?" asked Tom, noting that the workman was one of the new hands he had hired.

"Yes, sir, a little," was the respectful answer. "This hammer goes on a strike every now and then, and gets jammed. Your giant there forced it back into place, which is more than I could do with a big bar for a lever. He sure has some muscle."

"Yes," agreed Tom, "he's pretty strong. But what's this you said about wanting to give up this job, and go on the airship construction."

The man turned red under his coat of grime.

"I didn't intend him to repeat that to you, Mr. Swift," he said. "I was a little put out at the way this hammer worked. I lose so much time at it that I said I'd like to be transferred to the airship department. I've worked in one before But I'm not making a kick," he added quickly. "Work is too scarce for that."

"I understand," said Tom. "I have been thinking of making a change. Koku seems to like this hammer, and knows how to get it in order once it gets off the guides. You say you have had experience in airship construction?"

"Yes, sir. I've worked on the engines, and on the planes."

"Know anything about dirigible balloons?"

"Yes, I've worked on them, too, but the engineering part is my specialty. I'm a little out of my element on a trip-hammer."

"I see. Well, perhaps I'll give you a trial. Meanwhile you might break Koku in on operating this machine. If I transfer you I'll put him on this hammer."

"Thank you, Mr. Swift! I'll show him all I know about it. Oh, there goes the hammer again!" he exclaimed, for, as he started it up, as Tom turned away, the big piece of steel once more jammed on the channel-plates.

"Me fix!" exclaimed the giant eagerly, anxious for a chance to exhibit his great strength.

"Wait a minute!" exclaimed Tom. "I want to get a look at that machine."

He inspected it carefully before he signaled for Koku to force the hammer back into place. But, if Tom saw anything suspicious, he said nothing. There was, however, a queer look on his face as he turned aside, and he murmured to himself, as he walked away:

"So you want to be transferred to the airship department, do you? Well, we'll see about that We'll see."

Tom had more problems to solve than those of making an aerial warship that would be acceptable to the United States Government.

Ned Newton called on his chum that evening. The two talked of many things, gradually veering around to the subject uppermost in Tom's mind—his new aircraft.

"You're thinking too much of that." Ned warned him. "You're as bad as the time you went for your first flight."

"I suppose I am," admitted Tom. "But the success of the Mars means a whole lot to me. And that's something I nearly forgot. I've got to go out to the shop now. Want to come along, Ned?"

"Sure, though I tell you that you're working too hard—burning the electric light at both ends."

"This is just something simple," Tom said. "It won't take long."

He went out, followed by his chum.

"But this isn't the way to the airship shed," objected the young bank clerk, as he noted in which direction Tom was leading him.

"I know it isn't," Tom replied. "But I want to look at one of the trip-hammers in the forge shop when none of the men is around. I've been having a little trouble there."

"Trouble!" exclaimed his chum. "Has that plot Lieutenant Marbury spoke of developed?"

"Not exactly. This is something else," and Tom told of the trouble with the big hammer.

"I had an idea," the young inventor said, "that the man at the machine let it get out of order purposely, so I'd change him. I want to see if my suspicions are correct."

Tom carefully inspected the hammer by the light of a powerful portable electric lamp Ned held.

"Ha! There it is!" Tom suddenly exclaimed.

"Something wrong?" Ned inquired.

"Yes. This is what's been throwing the hammer off the guides all the while," and Tom pulled out a small steel bolt that had been slipped into an oil hole. A certain amount of vibration, he explained to Ned, would rattle the bolt out so that it would force the hammer to one side, throwing it off the channel-plates, and rendering it useless for the time being.

"A foxy trick," commented Tom. "No wonder the machine got out of kilter so easily."

"Do you think it was done purposely?"

"Well, I'm not going to say. But I'm going to watch that man. He wants to be transferred to the airship department. He put this in the hammer, perhaps, to have an excuse for a change. Well, I'll give it to him."

"You don't mean that you'd take a fellow like that and put him to work on your new aerial warship, do you, Tom?"

"Yes, I think I will, Ned. You see, I look at it this way: I haven't any real proof against him now. He could only laugh at me if I accused him. But you've heard the proverb about giving a calf rope enough and he'll hang himself, haven't you?"

"I think I have."

"Well, I'm going to give this fellow a little rope. I'll transfer him, as he asks, and I'll keep a close watch on him."

"But won't it be risky?"

"Perhaps, but no more so than leaving him in here to work mischief. If he is hatching a plot, the sooner it's over with the better I shall like it. I don't like a shot to hang fire. I'm warned now, and I'll be ready for him. I have a line on whom to suspect. This is the first clue," and Tom held up the incriminating bolt.

"I think you're taking too big a risk, Tom," his chum said. "Why not discharge the man?"

"Because that might only smooth things over for a time. If this plot is being laid the sooner it comes to a head, and breaks, the better. Have it done, short, sharp and quick, is my motto. Yes, I'll shift him in the morning. Oh, but I wish it was all over, and the Mars was accepted by Uncle Sam!" and Tom put his hand to his head with a tired gesture.

"Say, old man!" exclaimed Ned, "what you want is a day off, and I'm going to see that you get it. You need a little vacation."

"Perhaps I do," assented Tom wearily.

"Then you'll have it!" cried Ned. "There's going to be a little picnic to-morrow. Why can't you go with Mary Nestor? She'd like you to take her, I'm sure. Her cousin, Helen Randall, is on from New York, and she wants to go, also."

"How do you know?" asked Tom quickly.

"Because she said so," laughed Ned. "I was over to the house to call. I have met Helen before, and I suggested that you and I would take the two girls, and have a day off. You'll come, won't you?"

"Well, I don't know," spoke Tom slowly. "I ought to—"

"Nonsense! Give up work for one day!" urged Ned. "Come along. It'll do you good—get the cobwebs out of your head."

"All right, I'll go," assented Tom, after a moment's thought.

The next day, having instructed his father and the foremen to look well to the various shops, and having seen that the work on the new aerial warship was progressing favorably, Tom left for a day's outing with his chum and the two girls.

The picnic was held in a grove that surrounded a small lake, and after luncheon the four friends went for a ride in a launch Tom hired. They went to the upper end of the lake, in rather a pretty but lonesome locality.

"Tom, you look tired," said Mary. "I'm sure you've been working too hard!"

"Why, I'm not working any harder than usual," Tom insisted.

"Yes, he is, too!" declared Ned, "and he's running more chances, too."

"Chances?" repeated Mary.

"Oh, that's all bosh!" laughed Tom. "Come on, let's go ashore and walk."

"That suits me," spoke Ned. Helen and Mary assented, and soon the four young persons were strolling through the shady wood.

After a bit the couples became separated, and Tom found himself walking beside Mary in a woodland path. The girl glanced at her companion's face, and ventured:

"A penny for your thoughts, Tom."

"They're worth more than that," he replied gallantly. "I was thinking of—you."

"Oh, how nicely you say it!" she laughed. "But I know better! You're puzzling over some problem. Tell me, what did Ned mean when he hinted at danger? Is there any, Tom?"

"None at all," he assured her. "It's just a soft of notion—"

Mary made a sudden gesture of silence.

"Hark!" she whispered to Tom, "I heard someone mention your name then. Listen!"

A Night Alarm

Mary Nestor spoke with such earnestness, and her action in catching hold of Tom's arm to enjoin silence was so pronounced that, though he had at first regarded the matter in the light of a joke, he soon thought otherwise. He glanced from the girl's face to the dense underbrush on either side of the woodland path.

"What is it, Mary?" he asked in a whisper.

"I don't just know. I heard whispering, and thought it was the rustling of the leaves of the trees. Then someone spoke your name quite loudly. Didn't you hear it?"

Tom shook his head in negation.

"It may be Ned and his friend," he whispered, his lips close to Mary's ear.

"I think not," was her answer. "Listen; there it is again."

Distinctly then, Tom heard, from some opening in the screen of bushes, his own name spoken. "Did you hear it?" asked Mary, barely forming the words with her lips. But Tom could read their motion.

"Yes," he nodded. Then, motioning to Mary to remain where she was, he stepped forward, taking care to tread only on grassy places where there were no little twigs or branches to break and betray his presence. He was working his way toward the sound of the unseen voice.

There was a sudden movement in the bushes, just beyond the spot Tom was making for. He halted quickly and peered ahead. Mary, too, was looking on anxiously.

Tom saw the forms of two men, partially concealed by bushes, walking away from him. The men took no pains to conceal their movements, so Tom was emboldened to advance with less caution. He hurried to where he could get a good view, and, at the sight of one of the men, he uttered an exclamation.

"What is it?" asked Mary, who was now at his side. She had seen that Tom had thrown aside caution, and she had come up to join him.

"That man—I know him!" the young inventor exclaimed. "It is Feldman—the one who wanted to be changed from the trip-hammer to the airship department. But who is that with him?"

As Tom spoke the other turned, and at the sight of his face Mary Nestor said:

"He looks like a Frenchman, with that little mustache and imperial."

"So he is!" exclaimed Tom, in a hoarse whisper. "He must be the Frenchman that Eradicate spoke about. I wonder what this can mean? I didn't know Feldman had left the shop."

"You may know what you're talking about, but I don't, Tom," said Mary, with a smile at her companion. "Are they friends of yours?"

"Hardly," spoke the young inventor dryly. "That one, Feldman, is one of my workmen. He had charge of a drop-forge press and trip-hammer that—"

"Spare me the details, Tom!" interrupted Mary. "You know I don't understand a thing about machinery. The wireless you erected on Earthquake Island was as much as I could comprehend."

"Well, a trip-hammer isn't as complicated as that," spoke Tom, with a laugh, as he noticed that the two men were far enough away so they could not hear him. "What I was going to say was, that one of those men works in our shops. The other I don't know, but I agree with you that he does look like a Frenchman, and old Eradicate had a meeting with a man whom he described as being of that nationality."

"And you say they are not friends of yours?"

"I have no reason to believe they are."

"Then they must be enemies!" exclaimed Mary with quick intuition. "Oh, Tom, you will be careful, won't you?"

"Of course I will, little girl," he said, a note of fondness creeping into his voice, as he covered the small hand with his own large one. "But there is no danger."

"Then why were these men discussing you?"

"I don't know that they were, Mary."

"They mentioned your name."

"Well, that may be. Probably one of them, Feldman, who works for me, was speaking to his companion about the chance for a position. My father and I employ a number of men, you know."

"Well, I suppose it is all right, Tom, and I surely hope it is. But you will be careful, won't you? And you look more worried than you used to. Has anything gone wrong?"

"Not a thing, little girl. Everything is going fine. My new aerial warship will soon make a trial flight, and I'd be pleased to have you as a passenger."

"Would you really, Tom?"

"Of course. Consider that you have the first invitation."

"That's awfully nice of you. But you do look worried, Tom. Has anything troubled you?"

"No, not much. Everything is going all right now. We did have a little trouble at a fire in one of my buildings—"

"A fire! Oh, Tom! You never told me!"

"Well, it didn't amount to much—the only suspicious fact about it was that it seemed to have been of incendiary origin."

Mary seemed much alarmed, and again begged Tom to be on his guard, which he promised to do. Had Mary known the warnings uttered by Lieutenant Marbury she might have had more occasion for worry.

"Do you suppose that hammer man of yours came to these woods to meet that Frenchman and talk about you, Tom?" asked his companion, when the two men had strolled out of sight, and the young people were on their way back to the launch.

"Well, it's possible. I have been warned that foreign spies are trying to get hold of some of my patents, and also to hamper the government in the use of some others I have sold. But they'll have their own troubles to get away with anything. The works are pretty well guarded, and you forget I have the giant, Koku, who is almost a personal bodyguard."

"Yes, but he can't be everywhere at once. Oh, you will be careful, won't you, Tom?"

"Yes, Mary, I will," promised the young inventor. "But don't say anything to Ned about what we just saw and heard."

"Why not?"

"Because he's been at me to hire a couple of detectives to watch over me, and this would give him another excuse. Just don't say anything, and I'll adopt all the precautions I think are needful."

"I will on condition that you do that."

"And I promise I will."

With that Mary had to be content. A little later they joined Ned and his friend, and soon they were moving swiftly down the lake in the launch.

"Well, hasn't it done you good to take a day off?" Ned demanded of his chum, when they were on their homeward way.

"Yes, I think it has," agreed Tom.

"You swung your thoughts into a new channel, didn't you?"

"Oh, yes, I found something new to think about," admitted the young inventor, with a quick look at Mary.

But, though Tom thus passed off lightly the little incident of the day, he gave it serious thought when he was alone.

"Those fellows were certainly talking about me," he reasoned. "I wonder what for? And Feldman left the shop without my knowledge. I'll have to look into that. I wonder if that Frenchy looking chap I saw was the one who tried to pump Eradicate? Another point to settle."

The last was easily disposed of, for, on reaching his shops that afternoon, Tom cross-questioned the colored man, and obtained a most accurate description of the odd foreigner. It tallied in every detail with the man Tom had seen in the woods.

"And now about Feldman," mused Tom, as he went to the foreman of the shop where the suspected man had been employed.

"Yes, Feldman asked for a day off," the foreman said in response to Tom's question. "He claimed his mother was sick, and he wanted to go to see her. I knew you wouldn't object, as we were not rushed in his department."

"Oh, that's all right," said Tom quickly. "Did he say where his mother lived?"

"Over Lafayette way."

"Humph!" murmured Tom. To himself he added: "Queer that he should be near Lake Loraine, in an opposite direction from Lafayette. This will bear an investigation."

The next day Tom made it his business to pass near the hammer that was so frequently out of order. He found Feldman busy instructing Koku in its operation. Tom resolved on a little strategy.

"How is it working, Feldman?" he asked.

"Very well, Mr. Swift. There doesn't seem to be any trouble at all, but it may happen any minute. Koku seems to take to it like a duck to water."

"Well, when he is ready to assume charge let me know."

"And then am I to go into the aeroplane shop?"

"I'll see. By the way, how is your mother?" he asked quickly, looking Feldman full in the face.

"She is much better. I took a day off yesterday to go to see her," the man replied quietly enough, and without sign of embarrassment.

"That's good. Let me see, she lives over near Lake Loraine, doesn't she?"

This time Feldman could not repress a start. But he covered it admirably by stooping over to pick up a tool that fell to the floor.

"No, my mother is in Lafayette," he said. "I don't know where Lake Loraine is."

"Oh," said Tom, as he turned aside to hide a smile. He was sure now he knew at least one of the plotters

But Tom was not yet ready to show his hand. He wanted better evidence than any he yet possessed. It would take a little more time.

Work on the aerial warship was rushed, and it seemed likely that a trial flight could be made before the date set. Lieutenant Marbury sent word that he would be on hand when needed, and in some of the shops, where fittings for the Mars were being made, night and day shifts were working.

"Well, if everything goes well, we'll take her for a trial flight to-morrow," said Tom, coming in from the shops one evening.

"Guns and all?" asked Ned, who had come over to pay his chum a visit. Mr. Damon was also on hand, invoking occasional blessings.

"Guns and all," replied Tom.

Ned had a little vacation from the bank, and was to stay all night, as was Mr. Damon.

What time it was, save that it must be near midnight, Tom could not tell, but he was suddenly awakened by hearing yells from Eradicate:

"Massa Tom! Massa Tom!" yelled the excited colored man. "Git up! Git up! Suffin' turrible am happenin' in de balloon shop. Hurry! An' yo' stan' still, Boomerang, or I'll twist yo' tail, dat's what I will! Hurry, Massa Tom!"

Tom leaped out of bed.

THE CAPTURE

Tom Swift was something like a fireman. He had lived so long in an atmosphere of constant alarms and danger, that he was always ready for almost any emergency. His room was equipped with the end in view that he could act promptly and effectively.

So, when he heard Eradicate's alarm, though he wondered what the old colored man was doing out of bed at that hour, Tom did not stop to reason out that puzzle. He acted quickly.

His first care was to throw on the main switch, connected with a big storage battery, and to which were attached the wires of the lighting system. This at once illuminated every shop in the plant, and also the grounds themselves. Tom wanted to see what was going on. The use of a storage battery eliminated the running of the dynamo all night.

And once he had done this, Tom began pulling on some clothes and a pair of shoes. At the same time he reached out with one hand and pressed a button that sounded an alarm in the sleeping quarters of Koku, the giant, and in the rooms of some of the older and most trusted men.

All this while Eradicate was shouting away, down in the yard.

"Massa Tom! Massa Tom!" he called. "Hurry! Hurry! Dey is killin' Koku!"

"Killing Koku!" exclaimed Tom, as he finished his hasty dressing. "Then my giant must already be in the fracas. I wonder what it's all about, anyhow."

"What's up, Tom?" came Ned's voice from the adjoining room. "I thought I heard a noise."

"Your thoughts do you credit, Ned!" Tom answered. "If you listen right close, you'll hear several noises."

"By Jove! You're right, old man!"

Tom could hear his chum bound out of bed to the floor, and, at the same time, from the big shed where Tom was building his aerial warship came a series of yells and shouts.

"That's Koku's voice!" Tom exclaimed, as he recognized the tones of the giant.

"I'm coming, Tom!" Ned informed his chum. "Wait a minute."

"No time to wait," Tom replied, buttoning his coat as he sped down the hall.

"Oh, Tom, what is it?" asked Mrs. Baggert, the housekeeper, looking from her room.

"I don't know. But don't let dad get excited, no matter what happens. Just put him off until I come back. I think it isn't anything serious."

Mr. Damon, who roomed next to Ned, came out of his own apartment partially dressed.

"Bless my suspenders!" he cried to Tom, those articles just then dangling over his hips. "What is it? What has happened? Bless my steam gauge, don't tell me it's a fire!"

"I think it isn't that," Tom answered. "No alarm has rung. Koku seems to be in trouble."

"Well, he's big enough to look after himself, that's one consolation," chuckled Mr. Damon. "I'll be right with you."

By this time Ned had run out into the hall, and, together, he and Tom sped down the corridor. They could not hear the shouts of Eradicate so plainly now, as he was on the other side of the house.

But when the two young men reached the front porch, they could hear the yells given with redoubled vigor. And, in the glare of the electric lights, Tom saw Eradicate leading along Boomerang, the old mule.

"What is it, Rad? What is it?" demanded the young inventor breathlessly.

"Trouble, Massa Tom! Dat's what it am! Trouble!"

"I know that—but what kind?"

"De worstest kind, I 'spects, Massa Tom. Listen to it!"

From the interior of the big shed, not far from the house, Tom and Ned heard a confused jumble of shouts, cries and pleadings, mingled with the rattle of pieces of metal, and the banging of bits of wood. And, above all that, like the bellowing of a bull, was noted the rumbling voice of Koku, the giant.

"Come on, Ned!" Tom cried.

"It's suah trouble, all right," went on Eradicate. "Mah mule, Boomerang, had a touch ob de colic, an' I got up t' gib him some hot drops an' walk him around, when I heard de mostest terrific racket-sound, and den I 'spected trouble was comm."

"It isn't coming—it's here!" called Tom, as he sped toward the big shop. Ned was but a step behind him. The big workshop where the aerial warship was being built was, like the other buildings, brilliantly illuminated by the lights Tom had switched on. The young inventor also saw several of his employees speeding toward the same point.

Torn was the first to reach the small door of the shed. This was built in one of the two large main doors, which could be swung open when it was desired to slide the Mars in from the ground, and not admit it through the roof.

"Look!" cried Tom, pointing.

Ned looked over his chum's shoulder and saw the giant, Koku, struggling with four men—powerful men they were, too, and they seemed bent on mischief.

For they came at Koku from four sides, seeking to hold his hands and feet so that he could not fight them back. On the floor near where the struggle was taking place was a coil of rope, and it was evident that it had been the intention of the men to overcome Koku and truss him up, so that he would not interfere with what they intended to do. But Koku was a match for even the four men, powerful as they were.

"We're here, Koku!" cried Tom. "Watch for an opening, Ned!" he called to his chum.

The sound of Tom's voice disconcerted at least two of the attackers, for they looked around quickly, and this was fatal to their chances.

Though such a big man, Koku was exceptionally quick, and no sooner did he see his advantage, as two of the men turned their gaze away from him, than he seized it.

Suddenly tearing loose his hands from the grip of the two men who had looked around, Koku shot out his right and left fists, and secured good hold on the necks of two of his enemies. The other two, at his back, were endeavoring to pull him over, but the giant's sturdy legs still held.

So big was Koku's hands that they almost encircled the necks of his antagonists. Then happened a curious thing.

With a shout that might have done credit to some ancient cave-dweller of the stone age, Koku spread out his mighty arms, and held apart the two men he had grasped. In vain they struggled to free themselves from that terrible grip. Their faces turned purple, and their eyes bulged out.

"He's choking them to death!" shouted Ned.

But Koku was not needlessly cruel.

A moment later, with a quick and sudden motion he bent his arms, bringing toward each other the two men he held as captives. Their heads came together with a dull thud, and a second later Koku allowed two limp bodies to slip from his grip to the floor.

"He's done for them!" Tom cried. "Knocked them unconscious. Good for you, Koku!"

The giant grunted, and then, with a quick motion, slung himself around, hoping to bring the enemies at his back within reach of his powerful arms. But there was no need of this.

As soon as the other two ruffians had seen their companions fall to the floor of the shop they turned and fled, leaping from an open window.

"There they go!" cried Ned.

"Some of the other men can chase them," said the young inventor. "We'll tie up the two Koku has captured."

As he approached nearer to the unconscious captives Tom uttered a cry of surprise, for he recognized them as two of the new men he had employed.

"What can this mean?" he asked wonderingly.

He glanced toward the window through which the two men had jumped to escape, and he was just in time to see one of them run past the open door. The face of this one was under a powerful electric light, and Tom at once recognized the man as Feldman, the worker who had had so much trouble with the trip-hammer.

"This sure is a puzzle," marveled Tom. "My own men in the plot! But why did they attack Koku?"

The giant, bending over the men he had knocked unconscious by beating their heads together, seemed little worse for the attack.

"We tie 'em up," he said grimly, as he brought over the rope that had been intended for himself.

The First Flight

Little time was lost in securing the two men who bad been so effectively rendered helpless by Koku's ready, if rough, measures. One of them was showing signs of returning consciousness now, and Tom, not willing to inflict needless pain, even on an enemy, told one of his men, summoned by the alarm, to bring water. Soon the two men opened their eyes, and looked about them in dazed fashion.

"Did—did anything hit me?" asked one meekly.

"It must have been a thunderbolt," spoke the other dreamily. "But it didn't look like a storm."

"Oh, dere was a storm, all right," chuckled Eradicate, who, having left his mule, Boomerang outside, came into the shed. "It was a giant storm all right."

The men put their hands to their heads, and seemed to comprehend. They looked at the rope that bound their feet. Their forearms had been loosened to allow them to take a drink of water.

"What does this mean—Ransom—Kurdy?" asked Tom sternly, when the men seemed able to talk. "Did you attack Koku?"

"It looks as though he had the best of us, whether we did or not," said the man Tom knew as Kurdy. "Whew, how my head aches!"

"Me sorry," said Koku simply.

"Not half as sorry as we are," returned Ransom ruefully.

"What does it mean?" asked Tom sternly. "There were four of you. Feldman and one other got away."

"Oh, trust Feldman for getting away," sneered Kurdy. "He always leaves his friends in the lurch."

"Was this a conspiracy?" demanded Tom.

The two captives looked at one another, sitting bound on the floor of the shop, their backs against some boxes.

"I guess it's all up, and we might as well make a clean breast of it," admitted Kurdy.

"Perhaps it would be better," said Tom quietly. "Eradicate," he went on, to the colored man, "go to the house and tell Mrs. Baggert that everything is all right and no one hurt."

"No one hurt, Massa Tom? What about dem dere fellers?" and the colored man pointed to the captives.

"Well, they're not hurt much," and Tom permitted himself a little smile. "I don't want my father to worry. Tell him everything is all right."

"All right, Massa Tom. I'se gwine right off. I'se got t' look after mah mule, Boomerang, too. I'se gwine," and he shuffled away.

"Who else besides Feldman got away?" asked Tom, looking alternately at the prisoners.

They hesitated a moment about answering.

"We might as well give up, I tell you," spoke Kurdy to Ransom.

"All right, go ahead, we'll have to take our medicine. I might have known it would turn out this way—going in for this sort of thing. It's the first bit of crooked business I ever tried," the man said earnestly, "and it will be the last—believe me!"

"Who was the fourth man?" Tom repeated.

"Harrison," answered Kurdy, naming one of the most efficient of the new machinists Tom had hired during the rush.

"Harrison, who has been working on the motor?" cried the young inventor.

"Yes," said Ransom.

"I'm sorry to learn that," Tom went on in a low voice. "He was an expert in his line. But what was your object, anyhow, in attacking Koku?"

"We didn't intend to attack him," explained Ransom, "but he came in when we were at work, and as he went for us we tried to stand him off. Then your colored man heard the racket, and—well, I guess you know the rest."

"But I don't understand why you came into this shed at night," went on Tom. "No one is allowed in here. You had no right, and Koku knew that. What did you want?"

"Look here!" exclaimed Kurdy, "I said we'd make a clean breast of it, and we will. We're only a couple of tools, and we were foolish ever to go in with those fellows; or rather, in with that Frenchman, who promised us big money if we succeeded."

"Succeeded in what?" demanded the young inventor.

"In damaging your new aerial warship, or in getting certain parts of it so he could take them away with him."

Tom gave a surprised whistle.

"A frenchman!" he exclaimed. "Is he one of the—?"

"Yes, he's one of the foreign spies," interrupted Ransom. "You'd find it out, anyhow, if we didn't tell you. They are after you, Tom Swift, and after your machines. They had vowed to get them by fair means or foul, for some of the European governments are desperate."

"But we were only tools in their hands. So were Feldman and Harrison, but they knew more about the details. We were only helping them."

"Then we must try to capture them," decided Tom. "Ned, see if the chase had any results. I'll look after these chaps—Koku and I."

"Oh, we give in," admitted Kurdy. "We know when we've had enough," and he rubbed his head gently where the giant had banged it against that of his fellow-conspirator.

"Do you mean that you four came into this shop, at midnight, to damage the Mars?" asked Tom.

"That's about it, Mr. Swift," replied Kurdy rather shamefacedly. "We were to damage it beyond repair, set fire to the whole place, if need be, and, at the same time, take away certain vital parts

"Harrison, Feldman, Ransom and I came in, thinking the coast was clear. But Koku must have seen us enter, or he suspected we were here, for he came in after us, and the fight began. We couldn't stop him, and he did for us. I'm rather glad of it, too, for I never liked the work. It was only that they tempted me with a promise of big money."

"Who tempted you?" demanded Tom.

"That Frenchman—La Foy, he calls himself, and some other foreigners in your shops."

"Are there foreigners here?" cried Tom.

"Bless my chest protector!" cried Mn Damon, who had come in and had been a silent listener to this. "Can it be possible?"

"That's the case," went on Kurdy. "A lot of the new men you took on are foreign spies from different European nations. They are trying to learn all they can about your plans, Mr. Swift!"

"Are they friendly among themselves?" asked Tom.

"No; each one is trying to get ahead of the other. So far the Frenchman seems to have had the best of it. But tonight his plan failed."

"Tell me more about it," urged Tom.

"That's about all we know," spoke Ransom. "We were only hired to do the rough work. Those higher up didn't appear. Feldman was only a step above us."

"Then my suspicions of him were justified," thought Tom. "He evidently met La Foy in the woods to make plans. But Koku and Eradicate spoiled them."

The two captives seemed willing enough to make a confession, but they did not know much. As they said, they were merely tools, acting for others. And events had happened just as they had said.

The four conspirators had managed, by means of a false key, and by disconnecting the burglar alarm, to enter the airship shed. They were about to proceed with their work of destruction when Koku came on the scene.

The giant's appearance was due to accident. He acted as a sort of night watchman, making a tour of the buildings, but he entered the shed where the Mars was because, that day, he had left his knife in there, and wanted to get it. Only for that he would not have gone in. When he entered he surprised the four men.

Of course he attacked them at once, and they sprang at him. Then ensued a terrific fight. Eradicate, arising to doctor his mule, as he had said, heard the noise, and saw what was going on. He gave the alarm.

"Well, Ned, any luck?" asked Tom, as his chum came in.

"No, they got away, Tom. I had a lot of your men out helping me search the grounds, but it wasn't of much use."

"Particularly if you depended on some of my men," said Tom bitterly.

"What do you mean?"

"I mean that the place is filled with spies, Ned! But we will sift them out in the morning. This has been a lucky night for me. It was touch and go. Now, then, Koku, take these fellows and lock them up somewhere until morning. Ned, you and I will remain on guard here the rest of the night."

"I'm with you, Tom."

"Will you be a bit easy on us, considering what we told you?" asked Kurdy.

"I'll do the best I can," said Tom, gently, making no promises.

The two captives were put in secure quarters, and the rest of the night passed quietly. During the fight in the airship shed some machinery and tools had been broken, but no great amount of damage was done. Tom and Ned passed the remaining hours of darkness there.

A further search was made in the morning for the two conspirators who had escaped, but no trace of them was found. Tom then realized why Feldman was so anxious to be placed in the aeroplane department—it was in order that he might have easier access to the Mars.

A technical charge was made against the two prisoners, sufficient to hold them for some time. Then Tom devoted a day to weeding out the suspected foreigners in his place. All the new men were discharged, though some protested against this action.

"Probably I am hitting some of the innocent in punishing those who, if they had the chance, would become guilty," Tom said to his chum, "but it cannot be helped—I can't afford to take any chances."

The Mars was being put in shape for her first flight. The guns, fitted with the recoil shock absorbers, were mounted, and Lieutenant Marbury had returned to go aloft in the big aerial warship. He congratulated Tom on discovering at least one plot in time.

"But there may be more," he warned the young inventor. "You are not done with them yet."

The Mars was floated out of her hangar, and made ready for an ascent. Tom, Ned, Lieutenant Marbury, Mr. Damon, and several workmen were to be the first passengers. Tom was busy going over the various parts to see that nothing had been forgotten.

"Well, I guess we re ready," he finally announced. "All aboard!"

"Bless my insurance policy!" exclaimed Mr. Damon. "Now that the time comes I almost wish I wasn't going."

"Nonsense!" exclaimed Tom. "You're not going to back out at the last minute. All aboard! Cast off the ropes!" he cried to the assistants.

A moment later the Mars, the biggest airship Tom Swift had ever constructed, arose from the earth like some great bird, and soared aloft.

In Danger

"Well, Tom, we're moving!" cried Ned Newton, clapping his chum on the back, as he stood near him in the pilot-house. "We're going up, old sport!"

"Of course we are," replied Tom. "You didn't think it wouldn't go up, did you?"

"Well, I wasn't quite sure," Ned confessed. "You know you were so worried about—"

"Not about the ship sailing," interrupted Tom. "It was only the effect the firing of the guns might have. But I think we have that taken care of."

"Bless my pin cushion!" cried Mr. Damon, as he looked over the rail at the earth below. "We're moving fast, Tom."

"Yes, we can make a quicker ascent in this than in most aeroplanes," Tom said, "for they have to go up in a slanting direction. But we can't quite equal their lateral speed."

"Just how fast do you think you can travel when you are in first-class shape?" asked Lieutenant Marbury, as he noted how the Mars was behaving on this, the first trip.

"Well, I set a limit of seventy-five miles an hour," the young inventor replied, as he shifted various levers and handles, to change the speed of the mechanism. "But I'm afraid we won't quite equal that with all our guns on board. But I'm safe in saying sixty, I think."

"That will more than satisfy the government requirements," the officer said. "But, of course, your craft will have to come up to expectations and requirements in the matter of armament."

"I'll give you every test you want," declared Tom, with a smile. "And now we'll see what the Mars can do when put to it."

Up and up went the big dirigible aerial warship. Had you been fortunate enough to have seen her you would have observed a craft not unlike, in shape, the German Zeppelins. But it differed from those war balloons in several important particulars.

Tom's craft was about six hundred feet long, and the diameter of the gas bag, amidships, was sixty feet, slightly larger than the largest Zeppelin. Below the bag, which, as I have explained, was made up of a number of gas-tight compartments, hung from wire cables three cabins. The forward one was a sort of pilot-house, containing various instruments for navigating the ship of the air, observation rooms, gauges for calculating firing ranges, and the steering apparatus.

Amidships, suspended below the great bag, were the living and sleeping quarters, where food was cooked and served and where those who operated the craft could spend their leisure time. Extra supplies were also stored there.

At the stern of the big bag was the motor-room, where gas was generated to fill the balloon compartments when necessary, where the gasoline and electrical apparatus were installed, and where the real motive power of the craft was located. Here, also, was carried the large quantity of gasoline and oil needed for a long voyage. The Mars could carry sufficient fuel to last for over a week, provided no accidents occurred.

There was also an arrangement in the motor compartment, so that the ship could be steered and operated from there. This was in case the forward pilot-house should be shot away by an enemy. And, also, in the motor compartment were the sleeping quarters for the crew.

All three suspended cabins were connected by a long covered runway, so that one could pass from the pilot-house to the motor-room and back again through the amidship cabin

At the extreme end of the big bag were the various rudders and planes, designed to keep the craft on a level keel, automatically, and to enable it to make headway against a strong wind. The motive power consisted of three double-bladed wooden propellers, which could be operated together or independently. A powerful gasoline engine was the chief motive power, though there was an auxiliary storage battery, which would operate an electrical motor and send the ship along for more than twenty-four hours in case of accident to the gasoline engine.

There were many other pieces of apparatus aboard, some not completely installed, the uses of which I shall mention from time to time, as the story progresses. The gas-generating machine was of importance, for there would be a leakage and shrinking of the vapor from the big bag, and some means must be provided for replenishing it.

"You don't seem to have forgotten anything, Tom," said Ned admiringly, as they soared upward.

"We can tell better after we've flown about a bit," observed the young inventor, with a smile. "I expect we shall have to make quite a number of changes."

"Are you going far?" asked Mr. Damon.

"Why, you're not frightened, are you?" inquired Tom. "You have been up in airships with me before."

"Oh, no, I'm not frightened!" exclaimed the odd man. "Bless my suspenders, no! But I promised my wife I'd be back this evening, and

"We'll sail over toward Waterford," broke in Tom, "and I'll drop you down in your front yard."

"No, don't do that! Don't! I beg of you!" cried Mr. Damon. "You see—er—Tom, my wife doesn't like me to make these trips. Of course, I understand there is no danger, and I like them. But it's just as well not to make her worry-you understand!"

"Oh, all right," replied Tom, with a laugh. "Well, we're not going far on this trip. What I want to do, most of all, is to test the guns, and see if the recoil check will work as well when we are aloft as it did down on the ground. You know a balloon isn't a very stable base for a gun, even one of light caliber."

"No, it certainly is not," agreed Lieutenant Marbury, "and I am interested in seeing how you will overcome the recoil."

"We'll have a test soon," announced Tom.

Meanwhile the Mars, having reached a considerable height, being up so far, in fact, that the village of Shopton could scarcely be distinguished, Tom set the signal that told the engine-room force to start the propellers. This would send them ahead.

Some of Tom's most trusted workmen formed the operating crew, the young inventor taking charge of the pilot-house himself.

"Well she seems to run all right," observed Lieutenant Marbury, as the big craft surged ahead just below a stratum of white, fleecy clouds.

"Yes, but not as fast as I'd like to see her go, Tom replied. "Of course the machinery is new, and it will take some little time for it to wear down smooth. I'll speed her up a little now."

They had been running for perhaps ten minutes when Tom shoved over the hand of an indicator that communicated with the engine-room from the pilot-house. At once the Mars increased her speed.

"She can do it!" cried Ned.

"Bless my-hat! I should say so!" cried Mr. Damon, for he was standing outside the pilot-house just then, on the "bridge," and the sudden increase of speed lifted his hat from his head.

"There you are—caught on the fly!" cried Ned, as he put up his hand just in time to catch the article in question.

"Thanks! Guess I'd better tie it fast," remarked the odd man, putting his hat on tightly.

The aerial warship was put through several evolutions to test her stability, and to each one she responded well, earning the praise of the government officer. Up and down, to one side and the other, around in big circles, and even reversing, Tom sent his craft with a true hand and eye. In a speed test fifty-five miles was registered against a slight wind, and the young inventor said he knew he could do better than that as soon as some of the machinery was running more smoothly.

"And now suppose we get ready for the gun tests," suggested Tom, when they had been running for about an hour.

"That's what I'm mostly interested in," said Lieutenant Marbury. "It's easy enough to get several good types of dirigible balloons, but few of them will stand having a gun fired from them, to say nothing of several guns."

"Well, I'm not making any rash promises," Tom went on, "but I think we can turn the trick."

The armament of the Mars was located around the center cabin. There were two large guns, fore and aft, throwing a four-inch projectile, and two smaller calibered quick-firers on either beam. The guns were mounted on pedestals that enabled the weapons to fire in almost any direction, save straight up, and of course the balloon bag being above them prevented this. However, there was an arrangement whereby a small automatic quick-firer could be sent up to a platform built on top of the gas envelope itself, and a man stationed there could shoot at a rival airship directly overhead.

But the main deck guns could be elevated to an angle of nearly forty-five degrees, so they could take care of nearly any hostile aircraft that approached.

"But where are the bombs I heard you speaking of?" asked Ned, as they finished looking at the guns.

"Here they are," spoke Tom, as he pointed to a space in the middle of the main cabin floor. He lifted a brass plate, and disclosed three holes, covered with a strong wire netting that could be removed. "The bombs will be dropped through those holes," explained the young inventor, "being released by a magnetic control when the operator thinks he has reached a spot over the enemy's city or fortification where the most damage will be done. I'll show you how they work a little later. Now we'll have a test of some of the guns."

Tom called for some of his men to take charge of the steering and running of the Mars while he and Lieutenant Marbury prepared to fire the two larger weapons. This was to be one of the most important tests.

Service charges had been put in, though, of course, no projectiles would be used, since they were then flying over a large city not far from Shopton.

"We'll have to wait until we get out over the ocean to give a complete test, with a bursting shell," Tom said.

He and Lieutenant Marbury were beside a gun, and were about to fire it, when suddenly, from the stern of the ship, came a ripping, tearing sound, and, at the same time, confused shouts came from the crew's quarters.

"What is it?" cried Tom.

"One of the propellers!" was the answer. "It's split, and has torn a big hole in the gas bag!"

"Bless my overshoes!" cried Mr. Damon. "We're going down!"

All on board the Mars became aware of a sudden sinking sensation.

TOM IS WORRIED

"Steady, all!" came in even tones from Tom Swift. Not for an instant had he lost his composure. For it was an accident, that much was certain, and one that might endanger the lives of all on board.

Above the noise of the machinery in the motor room could be heard the thrashing and banging of the broken or loose propeller-blade. Just what its condition was, could not be told, as a bulge of the gas bag hid it from the view of those gathered about the gun, which was about to be fired when the alarm was given.

"We're sinking!" cried Mr. Damon. "We're going down, Tom!"

"That's nothing," was the cool answer. "It is only for a moment. Only a few of the gas compartments can be torn. There will soon enough additional gas in the others to lift us again."

And so it proved. The moment the pressure of the lifting gas in the big oiled silk and aluminum container was lowered, it started the generating machine, and enough extra gas was pumped into the uninjured compartments to compensate for the loss.

"We're not falling so fast now," observed Ned.

"No, and we'll soon stop falling altogether," calmly declared Tom. "Too bad this accident had to happen, though."

"It might have been much worse, my boy!" exclaimed the lieutenant. "That's a great arrangement of yours—the automatic gas machine."

"It's on the same principle as the air brakes of a trolley car," explained Tom, when a look at the indicators showed that the Mars had ceased falling and remained stationary in the air. Tom had also sent a signal to the engine-room to shut off the power, so that the two undamaged propellers, as well as the broken one, ceased revolving.

"In a trolley car, you see," Tom went on, when the excitement had calmed down, "as soon as the air pressure in the tanks gets below a certain point, caused by using the air for a number of applications of the brakes, it lets a magnetized bar fall, and this establishes an electrical connection, starting the air pump. The pump forces more air into the tanks until the pressure is enough to throw the pump switch out of connection, when the pump stops. I use the same thing here."

"And very clever it is," said Mr. Damon. "Do you suppose the danger is all over, Tom?"

"For the time being, yes. But we must unship that damaged propeller, and go on with the two."

The necessary orders were given, and several men from the engine-room at once began the removal of the damaged blades.

As several spare ones were carried aboard one could be put on in place of the broken one, had this been desired. But Tom thought the accident a good chance to see how his craft would act with only two-thirds of her motive force available, so he did not order the damaged propeller replaced. When it was lowered to the deck it was carefully examined.

"What made it break?" Ned wanted to know.

"That's a question I can't answer," Tom replied. "There may have been a defect in the wood, but I had it all carefully examined before I used it."

The propeller was one of the "built-up" type, with alternate layers of ash and mahogany, but some powerful force had torn and twisted the blades. The wood was splintered and split, and some jagged pieces, flying off at a tangent, so great was the centrifugal force, had torn holes in the strong gas bag.

"Did something hit it; or did it hit something?" asked Ned as he saw Tom carefully examining the broken blades.

"Hard to say. I'll have a good look at this when we get back. Just now I want to finish that gun test we didn't get a chance to start."

"You don't mean to say you're going to keep on, and with the balloon damaged; are you?" cried Mr. Damon, in surprise.

"Certainly—why not?" Tom replied. "In warfare accidents may happen, and if the Mars can't go on, after a little damage like this, what is going to happen when she's fired on by a hostile ship? Of course I'm going on!"

"Bless my necktie!" ejaculated the odd man.

"That's the way to talk!" exclaimed Lieutenant Marbury. "I'm with you."

There really was very little danger in proceeding. The Mars was just as buoyant as before, for more gas had been automatically made, and forced into the uninjured compartments of the bag. At the same time enough sand ballast had been allowed to run out to make the weight to be lifted less in proportion to the power remaining.

True, the speed would be less, with two propellers instead of three, and the craft would not steer as well, with the torn ends of the gas bag floating out behind. But this made a nearer approach to war conditions, and Tom was always glad to give his inventions the most severe tests possible.

So, after a little while, during which it was seen that the Mars was proceeding almost normally, the matter of discharging the guns was taken up again.

The weapons were all ready to fire, and when Tom had attached the pressure gauges to note how much energy was expended in the recoil, he gave the word to fire.

The two big weapons were discharged together, and for a moment after the report echoed out among the cloud masses every soul on the ship feared another accident had happened.

For the big craft rolled and twisted, and seemed about to turn turtle. Her forward progress was halted, momentarily, and a cry of fear came from several of the members of the crew, who had had only a little experience in aircraft.

"What's the matter?" cried Ned. "Something go wrong?"

"A little," admitted Tom, with a rueful look on his face. "Those recoil checks didn't work as well in practice as they did in theory."

"Are you sure they are strong enough?" asked Lieutenant Marbury.

"I thought so," spoke Tom. "I'll put more tension on the spring next time."

"Bless my watch chain!" cried Mr. Damon. "You aren't going to fire those guns again; are you, Tom?"

"Why not? We can't tell what's the matter, nor get things right without experimenting. There's no danger."

"No danger! Don't you call nearly upsetting the ship danger?"

"Oh, well, if she turns over she'll right herself again," Tom said. "The center of gravity is low, you see. She can't float in any position but right side up, though she may turn over once or twice."

"Excuse me!" said Mr. Damon firmly. "I'd rather go down, if it's all the same to you. If my wife ever knew I was here I'd never hear the last of it!"

"We'll go down soon," Tom promised. "But I must fire a couple of shots more. You wouldn't call the recoil checks a success, would you?" and the young inventor appealed to the government inspector.

"No, I certainly would not," was the prompt answer. "I am sorry, too, for they seemed to be just what was needed. Of course I understand this is not an official test, and I am not obliged to make a report of this trial. But had it been, I should have had to score against you.

"I realize that, and I'm not asking any favors. but I'll try it again with the recoil checks tightened up. I think the hydrostatic valves were open too much, also."

Preparations were now made for firing the four-inch guns once more. All this while the Mars had been speeding around in space, being about two miles up in the air. Tom's craft was not designed to reach as great an elevation as would be possible in an aeroplane, since to work havoc to an enemy's fortifications by means of aerial bombs they do not need to be dropped from a great height.

In fact, experiments in Germany have shown that bombs falling from a great height are less effective than those falling from an airship nearer the earth. For a bomb, falling from a height of two miles, acquires enough momentum to penetrate far into the earth, so that much of the resultant explosive force is expended in a downward direction, and little damage is done to the fortifications. A bomb dropped from a lower altitude, expending its force on all sides, does much more damage.

On the other hand, in destroying buildings, it has been found desirable to drop a bomb from a good height so that it may penetrate even a protected roof, and explode inside.

Once more Tom made ready to fire, this time having given the recoil checks greater resistance. But though there was less motion imparted to the airship when the guns were discharged, there was still too much for comfort, or even safety.

"Well, something's wrong, that's sure," remarked Tom, in rather disappointed tones as he noted the effect of the second shots. "If we get as much recoil from the two guns, what would happen if we fired them all at once?"

"Don't do it! Don't do it, I beg of you!" entreated Mr. Damon. "Bless my toothbrush—don't do it!"

"I won't—just at present," Tom said, ruefully. "I'm afraid I'll have to begin all over again, and proceed along new lines."

"Well, perhaps you will," said the lieutenant. "But you may invent something much better than anything you have now. There is no great rush. Take your time, and do something good."

"Oh, I'll get busy on it right away," Tom declared. "We'll go down now, and start right to work. I'm afraid, Ned, that our idea of a door-spring check isn't going to work."

"I might have known my idea wouldn't amount to anything," said the young bank clerk.

"Oh, the idea is all right," declared Tom, "but it wants modifying. There is more power to those recoils than I figured, though our first experiments seemed to warrant us in believing that we had solved the problem."

"Are you going to try the bomb-dropping device?" asked the lieutenant.

"Yes, there can't be any recoil from that," Tom said. "I'll drop a few blank ones, and see how accurate the range finders are.

While his men were getting ready for this test Tom bent over the broken propeller, looking from that to the recoil checks, which had not come up to expectations. Then he shook his head in a worried and puzzled manner.

An Ocean Flight

Dropping bombs from an aeroplane, or a dirigible balloon, is a comparatively simple matter. Of course there are complications that may ensue, from the danger of carrying high explosives in the limited quarters of an airship, with its flammable gasoline fuel, and ever-present electric spark, to the possible premature explosion of the bomb itself. But they seem to be considered minor details now.

On the other hand, while it is comparatively easy to drop a bomb from a moving aeroplane, or dirigible balloon, it is another matter to make the bomb fall just where it will do the most damage to the enemy. It is not easy to gauge distances, high up in the air, and then, too, allowance must be made for the speed of the aircraft, the ever-increasing velocity of a falling body, and the deflection caused by air currents.

The law of velocity governing falling bodies is well known. It varies, of course, according to the height, but in general a body falling freely toward the earth, as all high-school boys know, is accelerated at the rate of thirty-two feet per second. This law has been taken advantage of by the French in the present European war. The French drop from balloons, or aeroplanes, a steel dart about the size of a lead pencil, and sharpened in about the same manner. Dropping from a height of a mile or so, that dart will acquire enough velocity to penetrate a man from his head all the way through his body to his feet.

But in dropping bombs from an airship the damage intended does not so much depend on velocity. It is necessary to know how fast the bomb falls in order to know when to set the time fuse that will explode it; though some bombs will explode on concussion.

At aeroplane meets there are often bomb-dropping contests, and balls filled with a white powder (that will make a dust-cloud on falling, and so show where they strike) are used to demonstrate the birdman's accuracy.

"We'll see how our bomb-release works," Tom went on. "But we'll have to descend a bit in order to watch the effect."

"You're not going to use real bombs, are you, Tom?" asked Ned.

"Indeed not. Just chalk-dust ones for practice. Now here is where the bombs will be placed," and he pointed to the three openings in the floor of the amidship cabin. The wire nettings were taken out and one could look down through the holes to the earth below, the ground being nearer now, as Tom had let out some of the lifting gas.

"Here is the range-finder and the speed calculator," the young inventor went on as he indicated the various instruments. "The operator sits here, where he can tell when is the most favorable moment for releasing the bomb."

Tom took his place before a complicated set of instruments, and began manipulating them. One of his assistants, under the direction of Lieutenant Marbury, placed in the three openings bombs, made of light cardboard, just the size of a regular bomb, but filled with a white powder that would, on breaking, make a dust-cloud which could be observed from the airship.

"I have first to determine where I want to drop the bomb," Tom explained, "and then I have to get my distance from it on the range-finder. Next I have to know how fast I am traveling, and how far up in the air I am, to tell what the velocity of the falling bomb will attain at a certain time. This I can do by means of these instruments. some of which I have adapted from those used by the government," he said, with a nod to the officer.

"That's right—take all the information you can get," was the smiling response.

"We will now assume that the bombs are in place in the holes in the floor of the cabin," Tom went on. "As I sit here I have before me three buttons. They control the magnets that hold the bombs in place. If I press one of the buttons it breaks the electrical current, the magnet no longer has any attraction, and it releases the explosive. Now look down. I am going to try and drop a chalk bomb near that stone fence."

The Mars was then flying over a large field and a stone fence was in plain view.

"Here she goes!" cried Tom, as he made some rapid calculations from his gauge instruments. There was a little click and the chalk bomb dropped. There was a plate glass floor in part of the cabin, and through this the progress of the pasteboard bomb could be observed.

"She'll never go anywhere near the fence!" declared Ned. "You let it drop too soon, Tom!"

"Did I? You just watch. I had to allow for the momentum that would be given the bomb by the forward motion of the balloon."

Hardly had Tom spoken than a puff of white was seen on the very top of the fence.

"There it goes?" cried the lieutenant. "You did the trick, Swift!"

"Yes, I thought I would. Well, that shows my gauges are correct, anyhow. Now we'll try the other two bombs."

In succession they were released from the bottom of the cabin, at other designated objects. The second one was near a tree. It struck within five feet, which was considered good.

"And I'll let the last one down near that scarecrow in the field," said Tom, pointing to a ragged figure in the middle of a patch of corn.

Down went the cardboard bomb, and so good was the aim of the young inventor that the white dust arose in a cloud directly back of the scarecrow.

And then a queer thing happened. For the figure seemed to come to life, and Ned, who was watching through a telescope, saw a very much excited farmer looking up with an expression of the greatest wonder on his face. He saw the balloon over his head, and shook his fist at it, evidently thinking he had had a narrow escape. But the pasteboard bomb was so light that, had it hit him, he would not have been injured, though he might have been well dusted.

"Why, that was a man! Bless my pocketbook!" cried Mr. Damon.

"I guess it was," agreed Tom. "I took it for a scarecrow."

"Well, it proved the accuracy of your aim, at any rate," observed Lieutenant Marbury. "The bomb dropping device of your aerial warship is perfect—I can testify to that."

"And I'll have the guns fixed soon, so there will be no danger of a recoil, too," added Tom Swift, with a determined look on his face.

"What's next?" asked Mr. Damon, looking at his watch. "I really ought to be home, Tom."

"We're going back now, and down. Are you sure you don't want me to drop you in your own front yard, or even on your roof? I think I could manage that."

"Bless my stovepipe, no, Tom! My wife would have hysterics. Just land me at Shopton and I'll take a car home."

The damaged airship seemed little the worse for the test to which she had been subjected, and made her way at good speed in the direction of Tom's home. Several little experiments were tried on the way back. They all worked well, and the only two problems Tom had to solve were the taking care of the recoil from the guns and finding out why the propeller had broken.

A safe landing was made, and the Mars once more put away in her hangar. Mr. Damon departed for his home, and Lieutenant Marbury again took up his residence in the Swift household.

"Well, Tom, how did it go?" asked his father.

"Not so very well. Too much recoil from the guns."

"I was afraid so. You had better drop this line of work, and go at something else."

"No, Dad!" Tom cried. "I'm going to make this work. I never had anything stump me yet, and I'm not going to begin now!"

"Well, that's a good spirit to show," said the aged inventor, with a shake of his head, "but I don't believe you'll succeed, Tom."

"Yes I will, Dad! You just wait."

Tom decided to begin on the problem of the propeller first, as that seemed more simple. He knew that the gun question would take longer.

"Just what are you trying to find out, Tom?" asked Ned, a few nights later, when he found his chum looking at the broken parts of the propeller.

"Trying to discover what made this blade break up and splinter that way. It couldn't have been centrifugal force, for it wasn't strong enough."

Tom was "poking" away amid splinters, and bits of broken wood, when he suddenly uttered an exclamation, and held up something. "Look!" he cried. "I believe I've found it."

"What?" asked Ned.

"The thing that weakened the propeller. Look at this, and smell!" He held out a piece of wood toward Ned. The bank employee saw where a half-round hole had been bored in what remained of the blade, and from that hole came a peculiar odor.

"It's some kind of acid," ventured Ned.

"That's it!" cried Tom. "Someone bored a hole in the propeller, and put in some sort of receptacle, or capsule, containing a corrosive acid. In due time, which happened to be when we took our first flight, the acid ate through whatever it was contained in, and then attacked the wood of the propeller blade. It weakened the wood so that the force used in whirling it around broke it."

"Are you sure of that?" asked Ned.

"As sure as I am that I'm here! Now I know what caused the accident!"

"But who would play such a trick?" asked Ned. "We might all have been killed."

"Yes, I know we might," said Tom. "It must be the work of some of those foreign spies whose first plot we nipped in the bud. I must tell Marbury of this, but don't mention it to dad."

"I won't," promised Ned.

Lieutenant Marbury agreed with Tom that someone had surreptitiously bored a small hole in the propeller blade, and had inserted a corrosive acid that would take many hours to operate. The hole had been varnished over, probably, so it would not show.

"And that means I've got to examine the other two blades," Tom said. "They may be doctored too."

But they did not prove to be. A careful examination showed nothing wrong. An effort was made to find out who had tried to destroy the Mars in midair, but it came to nothing. The two men in custody declared they knew nothing of it, and there was no way of proving that they did.

Meanwhile, the torn gas bag was repaired, and Tom began working on the problem of doing away with the gun recoil. He tried several schemes, and almost was on the point of giving up when suddenly he received a hint by reading an account of how the recoil was taken care of on some of the German Zeppelins.

The guns there were made double, with the extra barrel filled with water or sand, that could be shot out as was the regular charge. As both barrels were fired at the same time, and in opposite directions, with the same amount of powder, one neutralized the other, and the recoil was canceled, the ship remaining steady after fire.

"By Jove! I believe that will do the trick!" cried Tom. "I'm going to try it."

"Good luck to you!" cried Ned.

It was no easy matter to change all the guns of the Mars, and fit them with double barrels. But by working day and night shifts Tom managed it. Meanwhile, a careful watch was kept over the shops. Several new men applied for work, and some of them were suspicious enough in looks, but Tom took on no new hands.

Finally the new guns were made, and tried with the Mars held on the ground. They behaved perfectly, the shooting of sand or water from the dummy barrel neutralizing the shot from the service barrel.

"And now to see how it works in practice!" cried Tom one day. "Are you with me for a long flight, Ned?"

"I sure am!"

The next evening the Mars, with a larger crew than before, and with Tom, Ned, Mr. Damon and Lieutenant Marbury aboard, set sail.

"But why start at night?" asked Ned.

"You'll see in the morning," Tom answered.

The Mars flew slowly all night, life aboard her, at about the level of the clouds, going on almost as naturally as though the occupants of the cabins were on the earth. Excellent meals were served.

"But when are you going to try the guns?" asked Ned, as he got ready to turn in.

"Tell you in the morning," replied Tom, with a smile.

And, in the morning, when Ned looked down through the plate glass in the cabin floor, he uttered a cry.

"Why, Tom! We're over the ocean!" he cried.

"I rather thought we'd be," was the calm reply. "I told George to head straight for the Atlantic. Now we'll have a test with service charges and projectiles!"

IN A STORM

Surprise, for the moment, held Mr. Damon, Ned and Lieutenant Marbury speechless. They looked from the heaving waters of the ocean below them to the young pilot of the Mars. He smiled at their astonishment.

"What—what does it mean, Tom?" asked Ned. "You never said you were going to take a trip as far as this."

"That's right," chimed in Mr. Damon. "Bless my nightcap! If I had known I was going to be brought so far away from home I'd never have come."

"You're not so very far from Water ford," put in Tom. "We didn't make any kind of speed coming from Shopton, and we could be back again inside of four hours if we had to."

"Then you didn't travel fast during the night?" asked the government man.

"No, we just drifted along," Tom answered. "I gave orders to run the machinery slowly, as I wanted to get it in good shape for the other tests that will come soon. But I told George, whom I left in charge when I turned in, to head for New York. I wanted to get out over the ocean to try the guns with the new recoil arrangement."

"Well, we're over the ocean all right," spoke Ned, as he looked down at the heaving waters.

"It isn't the first time," replied Tom cheerfully. "Koku, you may serve breakfast now," for the giant had been taken along as a sort of cook and waiter. Koku manifested no surprise or alarm when he found the airship floating over the sea. Whatever Tom did was right to him. He had great confidence in his master.

"No, it isn't the first time we've taken a water flight," spoke Ned. "I was only surprised at the suddenness of it, that's all."

"It's my first experience so far out above the water," observed Lieutenant Marbury, "though of course I've sailed on many seas. Why, we're out of sight of land."

"About ten miles out, yes," admitted Tom. "Far enough to make it safe to test the guns with real projectiles. That is what I want to do."

"And we've been running all night?" asked Mr. Damon.

"Yes, but at slow speed. The engines are in better shape now than ever before," Tom said. "Well, if you're ready we'll have breakfast."

The meal was served by Koku with as much unconcern as though they were in the Swift homestead back in Shopton, instead of floating near the clouds. And while it was being eaten in the main cabin, and while the crew was having breakfast in their quarters, the aerial warship was moving along over the ocean in charge of George Watson, one of Tom's engineers, who was stationed in the forward pilot-house.

"So you're going to give the guns a real test this time, is that it, Tom?" asked Ned, as he pushed back his plate, a signal that he had eaten enough.

"That's about it."

"But don't you think it's a bit risky out over the water this way. Supposing something should—should happen?" Ned hesitated.

"You mean we might fall?" asked Tom, with a smile.

"Yes; or turn upside down."

"Nothing like that could happen. I'm so sure that I have solved the problem of the recoil of the guns that I'm willing to take chances. But if any of you want to get off the Mars while the test is being made, I have a small boat I can lower, and let you row about in that until—"

"No, thank you!" interrupted Mr. Damon, as he looked below. There was quite a heavy swell on, and the ocean did not appear very attractive. They would be much more comfortable in the big Mars.

"I think you won't have any trouble," asserted Lieutenant Marbury. "I believe Tom Swift has the right idea about the guns, and there will be so small a shock from the recoil that it will not be noticeable."

"We'll soon know," spoke Tom. "I'm going to get ready for the test now.

They were now well out from shore, over the Atlantic, but to make certain no ships would be endangered by the projectiles, Tom and the others searched the waters to the horizon with powerful glasses. Nothing was seen and the work of loading the guns was begun. The bomb tubes, in the main cabin, were also to be given a test.

As service charges were to be used, and as the projectiles were filled with explosives, great care was needed in handling them.

"We'll try dropping bombs first," Tom suggested. "We know they will work, and that will be so much out of the way.

To make the test a severe one, small floating targets were first dropped overboard from the Mars. Then the aerial warship, circling about, came on toward them. Tom, seated at the range-finders, pressed the button that released the shells containing the explosives. One after another they dropped into the sea, exploding as they fell, and sending up a great column of salt water.

"Every one a hit!" reported Lieutenant Marbury, who was keeping "score."

"That's good," responded Tom. "But the others won't be so easy. We have nothing to shoot at."

They had to fire the other guns without targets at which to aim. But, after all, it was the absence of recoil they wanted to establish, and this could be done without shooting at any particular object.

One after another the guns were loaded. As has been explained, they were now made double, one barrel carrying the projectile, and the other a charge of water.

"Are you ready?" asked Tom, when it was time to fire. Lieutenant Marbury, Ned and Mr. Damon were helping, by being stationed at the pressure gauges to note the results.

"All ready," answered Ned.

"Do you think we'd better put on life preservers, Tom?" asked Mr. Damon.

"Nonsense! What for?"

"In case—in case anything happens."

"Nothing will happen. Look out now, I'm going to fire."

The guns were to be fired simultaneously by means of an electric current, when Tom pressed a button.

"Here they go!" exclaimed the young inventor.

There was a moment of waiting, and then came a thundering roar. The Mars trembled, but she did not shift to either side from an even keel. From one barrel of the guns shot out the explosive projectiles, and from the other spurted a jet of water, sent out by a charge of powder, equal in weight to that which forced out the shot.

As the projectile was fired in one direction, and the water in one directly opposite, the two discharges neutralized one another.

Out flew the pointed steel shells, to fall harmlessly into the sea, where they exploded, sending up columns of water.

"Well!" cried Tom as the echoes died away. "How was it?"

"Couldn't have been better," declared Lieutenant Marbury. "There wasn't the least shock of recoil. Tom Swift, you have solved the problem, I do believe! Your aerial warship is a success!"

"I'm glad to hear you say so. There are one or two little things that need changing, but I really think I have about what the United States Government wants."

"I am, also, of that belief, Tom. If only—" The officer stopped suddenly.

"Well?" asked Tom suggestively.

"I was going to say if only those foreign spies don't make trouble."

"I think we've seen the last of them," Tom declared. "Now we'll go on with the tests."

More guns were fired, singly and in batteries, and in each case the Mars stood the test perfectly. The double barrel had solved the recoil problem.

For some little time longer they remained out over the sea, going through some evolutions to test the rudder control, and then as their present object had been accomplished Tom gave orders to head back to Shopton, which place was reached in due time.

"Well, Tom, how was it?" asked Mr. Swift, for though his son had said nothing to his friends about the prospective test, the aged inventor knew about it.

"Successful, Dad, in every particular."

"That's good. I didn't think you could do it. But you did. I tell you it isn't much that can get the best of a Swift!" exclaimed the aged man proudly. "Oh, by the way, Tom, here's a telegram that came while you were gone," and he handed his son the yellow envelope.

Tom ripped it open with a single gesture, and in a flash his eyes took in the words. He read:

"Look out for spies during trial flights."

The message was signed with a name Tom did not recognize.

"Any bad news?" asked Mr. Swift.

"No—oh, no," replied Tom, as he crumpled up the paper and thrust it into his pocket. "No bad news, Dad."

"Well, I'm glad to hear that," went on Mr. Swift. "I don't like telegrams."

When Tom showed the message to Lieutenant Marbury, that official, after one glance at the signature, said:

"Pierson, eh? Well, when he sends out a warning it generally means something."

"Who's Pierson?" asked Tom.

"Head of the Secret Service department that has charge of this airship matter. There must be something in the wind, Tom."

Extra precautions were taken about the shops. Strangers were not permitted to enter, and all future work on the Mars was kept secret. Nevertheless, Tom was worried. He did not want his work to be spoiled just when it was about to be a success. For that it was a success, Lieutenant Marbury assured him. The government man said he would have no hesitation in recommending the purchase of Tom's aerial warship.

"There's just one other test I want to see made," he said.

"What is that?" Tom inquired.

"In a storm. You know we can't always count on having good weather, and I'd like to see how she behaves in a gale."

"You shall!" declared the young inventor.

For the next week, during which finishing touches were put on the big craft, Tom anxiously waited for signs of a storm. At last they came. Danger signals were put up all along the coast, and warnings were sent out broadcast by the Weather Bureau at Washington.

One dull gray morning Tom roused his friends early and announced that the Mars was going up.

"A big storm is headed this way," Tom said, "and we'll have a chance to see how she behaves in it."

And even as the flight began, the forerunning wind and rain came in a gust of fury. Into the midst of it shot the big aerial warship, with her powerful propellers beating the moisture-laden air.

Queer Happenings

"Say, Tom, are you sure you're all right?"

"Of course I am! What do you mean?"

It was Ned Newton who asked the question, and Tom Swift who answered it. The chums were in the pilot-house of the dipping, swaying Mars, which was nosing her way into the storm, fighting on an upward slant, trying, if possible, to get above the area of atmospheric disturbance.

"Well, I mean are you sure your craft will stand all this straining, pulling and hauling?" went on Ned, as he clung to a brass hand rail, built in the side of the pilot-house wall for the very purpose to which it was now being put.

"If she doesn't stand it she's no good!" cried Tom, as he clung to the steering wheel, which was nearly torn from his hands by the deflections of the rudders.

"Well, it's taking a big chance, it seems to me," went on Ned, as he peered through the rain-spotted bull's-eyes of the pilot-house.

"There's no danger," declared Tom. "I wanted to give the ship the hardest test possible before I formally offered her to the government. If she can't stand a blow like this she isn't what I thought her, and I'll have to build another. But I'm sure she will stand the racket, Ned. She's built strongly, and even if part of the gas bag is carried away, as it was when our propeller shattered, we can still sail. If you think this is anything, wait until we turn about and begin to fight our way against the wind."

"Are you going to do that, Tom?"

"I certainly am. We're going with the gale now, to see what is the highest rate of speed we can attain. Pretty soon I'm going to turn her around, and see if she can make any headway in the other direction. Of course I know she won't make much, if any speed, against the gale; but I must give her that test."

"Well, Tom, you know best, of course," admitted Ned. "But to me it seems like taking a big risk."

And indeed it did seem, not only to Ned, but to some of the experienced men of Tom's crew, that the young inventor was taking more chances than ever before, and Tom, as my old readers well know, had, in his career, taken some big ones.

The storm grew worse as the day progressed, until it was a veritable hurricane of wind and rain. The warnings of the Weather Bureau had not been exaggerated. But through the fierce blow the Mars fought her way. As Tom had said, she was going with the wind. This was comparatively easy. But what would happen when she headed into the storm?

Mr. Damon, in the main cabin, sat and looked at Lieutenant Marbury, the eccentric man now and then blessing something as he happened to think of it.

"Do you—do you think we are in any danger?" he finally asked.

"Not at present," replied the government expert.

"You mean we will be—later?"

"It's hard to say. I guess Tom Swift knows his business, though."

"Bless my accident insurance policy!" murmured Mr. Damon. "I wish I had stayed home. If my wife ever hears of this—" He did not seem able to finish the sentence.

In the engine-room the crew were busy over the various machines. Some of the apparatus was being strained to keep the ship on her course in the powerful wind, and would be under a worse stress when Tom turned his craft about. But, so far, nothing had given way, and everything was working smoothly.

As hour succeeded hour and nothing happened, the timid ones aboard began to take more courage. Tom never for a moment lost heart. He knew what his craft could do, and he had taken her up in a terrific storm with a definite purpose in view. He was the calmest person aboard, with the exception, perhaps, of Koku. The giant did not seem to know what fear was. He depended entirely on Tom, and as long as his young master had charge of matters the giant was content to obey orders.

There was to be no test of the guns this time. They had worked sufficiently well, and, if need be, could have been fired in the gale. But Tom did not want his men to take unnecessary risks, nor was he foolhardy himself.

"We'll have our hands full when we turn around and head into the wind," he said to his chum. "That will be enough."

"Then you're really going to give the Mars that test?"

"I surely am. I don't want any comebacks from Uncle Sam after he accepts my aerial warship. I've guaranteed that she'll stand up and make headway against a gale, and I'm going to prove it"

Lieutenant Marbury was told of the coming trial, and he prepared to take official note of it. While matters were being gotten in readiness Tom turned the wheel over to his assistant pilot and went to the engine-room to see that everything was in good shape to cope with any emergency. The rudders had been carefully examined before the flight was made, to make sure they would not fail, for on them depended the progress of the ship against the powerful wind.

"I rather guess those foreign spies have given up trying to do Tom an injury," remarked Ned to the lieutenant as they sat in the main cabin, listening to the howl of the wind, and the dash of the rain.

"Well, I certainly hope so," was the answer. "But I wouldn't be too sure. The folks in Washington evidently think something is likely to happen, or they wouldn't have sent that warning telegram."

"But we haven't seen anything of the spies," Ned remarked.

"No, but that isn't any sign they are not getting ready to make trouble. This may be the calm before the storm. Tom must still be on the lookout. It isn't as though his inventions alone were in danger, for they would not hesitate to inflict serious personal injury if their plans were thwarted."

"They must be desperate."

"They are. But here comes Tom now. He looks as though something new was about to happen."

"Take care of yourselves now," advised the young aero-inventor, as he entered the cabin, finding it hard work to close the door against the terrific wind pressure.

"Why?" asked Ned.

"Because we are going to turn around and fight our way back against the gale. We may be turned topsy-turvy for a second or two."

"Bless my shoe-horn!" cried Mr. Damon. "Do you mean upside down, Tom?"

"No, not that exactly. But watch out!"

Tom went forward to the pilot-house, followed by Ned and the lieutenant. The latter wanted to take official note of what happened. Tom relieved the man at the wheel, and gradually began to alter the direction of the craft.

At first no change was noticeable. So strong was the force of the wind that it seemed as though the Mars was going in the same direction. But Ned, noticing a direction compass on the wall, saw that the needle was gradually shifting.

"Hold fast!" cried Tom suddenly. Then with a quick shift of the rudder something happened. It seemed as though the Mars was trying to turn over, and slide along on her side, or as if she wanted to turn about and scud before the gale, instead of facing it. But Tom held her to the reverse course.

"Can you get her around?" cried the lieutenant above the roar of the gale.

"I—I'm going to!" muttered Tom through his set teeth.

Inch by inch he fought the big craft through the storm. Inch by inch the indicator showed the turning, until at last the grip of the gale was overcome.

"Now she's headed right into it!" cried Tom in exultation. "She's nosing right into it!"

And the Mars was. There was no doubt of it. She had succeeded, under Tom's direction, in changing squarely about, and was now going against the wind, instead of with it.

"But we can't expect to make much speed," Tom said, as he signaled for more power, for he had lowered it somewhat in making the turn.

But Tom himself scarcely had reckoned on the force of his craft, for as the propellers whirled more rapidly the aerial warship did begin to make headway, and that in the teeth of a terrific wind.

"She's doing it, Tom! She's doing it!" cried Ned exultingly.

"I believe she is," agreed the lieutenant.

"Well, so much the better," Tom said, trying to be calm. "If she can keep this up a little while I'll give her a rest and we'll go up above the storm area, and beat back home."

The Mars, so far, had met every test. Tom had decided on ten minutes more of gale-fighting, when from the tube that communicated with the engine-room came a shrill whistle.

"See what that is, Ned," Tom directed.

"Yes," called Ned into the mouthpiece. "What's the matter?"

"Short circuit in the big motor," was the reply. "We've got to run on storage battery. Send Tom back here! Something queer has happened!"

THE STOWAWAYS

Ned repeated the message breathlessly.

"Short circuit!" gasped Tom. "Run on storage battery! I'll have to see to that. Take the wheel somebody!"

"Wouldn't it be better to turn about, and run before the wind, so as not to put too great a strain on the machinery?" asked Lieutenant Marbury.

"Perhaps," agreed Tom. "Hold her this way, though, until I see what's wrong!"

Ned and the government man took the wheel, while Tom hurried along the runway leading from the pilot-house to the machinery cabin. The gale was still blowing fiercely.

The young inventor cast a hasty look about the interior of the place as he entered. He sniffed the air suspiciously, and was aware of the odor of burning insulation.

"What happened?" he asked, noting that already the principal motive power was coming from the big storage battery. The shift had been made automatically, when the main motor gave out.

"It's hard to say," was the answer of the chief engineer. "We were running along all right, and we got your word to switch on more power, after the turn. We did that all right, and she was running as smooth as a sewing-machine, when, all of a sudden, she short-circuited, and the storage battery cut in automatically."

"Think you put too heavy a load on the motor?" Tom asked.

"Couldn't have been that. The shunt box would have taken that up, and the circuit-breaker would have worked, saving us a burn-out, and that's what happened-a burn-out. The motor will have to be rewound."

"Well, no use trying to fight this gale with the storage battery," Tom said, after a moment's thought. "We'll run before it. That's the easiest way. Then we'll try to rise above the wind."

He sent the necessary message to the pilot-house. A moment later the shift was made, and once more the Mars was scudding before the storm. Then Tom gave his serious attention to what had happened in the engine room.

As he bent over the burned-out motor, looking at the big shiny connections, he saw something that startled him. With a quick motion Tom Swift picked up a bar of copper. It was hot to the touch—so hot that he dropped it with a cry of pain, though he had let go so quickly that the burn was only momentary.

"What's the matter?" asked Jerry Mound, Tom's engineer.

"Matter!" cried Tom. "A whole lot is the matter! That copper bar is what made the short circuit. It's hot yet from the electric current. How did it fall on the motor connections?"

The engine room force gathered about the young inventor. No one could explain how the copper bar came to be where it was. Certainly no one of Tom's employees had put it there, and it could not have fallen by accident, for the motor connections were protected by a mesh of wire, and a hand would have to be thrust under them to put the bar in place. Tom gave a quick look at his men. He knew he could trust them—every one. But this was a queer happening.

For a moment Tom did not know what to think, and then, as the memory of that warning telegram came to him, he had an idea.

"Were any strangers in this cabin before the start was made?" he asked Mr. Mound.

"Not that I know of," was the answer.

"Well, there may be some here now," Tom said grimly. "Look about."

But a careful search revealed no one. Yet the young inventor was sure the bar of copper, which had done the mischief of short-circuiting the motor, had been put in place deliberately.

In reality there was no danger to the craft, since there was power enough in the storage battery to run it for several hours. But the happening showed Tom he had still to reckon with his enemies.

He looked at the height gauge on the wall of the motor-room, and noted that the Mars was going up. In accordance with Tom's instructions they were sending her above the storm area. Once there, with no gale to fight, they could easily beat their way back to a point above Shopton, and make the best descent possible.

And that was done while, under Tom's direction, his men took the damaged motor apart, with a view to repairing it.

"What was it, Tom?" asked Ned, coming back to join his chum, after George Ventor, the assistant pilot, had taken charge of the wheel.

"I don't exactly know, Ned," was the answer. "But I feel certain that some of my enemies came aboard here and worked this mischief."

"Your enemies came aboard?"

"Yes, and they must be here now. The placing of that copper bar proves it."

"Then let's make a search and find them, Tom. It must be some of those foreign spies."

"Just what I think."

But a more careful search of the craft than the one Tom had casually made revealed the presence of no one. All the crew and helpers were accounted for, and, as they had been in Tom's service for some time, they were beyond suspicion. Yet the fact remained that a seemingly human agency had acted to put the main motor out of commission. Tom could not understand it.

"Well, it sure is queer," observed Ned, as the search came to nothing.

"It's worse than queer," declared Tom, "it's alarming! I don't know when I'll be safe if we have ghosts aboard."

"Ghosts?" repeated Ned.

"Well, when we can't find out who put that bar in place I might as well admit it was a ghost," spoke Tom. "Certainly, if it was done by a man, he didn't jump overboard after doing it, and he isn't here now. It sure is queer!"

Ned agreed with the last statement, at any rate.

In due time the Mars, having fought her way above the storm, came over Shopton, and then, the wind having somewhat died out, she fought her way down, and, after no little trouble, was housed in the hangar.

Tom cautioned his friends and workmen to say nothing to his father about the mysterious happening on board.

"I'll just tell him we had a slight accident, and let it go at that," Tom decided. "No use in causing him worry."

"But what are you going to do about it?" asked Ned.

"I'm going to keep careful watch over the aerial warship, at any rate," declared Tom. "If there's a hidden enemy aboard, I'll starve him out."

Accordingly, a guard, under the direction of Koku, was posted about the big shed, but nothing came of it. No stranger was observed to sneak out of the ship, after it had been deserted by the crew. The mystery seemed deeper than ever.

It took nearly a week to repair the big motor, and, during this time, Tom put some improvements on the airship, and added the finishing touches.

He was getting it ready for the final government test, for the authorities in Washington had sent word that they would have Captain Warner, in addition to Lieutenant Marbury, make the final inspection and write a report.

Meanwhile several little things occurred to annoy Tom. He was besieged with applications from new men who wanted to work, and many of these men seemed to be foreigners. Tom was sure they were either spies of some European nations, or the agents of spies, and they got no further than the outer gate.

But some strangers did manage to sneak into the works, though they were quickly detected and sent about their business. Also, once or twice, small fires were discovered in outbuildings, but they were soon extinguished with little damage. Extra vigilance was the watchword.

"And yet, with all my precautions, they may get me, or damage something," declared Tom. "It is very annoying!"

"It is," agreed Ned, "and we must be doubly on the lookout."

So impressed was Ned with the necessity for caution that he arranged to take his vacation at this time, so as to be on hand to help his chum, if necessary.

The Mars was nearing completion. The repaired motor was better than ever, and everything was in shape for the final test. Mr. Damon was persuaded to go along, and Koku was to be taken, as well as the two government officials.

The night before the trip the guards about the airship shed were doubled, and Tom made two visits to the place before midnight. But there was no alarm.

Consequently, when the Mars started off on her final test, it was thought that all danger from the spies was over.

"She certainly is a beauty," said Captain Warner, as the big craft shot upward. "I shall be interested in seeing how she stands gun fire, though."

"Oh, she'll stand it," declared Lieutenant Marbury. The trip was to consume several days of continuous flying, to test the engines. A large supply of food and ammunition was aboard.

It was after supper of the first day out, and our friends were seated in the main cabin laying out a program for the next day, when sudden yells came from a part of the motor cabin devoted to storage. Koku, who had been sent to get out a barrel of oil, was heard to shout.

"What's up?" asked Tom, starting to his feet. He was answered almost at once by more yells.

"Oh, Master! Come quickly!" cried the giant. "There are many men here. There are stowaways aboard!"

PRISONERS

For a moment, after hearing Koku's reply. neither Tom nor his friends spoke. Then Ned, in a dazed sort of way, repeated:

"Stowaways!"

"Bless my—" began Mr. Damon, but that was as far as he got.

From the engine compartment, back of the amidship cabin, came a sound of cries and heavy blows. The yells of Koku could be heard above those of the others.

Then the door of the cabin where Tom Swift and his friends were was suddenly burst open, and seven or eight men threw themselves within. They were led by a man with a small, dark mustache and a little tuft of whiskers on his chin—an imperial. He looked the typical Frenchman, and his words, snapped out, bore out that belief.

What he said was in French, as Tom understood, though he knew little of that language. Also, what the Frenchman said produced an immediate result, for the men following him sprang at our friends with overwhelming fierceness.

Before Tom, Ned, Captain Warner, Mr. Damon or Lieutenant Marbury could grasp any weapon with which to defend themselves, had their intentions been to do so, they were seized.

Against such odds little could be done, though our friends did not give up without a struggle.

"What does this mean?" angrily demanded Tom Swift. "Who are you? What are you doing aboard my craft? Who are—"

His words were lost in smothered tones, for one of his assailants put a heavy cloth over his mouth, and tied it there, gagging him. Another man, with a quick motion, whipped a rope about Tom's hands and feet, and he was soon securely bound.

In like manner the others were treated, and, despite the struggles of Mr. Damon, the two government men and Ned, they were soon put in a position where they could do nothing—helplessly bound, and laid on a bench in the main cabin, staring blankly up at the ceiling. Each one was gagged so effectively that he could not utter more than a faint moan.

Of the riot of thoughts that ran through the heads of each one, I leave you to imagine.

What did it all mean? Where had the strange men come from? What did they mean by thus assaulting Tom and his companions? And what had happened to the others of the crew—Koku, Jerry Mound, the engineer, and George Ventor, the assistant pilot?

These were only a few of the questions Tom asked himself, as he lay there, bound and helpless. Doubtless Mr. Damon and the others were asking themselves similar questions.

One thing was certain—whatever the stowaways, as Koku had called them, had done, they had not neglected the Mars, for she was running along at about the same speed, though in what direction Tom could not tell. He strained to get a view of the compass on the forward wall of the cabin, but he could not see it.

It had been a rough-and-tumble fight, by which our friends were made prisoners, but no one seemed to have been seriously, or even slightly, hurt. The invaders, under the leadership of the Frenchman, were rather ruffled, but that was all.

Pantingly they stood in line, surveying their captives, while the man with the mustache and imperial smiled in a rather superior fashion at the row of bound ones. He spoke in his own tongue to the men, who, with the exception of one, filed out, going, as Tom and the others could note, to the engine-room in the rear.

"I hope I have not had to hurt any of you," the Frenchman observed, with sarcastic politeness. "I regret the necessity that caused me to do this, but, believe me, it was unavoidable."

He spoke with some accent, and Tom at once decided this was the same man who had once approached Eradicate. He also recognized him as the man he had seen in the woods the day of the outing.

"He's one of the foreign spies," thought Tom "and he's got us and the ship, too. They were too many for us!"

Tom's anxiety to speak, to hold some converse with the captor, was so obvious that the Frenchman said:

"I am going to treat you as well as I can under the circumstances. You and your other friends, who are also made prisoners, will be allowed to be together, and then you can talk to your hearts' content."

The other man, who had remained with the evident ringleader of the stowaways, asked a question, in French, and he used the name La Foy.

"Ah!" thought Tom. "This is the leader of the gang that attacked Koku in the shop that night. They have been waiting their chance, and now they have made good. But where did they come from? Could they have boarded us from some other airship?"

Yet, as Tom asked himself that question, he knew it could hardly have been possible. The men must have been in hiding on his own craft, they must have been, as Koku had cried out— stowaways—and have come out at a preconcerted signal to overpower the aviators.

"If you will but have patience a little longer," went on La Foy, for that was evidently the name of the leader, "you will all be together. We are just considering where best to put you so that you will not suffer too much. It is quite a problem to deal with so many prisoners, but we have no choice."

The two Frenchmen conversed rapidly in their own language for a few minutes, and then there came into the cabin another of the men who had helped overpower Tom and his friends. What he told La Foy seemed to give that individual satisfaction, for he smiled.

"We are going to put you all together in the largest storeroom, which is partly empty," La Foy said. "There you will be given food and drink, and treated as well as possible under the circumstances. You will also be unbound, and may converse among yourselves. I need hardly point out," he went on, "that calling for help will be useless. We are a mile or so in the air, and have no intention of descending," and he smiled mockingly.

"They must know how to navigate my aerial warship," thought Tom. "I wonder what their game is, anyhow?"

Night had fallen, but the cabin was aglow with electric lights. The foreigners in charge of the Mars seemed to know their way about perfectly, and how to manage the big craft. By the vibration Tom could tell that the motor was running evenly and well.

"But what happened to the others—to Mound, Ventor and Koku?" wondered Tom.

A moment later several of the foreigners entered. Some of them did not look at all like Frenchmen, and Tom was sure one was a German and another a Russian.

"This will be your prison—for a while," said La Foy significantly, and Tom wondered how long this would be the case. A sharp thought came to him—how long would they be prisoners? Did not some other, and more terrible, fate await them?

As La Foy spoke, he opened a storeroom door that led off from the main, or amidship, cabin. This room was intended to contain the supplies and stores that would be taken on a long voyage. It was one of two, being the larger, and now contained only a few odds and ends of little importance. It made a strong prison, as Tom well knew, having planned it.

One by one, beginning with Tom, the prisoners were taken up and placed in a recumbent position on the floor of the storeroom. Then were brought in the engineer and assistant pilot, as well as Koku and a machinist whom Tom had brought along to help him. Now the young inventor and all his friends were together. It took four men to carry Koku in, the giant being covered with a network of ropes.

"On second thought," said La Foy, as he saw Koku being placed with his friends, "I think we will keep the big man with us. We had trouble enough to subdue him. Carry him back to the engine-room."

So Koku, trussed up like some roped steer, was taken out again.

"Now then," said La Foy to his prisoners, as he stood in the door of the room, "I will unbind one of you, and he may loose the bonds of the others."

As he spoke, he took the rope from Tom's hands, and then, quickly slipping out, locked and barred the door.

APPREHENSIONS

For a moment or two, after the ropes binding his hands were loosed, Tom Swift did nothing. He was not only stunned mentally, but the bonds had been pulled so tightly about his wrists that the circulation was impeded, and his cramped muscles required a little time in which to respond.

But presently he felt the tingle of the coursing blood, and he found he could move his arms. He raised them to his head, and then his first care was to remove the pad of cloth that formed a gag over his mouth. Now he could talk.

"I—I'll loosen you all in lust a second," he said, as he bent over to pick at the knot of the rope around his legs. His own voice sounded strange to him.

"I don't know what it's all about, any more than you do," he went on, speaking to the others. "It's a fierce game we're up against, and we've got to make the best of it. As soon as we can move, and talk, we'll decide what's best to do. Whoever these fellows are, and I believe they are the foreign spies I've been warned about, they are in complete possession of the airship."

Tom found it no easy matter to loosen the bonds on his feet. The ropes were well tied, and Tom's fingers were stiff from the lack of circulation of blood. But finally he managed to free himself. When he stood up in the dim storeroom, that was now a prison for all save Koku, he found that he could not walk. He almost toppled over, so weak were his legs from the tightness of the ropes. He sat down and worked his muscles until they felt normal again.

A few minutes later, weak and rather tottery, he managed to reach Mr. Damon, whom he first unbound. He realized that Mr. Damon was the oldest of his friends, and, consequently, would suffer most. And it was characteristic of the eccentric gentleman that, as soon as his gag was removed he burst out with:

"Bless my wristlets, Tom! What does it all mean?"

"That's more than I can say, Mr. Damon," replied Tom, with a mournful shake of his head. "I'm very sorry it happened, for it looks as though I hadn't taken proper care. The idea of those men stowing themselves away on board here, and me not knowing it; and then coming out unexpectedly and getting possession of the craft! It doesn't speak very well for my smartness."

"Oh, well, Tom, anyone might have been fooled by those plotting foreigners," said Mr. Damon. "Now, we'll try to turn matters about and get the best of them. Oh, but it feels good to be free once more!"

He stretched his benumbed and stiffened limbs and then helped Tom free the others. They stood up, looking at each other in their dimly lighted prison.

"Well, if this isn't the limit I don't know what is!" cried Ned Newton.

"They got the best of you, Tom," spoke Lieutenant Marbury.

"Are they really foreign spies?" asked Captain Warner.

"Yes," replied his assistant. "They managed to carry out the plot we tried to frustrate. It was a good trick, too, hiding on board, and coming out with a rush."

"Is that what they did?" asked Mr. Damon.

"It looks so," observed Tom. "The attack must have started in the engine-room," he went on, with a look at Mound and Ventor. "What happened there?" he asked.

"Well, that's about the way it was," answered the engineer. "We were working away, making some adjustments, oiling the parts and seeing that everything was running smoothly, when, all at once, I heard Koku yell. He had gone in the oil room. At first I thought something had gone wrong with the ship, but, when I looked at the giant, I saw he was being attacked by four strange men. And, before I, or any of the other men, could do anything, they all swarmed down on us.

"There must have been a dozen of them, and they simply overwhelmed us. One of them hit Koku on the head with an iron bar, and that took all the fight out of the giant, or the story might have been a different one. As it was, we were overpowered, and that's all I know until we were carried in here, and saw you folks all tied up as we were."

"They burst in on us in the same way," Tom explained. "But where did they come from? Where were they hiding?"

"In the oil and gasoline storeroom that opens out of the motor compartment," answered Mound, the engineer. "It isn't half full, you know, and there's room for more than a dozen men in it. They must have gone in some time last night, when the airship was in the hangar, and remained hidden among the boxes and barrels until they got ready to come out and overpower us."

"That's it," decided Tom. "But I don't understand how they got in. The hangar was well guarded all night."

"Some of your men might have been bribed," suggested Ned.

"Yes, that is so," admitted Tom, and, later, he learned that such had been the case. The foreign spies, for such they were, had managed to corrupt one of Tom's trusted employees, who had looked the other way when La Foy and his fellow-conspirators sneaked into the airship shed and secreted themselves.

"Well, discussing how they got on board isn't going to do us any good now," Tom remarked ruefully. "The question is—what are we going to do?"

"Bless my fountain pen!" cried Mr. Damon. "There's only one thing to do!"

"What is that?" asked Ned.

"Why, get out of here, call a policeman, and have these scoundrels arrested. I'll prosecute them! I'll have my lawyer on hand to see that they get the longest terms the statutes call for! Bless my pocketbook, but I will!" and Mr. Damon waxed quite indignant.

"That's easier said than done," observed Torn Swift, quietly. "In the first place, it isn't going to be an easy matter to get out of here."

He looked around the storeroom, which was then their prison. It was illuminated by a single electric light, which showed some boxes and barrels piled in the rear.

"Nothing in them to help us get out," Tom went on, for he knew what the contents were.

"Oh, we'll get out," declared Ned confidently, "but I don't believe we'll find a policeman ready to take our complaint. The upper air isn't very well patrolled as yet."

"That's so," agreed Mr. Damon. "I forgot that we were in an airship. But what is to he done, Tom? We really are captives aboard our own craft."

"Yes, worse luck," returned the young inventor. "I feel foolish when I think how we let them take us prisoners."

"We couldn't help it," Ned commented. "They came on us too suddenly. We didn't have a chance. And they outnumbered us two to one. If they could take care of big Koku, what chance did we have?"

"Very little," said Engineer Mound. "They were desperate fellows. They know something about aircraft, too. For, as soon as Koku, Ventor and I were disposed of, some of them went at the machinery as if they had been used to running it all their lives."

"Oh, the foreigners are experts when it comes to craft of the air," said Captain Warner.

"Well, they seem to be running her, all right," admitted the young inventor, "and at good speed, too. They have increased our running rate, if I am any judge."

"By several miles an hour," confirmed the assistant pilot. "Though in which direction they are heading, and what they are going to do with us is more than I can guess."

"That's so!" agreed Mr. Damon. "What is to become of us? They may heave us overboard into the ocean!"

"Into the ocean!" cried Ned apprehensively. "Are we near the sea?"

"We must be, by this time," spoke Tom. "We were headed in that direction, and we have come almost far enough to put us somewhere over the Atlantic, off the Jersey coast."

A look of apprehension was on the faces of all. But Tom's face did not remain clouded long.

"We won't try to swim until we have to," he said. "Now, let's take an account of stock, and see if we have any means of getting out of this prison.

ACROSS THE SEA

With one accord the hands of the captives sought their pockets. Probably the first thought of each one was a knife—a pocket knife. But blank looks succeeded their first hopeful ones, for the hands came out empty.

"Not a thing!" exclaimed Mr. Damon. "Not a blessed thing! They have even taken my keys and—my fountain pen!"

"I guess they searched us all while they were struggling with us, tying us up," suggested Ned. "I had a knife with a big, strong blade, but it's gone.

"So is mine," echoed Tom.

"And I haven't even a screwdriver, or a pocket-wrench," declared the engineer, "though I had both."

"They evidently knew what they were doing," said Lieutenant Marbury. "I don't usually carry a revolver, but of late I have had a small automatic in my pocket. That's gone, too."

"And so are all my things," went on his naval friend. "That Frenchman, La Foy, was taking no chances."

"Well," if we haven't any weapons, or means of getting out of here, we must make them," said Tom, as hopefully as he could under the circumstances. "I don't know all the things that were put in this storeroom, and perhaps there may be something we can use."

"Shall we make the try now?" asked Ned. "I'm getting thirsty, at least. Lucky we had supper before they came out at us."

"Well, there isn't any water in here, or anything to eat, of so much I am sure," went on Tom "So we will have to depend on our captors for that."

"At least we can shout and ask for water," said Lieutenant Marbury. "They have no excuse for being needlessly cruel."

They all agreed that this might not be a bad plan, and were preparing to raise a united shout, when there came a knock on the door of their prison.

"Are you willing to listen to reason?" asked a voice they recognized as that of La Foy.

"What do you mean by reason?" asked Tom bitterly. "You have no right to impose any conditions on us."

"I have the right of might, and I intend exercising it," was the sharp rejoinder. "If you will listen to reason—"

"Which kind—yours or ours?" asked Tom pointedly.

"Mine, in this case," snapped back the Frenchman. "What I was going to say was that I do not intend to starve you, or cause you discomfort by thirst. I am going to open the door and put in food and water. But I warn you that any attempt to escape will be met with severe measures.

"We are in sufficient force to cope with you. I think you have seen that." He spoke calmly and in perfect English, though with a marked accent. "My men are armed, and will stand here ready to meet violence with violence," he went on. "Is that understood?"

For a moment none of the captives replied.

"I think it will be better to give in to him at least for a while," said Captain Warner in a low voice to Tom. "We need water, and will soon need food. We can think and plan better if we are well nourished."

"Then you think I should promise not to raise a row?"

"For the time being—yes."

"Well, I am waiting!" came in sharp tones from the other side of the portal.

"Our answer is—yes," spoke Tom. "We will not try to get out— just yet," he added significantly.

A key was heard grating in the lock, and, a moment later, the door slid back. Through the opening could be seen La Foy and some of his men standing armed. Others had packages of food and jugs of water. A plentiful supply of the latter was carried aboard the Mars.

"Keep back from the door!" was the stern command of La Foy. "The food and drink will be passed in only if you keep away from the entrance. Remember my men are armed!"

The warning was hardly needed, for the weapons could plainly be seen. Tom had half a notion that perhaps a concerted rush would carry the day for him and his friends, but he was forced to abandon that idea.

While the guards looked on, others of the "pirate crew," as Ned dubbed them, passed in food and water. Then the door was locked again.

They all felt better after drinking the water, which was made cool by evaporation, for the airship was quite high above the earth when Tom's enemies captured it, and the young inventor felt sure it had not descended any.

No one felt much like eating, however, so the food was put away for a time. And then, somewhat refreshed, they began looking about for some means of getting out of their prison.

"Of course we might batter down the door, in time, by using some of these boxes as rams," said Tom. "But the trouble is, that would make a noise, and they could stand outside and drive us back with guns and pistols, of which they seem to have plenty."

"Yes, and they could turn some of your own quick-firers on us," added Captain Warner. "No, we must work quietly, I think, and take them unawares, as they took us. That is our only plan."

"We will be better able to see what we have here by daylight," Tom said. "Suppose we wait until morning?"

That plan was deemed best, and preparations made for spending the night in their prison.

It was a most uncomfortable night for all of them. The floor was their only bed, and their only covering some empty bags that had contained supplies. But even under these circumstances they managed to doze off fitfully.

Once they were all awakened by a violent plunging of the airship. The craft seemed to be trying to stand on her head, and then she rocked violently from side to side, nearly turning turtle. "What is it?" gasped Ned, who was lying next to Tom.

"They must be trying some violent stunts," replied the young inventor, "or else we have run into a storm."

"I think the latter is the case," observed Lieutenant Marbury.

And, as the motion of the craft kept up, though less violently, this was accepted as the explanation. Through the night the Mars flew, but whither the captives knew not.

The first gray streaks of dawn finally shone through the only window of their prison. Sore, lame and stiff, wearied in body and disturbed in mind, the captives awoke. Tom's first move was toward the window. It was high up, but, by standing on a box, he could look through it. He uttered an exclamation.

"What is it?" asked Ned, swaying to and fro from the violent motion ef the aerial warship.

"We are away out over the sea," spoke Tom, "and in the midst of a bad storm."

THE LIGHTNING BOLT

Tom turned away from the window, to find his companions regarding him anxiously.

"A storm," repeated Ned. "What sort?"

"It might turn into any sort," replied Tom. "All I can see now is a lot of black clouds, and the wind must be blowing pretty hard, for there's quite a sea on."

"Bless my galvanometer!" cried Mr. Damon. "Then we are out over the ocean again, Tom?"

"Yes, there's no doubt of it."

"What part?" asked the assistant pilot.

"That's more than I can tell," Tom answered.

"Suppose I take a look?" suggested Captain Warner. "I've done quite a bit of sailing in my time."

But, when he had taken a look through the window at which Tom had been standing, the naval officer descended, shaking his head.

"There isn't a landmark in sight," he announced. "We might be over the middle of the Atlantic, for all I could tell."

"Hardly as far as that," spoke Tom. "They haven't been pushing the Mars at that speed. But we may be across to the other side before we realize it."

"How's that?" asked Ned.

"Well, the ship is in the possession of these foreign spies," went on Tom. "All their interests are in Europe, though it would be hard to say what nationality is in command here. I think there are even some Englishmen among those who attacked us, as well as French, Germans, Italians and Russians."

"Yes, it seems to be a combination of European nations against us," admitted Captain Warner. "Probably, after they have made good their seizure of Tom's aerial warship, they will portion her out among themselves, or use her as a model from which to make others."

"Do you think that is their object?" asked Mr. Damon.

"Undoubtedly," was the captain's answer. "It has been the object of these foreign spies, all along, not only to prevent the United States from enjoying the benefits of these progressive inventions, but to use them for themselves. They would stop at nothing to gain their ends. It seems we did not sufficiently appreciate their power and daring."

"Well, they've got us, at any rate," observed Tom, "and they may take us and the ship to some far-off foreign country."

"If they don't heave us overboard half-way there," commented Ned, in rather gloomy tones

"Well, of course, there's that possibility," admitted Tom. "They are desperate characters."

"Well, we must do something," declared Lieutenant Marbury. "Come, it's daylight now, and we can see to work better. Let's see if we can't find a way to get out of this prison. Say, but this sure is a storm!" he cried, as the airship rolled and pitched violently.

"They are handling her well, though," observed Tom, as the craft came quickly to an even keel. "Either they have a number of expert birdmen on board, or they can easily adapt themselves to a new aircraft. She is sailing splendidly."

"Well, let's eat something, and set to work," proposed Ned.

They brought out the food which had been given to them the night before, but before they could eat this, there came a knock on the door, and more food and fresh water was handed in, under the same precautions as before.

Tom and his companions indignantly demanded to be released, but their protests were only laughed at, and while the guards stood with ready weapons the door was again shut and locked.

But the prisoners were not the kind to sit idly down in the face of this. Under Tom's direction they set about looking through their place of captivity for something by which they could release themselves. At first they found nothing, and Ned even suggested trying to cut a way through the wooden walls with a fingernail file, which he found in one of his pockets, when Tom, who had gone to the far end of the storeroom, uttered a cry.

"What is it—a way out?" asked Lieutenant Marbury anxiously.

"No, but means to that end," Tom replied. "Look, a file and a saw, left here by some of my workmen, perhaps," and he brought out the tools. He had found them behind a barrel in the far end of the compartment.

"Hurray!" cried Ned. "That's the ticket! Now we'll soon show these fellows what's what!"

"Go easy!" cautioned Tom. "We must work carefully. It won't do to slam around and try to break down the door with these. I think we had better select a place on the side wall, break through that, and make an opening where we can come out unnoticed. Then, when we are ready, we can take them by surprise. We'll have to do something like that, for they outnumber us, you know."

"That is so," agreed Captain Warner. "We must use strategy."

"Well, where would be a good place to begin to burrow out?" asked Ned.

"Here," said Tom, indicating a place far back in the room. "We can work there in turns, sawing a hole through the wall. It will bring us out in the passage between the aft and amidship cabins, and we can go either way."

"Then let's begin!" cried Ned enthusiastically, and they set to work.

While the aerial warship pitched and tossed in the storm, over some part of the Atlantic, Tom and his friends took turns in working their way to freedom. With the sharp end of the file a small hole was made, the work being done as slowly as a rat gnaws, so as to make no noise that would be heard by their captors. In time the hole was large enough to admit the end of the saw.

But this took many hours, and it was not until the second day of their captivity that they had the hole nearly large enough for the passage of one person at a time. They had not been discovered, they thought.

Meanwhile they had been given food and water at intervals, but to all demands that they be released, or at least told why they were held prisoners, a deaf ear was turned.

They could only guess at the fate of Koku. Probably the giant was kept bound, for once he got the chance to use his enormous strength it might go hard with the foreigners.

The Mars continued to fly through the air. Sometimes, as Tom and his friends could tell by the motion, she was almost stationary in the upper regions, and again she seemed to be flying at top speed. Occasionally there came the sound of firing.

"They're trying my guns," observed Tom grimly.

"Do you suppose they are being attacked?" asked Ned, hopefully.

"Hardly," replied Captain Warner. "The United States possesses no craft able to cope with this one in aerial warfare, and they are hardly engaging in part of the European war yet. I think they are just trying Tom's new guns."

Later our friends learned that such was the case.

The storm had either passed, or the Mars had run out of the path of it, for, after the first few hours of pitching and tossing, the atmosphere seemed reduced to a state of calm.

All the while they were secretly working to gain their freedom so they might attack and overpower their enemies, they took occasional observations from the small window. But they could learn nothing of their whereabouts. They could only view the heaving ocean, far below them, or see a mass of cloud-mist, which hid the earth, if so be that the Mars was sailing over land.

"But how much longer can they keep it up?" asked Ned.

"Well, we have fuel and supplies aboard for nearly two weeks," Tom answered.

"And by the end of that time we may all be dead," spoke the young bank clerk despondently.

"No, we'll be out of here before then!" declared Lieutenant Marbury.

Indeed the hole was now almost large enough to enable them to crawl out one at a time. They could not, of course, see how it looked from the outside, but Tom had selected a place for its cutting so that the sawdust and the mark of the panel that was being removed, would not ordinarily be noticeable.

Their set night as the time for making the attempt—late at night, when it was hoped that most of their captors would be asleep.

Finally the last cut was made, and a piece of wood hung over the opening only by a shred, all ready to knock out.

"We'll do it at midnight," announced Tom.

Anxious, indeed, were those last hours of waiting. The time had almost arrived for the attempt, when Tom, who had been nervously pacing to and fro, remarked:

"We must be running into another storm. Feel how she heaves and rolls!"

Indeed the Mars was most unsteady.

"It sure is a storm!" cried Ned, "and a heavy one, too," for there came a burst of thunder, that seemed like a report of Tom's giant cannon.

In another instant they were in the midst of a violent thunderstorm, the airship pitching and tossing in a manner to almost throw them from their feet.

As Tom reached up to switch on the electric light again, there came a flash of lightning that well nigh blinded them. And so close after it as to seem simultaneous, there came such a crash of thunder as to stun them all. There was a tingling, as of a thousand pins and needles in the body of each of the captives, and a strong smell of sulphur. Then, as the echoes of the clap died away, Tom yelled:

"She's been struck! The airship has been struck!"

FREEDOM

For a moment there was silence, following Tom's wild cry and the noise of the thunderclap. Then, as other, though less loud reverberations of the storm continued to sound, the captives awoke to a realization of what had happened. They had been partially stunned, and were almost as in a dream.

"Are—are we all right?" stammered Ned.

"Bless my soul! What has happened?" cried Mr. Damon.

"We've been struck by lightning!" Tom repeated. "I don't know whether we're all right or not."

"We seem to be falling!" exclaimed Lieutenant Marbury.

"If the whole gas bag isn't ripped to pieces we're lucky," commented Jerry Mound.

Indeed, it was evident that the Mars was sinking rapidly. To all there came the sensation of riding in an elevator in a skyscraper and being dropped a score of stories.

Then, as they stood there in the darkness, illuminated only by flashes from the lightning outside the window, waiting for an unknown fate, Tom Swift uttered a cry of delight.

"We've stopped falling!" he cried. "The automatic gas machine is pumping. Part of the gas bag was punctured, but the unbroken compartments hold!"

"If part of the gas leaked out I don't see why it wasn't all set on fire and exploded," observed Captain Warner.

"It's a non-burnable gas," Tom quickly explained. "But come on. This may be our very chance. There seems to be something going on that may be in our favor."

Indeed the captives could hear confused cries and the running to and fro of many feet.

He made for the sawed panel, and, in another instant, had burst out and was through it, out into the passageway between the after and amidship cabins. His companions followed him.

They looked into the rear cabin, or motor compartment, and a scene of confusion met their gaze. Two of the foreign men who had seized the ship lay stretched out on the floor near the humming machinery, which had been left to run itself. A look in the other direction, toward the main cabin, showed a group of the foreign spies bending over the inert body of La Foy, the Frenchman, stretched out on a couch.

"What has happened?" cried Ned. "What does it all mean?,'

"The lightning!" exclaimed Tom. "The bolt that struck the ship has knocked out some of our enemies! Now is the time to attack them!"

The Mars seemed to have passed completely through a narrow storm belt. She was now in a quiet atmosphere, though behind her could be seen the fitful play of lightning, and there could be heard the distant rumble of thunder.

"Come on!" cried Tom. "We must act quickly, while they are demoralized! Come on!"

His friends needed no further urging. Jerry Mound and the machinist rushed to the engine-room, to look after any of the enemy that might be there, while Tom, Ned and the others ran into the middle cabin.

"Grab 'em! Tie 'em up!" cried Tom, for they had no weapons with which to make an attack.

But none were needed. So stunned were the foreigners by the lightning bolt, which had miraculously passed our friends, and so unnerved by the striking down of La Foy, their leader, that they seemed like men half asleep. Before they could offer any resistance they were bound with the same ropes that had held our friends in bondage. That is, all but the big Frenchman himself. He seemed beyond the need of binding.

Mound, the engineer, and his assistant, came hurrying in from the motor-room, followed by Koku.

"We found him chained up," Jerry explained, as the big giant, freed from his captivity, rubbed his chafed wrists.

"Are there any of the foreigners back there?,'

"Only those two knocked out by the lightning," the engineer explained. "We've made them secure. I see you've got things here in shape."

"Yes," replied Tom. "And now to see where. we are, and to get back home. Whew! But this has been a time! Koku, what happened to you?,"

"They no let anything happen. I be in chains all the while," the giant answered. "Jump on me before I can do anything!"

"Well, you're out, now, and I think we'll have you stand guard over these men. The tables are turned, Koku."

The bound ones were carried to the same prison whence our friends had escaped, but their bonds were not taken off, and Koku was put in the place with them. By this time La Foy and the two other stricken men showed signs of returning life. They had only been stunned.

The young inventor and his friends, once more in possession of their airship, lost little time in planning to return. They found that the spies were all expert aeronauts, and had kept a careful chart of their location. They were then halfway across the Atlantic, and in a short time longer would probably have been in some foreign country. But Tom turned the Mars about.

The craft had only been slightly damaged by the lightning bolt, though three of the gas bag compartments were torn, The others sufficed, however, to make the ship sufficiently buoyant.

When morning came Tom and his friends had matters running almost as smoothly as before their capture.

The prisoners had no chance to escape, and, indeed, they seemed to have been broken in spirit. La Foy was no longer the insolent, mocking Frenchman that he had been, and the two chief foreign engineers seemed to have lost some of their reason when the lightning struck them.

"But it was a mighty lucky and narrow escape for us," said Ned, as he and Tom sat in the pilot-house the second day of the return trip.

"That's right," agreed his chum.

Once again they were above the earth, and, desiring to get rid as soon as possible of the presence of the spies, a landing was made near New York City, and the government authorities communicated with. Captain Warner and Lieutenant Marbury took charge of the prisoners, with some Secret Service men, and the foreigners were soon safely locked up.

"And now what are you going to do, Tom?" asked Ned, when, once more, they had the airship to themselves.

"I'm going back to Shopton, fix up the gas bag, and give her another government trial," was the answer.

And, in due time, this was done. Tom added some improvements to the aircraft, making it better than ever, and when she was given the test required by the government, she was an unqualified success, and the rights to the Mars were purchased for a large sum. In sailing, and in the matter of guns and bombs, Tom's craft answered every test.

"So you see I was right, after all, Dad," the young inventor said, when informed that he had succeeded. "We can shoot off even bigger guns than I thought from the deck of the Mars."

"Yes, Tom," replied the aged inventor, "I admit I was wrong."

Tom's aerial warship was even a bigger success than he had dared to hope. Once the government men fully understood how to run it, in which Tom played a prominent part in giving instructions, they put the Mars to a severe test. She was taken out over the ocean, and her guns trained on an obsolete battleship. Her bombs and projectiles blew the craft to pieces.

"The Mars will be the naval terror of the seas in any future war," predicted Captain Warner.

The Secret Service men succeeded in unearthing all the details of the plot against Tom. His life, at times, had been in danger, but at the last minute the man detailed to harm him lost his nerve.

It was Tom's enemies who had set on fire the red shed, and who later tried to destroy the ship by putting a corrosive acid in one of the propellers. That plot, though, was not wholly successful. Then came the time when one of the spies hid on board, and dropped the copper bar on the motor, short-circuiting it. But for the storage-battery that scheme might have wrought fearful damage. The spy who had stowed himself away on the craft escaped at night by the connivance of one of Tom's corrupt employees.

The foreign spies were tried and found guilty, receiving merited punishment. Of course the governments to which they belonged disclaimed any part in the seizure of Tom's aerial warship.

It came out at the trial that one of Tom's most trusted employees had proved a traitor, and had the night before the test, allowed the foreign spies to secrete themselves on board, to rush out at an opportune time to overpower our hero and his friends. But luck was with Tom at the end.

"Well, what are you going to tackle next, Tom?" asked Ned, one day about a month after these exciting experiences.

"I don't know," was the slow answer. "I think a self-swinging hammock, under an apple tree, with a never-emptying pitcher of ice-cold lemonade would be about the thing."

"Good, Tom! And, if you'll invent that, I'll share it with you."

"Well, come on, let's begin now," laughed Tom. "I need a vacation, anyhow."

But it is very much to be doubted if Tom Swift, even on a vacation, could refrain from trying to invent something, either in the line of airships, water, or land craft. And so, until he again comes to the front with something flew, we will take leave of him.

Printed in Great Britain
by Amazon